The Grey Man
-Twilight-

JL Curtis

All rights reserved. No part of this publication may be reproduced, distributed or transmitted in any form or by any means, including photocopying, recording, or other electronic or mechanical methods, without the prior written permission of the publisher, except in the case of brief quotations embodied in critical reviews and certain other noncommercial uses permitted by copyright law. For permission requests, contact the author, addressed "Attention: Permissions Coordinator," at the address below:

Oldnfo@gmail.com

Author's Note: This is a work of fiction. Names, characters, places, and incidents are a product of the author's imagination. Locales and public names are sometimes used for atmospheric purposes. Any resemblance to actual people, living or dead, or to businesses, companies, events, institutions, or locales is completely coincidental.

Published by JLC&A. Available from Amazon.com in Kindle format or soft cover book. Printed by CreateSpace.

The Grey Man-Twilight/ JL Curtis. -- 1st ed.
ISBN-13:978-1985279780
ISBN-10:1985279789

DEDICATION

Captain W.M. "Bill" Moore, End of Tour, May 3, 2017.

"A man *that hath* friends must shew himself friendly: and there is a friend *that* sticketh closer than a brother."

Proverbs 18:24 KJV

ACKNOWLEDGMENTS

Thanks to the usual suspects.

Special thanks to my editor, Stephanie Martin.

Cover art by Tina Garceau.

The characters of Jake Devreau and Ramon Alvarez are © 2012 by J. D. Kinman, used with permission of the author.

Table of Contents

Prologue...7
Dressing for the Occasion...16
Setting up the Range...24
Boring..34
Surprise, surprise..44
Tricks of the Trade..56
Dealing with Issues...66
Dead Man in the Patch...77
Chasing...87
Grand Opening..98
Clay Retires..109
Insults and Injury..121
July 4th...132
Grinding Through...144
Fun and Games..155
Laredo...168
Marine Corps Ball...179
Conversations..191
Underfoot...202
Threats..212
Shootist...225
Petty Tyrants...235
By Any Means..245
Missed Opportunity..256
A Strange Meeting..268
Undercover..280
Learning Experience...291
An Old Gun..304
Trouble...316
Florida..328
Good News, Bad News..340

One More Time	350
Site and Situation	361
Shootout	376
Retired	389
Trading Longhorns	400
Epilogue	413

Prologue

Jesse Miller, now thirty, striking, still trim and fit, sat contentedly in the rocker on the front porch of the ranch house. Comfortably dressed in jeans, boots, and a western blouse, she was joined by Felicia Carter; small, petite, and beautiful. She was dressed in a casual Spanish skirt and blouse and sat in the other rocker, idly sipping iced tea as the kids and dogs played around their feet. The metronomic *crack* of rifles punctuated their conversation, but it was far enough away that, other than Jace, the kids didn't even notice it. Felicia sighed, "It's hard to believe it's been three years." Yogi whined, and Felicia looked down, then said sharply, "Esmerelda! Stop hitting the dog, please."

Jesse laughed, "Poor Yogi and Boo Boo. Too many kids, too much going on." Stretching, she smiled. "Yes, three *good* years. I've got Jace and Kaya, you've got Esme and Matt Junior. We've been lucky all the way around. Aaron's loving the sheriff's office, they seem to like him, Matt is doing a great job managing the ranch, you've been a great help keeping two sets of home fires burning, and Papa's about to retire. Maybe."

It was Felicia's turn to laugh. "Well, some fires are easier than others to keep burning. I'm happy here. Matt's happy too, although I wasn't sure he would make it through the first year."

"With Aaron's retirement, then Matt coming right behind him, it wasn't easy for either of them. And Matt trying to pick up all the subtleties of running a ranch from a cold start didn't help. Papa spent a lot of time with him, and a lot of hours in the saddle."

Felicia snickered, "Oh yes, the saddle sores. For the first month, he could hardly walk. His becoming a reserve deputy like you helped him though. It gave him something other than the ranch to focus on."

"Kaya, stop hitting your brother. Esme, please stop hitting Boo Boo." Matt Junior, lying in a donut between the two dogs gurgled happily and grabbed handfuls of fur from each dog, prompting both of them to start licking him. Both women shook their heads and started untangling the kids as the shooting stopped, punctuated by a loud, "Dammit!"

Jesse cocked her head, "Was that Matt or Aaron?"

Felicia blew hair out of Matt Junior's reach and replied, "I think that was Aaron."

"That means he lost, again. Well, let's go get lunch on the table."

***

John Cronin, now in his mid-70s, and winding down his career with the Pecos County Sheriff's Office, was still the office's lead investigator. He looked intently at Aaron and asked, "So, run that by me again. This all started at the border?"

Aaron stopped bouncing Jace on his lap, and looked up as he answered, "Yep, he jumped the inspection station at Boquillas, got ahead of the CBP Tahoe and, as usual, the Greenies at the Big Bend entrance were no help. They didn't even close the gate like CBP asked, so he got on three eighty five north, apparently hauling ass. Martinez from Brewster County tried to get position to stop him south of Marathon, but he got around him."

He put Jace down, took another swig of iced tea, and continued, "Martinez got turned around, took up the chase, and followed him through Marathon. Two other officers, not sure who, were coming from the west and the east on ninety, so this guy hooked it onto three eighty five north again, and we got a call on Law-1 about a green, late model Mustang, male Hispanic driving, heading north, with a full pursuit behind him. I was in Sector Two and heading south already, Ortiz was about a mile behind me. Sergeant Wilson was ahead of me, but I didn't know it. We were going to do stop sticks, until I heard Michelle, out of the car, with her set." Aaron paused, and the old man motioned, so Aaron continued, "So we set up a roadblock at Longfellow Road, pretty much got the entire road blocked for a change."

Matt and Jessie snickered at that, knowing the area and how flat it was. Aaron looked at her with a hurt expression, "No, really, we *did* get it blocked."

The old man growled, "Y'all shut up. I'm trying to get a sense of what happened here."

Aaron cocked his head, arranging what had happened into its proper order. "So, we're set up, I hear Michelle say she got the strip down, and took out at least one tire. That was about a mile south of us. We could hear sirens coming at us, so we had some pacing."

Sipping iced tea again, he glanced at Jesse then turned back to the old man. "We see the car come sliding around the curve out there, and it slides to a stop. The guy pops off two rounds through the windshield at us, jumps out of the car and stands there with what looked like a chrome plated 1911 in his hand. Ortiz and I both had our carbines on him, but with Martinez, CBP and Michelle coming up behind him, we really didn't have a shot." He rubbed his hand over his face and sighed, "Martinez jumped out of his car, yelled at him to drop the weapon and prone out."

The old man interrupted, "In English or Spanish?"

"Spanish. The guy didn't comply and brought the pistol up, pointing it at Martinez. He fired two rounds, center of mass and put the guy down."

"So neither you nor Ortiz fired any rounds?"

"Nope, crossfire issue. Martinez had a clean shot, as we were clear of his line of fire."

Jesse reached across the table and squeezed Aaron's hand as Matt shook his head, "Way too damn close, bro."

Aaron shrugged, "Not like we haven't been there before. I called for an ambulance, but we ended up cancelling it, 'cause he was DRT. Sheriff Moyer showed up and said he'd already called the sheriff, and they would take the case, even though it terminated in our county. We waited until Ranger Boone and his replacement got there, gave our statements and went back on patrol."

The old man cocked his head, "Clay's replacement? Yeah, I guess it's that time. He's officially retiring in two months. Who was the replacement?"

"Levi Michaels. He apparently was a Trooper sergeant down here."

Nodding the old man replied, "Yep, good guy. Smart as a whip. He knows the area too, which is a bonus," he thought for a second then continued, "Did any rounds hit either of our vehicles?"

"Not that we could find. Both Tahoes were clean," Aaron leaned back. "Oh yeah, and he had twelve keys of heroin in the trunk of the Mustang."

Jesse and Matt both whistled at that, and Felicia looked up with a worried expression. "Why? Why would he?"

The old man rubbed his thumb and index finger together. "Money, Felicia, money. I'm betting he thought there would be a decoy there to get everybody distracted while he eased on through." Turning back to Aaron he asked, "Anything else?"

Aaron shook his head, "Not that I can think of. Just another day at the office."

***

Jesse and Felicia had gotten the kids down for naps, and were cleaning up the remnants of lunch and washing dishes while the old man, Matt, and Aaron sat at the table discussing the morning's shooting.

Aaron mumbled something that Jesse didn't hear, but the old man answered, "Old and cunning beats young and idealistic every time."

Matt laughed, but Aaron said ruefully, "I know, but dammit, I'm tired of getting beat every time we shoot. Hell, I'm thirty years younger than you are John, I should…"

"Maybe you should, but you haven't shot out here for sixty years like I have. I know the wind, I know how to read it, and I know what my old mongrel of a rifle is going to do."

Matt chimed in, "It's different when you don't have a spotter. Granted our rifles *should* be better than John's, but that local course knowledge obviates any advantage we have through equipment or age."

Aaron grumbled, "Shit, Matt, we've been trained by the Marines in one of the toughest sniper courses there is, we've been in combat more than once. Dammit, we were a team for what, almost six years?"

Matt laughed, "Yep, and now we're both retired and living in Texas, out where the wind blows free, and the only thing slowing it down is a barbed wire fence in Montana."

Aaron replied, "I know, but dammit, when my own *wife* outshoots me…"

The old man chuckled at that. "Well, she's been shooting out here since she was little, and she knows how to read the grass too."

"Read the grass?"

Jesse dried her hands and stepped over to the coffee pot. "The grass out here will tell you what's happening with the wind, and, if you can see far enough, what's about to happen." Pouring a cup of coffee, she handed one to Felicia, then poured herself second one and sat down next to Aaron.

Felicia shook her head. "I don't think I know of any other dining table that has these kinds of conversations over lunch."

Matt cocked an eyebrow. "What do you mean?"

Felicia started counting as she said, "Well, a traffic stop where Aaron gets shot at and a man dies, shooting rifles at what, a thousand yards today? I don't know of too many people that have their own personal rifle and pistol ranges in their front yards."

Jesse laughed. "Well, Marines… Duh!"

Felicia rolled her eyes. "I know, I know…" Whatever she was going to say was interrupted by one, then two babies crying, and she and Jesse made for the back bedroom to check on the kids.

Aaron took the opportunity to quickly drop his pants and strip off the prosthetic, scratching the stump below the knee and sighing, "Oh damn, I *hate* getting that damn grass seed down in the sock. That shit itches like hell!"

The old man asked, "How bad is it?"

Aaron cocked his head. "Honestly, I don't know how much of it is real, and how much of it is phantom itching from the missing parts."

Matt said, "What did Doc Truesdale say?"

"What I just said, partially psychosomatic, part real. Maybe it's an allergy, and he gave me some cream to put on it. But he's sending me back to Fort Sam for a consult on the fit. I'm about due for a new leg anyway."

"What are you going to do about a new riding leg?"

Aaron shrugged. "I'll figure something out. Eddie's idea worked pretty well, and the one time I fell off Monday, it worked good."

Matt shook his head. "Yeah, that is one strange horse, butt ugly, hair sticking up everywhere, piebald, bucks you off, then nuzzles you."

"In other words, Monday as in Monday morning…"

The old man laughed, "Well, that's *one* way to name a horse."

"Well, at least mine isn't named Devil!"

"Diablo, not Devil."

Aaron threw up his hands and Matt laughed. "Either-or. That damn horse doesn't like any of us guys. Well, I take that back: he likes Toad, right?"

The old man laughed, "Yeah, talk about babes in the woods around horses. Toad just ignored him, then popped him on the nose when Diablo lipped his hair. I thought sure as hell I'd be shooting Diablo to be able to get to the body in time to save him, but Diablo let him get away with it."

Jesse came back in the kitchen carrying Kaya. "Remember when he reached across the fence and bit Uncle Billy's pony tail?"

The old man smiled. "Yep, but I think that was payback for Billy teasing him with the carrots."

Aaron said. "Mr. Moore was teasing him with carrots?"

Jesse laughed, "Uncle Billy was on a health kick, he had a couple of carrots in his pocket and was munching on them as he wandered around outside. He didn't know Diablo *loves* carrots. And I don't think he knew Diablo was right behind him, following him down the corral fence either. He'd made a couple of tries to get a carrot, but Uncle Billy apparently didn't notice him. Anyway, Diablo bit the hell out of Uncle Billy's pony tail, took about four inches of it off, and put his butt on the ground."

Everybody at the table laughed and the old man shook his head. "Yep, thought I was gonna have to hog-tie Billy there for a while…"

Dressing for the Occasion

Aaron came out of the bedroom, stretching his neck in the unaccustomed suit and tie. As he walked into the kitchen, the old man asked, "What the hell are you doing?"

Aaron stopped short. "Uh, I've got to go to court today, I'm testifying. Remember, I told you last night."

"Not dressed like that you aren't. Get that damn monkey suit off. Jeans and a pressed white shirt. BBQ belt, holster and gun. Where's your hat? Go get your good Silver Belly out of the box. Now, vamoose. I'll explain later."

Aaron said, "Can I at least get a cup of coffee first?"

The old man chuckled, "I guess so. And I guess we need to have a chat about dressing for court when you get back."

Fifteen minutes later, Aaron was back, wearing a tan long sleeved shirt, with pressed Wranglers over his boots. The old man looked him up and down critically, "Need to run a brush over the boots. A cowboy may only have one pair of boots, and they may be run down, but he'll do his damnest to put a shine on them."

Aaron retreated once again, and ten more minutes went by before he reappeared. "How's this?" he asked as he flipped his tooled leather gun belt around his waist and buckled it, dropping the engraved 1911 in the holster.

"That'll do," the old man replied. "Now sit down and drink your coffee."

Aaron filled his cup and took a seat at the table as Jesse came in drowsily, carrying Kaya in her arms. Jesse plopped her in the old man's arms and mumbled unintelligibly as she headed for the coffee pot. Aaron asked, "Why the jeans? When we went through testifying class in the academy, they specified being well dressed and professional looking. To me, that's a suit."

The old man sighed, "That's typical of the Houston PD mentality. They aren't in cow country. They're in an urban environment. Hell, Austin and Dallas are the same way, but anywhere else in Texas, you go in wearing a suit and the jury is gonna be against you."

Jesse flopped down across from Aaron. "Bankers, right Papa?"

"Bankers?" Aaron asked.

"Yep. Anybody that looks like a banker is gonna remind those jurors of the damn bankers that took their pappy or grand pappy's land back in the day. That is the *wrong* foot to get off on with any jury."

"What about the lawyers?"

The old man chuckled. "Always wanted to get defense lawyers that dressed like that. Guaranteed the jury would hate them for cross-examining us poor ol' hardworking deputies."

Aaron said, "But Attorney Randall dresses well, right?"

The old man laughed this time. "Nan Randall dresses only well enough to be seen as a hard-working county attorney. She doesn't wear fancy dresses here. Matter of fact, she gets them off the rack at the local department store. That way, if there are women on the jury, they'll recognize that dress. Hell, they might even *have* that dress in their closet. Makes 'em comfortable with her, knowing she's not putting on airs."

"Jeezus… What *else* did I get taught that was wrong?"

Jesse patted his hand and laughed, "Probably half the stuff. Urban versus rural. HPD does all urban, leaving us poor rural deputies to learn the hard way."

Jace wandered into the kitchen rubbing his eyes. "Daddy, you go work?"

Aaron tousled his hair affectionately. "Yes, Jace. Daddy is *going* to work."

Jace ran his hand over the butt of the 1911 on Aaron's belt. "Daddy wearing pretty gun today."

The old man coughed to cover a laugh as Jesse said, "Jace, come here. You want breakfast? And what do you do if you see a gun laying out?"

Jace smiled. "No touch, tell a big person. Can I have cereal? With choco… Chocolate milk? Please?"

Jesse said, "That's right. No touch, and tell an adult. Are guns in this house loaded?" she asked as she got up to fix him a bowl of cereal.

Jace nodded solemnly. "Guns are always loaded. Especially the ones hanging on the wall. They make loud noise!"

Jesse smiled at him. "Yes they do, don't they! What are you supposed to do before you eat?"

Jace stood, hands on hips, prompting another cough from the old man and a chuckle from Aaron. "Oh, I gotta feed Yogi and Boo Boo!" He scrambled across the kitchen, then came back for the bowls, carrying them to the dog food bin by the back door, closely followed by the dogs.

Filling them carefully, he tried to carry both of them back, but finally carried one at a time, sitting them in place next to the water dishes as the dogs whined. "Eat, doggies," Jace said proudly.

Aaron smiled at him. "Good job, buddy! Now you can eat, too!"

Kaya took that as a challenge to start crying, prompting the old man to look at her. "Hey now, I'm not your mommy. You want food, go talk to her." He set her down at watched her toddle toward Jesse, "Incoming."

Jessie looked down, "Okay baby, give me a couple of minutes." Kaya reached Jesse and started trying to climb her sweatpants, almost pulling them off. Jesse swatted her lightly. "Hey, mommy is not doing the strip tease here. Aaron?"

Aaron picked up Kaya, planted her in her high chair, and thought, *I wonder how old this high chair is? I know Jesse used it, I wonder if it was John's too. There are a lot of pieces of furniture in these houses that are at least a hundred years old. Real wood and handmade. Hell, other than the appliances, I think the newest things in here are our bedroom suite.*

With the kids fed, Jesse took them back to their room to get them dressed, as Aaron got up. "Time to go do battle."

He heard a whistle as the old man started to answer, turned, and saw Matt come in the back door. "Don't you look purty today! All dressed up and no place to go?"

Aaron replied, "Gotta go over to Alpine, testifying on that chase that started at the border and ended up crashing at Longfellow Road."

The old man chimed in. "Remember, follow Clay's advice: make sure you get with him before you go in. They'll call you last, since you initiated the final stop. Just give them the facts as you knew them at the time. *Do not* add any of the after the fact, at that point you were just an assist."

Aaron nodded, "I'll call Clay as soon as I get close to Alpine." Aaron headed for the door. "Y'all have fun."

Jesse came back with the kids dressed to find the old man chuckling, "Kids. Gotta teach 'em how to dress."

"Papa, he's trying. I didn't think about it that way either, until you said something."

***

Aaron pulled into the diner in Alpine, saw Clay Boone's unmarked car, and parked next to it. Feeling a bit self-conscious, he walked into the diner, and saw Clay waving from a booth at the back of the diner, along with Levi Michaels. "Morning, Rangers. Captain Cronin said to make sure I talked to you."

Clay stuck out a hand. "Sit, Aaron, sit. Yeah, just want to make sure you know what to expect this morning. Coffee?"

Aaron nodded, and Clay waved his coffee cup at the waitress then pointed to Aaron. "Angie, another one please."

Aaron slid into the booth, noted the seating arrangement, and chuckled. "Normally, I try to sit facing the door, but I guess I'm out ranked, aren't I?"

Clay and Levi both laughed. "Yep. John is worse than I am about it. Now, the court down here is basically the same as Fort Stockton, but it's Judge Cameron down here. He's by the book, doesn't like a bunch of BS in his courtroom, and he's already pissed off at this case and the officer involved shooting, since the CBP didn't do their jobs. Not that he'll ever admit that, but I've known him for thirty years. The change of venue motion didn't go over well, nor did that highfalutin' immigration lawyer from Houston."

Angie delivered Aaron's coffee and refilled Clay's. "Honey, you want anything to eat?"

"No, ma'am. I had breakfast this morning, just need coffee."

She smiled and sauntered back to the counter, pouring refills as she went. Clay detailed the expectations for the trial, including the fact that, even though the chase had started in Brewster County, it ended in Pecos County, with the one perp dead at the roadblock he and Ortiz had set up, and the other in custody in the hospital with multiple broken bones.

Clay stopped and sipped his coffee. Aaron asked, "So just to confirm, all I talk to is the end of the pursuit, nothing after. I know when they deposed me, they wanted a copy of my wheel book, but they only got the pages with the notes for this chase, broken down by timeline."

Clay nodded. "Remember to ask for a copy of your deposition to refer to. Don't let them catch you out. I'll guarantee they're going to try." Clay looked at his watch. "We better go. Ain't no point in being late and pissing the judge off any more than he already is. I got the coffee, you two get the tip."

The three of them got up, and Aaron dropped two dollars on the table, tipping his hat to Angie as they headed for the door.

***

Thirty minutes into his testimony and cross examination, Mr. Klapp, the prosecutor, wearily got up. "Objection again, your Honor. Deputy Miller was not involved in the subsequent arrest of Mr. Holmes, or the search that was conducted by Brewster County personnel, even though that happened in Pecos County."

Judge Cameron rapped his gavel. "Sustained. Mr. Maginault, I've told you three times to keep your questioning relevant. Am I not getting through to you?"

Maginault, the lawyer hired by Holmes' parents, didn't even look at the judge. "No further questions." He sat carefully back down, straightening his Armani jacket and smoothing his styled hair in what Aaron had determined was a nervous tic.

"Prosecution calls Deputy Grayson."

Aaron returned to his seat in the back of the courtroom, next to Ranger Mitchell, as they waited for Deputy Ortiz and Ranger Boone to testify. The Ranger gave him a thumbs-up and leaned over. "Fun ain't it, Amigo?"

Aaron said softly, "Yeah, 'bout as much fun as a surprise inspection in the Corps. Glad that's over." He zoned out on Grayson's testimony, just remembering the flashing blue and red lights of the roadblock, the car's frantic braking, the perp jumping out, and ducking the shots at them.

Setting up the Range

Jesse finished up the dishes and started getting the kids ready for bed, as Matt and Aaron settled in with a cup of coffee each. Aaron jumped up, headed to the office, and came back with a topo map and some acetate overlays. Unrolling them on the table, Aaron said quietly, "You wanted to know what we could come up with, and I think we have it, or at least a damn good idea of a way to go."

The old man leaned back. "Okay, explain it to me. Why do I need to do anything out here?"

Aaron glanced over at Matt, sighed, and said, "It's not a matter of need. There isn't a real range in the area where folks can safely shoot to much over three hundred yards. The closest long-range facilities are either in Las Cruces or San Antonio. We've been chatting with some folks we worked with, and Toad has also been in on the planning for this." Steeling himself, Aaron continued, "We, that is Matt, Toad, and I, believe there is a market for a range, and the possibility of teaching classes out here, not just long range rifle, but pistol, too. All of us, including Jesse, are NRA instructors, and Matt and I have instructed at the school house in Quantico for sniping and long-range shooting. Toad was also an instructor in weapons maintenance, and…"

The old man held up his hand, "So, what you're saying is, you want to turn the south forty into a gun range?"

Matt and Aaron nodded as Jesse walked back into the kitchen. The old man looked up at her, "You agree with this, Jesse?"

Jesse replied, "I do, Papa. You've never put cows in the south forty, and it hasn't been farmed, that I've ever known of. I saw what can happen when you offer help to women, when I taught those classes out in California, and I know there is at least some market for that here, too."

"How big are we talking?"

Aaron pulled out a floorplan and handed it to Jesse with a gesture to show it to the old man. She put it on the table in front of him. "We're looking at forty by eighty for the main building. We'd put it down where the middle culvert crosses into the south forty, set back about three hundred feet from the road, right at the top of the little bench down there."

The old man leaned back, then got up and walked over to the counter, pouring another cup of coffee. He turned, and said, "Why now?"

Jesse sat down. "Papa, money is cheap right now. We'd do an LLC, do a ninety-nine year lease, and take a loan from the operating account to put it together. For less than seventy-five thousand dollars, we would have a functional, operating business that would give us the flexibility to continue to do what we're doing, and still get additional income coming in."

"What about insurance? Licensing? FFLs? I get doing the LLC, and that stuff to separate it from the ranch, but what's the break-even? Or will it *ever* break-even?"

Aaron spoke up. "The going rate for a two-day sniper class is a thousand dollars per student. We could do a maximum of twelve students, so that's twelve grand for two days work. If we lease out the range facilities, we'd probably net three hundred per student. Say you do one class every other month, plus rent the range out once a month, that's a little over ninety-three thousand in a year, by itself. If we did pistol classes, lane rentals, and the other stuff, it should be fairly easy for the business to make its nut every month. Jesse's run those figures, and…"

"What do you want me to do?"

Matt finally spoke up. "John, we don't *want* you to do anything. Other than agree, that is. What got us started was Charlie Melton calling me and asking if we knew of a range he could use to teach a class at. That got us looking at what is available, and it's not a lot. Granted, the ranch doesn't *need* any additional income, but it's a little bit of diversification into a field that Aaron, Toad, and I know something about. Toad wants to have a real gunsmithing area, and he's willing to pony up to get the equipment and tools he needs, not only to repair things, but also build custom rifles."

The old man walked slowly back to the table and sat down, pulling the floorplan to him. "What is this vault thing?"

Matt said, "It's basically a bank vault. It'd be storage for weapons, and also a safe room if we needed one for tornadoes. It'd be big enough at fifteen by fifteen to hold all the inventory, and have a real vault door on it, which is its own kind of anti-theft device."

"And you want to do how many ranges?"

Matt spun the topo map around, flipping an acetate overlay down on it. "Twenty pistol, out to twenty-five yards, ten pistol/rifle out to fifty yards under this set of awnings. This set," he continued, pointing to a three-part awning, "will have ten at one hundred, ten at six hundred, then six at a thousand over here on the right."

"Okay, what about safety?"

Matt flipped an acetate overlay with the ranges on it, up and down. "See, if we do that, it's six miles to eleven seventy-six, so we're good in that direction."

The old man pointed to a couple of tracks that ran between Hwy 18 and 1178, "What about these?"

"I've talked to Halverson and Ortega, they don't use them. Matter of fact," Matt continued, tracing one of the tracks, "Halverson has blocked this one at his ranch entrance. It's thirteen hundred, almost fourteen hundred yards deep, here. Doesn't impact any wells or fields that are in use for anything. It's pretty much mesquite, which needs to be grubbed out anyway."

The old man nodded. "Okay, I'll buy that. What else are you planning?"

Aaron said, "Get a few guns in to sell, depending on which distributor we go with. For the higher end ARs and such, Axleson Tactical out of Nevada. They are part of a group of Veteran-owned businesses that give back to the vets. We'd like to be part of that, and they do some damn nice gear!"

Matt chimed in, "If we're going to have folks out here, I'd rather have a safe shooting environment.

And, we really do need to knock down that mesquite. Us shooting is one thing, we are all professionals. We're not going to lose rounds into the middle of nowhere. There really isn't a range, per se, in the area where people can learn. I think we can make some money on it, hell, we can even rent it to the PD and sheriff's offices for training and qualification, since neither one has their own range."

The old man shrugged, "Okay. if that's what y'all want, go ahead."

Jesse hugged him, and said, "I'll get with Uncle Billy to get the papers drawn up. Thank you, Papa."

The old man thought, *Dunno if I'm doing the right thing, but what the hell, they've got a plan, and this is all going to be Jesse and Aaron's soon enough anyway. At least this way, they're working from home, and I'll get to see them more often. That's not a bad thing!*

***

Two weeks brought significant changes in the south forty. The old man sat on the front porch, sipping a cup of coffee as he watched the Gonzales brothers unloading equipment, still marveling at the speed with which Jesse had gotten everything arranged. The paperwork was filed, the steel building ordered, they were pouring foundation either today or tomorrow, and the county truck sitting on the side of the road had to be the power guy. While he appreciated Aaron's willingness to pay for the mesquite abatement, that was really a ranch cost, and would be a deduction that they could use later.

Jesse slipped out on the porch, followed by Yogi and Boo Boo. A cup of coffee in hand, she slumped gratefully into a chair. "Wow, the kids are on a roll this morning!"

"Didn't want to go down for a nap?"

"Not even close! And the dogs were no help, either!" Maybe if they are out here, the kids will sleep more than fifteen minutes." Jesse glanced out at the south forty, "Looks like they are busy this morning."

Waving his arm, he said, "Can't believe what's happening down there. At least the weather is holding off, for now."

Jesse looked at the equipment and sighed. "You're still not sure, are you Papa?"

"Well, y'all have a plan. All I have is old…"

A breeze ruffled Jesse's hair and she shivered a little. "Papa, we're just looking at what we can do to diversify operations a little bit. If worse comes to worst, it's a tax write off, and a lesson learned. I think Aaron and Matt are thinking about getting some military folks out here, too. I know they do train at civilian facilities…"

The old man laughed, "Y'all haven't even got the first target butt up, and you're already looking at bringing military teams in? What are the odds of that…"

Jesse smiled sadly. "That's how I met Aaron, remember? That was military teams at a civilian range. There is no guarantee we're going to do this perfectly, but we're at least going to try. I finally got all the damn FFL paperwork submitted, and that was a real pain in the ass. Had to go by the county clerk's office and get her to assign us an actual physical address, I never knew there weren't addresses out in the county until the 1970s. I'd never thought about 911 being the cause of that implementation."

The old man chuckled. "Our address used to be Star Route One. That was it. Before that, grandpa used to have to go to town to get mail. And that was damn near a day's ride in a buggy or wagon." He turned to face Jesse. "I just want y'all to succeed. That's it. I don't see Aaron doing a long career in law enforcement, not with that leg, even if the prosthetics are as good as they can be made. It wears on him every day. I see it. I've seen how much he's aged, just since the injury. I know how bad I hurt on mornings like this, when it's nippy and the humidity is up. I stayed in law enforcement because I didn't know anything different, Jesse. Hell, I still don't. It's this or the ranch. I don't have y'alls' skills with computers, nor your education. I looked at the minimum qualifications for Peace Officer, and I can't even meet them today. I don't want to be a drain on y'all, either."

Jesse got up and walked around the chair to hug the old man. "Papa, Papa. You're not a drain. What you've done, few people could ever think about doing. You're leaving one helluva legacy in law enforcement, not just at the local level, but on both national and international levels. I know you still get calls from your NA buddies, and you could be on the road teaching all the time, if you wanted to. *That* is not being a drain!"

His eyes were suspiciously wet when he said gruffly, "Let go of me girl, I've got to get to work.

You just take care of the kids, and let us do the rest." Shoving himself up out of the chair, he went back to the kitchen, deposited the cup in the sink. He went into the office, grabbed his gunbelt, swung it around his hips, plucked the radio out of its charger and slipped it on his belt, and picked up his hat, setting it squarely on his head as he walked out to the car. "Yogi, let's go!"

Yogi bounded around the corner of the house, jumped in the back seat, and woofed softly, as the old man shut the back door and climbed in the driver's seat. He looked up as he started the car. *Another bluebird day. Hopefully it'll warm up a little bit, but at least it isn't raining, and none is in the forecast.*

Jesse stood just inside the front door, hugging herself, *I don't know what's gotten into Papa. He's not been his usual self. I wonder if it's all his friends retiring, and knowing he's going to retire too. I know people do fear change, but dammit, he… He should have retired eight years ago! Maybe if I fix meatloaf, green beans, and mashed potatoes for dinner… I could use some comfort food about now…*

***

The old man pulled into the parking lot, let Yogi water his favorite tree, and eased in the back door. Sticking his head in dispatch, he said, "Morning, ladies, anything interesting last night?"

Lisa paged back through the logs. "Nope, nothing of interest, Captain. Just the usual: a couple of drunks, one assist, one domestic, and two busts for possession on ten. That's it."

"Good! I need to catch up on paperwork today."

Lisa laughed, "I'll try not to give you any more then."

The old man deposited Yogi in his office, picked up his coffee cup, and strolled back to the kitchen. Pouring a cup of coffee, he glanced over the bulletin board, didn't see anything of interest, and headed back down the hall. The sheriff stuck his head out the door. "John? Got a minute?"

"Sure, what's up?"

"When are you going to have your range finished?"

The old man thought for a minute. "Shootable, or completely finished?" Then continued, "Probably shootable next week, completely finished, probably at least a month. Why?"

"Would you be willing to sign a lease with us for use of it?"

"Why? You can just come use it anytime you need to, Jose. Anybody on the force can."

The sheriff waved his hand. "No, I know we can. But the issue is for compliance: we need a contract with a range facility to maintain our currency and keep our certification."

The old man shook his head. "Um. Sure, just talk to Jesse and work it out with her. She's going to be the de facto manager."

The sheriff smiled. "I can do that, but I'm sure it's going to cost me…"

The old man laughed. "That's why I said deal with her. She's the CPA in the family."

"Go to work, John."

"Workin' over here, boss," the old man said with a grin as he headed for his office.

Two hours later, paperwork caught up for now, the old man pulled up the pdf file Aaron had sent him on range design from the NRA. He opened it and started reading. *Damn, Aaron and Matt do know what they're talking about. They must have followed this… book? Chapter and verse. But they both instructed at Quantico, and I'm sure they had to qualify as range officers there. I wonder, maybe they can make some money with it, and it's not like the south forty was used for much else…*

Yogi whined, interrupting his train of thought. "Want to go out? Is that what you want?"

Yogi whined again, then woofed softly. "Okay, okay… I'm coming dog." The old man got up slowly, rolled his shoulders to try to loosen them up, and took Yogi out to his tree. *What are we going to do about the kids and dogs with the range? I wonder if they make earmuffs for dogs? Hell, I know they do, saw them downrange… But do they make 'em for kids?*

Boring

Aaron pushed hard on the steering wheel, trying to get his back to loosen up as he pulled back onto I-10 heading west. Two more hours on shift and he could head home. *I'll hit the rest area, then swing south on Hovey, check the rigs, and back up sixty-seven. That should kill an hour and half or so.* He wiggled his butt in the seat, grumbling out loud, "I don't care what vehicle it is, eight hours a day just sucks in the seats."

Swinging into the rest area, he slowed down and scanned the area side to side. Pulling into the bathrooms, he got out and stretched, felt his back crack, and sighed with relief. *Damn, I needed that!* After a quick piss, he stepped back out of the bathroom, noting an older woman coming out of the women's side, "Ma'am, any problems in the ladies? Everything look okay?"

A little flustered, the lady said, "Oh, uh, it's fine as far as I'm concerned. Texas does a pretty good job of keeping the areas clean."

Aaron tipped his hat to her, "Good, y'all travel safe."

Hopping back in the Tahoe, he backed out and accelerated out of the rest area. A mile down the road, he saw a bike off on the emergency lane. With a quick glance, he pulled over behind it, flipped on his traffic backers and eased out of the truck. He saw a bearded male with a skull patterned do-rag on his head crouched, working on something on the bike, a small tool kit spread out on the ground. "Got a problem, sir?"

The startled biker turned, "Oh, well yeah. Damn coil wire vibrated loose again. I'm fixing it for the umpteenth time."

As the biker stood up, leaning on his bike for balance, his jacket swung open and Aaron saw the butt of a pistol on his right side. Since the biker had a pair of pliers in his right hand, he didn't react, noting the biker wasn't acting suspiciously. Unconsciously, Aaron noted the tag, and a quick visual of the bike didn't show any violations, so he asked politely, "You have a permit for the pistol?"

The biker's look of surprise was followed by a chagrined expression. "Yes, sir. Would you like to see it?"

"If you don't mind. Where are you headed?"

The biker pulled a chained wallet from his left rear pocket, laying the pliers carefully on the bike's seat. He opened the wallet and extracted two IDs, passing them over as he said, "El Paso. Trying to beat the rain."

"You're a ways from home, aren't you, Mr. Harris?" Aaron asked as he scanned the IDs, noting the veteran status on the driver's license and that they were the same age.

"Call me Mike. Mr. Harris was my dad. Been over to Houston to interview for a job with TPO. Now that the patch is picking back up, I'm hoping to get back in the field. I'm a welder and pipefitter, do rig construction and maintenance."

Aaron handed the license and permit back, "TPO? Trans-Pecos Oil? I see you're a veteran too."

Mike stretched his shoulders, "Yeah, TPO. I was in hundred and first. Got fucked up in an IED attack in oh-six in Ramadi."

Aaron winced. "Back?"

"That, and shrapnel in the left leg, some TBI and PTSD. I was in the right rear, the Hummer hit the IED with the left front wheel. Flipped it and blew the front end off." Mike stared into the past. "I was the only survivor. You?"

"Marines. Fallujah, Helmund, FOBs up on the border." Bending down he rapped the prosthetic, "They got my leg."

"Shit, man, you got a pros, and you're still a cop?"

Aaron nodded. "I work for a good sheriff. He looked at the total man, not just the missing pieces. You gonna get it fixed?" he asked pointing to the bike.

"I think I've got it." Mike reached over and hit the starter, and the bike rumbled to life. He shut it back down. "Yep, that got it."

Aaron looked at the sky and said, "Well, you better get going; otherwise you're gonna get wet. Take care of yourself, and don't do anything stupid, okay?"

Mike zipped his jacket back up, put his helmet on and said, "This is my Zen, man. Can't stand being in a cage anymore. I'll be careful, Deputy." Throwing a leg over the bike, he looked back over his shoulder, hit the turn signal, and rumbled onto the Interstate.

Aaron shook his head. *Not on a bet. Jesse would kill me if I ever thought about a bike. But that can't be good for his back either. Hope he makes it okay.* Hopping back in the Tahoe, he went up to Hovey Road, turned south and checked the pump jacks, noting the new rigs in the area. Two new ones were going in down by sixty-seven and he took pictures with his cell phone and backed them up with his issued camera, noting that both rigs were from TPO. *Maybe he, Mike… yeah, Mike will get lucky and get back on the patch.*

Just as he turned back north on sixty-seven, the bottom fell out and the rain came pouring down. Aaron slowed down, knowing how slick these Texas roads got in the first half hour or so of rain as all the oil percolated to the surface. Thankfully, he made it back to the sheriff's office without incident, since he realized he'd forgotten to put any rain gear in his go bag. He pulled into the parking area, timing the rain and made a run for it during a lull in the downpour.

Dropping his go bag in his truck, he made it to the back door just as the rain started pelting down again, and the clouds got darker. Shaking the rain off his hat, he set his folder and computer on the desk in patrol, nodding to Kathy Fargo, one of the new deputies. "Hey, Kathy. Which sector have you got tonight?"

She grumbled, "Two. Middle of nowhere on a rainy night. Just how I wanted to spend my Friday night!"

Aaron laughed. "Well, it'll be quiet. Nothing but cows and idiots on I-10."

"The idiots I can deal with, it's the damn cows that I don't get along with. Anything new?"

"Two new TPO rigs going in down on Hovey Road. Other than that, nothing much. Watch out for the wash outs down at the end just before sixty-seven."

"Okay, thanks. How much gas did you leave me?"

Aaron laughed, "I filled it up. I wouldn't do that to you."

Kathy smiled. "You're one of the few! You off for the weekend?"

"Yep, flipping to second shift Monday night."

"Oh, fun…"

Aaron laughed as he headed down the hall, "At least it's not third shift!" He stopped in the kitchen and grabbed a cup of coffee after sniffing the pot to figure out how old the current coffee was, then walked back down to the old man's office and knocked on the door. "Captain?"

The old man looked up. "Come on in, Aaron. What can I do for you?"

"It's raining cats and dogs, don't feel like making a dash for the truck just yet. And I've got a question."

"Shoot."

"All this hoorah about the new oil find, Wolfcamp Shale? Yeah, that one. Is that why we're seeing more rigs starting to go in?"

The old man leaned back and grinned. "Well, *technically* that find isn't down here, it's Midland and the eight counties that surround it, but lots of folks 'think' it's the whole basin."

"But I saw two more rigs going in down off Hovey Road today."

"Probably TPO, right? They're getting pretty froggy about getting new wells down. Don't think they're going to find much new, but the Midland area's blowing up. Some amazing lease prices up there, all betting on the come."

"So, it really shouldn't affect us, right?"

"No, not on the ranch, what we'll see is the impact of the drugs on the department. Lots of drugs going into the patch these days, which means we're going to see more and more of them transiting our county, probably on the back roads, three-eighty-five, and three-forty-nine. Reminds me, I need to talk to the sheriff about rolling some extra officers on the back roads for a while. Want some overtime?"

Aaron laughed. "I don't know if my butt will take it! Jesse'd probably like it though. I can't believe how many clothes the kids are going through!"

The old man grinned. "Yep, and it ain't gonna get any better. Shoes, clothes, diapers, all those fun things"

"And they all cost money. Dammit." Aaron glanced out the window. "Looks like the rain is letting up, I'm gonna make a run for it. See you at the house."

The old man glanced up. "Go. I'm going to be a while, got to get this paperwork done."

***

The old man pulled into the yard, slogged through the rain to the house and was met at the door by a bedraggled Jesse. "A couple of the steers are out. Matt, Aaron, and Ernesto are trying to get them back in the north forty."

"Dammit! Any idea what happened?"

"I was coming back from Monahans, and saw the fence down up by the cemetery. I'd seen some lightning as I came down eighteen, maybe they spooked."

"They got any fencing or posts with them?"

"No, they took horses."

"Sonofa… Okay, I'll load the Gator and head up there." The old man changed out hats, grabbing one that was waterproof and threw on a slicker as he headed out the back door. Slogging through the rain to the barn, he backed the Gator out of its hole, then backed up to the storage door. Opening it, he got a dozen metal poles and two rolls of barbed wire, threw them in the back and pulled the pole driver, wire wrap, hammer, and fence pliers off the pegboard. Laying them in the bed, he jumped in and pulled out of the barn, heading north on Hwy 18 in the pouring rain.

Fifteen minutes later, he slowed down as he saw horses in the headlights and one steer, head lowered staring at the three horses. Cussing under his breath, the old man got out of the Gator and opened his slicker, "Sumbitch won't go back through the fence will he?"

Matt answered, "Not so far. He's tried to gore Ernesto's and my horse both."

Ernesto chimed in, "*Señor*, he did no get me. This *cabron*, he needs to go away!"

The old man nodded. "My thoughts exactly Ernesto, y'all cover your ears." Drawing his 1911, the old man knelt on one knee and shot the steer twice through the eye socket. The steer bawled and shook his head, then dropped to his knees and finally fell over. The old man walked up and put a third round through the back of the skull, just to make sure and reholstered the gun, grumbling, "Now I gotta go back and clean the damn pistol. Okay, how much fence is down?"

Aaron replied, "Looks like three posts and maybe thirty feet. You want me to ride further and check?"

"Please. Probably a hundred yards in either direction. Make sure they didn't pull anything else loose further away." Matt and Ernesto dismounted, tied their horses to the Gator's bumper and started unloading the posts and wire, while the old man got on his phone. "Jesus, this is John Cronin. Had to put a steer down." He listened for a minute, then said, "No, this one is right on the side of eighteen, up by my north forty. Yeah, I'll still be here. Just look for my Gator."

Matt looked at him curiously, "Jesus?"

"Jesus Ramos, the ones that do the fandango meat for us. He and Jorge are going to come get this bastard and process him. Guess we're going to be having an early fandango this year, maybe around the fourth."

Aaron came back, trotted past as he yelled, "All good to the north, lemme go check the south." The old man waved, then grabbed the stretchers.

Walking over to a post that was still upright, he hooked the stretcher into the wire and pulled. Grunting with effort, he got maybe six inches of wire and laughed, "Thank God, looks like all they did was push the posts down. We may have gotten lucky and they didn't break any wire!"

Aaron came back, tied Monday off to the back of the Gator and walked up, "Four posts down to the north, the south all looks good. I didn't see any busted wire either."

"Okay, load everything back up and we'll go replace posts, then re-stretch every strand."

Forty minutes later, they were working on the pounding the last pole in with the pole driver when they saw headlights coming up Hwy 18. Matt hit the pole one more time then dropped the pole driver. "Damn! I'm out of shape. It shouldn't be that hard to pound a steel pole four-feet into the ground!"

A hiss of airbrakes interrupted him as Jesus and Jorge climbed out of their rollback wrecker. "*Hola, Señor!* What did this poor steer do to deserve this fate on such a beautiful night?"

The old man laughed. "Sumbitch wouldn't go back in the fence. I wasn't in the mood to put up with his shit tonight. I'd been eyeing him for the fandango, anyway."

"So we are moving it up, *Señor*?"

"Yeah, let's shoot for roughly a month from this coming weekend. July second, I think it is. Usual split?"

Two big grins appeared. "*Sí Señor.* You are more than generous!"

"No, your willingness to come get this bastard more than makes up for it."

Backing the wrecker around, they dropped the rollback bed back, got a pair of wide straps and wire cables and laid them out on the ground. With everyone's help, they got the steer rolled over and hooked the straps to the wire cables and to the winch. They slowly winched the steer up on the bed of the tow truck, raised the bed, and with a wave, took off into the night.

Aaron mused, "Huh, never saw a setup like that. But that worked, didn't it!"

The old man chuckled, "Old age and ingenuity beats youth and enthusiasm every time. Let's go to the house. I'm hungry!"

Untying their horses, Matt, Aaron, and Ernesto mounted up and cantered back toward the ranch as the old man followed in the Gator, as the rain finally let up.

Surprise, surprise

Jesse and Felicia loaded up the Suburban with the kids. Felicia hopped in the back seat and they headed to town, leaving the men in the south forty with the Gonzales brothers, a D-8 Cat, a backhoe, a dump truck, and the dogs getting underfoot at every opportunity. "Damn, they're a bunch of assholes this morning." Jesse sighed.

Felicia laughed, "They want the work done and over with. Matt was grumpy last night, more so after Matt Junior woke up at three, screaming at the top of his lungs. Matt tried to get him to calm down, but he finally admitted defeat and gave him to me."

"I remember those days, both with Jace and Kaya. But it's all pretty much a blur to Aaron. I swear that man could sleep through a damn tornado hitting the house!"

"Speaking of that, I brought the shopping list. What are we going to do first?"

Jesse chuckled, "First is get rid of the kids. We're going to drop them at Cherie Lynn's and then shop at our leisure. I've got to go get something done with this hair and Melaina said she could get me in before noon."

"Cherie Lynn's?"

"Yep, she took over the day care center. She's got a couple of *Abuelas* in there, along with some of the good high school kids. Remember, Lucy is working there."

"*Sí*, she's working there to save money for college."

"And it's spring break, so Cherie Lynn's son is home from college."

Felicia cocked her head. "And this means something?"

Jesse laughed. "Apparently Khalil is a budding basketball star at Sul Ross. He's six feet something, great with the little ones, and apparently the girls are falling all over him."

Rolling her eyes, Felicia asked, "Are you sure the kids will be okay?"

"Oh yes, she rules that place with an iron hand. Hormones *will not* interfere with the kids' care."

"How did you find out about her?"

"Angelina. She told me if we needed a break, she was a good one with the kids. Accredited, and all the folks in town that don't have other child care use her. She isn't an ass about it if you're late, or have to pick up early."

Pulling into the covered drive, she stopped the Suburban and started taking kids from Felicia as she unlatched them from their car seats. Telling Jace and Kaya to hold hands, she took Esme's hand and led them to the door, which was being held open by a tall young man. "You must be Khalil."

"Yes, ma'am. You need any help with anything else?"

Jesse glanced over her shoulder, seeing Felicia with Matt Junior she replied, "I don't think so."

Khalil held the door for them, then followed them into the lobby. "Did y'all schedule a drop off today?"

Lucy came around the corner, and Jace bolted for her, chanting, "Uci, Uci!"

She scooped him up and blew a raspberry in his neck, causing Jace to giggle. "Hi, Jesse, Aunt Felicia." Coming behind the counter, she sat Jace on it, saying, "I'll check them in. I've babysat all four of them."

Khalil smiled and handed over the pen, then disappeared around the corner.

***

Back at the ranch, Aaron and Matt stood over spread out plans on the dozer's tracks, going over with Miguel Gonzales what they wanted and pointing out the various stakes they'd driven to mark the corners of the various ranges. The old man leaned against the backhoe chatting with Miguel's brother Pedro. "So, business is going pretty good for y'all?"

Pedro grinned. "Oh yes, *Señor!* We start Monday up north of Rankin off twenty-four oh-one, putting in cuts for them to start drilling up there, and when we finish that one, we've got two more. One north of Garden City, and one south of Big Spring."

"They all for TPO?"

"*Sí, Señor.*"

"They sure are betting on the come, guess they went whole hog on the reports that Wolfcamp is the real deal."

Pedro shrugged and grinned. "We don't care, *Señor*, we're getting work. And good paying work at that. It's not going to buy us new equipment, but it will give us a float for the bad months."

"What do you think about what the boys are doing up here?"

Pedro laughed. "Everybody is excited! A nice place to shoot, out of the sun? What's not to like! And your family has always been fair to us, more than fair. Jesus told us what you did with them on the steer."

The old man waved it off. "Not a big thing. They came out in the rain and got it, least I could do."

Miguel climbed into the driver's seat of the big D-8, fired it up, then trundled down the lane they had decided would be the thousand-yard range. Aaron jogged down to a point about six hundred yards out, marking the point where they wanted Miguel to start flattening the ground. Pedro looked over and saw Matt waving at him. "Well, I guess I better get to work. We'll knock as much of this out today as we can, *Señor*."

"*Gracias*, Pedro," the old man said, as he stepped away from the backhoe and called the dogs to him. Since he was nothing but a fifth wheel in this evolution, he decided another cup of coffee and a leftover cinnamon roll sounded good. He strode back up toward the house, dogs in tow, leaving Matt and Aaron to do their thing.

***

Jesse pulled into the strip center with the Spa in it, and Felicia said, "Oh, Second Hand Rose! I've heard about that place. I may go see what they have while you get your hair done."

"Go ahead. I'm probably going to be at least forty-five minutes, maybe an hour," Jesse parked one row out from the Spa, and hopped out. "If you get bored, come on down and sit with me."

Felicia waved. "Okay."

Jesse smiled to herself as she walked across the parking lot to the Spa, glancing around before she walked through the door, stepping quickly to the side. It wasn't all that dark inside, but coming from the bright sun, it took her a second to see everything. Mrs. Halvorson was in the first chair by the door, with Linda working on her perm. Rebecca was sitting in her chair, sipping a cup of coffee, and Melaina was just ringing up an older lady Jesse didn't recognize.

Melaina waved to Jesse. "Have a seat, I'll be with you in a minute."

Jesse nodded and sat in the chair, spinning it around so she could see the door, "Take your time. We're kid free this morning. Hi, Mrs. Halvorson, how are you doing?"

Mrs. Halvorson, in her mid-80s, and a bird-like little lady smiled. "Good, Jesse. I'm above ground and I give thanks for that every day. Linda is doing her best with this rag mop I call a head of hair."

Linda chimed in. "Well, if you'd come in more than once every three months…"

Mrs. Halvorson chuckled, "Honey, at my age, I'm happy to *make* it three months."

Melaina led Jesse over to the sinks, "Shampoo or just a rinse?"

"Um, rinse. I shampooed this morning." Melaina quickly rinsed Jesse's hair, and draped a towel around her head, as Jesse got up and went back to the chair.

Picking up the drape, she placed it around Jesse's neck, fluffed her hair and asked, "What do you want me to do, Jesse?"

"Well, it's coming on spring, so maybe shoulder length, clean up the bangs, and that should do it."

Melaina fluffed it again, and started combing it out, "Any color?"

Jesse huffed. "No." Reaching up, she touched her temple where the white hair covered her scar from being shot. "This never colors right, and it makes me look stupid until it washes out. I'm stuck with what I have."

Melaina replied, "Okay, trim, bangs, and a wash it is." Picking up her scissors, she started trimming Jesse's hair as they chatted about the everyday trials and tribulations of raising kids. Melaina laughed at Jesse's comments about Jace and Kaya, reminding Jesse she was almost a grandmother, and that Jesse had a long way to go.

Suddenly the door banged open and a skinny white male charged through it, waving a pistol erratically. "This is a holdup bitches! Gimme your money!" The man turned first toward Rebecca, then saw Mrs. Halvorson and Linda. "Give it up bitches! Money, jewelry, credit cards. I want it now!" He scraped the hand holding the pistol up and down the other arm, then glanced over his shoulder, seeing Melaina and Jesse basically frozen in position, "Don't you two move. I'll get you in a minute."

Jesse slipped her hands under the drape and started easing her purse open. As he turned back to Mrs.

Halvorson and Linda, he yelled, "I said move! Give it up!"

Linda, hands in the air, said, "I don't have any money on me. It's…"

He viciously slapped her with the pistol, causing it to fire a round into the ceiling. Linda collapsed without a word, and he reached for Mrs. Halvorson. "Pretty ear rings, bet those are real diamonds, aren't they bitch?"

He jerked one out of her right ear, causing Mrs. Halvorson to yelp. Jesse yelled, "You, leave her alone, you bastard!" as she pulled her Python from her purse and started bringing it out from under the drape. *Fucking meth heads*, Jesse thought as she got a good look at the man as he turned, *No teeth, what looks like a bad case of acne, and I'm going to have to shoot that poor sonofabitch!*

Spinning toward her, he popped off another round that went into the wall just to Melaina's left. Jesse leaned right to make sure her line of fire was clear, and the brick front wall was behind her shot. As she fired the first round to his center of mass, she heard a pop and saw a flash of light off to the side. As he continued to turn she thought, *Damn that was loud! This sonofabitch is higher than hell. That didn't even phase him. I wonder if this is where I die?* She put a second round through his chin that angled up and took out the back of his head as he crumpled between the chairs, still twitching.

Jesse bolted out of the chair, stomping on his gun hand as she yelled, "Everybody okay?"

She dimly heard responses, and looked around to physically check. She saw Mrs. Halvorson, holding a snub nosed .38 in a two-handed grip, blood dripping from her ear, and shaking. Linda sat up slowly, bleeding from her cheek and moaning. Rebecca still sat with her hands up and she finally glanced at Melaina, who had grabbed her 20ga from wherever she'd had it stashed. "Are you okay?" When Melaina nodded, she said, "Call 911. Tell them shots fired, officer involved shooting, one down, and give your address, okay? And tell them to send an ambulance."

Melaina nodded and picked up the portable phone off the counter, as Felicia burst through the door, her pistol in hand. Jesse started swinging towards the movement bringing her pistol up from low ready, and jerked it up. "Dammit, Felicia! You almost got shot!"

Felicia looked at the body, Jesse still standing on his hand and sobbed, "I was afraid you were…"

"I'm not. Now, put your pistol up. Mrs. Halvorson, put yours up too." Jesse heard the rising wail of sirens, looked at Felicia, and said, "Go call Papa and Aaron. Let them know we're alright and… And, I had to shoot. Nothing else."

Felicia nodded and stepped back out the door as Mrs. Halvorson put her pistol back in her purse. "Is that bastard dead?"

Jesse leaned down and felt for a pulse. Not feeling one, she took her foot off his hand and slowly removed the pistol from it. "Yes ma'am, I think he is. Melaina, can you help Linda, please? Rebecca, can you prop the door open?"

Jesse laid her pistol in the chair, careful to point it away from anyone with the cylinder open, "I don't know who is responding, so everyone stay where you are. I'm going to go stand outside the door."

Jesse had just stepped outside, waving to Felicia when the first city car slid to a stop, two doors up from the Spa. Sergeant Alvarez jumped out, running toward the front door, gun drawn. Jesse held up her hands. "It's all over Miguel. One probable meth head down. He's ten-seven."

A second car slid to a stop, and another city officer jumped out, followed by one of the county Tahoes, driven by Deputy Johnny Hart. Sergeant Alvarez waved at them. "Scene is secure." Turning to Jesse he said, "You want to show me? And who needed the ambulance?" Over his shoulder he said, "Jordan, call the coroner. He'll need to pronounce this one here."

Officer Jordan spoke quietly into his radio as Hart caught up with them, "You okay, Jesse?"

She shrugged, "I don't know yet. But the adrenalin dump has given me one hell of a headache."

Alvarez asked, "You want a lawyer present, Jesse?"

"Not right now. There are witnesses a plenty."

The ambulance crew rolled in a stretcher, checking both Linda and Mrs. Halvorson, as Jesse walked all three officers through what had happened. Doc Truesdale came through the door, asking, "What have we got?"

Alvarez pointed to the body on the floor, "Probable meth head."

Doc Truesdale nodded, as he pulled out his gloves, "You got your basic pics? I'll need to roll him."

Jordan replied, "I've got enough to start. Let me chalk him, then you can do what you need to do."

Doc looked at the body then asked curiously, "Who shot him in the side?"

Jesse started, "What?"

Doc pointed to a hole in the shirt with some blackening around it, "Somebody got a round into him from a short distance."

Mrs. Halvorson, now being treated by the medics said, "That was me. I couldn't get my gun out any sooner. When he started turning away, I didn't want him to shoot Jesse, so I shot him first."

That reminded Jesse of the round that had gone through the wall, "Need to send somebody next door, one round went through the wall just about head high, between these two stations."

Deputy Hart said, "I'll take care of that," as he stalked out the door.

Doc Truesdale and the EMT turned the body, and he looked up at Jesse, "Two rounds?"

Jesse nodded, "One to center mass but he kept coming. Figured he was high, so I went to the head shot."

Doc nodded and said, "Yep, he's DRT. Massive head trauma due to interacting with a, what, one fifty-eight grain Jesse?" She nodded. "One fifty-eight grain JHP to the brain pan. Once y'all get done, I'll haul him and do a full autopsy. And with that, I'm outta here, I've got patients waiting!"

As the medics put the body in a body bag, Melaina said, "Now I gotta get the blood up, dammit."

Mrs. Halvorson replied, "Bleach. Just be glad it's not on carpet. That is a real bitch."

"I can do that. We use bleach every two weeks on the floor as a disinfectant."

Johnny Hart came back in shaking his head, "It's all good next door, nobody hit. The round just broke a mirror."

Alvarez chuckled, "Well, at least he won't have seven years of bad luck," as he dropped both Mrs. Halvorson's and Jesse's unloaded pistols in evidence bags. "There shouldn't be any issues with you getting them back pretty quick, okay, ladies?" He then proceeded to bag up the white male's pistol and his pocket lint.

"No ID?" asked Jesse. Alvarez shook his head, and started loading his evidence kit and camera back in the bag.

Melaina said, "I'll finish you up whenever you can come back, Jesse. Thank you for what you did."

Jesse nodded as she was lead out the door. Two hours later, Aaron and Mr. Halvorson were finally allowed to pick Jesse and Mrs. Halvorson up from the Police Department. After hugging Aaron, the first question Jesse asked was, "Did Felicia pick up Jace and Kaya?"

"Yes, they're at home now. How are you doing?"

"I killed a man today. How do you think I feel?"

Aaron hugged her hard. "It's okay. Let's get you home, then we'll talk."

Jesse leaned into Aaron as they walked slowly to the truck, arms around each other.

Tricks of the Trade

"Hey Captain, you might want to go over to booking," Lisa said as the old man stepped into dispatch.

"Why?"

"Looks like your Aaron and Johnny Hart got a biggie. They're coming in with four cartel guys, a lot of meth, and some coke."

"He's not mine, he's Jesse's, but I just might wander that way. What's their ETA?"

"Wait one," Lisa said. "Two-oh-two, dispatch, ETA?"

The old man heard Aaron respond, "Two-oh-two, in fifteen. Tow truck just got here and he's hooking up now. Need a drug dog to meet us at the sheriff's office."

"Dispatch copies, drug dog is on the way." Lisa turned to the old man. "Captain, why didn't you put Yogi through the training?"

The old man shrugged. "Never really thought about it. And I don't think he's really got the temperament for it." Yogi whined at him and the old man laughed, "Yes, we're talking about you, dog. Let me take him out and if you don't mind, I'll leave him with you when I come back in."

Lisa smiled. "Not a problem, Captain."

The old man took Yogi out to his favorite tree and let him do his business, cleaned up after him and dropped him off with dispatch. Walking over to the jail side, he stepped into the control room and watched the monitors as Aaron and Deputy Hart brought the four male Hispanics into booking. The old man did a double take as the last one was escorted in by Aaron, prompting Sergeant Kamp to ask, "You recognize him, Captain?"

"Hell, yes. That's Ernesto Rivas, he's a major mover for Sínaloa. What the hell is he doing north of the border?" Turning to the sergeant, he said, "Do me a favor and call the Rangers. I think they're going to want him more than we do, and I'm pretty sure they've got murder warrants out for him."

The old man looked around the control room. "You got any PR[1] bond paperwork over here?"

"No, sir. That's all kept over on y'all's side of the office."

"Dammit… Lemme out the back way and tell Aaron and Johnny to slow-roll the booking."

Sergeant Kamp cocked her head, but said, "Uh, anything you say, Captain. How long do you want them to delay?"

"At least fifteen minutes, maybe twenty."

The old man slid out the back way and hustled back over to his office, grabbed a blank PR bond, filled in Rivas' name in block letters, and walked quickly down to the sheriff's office. "Jose, we got a

---

[1] Personal Recognizance

big fish in booking right now. I want to play him before we turn him over to the Rangers."

Ten minutes later, the sheriff was laughing and nodding as the old man asked, "Good to go?"

"Do it, John. I'll review the tape later, and I'll make damn sure the sally port camera is recording, too. Who's coming to make the arrest for the Rangers?"

"Dunno, probably Clay and Levi."

The old man walked into booking, glanced at the four Hispanics, and did a double take. "Ernesto? Is that you, *mi amigo*?" Glancing at Aaron, he winked and continued, "Deputy, why is this man in cuffs? He is not a danger to us. Release him and give me his paperwork."

Aaron walked over slowly. "Release him?"

"Yes, he is not to be cuffed. His paperwork?"

"Uh, almost done."

Imperiously, the old man added, "As soon as it is finished, he must be segregated for his safety, understand?"

"Yes, sir."

"I must go prepare his release paperwork. I will be back shortly."

Aaron, his back to the four prisoners mouthed, "What?"

"He's an I, A, O."

"Gotcha, Captain. I think the DWI cell is empty, will that be good enough?"

"As long as it's clean."

The old man walked out of the booking area, a smile on his face as he watched the interactions among the four men. Pulling out his cell, he selected the speed dial for Clay, hit speaker, and waited for him to answer. "Boone."

"Clay, it's John. What's your ETA?"

"We should be there in twenty minutes. Is it really Rivas?"

"If he's not, he's the twin brother, right down to the tats."

"What did they get him for?"

"Speeding and drugs."

"How much?"

"Does it matter?"

"Not really… Just curious."

"I need to kill a few minutes, so I'll go find out. Park out of sight and stay out of booking when you get here. I'll walk him out the sally port, then y'all can take him."

"K. See you in a bit."

The old man punched his phone off, and headed around the side of the building to the parking and impound area. There was a DPS car parked next to a van still hooked to a tow truck, and he walked slowly over to it. "Trooper Lambert! How are you this fine day?"

Lambert, tall, dark and lugubrious, methodically hooked up the leash to his drug dog. "Above the ground, Captain. Can't say much more than that. Sit, Fang!"

Fang, the mixed breed drug dog immediately sat and woofed softly at the old man, as Lambert asked, "This the vehicle?"

The tow truck driver replied, "Yep, picked it up just east of Hovey Road. Deputies said it's loaded with probable drugs," as he dropped the van to the ground. "Here's the keys. I used gloves to do what I needed to for steering and putting the van in neutral."

Lambert just nodded as he took the keys, then led Fang around the vehicle. Fang sat down five or six times, but didn't do anything else, and the old man began to worry. Lambert made a couple of notes in his wheel book, then unlocked the back door of the van, swinging the doors all the way open. The back of the van was a mess of dirty clothes, four suitcases, and underneath that, multiple wrapped packages.

The old man asked, "Drugs or not?"

Lambert nodded. "Lots."

The old man asked, "But Fang didn't alert, did he?"

Lambert said dourly, "Oh yeah, multiple times. But I'm not going to tell you what the alert is."

The old man laughed, "Fine, whatever. Rangers are on the way, I just needed to confirm we have enough to hold the other three."

Lambert nodded and turned back to the van, and the old man headed back into booking. He walked in to see the other three Hispanics still sitting in booking, an Aaron walking back around the corner. "Captain, *Señor* Rivas has been moved."

"Thank you, Deputy." The old man picked up the PR paperwork from the back counter, walked around to the DWI cell, and motioned for the control room to open the door. It clanged open and he stepped in, eyeing Rivas as he sat languidly on the bench. "You ready to go Ernesto?" Fanning the paperwork in his hand, he said, "I've got your personal recognizance bond right here."

Rivas looked up at the old man in amazement. "What chu talkin' about, man?"

"I'm going to walk you out through booking, stop in the sally port, slap you on the back, loudly tell you how good a job you did, hand you this PR paperwork, and let your happy ass go, Ernesto."

Rivas laughed, "You're crazy, man! You can't do that. They won't let you!"

Smiling, the old man said, "Your choice. Talk to me, or walk free. Now get your ass up, and let's go."

Rivas sat up, paled and said fearfully, "*Mijo*, you can't do this to me. You're going to get me killed!"

"Not my problem, *Mijo*. Let's go." The old man got a compliance grip on Rivas, levered him up off the bench, and marched him back through booking, saying loudly, "Thanks Ernesto, we'll take it from here. I've got your PR paperwork right here. As soon as we get outside, I'll release you."

He marched Rivas out the door to the sally port, took his handcuffs off and slapped him on the back as he handed him the bond paperwork, then turned and headed back toward the door to booking. Rivas looked around, and walked around the corner.

The other three Hispanics started talking among themselves, but were quickly separated by the deputies, each going to a separate isolation cell. What they didn't see was Levi Michaels wrestling Rivas to the ground, and arresting him on the side of the building.

***

The old man and Nan Randall high fived each other as the third of the men with Rivas was escorted back to the jail. "Damn, that worked out better than I could possibly have believed. Captain, you are truly crazy like a fox."

The old man laughed, "Well, given a drug bust or a murder rap, it was a pretty easy decision to make. The Rangers got him, and he'll go down for murder. We got, what, three hundred kilos of drugs off the street, and," he continued, looking down at his notes, "probably three good busts, at a minimum, plus all three of these drug runners will be doing hard time. Rivas' name will be mud with the cartel, and they'll probably try to hit him, but that's *not* our problem. Plus, that's going to make all of them nervous, especially when the cartel lawyers show up to rep these three."

Randall asked, "Why?"

"Well, those lawyers are going to run back to the cartel and tell them we released Rivas, and were friendly with him. They'll put two and two together, and get five."

"Five?"

"Yeah, five. In their minds, Rivas will become a CI for us, so they'll take down anyone close to him, and if these busts happen quickly in Arizona and Louisiana, they're going to think Rivas tipped them. That should make them look sideways at each other for a while."

Randall cautioned, "But some people may die."

The old man smiled. "Yep, that they will. And that's all for the good."

Nan Randall thought to herself, *Captain Cronin is not a nice man. That wasn't a smile, that was the monster that lives just below the surface getting some of its own back.* She shivered, even though it wasn't that cold, and followed the old man as he headed for the sheriff's office.

After they'd debriefed the sheriff, the old man headed back to his office and called Bucky, passing along what they'd gotten from the other three cartel guys, along with the info to leak that Rivas had been PR'ed out, and had left town.

***

Over dinner, Aaron finally asked, "John, I gotta ask, that whole thing you pulled day before yesterday, with… Rivas?"

"Yes?"

"Where… I mean you didn't really let him go, did you?"

The old man laughed, "Oh, no. He's in protective custody with the Rangers, while they prepare to bring him up on murder charges in El Paso."

"I almost blew it, didn't I?"

"Nope, I figured you'd pick up on the IAO clue and run with it, which was exactly what I wanted you to do."

Jesse asked curiously, "IAO?"

Matt and Aaron chorused, "Improvise, adapt, and overcome." Matt laughed, "The unofficial creed of the Marine Corps."

"Oh. Okay."

Aaron added, "I knew something was up, I just didn't know what. I didn't know how big a fish we had, and couldn't figure out why it was playing out like it was." Looking over at the old man he asked, "You've done that before, haven't you?"

"Might have, back in the day. It's all good. Phoenix got a good hit on the drug house there, and apparently the Staties and DEA hit a home run over in New Orleans. Apparently, the ninth ward hasn't changed their stripes since Katrina wiped it most of the way out. They got three houses, fifteen people, over a hundred kilos of product, almost a half million in cash, and something like nine Mercedes, Escalades, Audis, and one old Rolls."

Everybody shook their heads and said various things under their breath at that, until Felicia finally asked, "Why all the cars?"

Matt said, "Hon, when a car contains drugs, it can be confiscated. Now those cars will either be sold, or used as unmarked or undercover cars for new investigations."

"What about the houses?"

Matt deferred to the old man. "Well, it's the ninth ward, so they'll either be torn down or sold by the government. They were burned as drug houses, so the government really can't use them."

"What about the people?"

The old man laughed, "Oh, they were only the major distribution ring in South Louisiana, and tied into both St. Louis and Chicago going north, and Georgia and Florida going east. Maybe they'll get one or two of them to roll, and who knows how many more might get picked up."

Aaron laughed, "So, I did something right? Didn't I?"

The old man smiled. "That you did, and learned another trick of the trade. We'll make a cop out of you yet."

Dealing with Issues

Ranger Boone and the sheriff sat in the conference room as Jesse came in. "You wanted to see me, Sheriff? Hello, Clay."

Clay nodded. "Jesse."

The sheriff said, "Yes we do, Jesse. Take a seat."

She tentatively sat facing the two of them, and the sheriff continued, "This is about the shooting last month. Clay has finished the investigation, the grand jury no billed it, and you're cleared to return to duty. It was a good shoot, line of duty. Mrs. Halvorson won't be charged either."

Jesse almost sobbed in relief, and wiped her suddenly wet eyes. "Thank you. Why did it take so long?"

Clay replied, "The perp had a record a mile long, and it took a while to piece all his actions together, he was detoxing, so he was desperate. Once that was done, then it was a matter of interviewing the witnesses. Remember what I said about no two witnesses seeing the same thing?"

Jesse nodded.

"Well, that was the case here. You, Melaina, and Mrs. Halvorson basically *saw* the same thing. Linda didn't remember much, and what she did remember, contradicted y'all. Granted she was pistol whipped and down on the ground, so that had to be taken into account, without seeming to coerce her into a false statement. And all of that had to go to the grand jury."

The sheriff added, "Clay kept me in the loop the whole time, but I didn't think you'd want to be given bits and pieces. That's why I didn't say anything until it was all said and done."

Jesse bowed her head, saying softly, "Thank you. Thank you both." Looking up at the sheriff, she said, "I guess I need to get back in the saddle, the quicker the better."

The sheriff nodded. "You'll be on the schedule for Saturday. That's all I have for you."

Jesse got up and started for the door. "Thank you for the trust. It means a lot."

The two men nodded as Jesse walked out. Jesse got to her car before she cried, and she sat for a few minutes as the tension drained out of her. She finally took out her phone and called Aaron. "I'm cleared on the shooting. I'll be back on duty Saturday." After a couple of minutes, Jesse headed home, finally smiling a little bit.

***

Jesse tossed and turned, and finally got up, careful not to wake Aaron. She'd had trouble sleeping the last couple of nights, nightmares interrupting her sleep and making her feel like crap. She wandered into the kitchen saw that it was five thirty in the morning and decided to make a pot of coffee.

As the pot gurgled and spit, she leaned against the counter morosely staring into the darkness. "Can't sleep again?" the old man asked quietly as he walked in the kitchen.

Startled, Jesse whipped around. "No, dammit. Can't sleep, my head is killing me, I feel like shit and the kids are…"

"Whoa, whoa," the old man said, holding up his hands. "It's only been a little over a month since you had that shootout, and you just got cleared yesterday."

"I know, Papa, but I didn't feel like this last time." She poured two cups of coffee, handing him one. "Why is this time so different?"

"Thanks," he said, taking the coffee. "Every time is different. At least, it has been for me."

"I know you said don't dwell on it, but I can't…"

The old man sat down at the table, shrouded in darkness. "It's not something I can change. Matt's even noticed you're touchier."

Jesse sat with a sigh. "I know, I know. Even Aaron is kinda avoiding me."

The old man cupped his coffee. "Jesse, you need to follow your regular routine. Remember the good. Remember saving Mrs. Halvorson. Saving Linda and Melaina. *That* is what is important."

Jesse got up and hugged the old man. "Thanks, Papa. I know I can always come to you with a problem, and you'll listen."

He awkwardly hugged her back, saying nothing, figuring that was the best option at the moment. Jesse pulled back and moved around the table to flip on the kitchen lights. "What do you want for breakfast, Papa?"

"Bacon and eggs? Biscuits?"

Jesse laughed. "I don't know why I even ask. I think you would eat that every day, given the choice."

They ate breakfast as the sun peeked over the horizon, warming the kitchen with the morning light. Aaron came in a few minutes later, looking for coffee and said, "Kaya is wanting you. Jace is still asleep."

Jesse set Aaron's plate on the table and said, "Thank you. Eat, and I'll take care of the kids."

***

Jesse turned to Felicia. "Would you mind watching Jace and Kaya for a little bit? I need to get out of the house for a little while."

Felicia glanced up from peeling the potatoes in the sink. "Uh, sure. Are you okay?"

Jesse shrugged. "I don't know. I feel like crap. We're out of aspirin, so I'm going to run into town and get some. You need anything?"

"Masa harina. I'm doing tamales tomorrow and I'm just about out. A five-pound bag would be nice."

"I can do that." Jesse smiled wanly, grabbed her car keys off the hook and headed out the front door, as Matt came in the back door.

"What was that all about?" he asked.

"She needs some 'me time', I guess. She's not looking good. I don't think she's sleeping real good."

"She's grouchy, too. I think the shooting is getting to her."

Felicia looked at him sharply. "Can't you do anything? Can't you help?"

Matt shrugged. "If she'd give me the chance, maybe. But Aaron says she doesn't want to discuss it, period."

"Dammit. She has *never* left the kids like this. Not in this kind of mood, Matt I'm getting worried."

"I'll talk to John, maybe he knows somebody she will talk to."

Felicia hugged him. "Thank you. Now finish the potatoes while I get the kids down for their naps."

Matt rolled his eyes, but picked up the potato peeler and set to work, mumbling to himself.

***

Jesse drove aimlessly for a while, almost as if she was patrolling sector 2, but finally turned back toward town after her stomach growled. She felt a little better, and decided to stop and get some lunch before heading back to the ranch. She parked in front of Miguel's place, and walked slowly toward the door, until she heard, "Jesse, come, sit with me."

Padre Augustin, plump, balding, with a fringe of white hair, dressed all in black, sat in the shade at one of the smaller outdoor tables, a glass of beer on the table in front of him. Jesse smiled wanly, as she sat. "Padre."

"My child, you look tired."

Jesse laughed ruefully. "If you only knew."

Miguel bustled over with an iced tea, another bowl of chips, and a bowl of queso, asking, "Your usual, Jesse?"

"Sure, the two-taco plate sounds good."

"I'll get that right in. Padre, yours will be up in a minute."

The padre waved him off with a smile. "Take your time Miguel, I have all day."

Miguel laughed, "You may, but if *I* take all day, I'm going to lose business."

Jesse and the padre both laughed as Miguel turned away, asking another table how they were doing. Padre Augustin looked closely at Jesse. "Do you want to talk?"

Jesse looked around, then said softly. "I guess I need to. Would you mind?"

"No, my child. I never mind talking to my flock, even if technically you are not one of mine. But I sense you'd like a little more privacy?" Jesse nodded, and he continued, "Then we shall adjourn to my luxurious rectory after a delicious meal."

Jesse laughed, "And how many beers have you had, Padre? Especially to be calling your rectory luxurious?"

He shrugged. "It's dry, the roof is good, the AC works, and Maria cooks. What more can a humble parish priest ask for?"

"Well, those *are* good points."

Miguel delivered their lunches, and they ate quietly, each lost in their own thoughts. Fifteen minutes later, the padre pushed back from the table with a groan. "I know better. I really do. But that *carne asada* is *so* good! But I will pass on dessert, since I know Maria is baking chocolate chip cookies."

Jesse grinned. "I would agree, Miguel's *flan* is good, but *chocolate*!

The padre wiggled his eyebrows. "The better to entice you into my lair, my child."

Jesse asked curiously, "Are you a regular Catholic, Padre?"

"Why? Don't I act like one?"

Jesse said thoughtfully, "No… You're different from Padre Louis. I mean, I know you're both Hispanic, but…"

The padre quickly paid the lunch bill, over Jesse's protestations, and said, "Come, walk with me. It's only a block."

Jesse got up, saying, "You didn't answer my question…"

The padre looked at her sharply. "No, I didn't. I'm actually a lot different from Padre Louis. I'm actually a Jesuit, for starters. Secondly, I have not always been a peaceful man."

Jesse mulled that over as they completed the short walk, and Padre Augustin didn't say anything else until they were seated on the couch in his austere office, Maria dispatched to bring coffee and cookies.

"Padre, I need… Well… I… I need to talk to somebody about what happened a couple of weeks ago."

"The shooting?"

"Yes," Jesse said softly.

"Let me guess. Insomnia, you're jumpy as hell, you don't want to be with… Aaron, right?"

Jesse nodded. "I… I'm carrying, but I'm almost afraid I'm going to shoot somebody by accident."

"But at the same time, you're overprotective of the kids?"

Jesse shuddered. "Paranoid doesn't begin to describe it, I rememb…"

The padre held up his hand. "Stop right there!"

Jesse looked at him with a shocked expression. "But I need…"

"No, you *do not* need to relive the incident. Don't dwell on it. Only in the broadest terms, should you remember it. You don't drink do you?"

"Um, not really. An occasional beer or a glass of wine."

"Good! The other thing you need to do is follow your usual routine."

Jesse smiled ruefully. "With young kids? Routine? Really, Padre?"

The padre laughed. "Well, as close as you can. Since I have not had that pleasure, well, suffice to say I can imagine, and have heard many things at confession…"

Maria bustled in, pushing a small cart with a carafe, two cups, and two saucers with cookies on them. She set the padre's cup and saucer in front of him, then repeated it with Jesse, finally setting the carafe of coffee between them. The padre and Jesse both thanked her, and she smiled as she pushed the cart out the door.

Jesse asked, "But according to the Bible, we aren't supposed to take another's life. And this isn't the first time…"

The padre cocked an eyebrow, stopping Jesse in mid-sentence, "Ezekiel thirty-three verse six says, *But if the watchman sees the sword coming and does not blow the trumpet, and the people are not warned, and a sword comes and takes a person from them, he is taken away in his iniquity; but his blood I will require from the watchman's hand.* In this case, you were that watchman. You did blow the trumpet, in a manner of speaking, preventing him from taking a person."

He took a bite of his cookie, and a sip of coffee before he continued, "In Exodus twenty-thirteen, it says…"

Jesse said, "The seventh commandment, *You shall not murder.* Which I did."

"No, you didn't. Yes, you took a life, but you *did not* murder anyone. Now take it one step further: Exodus twenty-two two says, *If the thief is found breaking in, and he is struck so that he dies, there shall be no guilt for his bloodshed.* That is where you are. You are the watchman. Yes, you took a life, but you did so in defense of others. You have not sinned against God for that."

A tear rolled slowly down Jesse's cheek, as she bowed her head, saying very softly, "Thank you, Padre."

"Jesse, you are much like your grandfather. He and I have had many conversations over the years about this very thing, even before I became a priest."

Jesse looked up. "You, but you've only been here, what, ten years?"

The padre grimaced. "Remember, I said I was not a nice man? That was when I knew your grandfather. We… We fought the drug kingpins together in South America. I was… a Kaibil- Guatemalan Special Operations. I was in the first class, and was sent to support the border operations against the Colombians, then picked up for the Narcoterrorism force headed by your DEA. Your grandfather and I worked together for almost a year, off and on."

"Papa never talks about those times, well, not specifically."

"Nor will he ever. We did things that…, that weren't pretty. Even then, I was a good Catholic boy. I had thought about the seminary, but my family was poor. The military allowed me to support them, at least until they were killed."

Jesse reached out. "Oh, Padre. I'm so sorry."

He shrugged. "It was, and is, life in Central America. The poor are fodder for the rich or the criminals. Either way, they are caught in the middle, and some do not survive."

A knock on the door interrupted him, and Maria stuck her head in. "Padre, you have a call."

"Give me one minute, Maria." Turning to Jesse, he said hurriedly, "Jesse, I know what you are feeling. I have been there and felt it. Follow your routine, don't dwell on what happened. Remember the good, and why you did what you did. You will get over it, maybe not today or tomorrow, but soon. You are strong, and you have strong people around you who care for and support you. They have all been where you are. Lean on them. Bless you my child, now if you will excuse me?"

The padre got up and she impulsively hugged him. "Thank you, Padre, thank you!"

Maria stuck her head back in. "The phone, Padre, Miss Jesse?"

Jesse nodded, moving toward the door. "Lead on, Maria. I'd better be getting home. Please remind the padre that y'all are invited to the fandango on the second of July."

Maria smiled. "I will. Say hello to Felicia for me, please."

Jesse nodded, "I will. She is such a help."

Oh God, I've pushed the kids off on her way too much. I'm thankful she's willing to help, and I need to find a way to thank her. And I need to start being a mother again.

Dead Man in the Patch

Jesse sighed and banged on the dash of two-fourteen yet again, mumbling, "Damn squeaks!" She was answered by an elongated spiteful squeal from the dash as she turned down Hovey Road. Dreading the next eight hours of patrol, and knowing if she let it get to her, it would drive her nuts, she tried to think of something to do. As she fiddled with the dash, she almost missed the open gate on TPO 37. She slammed on the brakes, backed around and stopped, facing into the patch. She looked around, didn't see anyone, nor any vehicles, but there were two buzzards circling up near the rig. Getting out, she walked carefully over to the track, noting a set of dually tracks coming out of the patch, and what might have been a single track underneath it in a couple of spots.

"Dispatch, two-fourteen, I'm out at Trans Pecos Oil thirty-seven off Hovey Road. Got an open gate, and buzzards. Maybe nothing, but roll backup, if you would. I'm out on the handheld."

"Two-fourteen, dispatch. Copied all. TPO thirty-seven off Hovey Road." She heard the countywide tone, then dispatch again, "Who's closest to Hovey Road? Two-fourteen is requesting backup for investigation."

She heard Matt answer, "Two-oh-four, I'm in sector one. I can be there in ten."

"Roger, two-oh-four. Proceed. Two-fourteen, two-oh-four ETA is ten minutes."

"Roger dispatch, two-fourteen." Jesse took a deep breath, dug a set of gloves out of her pants pocket and put them on, loosened the Python in her holster, and slipped through the gate, stepping off to the side of the track as she walked slowly toward the rig, scanning for all she was worth. She was concentrating so hard, she didn't hear the semis pulling up on Hovey Road, and jumped when one of them blew their air horn. She waved at them, and started to turn back around, when the horn was blown again, *What the hell? Dammit, I don't need this right now...* She turned and started walking back toward her car, picking up speed when she saw one of the drivers getting out of the first semi.

Holding up her hand, she yelled, "Stop right there! Do not step off the road!"

The driver ignored her and started to walk around two-fourteen, and she yelled again, "Stop! Stop right there!"

The driver weaved a little bit, then leaned against the hood of two-fourteen, smirking, "Hey, honey, you're blocking my route. I need to get in there and drop these loads off."

"Sorry, but right now you can't go in there. We have to check something out, first."

The driver stood up, and Jesse realized how big he was, probably 6'4", maybe 6'5", heavily muscled, deeply tanned, dressed in the typical oil field khakis, with run down steel-toed boots. "Hey, where's Rick? He's 'sposed to be here to meet us?"

He started forward again, and Jesse put out her arm. "Sir, I'm sorry you can't…"

He knocked her arm aside. "Where's Rick? Don' see his truck. He's 'sposed to be here. Gotta check on m'buddy."

He continued walking forward and Jesse drew her Taser. "Sir, if you don't stop I'm going to have to Taser you. You *cannot* go down there."

He looked over his shoulder. "Fuck you bitch. Gotta find Rick."

Jesse shrugged. "Sir, I'm going to Taser you." When he kept going, she hit him squarely between the shoulder blades with one dart going high, and one low. The five second cycle from the Taser put him on the ground, flopping and moaning. She quickly cuffed him, leaving him groaning, face down on the ground, as she heard footsteps behind her. She hopped up and turned, to see the other drivers and workers coming around the back of her unit, sounding angry. She keyed her mic, "Two-oh-four, pick it up. Got a situation here." Holding up her hands, she said, "Please stop where you are. You cannot go down there, not until we do some investigating of a possible situation."

She half heard a couple of comments in Spanish, but couldn't make them out. One of the other drivers, young and scruffy, said, "Hey, why'd you tase Rob? He wasn't doing anything to you?"

"I told him, and I'm telling y'all, you *cannot* go down there."

"Is there something wrong? What are you not telling us? Where's the pusher that's supposed to be here?" the scruffy driver asked.

Jesse heard a distant chirping noise, but it was overridden by the rising wail of a siren, and she replied, "I don't know, and you need to go back and sit quietly in your trucks. Rob here decided not to obey my commands, that's why he got tased and cuffed. He's going to stay that way until we figure out what is going on, okay?"

Although Jesse didn't realize it, she'd taken a half step back, put her hand on her pistol and started to crouch. The scruffy driver, realizing she was serious and not going to take any crap, decided common sense was the better action, motioning the others back to the trucks, "We're going. But we want answers!"

Matt slid two-oh-four to a stop and came out of the car quickly, which hastened the driver's and others' return to their trucks. "What have you got?" he asked, pointing to the cuffed and moaning driver, lying on the ground.

Jesse shrugged, saying, "Not sure, other than one asshole who disregarded commands and got his ass tased for the trouble. I'd just started to walk down there when these bozos showed up. I saw the gate open, and buzzards."

"Well, let's go see what's what. Since you'd already started, you lead, that way I can follow your tracks. This asshole can wait."

Jesse nodded. "Glove up, we'll go down the left side. Let's go." They walked carefully back down the side of the track, looking to both sides, until Jesse saw what she first thought was a big paper bag. As she got closer, the odor hit her. "Damn, got a body. Ten yards ahead." She drew her pistol as Matt came up behind her. "You go right, I'll go left."

Matt drew his pistol, looked at the track, and stepped carefully over the tire tracks until he was clear of the track, nodding at Jesse, they started moving forward in turn. The shack was clear, and the two storage containers sitting on site were locked. As they approached the body, Matt saw an oily patch in the dirt. "Something was parked there. And looks like multiple foot prints. Your angle is better, I'll come around to your side." As Matt started around the body, the chirping started again, and Matt stopped. "Hear something?"

Jesse nodded, "Something chirping? Yeah."

Matt scanned around, then stepped over a couple of feet, because he saw a small phone lying on the ground. "Got it, it's a phone. Going to answer it." Matt picked it up, and hit speaker, Hello?"

A tinny voice sounded, yelling, "Dammit, Rick, where you been? I've been calling for an hour."

"Who is this?"

"Dammit Rick, you know damn well this is Jim, your fucking boss! Did the trucks get there yet? I had a flat, but I'll be there in ten minutes."

Matt looked at Jesse, who raised her eyebrows, miming come on.

Matt grimaced. "Sir, this is Deputy Sheriff Carter. We have a situation here. I would appreciate it if you would identify yourself and come on here. It would save us all a lot of trouble."

There was silence for a few seconds, then a dull answer. "My name is Jim Owens. I'm the district manager for TPO. If you have Rick's phone, this is not good. I will be there in ten minutes."

"Thank you, sir. While I cannot verify this, I would appreciate it if you would not make any phone calls until you come here and talk to us."

"Shit. Rick… Rick Deen is dead, isn't he?"

"Mr. Owens, if you would just come on out here."

"Soon as I can."

***

Clay and Levi, along with the old man, Aaron, and Doc Truesdale huddled off to the side of the track. Clay nodded at Levi. "This is the way it's supposed to work. Deputies that pay attention to procedure, document the hell out of the scene, and more importantly, think outside the box. Don't get used to it."

That generated a round of laughter, and Doc asked, "Okay, y'all got what you need? I'll go ahead and haul the body. I'll do an autopsy, but we know the findings are going to be death caused by gun shot. I'm assuming y'all will want an autopsy. Probable TOD is going to be sometime yesterday evening, no defense marks that I can see."

Levi looked around. "Yep, autopsy, please. Anybody see anything different?"

The old man looked at Aaron, who said, "Not that *I* see. We got casts of the boot prints here, the tire tracks, a sample of the dropped oil, and the probable motorcycle track up at Hovey Road. Photos of all of that, from different angles, photos of where somebody brushed out the probable motorcycle tracks down here, one spent shell case, and one satellite cell phone. I've got a list from Mr. Owens of what company stuff is probably missing, like the truck and computers, but I'm not sure how to account for the amount of missing money. Oh yeah, and printed all the doors, door handles and the tops of the tables."

The old man said, "Well, let's ask him again." The group walked slowly back up to the gate, where a disconsolate Jim Owens, tall, wiry and white haired, sat on the hood of his truck, staring at his phone. The old man said, "Mr. Owens, one more question, if you don't mind. You said Mr. Deen always had an envelope full of cash with him?"

Jim Owens looked up sadly. "Yeah, Rick was an old oilfield guy. Always paranoid about getting caught without any cash. He'd always cash his check and get a thousand in cash. It was always the same: five hundreds, four fifties, and the rest twenties. That way if he needed something, he could get it without waiting, or fighting with getting folks to take a credit card."

"Did he keep it with him?"

Owens hung his head, "Most times it was in his left shirt pocket. Everybody knew it, if they knew Rick. It wasn't like he hid it. If he had leftovers from the last paycheck, lot of times, he'd throw the envelope in the glove box."

"So you really don't know how much cash he had?"

Owens shrugged. "Well, yesterday was payday, so he had a least a thousand. Could have been more in the truck. Earlier this year, we went to a meeting in his truck, and I was looking for something and opened the glove box, there were five or six envelopes in there. Most of them with money in them."

"Thank you."

Owens raised a hand. "Why? Who would have done this? Rick was a good tool pusher. He was well respected… I can't…

Clay said, "Sir, we don't know. You said it wasn't unusual for him to come out early to a rig, but that it wasn't required."

Owens shook his head. "No, nothing was *scheduled* until this morning. But Rick liked to get the computers set up, get the air on, and have cold water in the fridge for the roustabouts. He was between girlfriends again, so…"

Levi said, "So that is why he picked the company truck up yesterday afternoon. He probably came straight out here, so the earliest he could have gotten here is probably five p.m. And nobody knew he would do that, right?"

"No, sir. I mean, I would have figured he would, but we've worked together for almost fifteen years."

"Thank you, sir. We're going to release the scene, so you can go ahead and get your equipment moved in. Hopefully you have a spare driver, since Robert Walls is going to reside in our jail until his hearing for DWI, assaulting an officer, and interference with the duty of a peace officer."

Owens laughed bitterly. "Walls… Damn druggie. That should have gotten him fired, for being drugged up on the rig, but they sent him to rehab, and put him driving a semi. He's gone now, for sure. Back in the day, it was booze. You could at least search for that, and take it. Now days, it's meth. You can search all damn day and not find it. Shit's going to get people killed."

"Let us move our cars, and it's all yours, sir."
***

The semis pulled through the gate as the group gathered by Hovey Road, with Levi asking, "Anybody else think this one is a tad strange?"

The old man chuckled. "Strange isn't the word for it. It smells to high heaven. It looks to me like a targeted robbery."

Matt asked, "What makes you think that John? I mean…"

The old man ticked off on his fingers, "One shot, up close and personal. No indication of a confrontation or a fight. Did he know whoever it was? Maybe… All the things missing are easy to sell or move, at least three computers, a hundred bucks apiece. A 2016 Dodge Ram 3500 field truck, full of equipment, that's five, ten grand right there, other than the truck, mostly untraceable. Part the truck out, that's ten, twenty grand. Or they run it across the border, sell it PEMEX as is, twenty-five grand for the whole deal. Poof…"

Clay chimed in, "Nothing taken from the body, other than money. No credit cards. And they left the phone."

Aaron said slowly, confused, "That I don't get. Those phones are expensive!"

Clay replied, "And traceable. Iridium is also a defacto military network. "

Aaron said, "I know. We used to carry them in the field…"

Clay smiled, "Lots of oilfield folks do too. There are a lot of patches that have no cell coverage, or real spotty. A stolen sat phone, we make one call, and the network folks jump right on tracking it. Thieves, especially those that work the patch, know that. That's why they leave them."

Levi added, "So, we've got an unknown, possibly oil field worker or thief, motorcycle rider, who either stumbled on Mr. Deen, or followed him out here, did the deed, loaded up the bike and computers, and drove away. And El Paso PD says nothing was missing at the apartment Mr. Deen rented. Fridge was empty, AC was turned up, just like he expected to be gone for a while, which matches what Mr. Owens said."

Clay smiled at Levi. "You're gonna have fun with this one. Jesse, Matt, thanks for a good job on the scene. The only thing I would have done different, is I wouldn't have answered the phone. I'd have written down the number, and called it from my phone."

Matt nodded. "Lesson learned."

Levi looked around. "Well, I think we're done here. Thanks, folks. John, do I call you or the sheriff for follow-up?"

The old man replied, "Call me. I'm not retired yet, and I'll pass anything to Jose that you get."

Chasing

The old man cautioned Matt about letting the defense attorney try to get him to say anything about what happened after the wreck, including the drugs Deputy Ortiz had found after Matt called for backup when he saw the package thrown from the Challenger. Luckily, it had been caught on video with a road sign, allowing them to pinpoint exactly where it had been thrown out.

As Matt drove over to the courthouse, he couldn't help but think back to that night, six months ago. It was a quiet Saturday, and he'd been ready to call it a night, sector four was boring as usual, but it still had to be patrolled. He'd been all the way down at the county line, getting ready to turn around when the Challenger had gone past heading north. He'd flipped on the lights, just in case somebody else was coming north, as he swung around and started back up two eighty-five.

What he hadn't expected to see was the tire smoke from the Challenger accelerating hard up two eighty-five. *What the hell? All, I'm doing is turning… Shit, I'm not going to catch him in this old beater…*

"Dispatch, two-oh-eight, northbound two eighty-five, late model dark grey or black Challenger, rabbited when I turned around at the county line.

Speed unknown, I'm at eighty and he's still pulling away."

Dispatch replied, "Roger, two-oh-eight. Anybody assist two-oh-eight on two eighty-five north?"

He continued accelerating hard after the car, but at 95 the old Ford started shimmying and he backed off to 90. "Dispatch, he's in excess of ninety."

He heard Deputy Ortiz answer, "Two-oh-one, I'm southbound out of town."

Matt thought he saw something come out of the side window and said, "Think the driver just threw something out. Coming up on…" A huge cloud of dust appeared in his headlights, and he continued, "Think the car is off at the curve just north of twenty-four hundred."

Matt jumped on the brakes, cussing the old Ford as it nosedived and swayed side to side, but he got slowed down enough to see a taillight fifty or sixty yards out in the brush. "Dispatch, car is off in the brush just north of twenty-four hundred. I'm out of the car, and in pursuit. Two-oh-one, I see your lights."

Matt jumped out, grabbing his Maglite and headed into the brush, following the tracks of the car as he heard Ortiz slide to a stop. Just as he got to the car, and saw the open driver's side door, he heard Ortiz yell, "Matt! Get out of there! Come back! *Mala Mujer*! *Mala Mujer*!"

Matt turned around. "What?" Just about that time, his legs began to sting, and he shined his light down, to see he was standing in a bunch of green plants with white flowers. "What about the driver?" The stinging got worse, and Matt headed back for the road, as they both heard screaming starting deeper in the brush.

He heard Ortiz calling for an ambulance, but wasn't sure why, then heard Ortiz yell, "You. Driver! Come back to the road with your hands on top of your head! Do it now! We have an ambulance on the way. You have been stung, and require immediate treatment! Come out *now*!"

Matt's legs were really burning and itching now, and he was tearing up. "Danny, what the hell is *Mala*…"

Ortiz hung his head. "Uh, what you call bull nettles. You've got them embedded in your pants. They're what's stinging you. Let me get the shears out of my medical kit, and we'll cut your pants legs off. That should…"

They heard another scream from the brush, and a sobbing voice said, "Oh my God, help me. *Help me*! I'm dying!"

Ortiz called out, "Come back to the road with your hands on top of your head! Do it now! We have an ambulance on the way. You have been stung, and require immediate treatment! Come out *now*! We are *not* coming in to get you."

A sobbing voice said weakly, "I… I'm coming out. Oh God, help me!"

Ortiz handed Matt the shears and said, "Cut them off higher than you were deep, I'm going to see where this asshole is."

Matt handed the shears back, wincing in pain, and tearing up. "I'll go get him. I'm already screwed up. At least you can arrest his ass and take him in. I don't need an ambulance." Matt sighed, flipped his Maglite back on and scanned the area, finally seeing a scrawny white male in dark shorts, without a shirt, staggering toward the road. Flipping the light beam over him, he said, "Come to the light. Keep your hands out where we can see them."

As the man turned, Matt could see the welts already rising on the man's chest, and he winced in sympathy. Hearing the warble of another siren in the distance, he said, "The sooner you get here, the sooner the ambulance crew can treat you. Keep coming!"

Instead, the man collapsed with a moan, going face down in the nettles. Cursing, Matt ran to him, shoved a gloved hand under his armpit and lifted him to his feet. "Walk, you son of a bitch! I am *not* going to carry you!" They finally stumbled to the side of the road, just as the ambulance pulled, up, and the medics got out, gloving up and asking, what the issue was.

Ortiz said, "Bull nettles."

The senior medic replied, "Shit. Okay, we're going to have to put on biohazard gear." Turning to the EMT, he continued, "Get the gurney out while I throw on a suit. You stay clear. Deputy, can you sit him on the gurney? Do you need treatment too?"

Matt led the man over to the gurney and deposited him on it, "Yeah, I got into them too, not as bad as this guy. He's hurting."

Ortiz said, "Check his pocket, let's see if…"

The medic looked at the man as he paled and fell over on the gurney, and said, "Shit, he's coding. Histamine reaction. Joey! Help me load him." They quickly threw the man in the back, as the medic frantically worked to fasten the straps, they heard him yell, "Run code three, tell the hospital one coding, histamine reaction to bull nettles. Will need decon." The siren drowned out anything else he might have said, as the ambulance threw gravel heading for the hospital.

Matt slumped against the front of the car, tears running down his face, as he moaned in pain. Ortiz said, "Cut your pants off, and if I were you, I'd dump my boots too. One thing you could do… Well, is piss on yourself. If you want to do that, I've got a gallon of water you can wash down with."

Matt nodded, "At this point, anything that helps. God this hurts! It hurts worse than being shot! It's not like anybody is going to see me." Matt started cutting away his pant legs, then splitting them down the seams, until he was standing in a ragged pair of shorts. Reaching down, he untied his shoes, then peeled off his socks, cussing the gravel on the side of the road, "Water?"

Ortiz nodded, "Be right back."

Matt stripped off his gloves and dropped them on top of his shoes, then turned away and pissed down both legs, using his hands to brush the urine down the back of his legs. Ortiz came back with a gallon jug of water, and asked, "Feel any better?"

"Some, now I just want to gnaw my legs off, instead of taking the shotty to them."

"Wait a few minutes, then rinse off. I've got a wrecker coming, and they can haul the car out. You need to go on to the hospital."

"Yeah, I am. Oh, I think the asshole threw something out just prior to the curve. It should be on the video."

"I'll check it, go!"

"Thanks, Danny."

***

Matt sat on the exam table in the ER, as he waited for the resident to come check on him. An older, grumpy PA had checked on him, then handed him some wipes, and told Matt to wipe them down his legs and down his right arm, where there were some bumps. The PA cautioned him to only wipe once, and throw them in the trash. He felt pretty foolish, sitting there in a uniform top, cut off 5.11 pants and his gunbelt, but he had to admit whatever the wipers were, it didn't hurt as badly as it had earlier.

The resident finally bustled in, flipped his glasses down, and asked, "Carter? What the hell possessed you to wallow around in nettles?"

Matt bristled. "I was chasing a guy, didn't realize what it was, as I was more worried about where the guy was, and what he had in the car."

"Well, you're in better shape than he is. What did you do, throw him down in them? He's in ICU, he's coded twice, and apparently is an asthmatic on top of everything else. Although that doesn't explain why he's…"

"Why he's what?"

The resident shrugged. "He's got a medical marijuana card from Colorado in his wallet. Kinda contra-indicated."

Matt replied, "I need to see that wallet, as we still haven't ID'ed him. It was more important to get him here."

"Are you the arresting officer?"

Matt's thoughts were interrupted when Ortiz came in. "How you doing?"

Matt cocked his head. "Better? For versions of better, anyway."

Ortiz turned to the resident, "Do you have the property of the white male in black shorts that was brought in an hour or so ago?"

The resident said, "The nurses have it at the ICU. That's where he is." Glancing at Matt he said, "You can go home. I'm going to give you a shot of Benadryl, and I'd suggest you be ready for bed in a half hour. You should be good to go tomorrow. If you have any problems, come back in."

"Okay, Doc."

***

Matt sat quietly in Judge Cotton's courtroom, waiting to be called as he started the proceedings against Claude 'CJ' Ryan, for possession with the intent to distribute marijuana, cocaine, and methamphetamine. Ryan had finally been released from the hospital, bonded out, and apparently required further treatment in Midland. He'd had a haircut, and was dressed in a coat and tie, obviously at the direction of his lawyers.

Danny Ortiz slipped in beside him. "Nothing yet?"

"Just starting. They cleaned the kid up, didn't they?"

Ortiz sighed, "They always do. Little choirboys."

Matt snorted, "Yeah, right. I hope this is quick, I've got cows to move and people waiting on me."

Judge Cotton went through the litany of proposed charges for young Mr. Ryan, and turned to the DA. "Mr. Newton, you want to call your witnesses?"

Paul Newton, the lanky DA known as 'Ichabod,' stood. "Yes, sir. I call Deputy Matthew Carter to the stand."

After Matt was sworn in, Newton said, "Deputy Carter, please state your qualifications for the Judge."

Matt rattled off his quals, his history, and the average numbers of hours he patrolled a month. Newton then asked, "Can you provide the details of the events of the night of the nineteenth of August please?"

Matt glanced down at his notes, saying, "I was at the end of the shift, patrolling sector four, which reaches to the south edge of the county and encompasses approximately six hundred square miles. I was at the county line on two-eighty-five, and observed one dark late model Challenger go by me heading north. I flipped on my overheads to turn around, and…"

Five minutes later, he concluded his recitation of the traffic stop, saying he'd turned the actual arrest and follow-up to Danny Ortiz, due to being stung by the bull nettles.

"Thank you, Deputy Carter, I have no further questions."

Matt started to get up, but the lawyer sitting at the defense table with Ryan said, "I have some questions." Matt watched him get up, then glance over his shoulder at an older, florid faced man sitting directly behind the defense table.

He walked over to stand directly in front of Matt, asking, "So you aren't really a deputy, are you? You're just a part-timer, playing at being a cop?"

Matt stiffened, but replied politely, "As I said, I am a reserve deputy, I have met all Texas peace officer training requirements, and I maintain all of the certifications required to be a peace officer. I have been a reserve deputy…"

The lawyer cut him off. "Whatever. Why did you pursue my client and run him off the road? Were you trying to kill him?"

Matt held his temper. "I pursued Mr. Ryan because he was exceeding the speed limit. The fact that he ran off the road was due to his losing control of the vehicle, I never got close to him."

"But you claimed you were close enough to see my client *throw* something out of the car, didn't you?"

"I did believe I saw an object thrown from the car."

"So what did my client supposedly throw out? Or did you throw something out of *your* car, *Deputy* Carter?"

Matt bristled, and started to answer when Judge Cotton said, "Mr. Lyons, do you actually have any pertinent questions? You're impugning a deputy in my court, which is not a good thing, unless you actually have some proof."

"No further questions, your honor," Lyons walked back to the defense table, shrugging as he looked at the florid faced man.

Judge Lyons said, "You're dismissed Deputy. Mr. Newton, call your next witness."

Matt sat back down as the DA called Ortiz, and listened as Danny recited the rest of the arrest, including finding one package of meth in the car, and a package of cocaine and another of marijuana in the roadside ditch where Matt had indicated something was thrown out. When Lyons, the defense lawyer tried to go after the packages and their ownership, Ortiz was able to show they had Ryan's fingerprints on them, and he had a list of drugs to buy in his wallet. Matt chuckled to himself at that, and listened with interest as the DA listed the drugs recovered from the scene and the car, then reading the indictment of Claude Ryan on felony drug charges, possession with intent to distribute, and possession of a weapon without a license of carry. It appeared they'd dropped the speeding charge.

Judge Cotton called a recess before the defense started their case, and Matt and Ortiz left to head back to work.

As they were leaving the court house, the florid faced man Matt had noticed sitting behind the defense table came up, blustering, "I'll see your ass fired, and run out of this county for trying to kill my boy!" Turning on Ortiz he continued, "And you, you fucking Spic! You probably planted those drugs on my boy, didn't you?"

Matt replied, "I don't know who you are, but you realize you are threatening duly sworn officers, don't you?"

The man got even redder in the face, "I'm Charles Ryan. I can buy and sell your asses. I'm going…"

The attorney, Lyons, grabbed him by the arm, "Charles, not now! Come on, *come on*!" Turning to the deputies, he said, "My client is overwrought, he didn't mean…"

Ryan yanked away from Lyons, "Go talk to him. I'm going back to Midland, and I'm going to take care of this problem." He stomped off, closely followed by Lyons, who was talking fast.

Matt looked at Danny, "Could that be considered a threat?"

Bemused, Ortiz replied, "Yeah, I think so. I can't believe he called me a Spic, that's not the usual insult down here. And that accent isn't a Texas one."

"Guess we better let the Captain know about it, shouldn't we?"

Ortiz nodded. "Yep, let's go tell him. He's gonna *love* this one!"

Grand Opening

Jesse and the old man walked down to the new gun range from the house, with Jesse listing the work that had been done, as the old man took in the completed building. It was a brown steel building, but looked more like an office than the ones he was used to seeing. It had windows, a porch, and green metal roof. Stepping up on the porch, Jesse opened the door and laughed, "Enter and sign in please!"

The old man stopped just inside the front door in amazement. "Damn, I can't believe…" He looked at the wooden display cases, the wooden wall racks, and the seating area. "Who?"

Jesse laughed delightedly. "Felix. He came out and built them for us. The glass fronts and tops came out of the old Franklin store in town, and didn't cost us much." Grabbing his hand, she led him down the hall, opened a door and continued, "This is Toad's play room, as he calls it."

The old man looked around, sniffed and said, "Hoppe's and machine oil. Can't go wrong with that." He walked over to the metal lathe set up in the back corner, scratched his head, and said, "Huh, never heard of Monarch. But it's an old one, no question."

There was a Monarch milling machine over there too. He saw workbenches, obviously used, but clean, what looked like a dip tank, a small sandblasting unit, and various other things he couldn't identify. One vise held a barrel and an engine turned bolt action, but he didn't recognize it. Turning to Jesse he asked, "Toad brought all of this and set it up?"

"Yep. He said he bought out some old gunsmith over in New Mexico. He brought all this stuff the week you were down in Laredo instructing." Pointing to the barrel and action, she continued, "He's got some project for somebody that he started. I forgot you haven't been in here since we got the shell up around the vault."

The old man shook his head as they walked to the roll up door in the back, where a number of target stands, with stakes and target backers were arranged, ready to go out the door. Pallets of ammunition were lined up on the back wall, along with boxes of targets. "When are y'all going to open this place?"

Jesse thought for a minute. "We're looking at mid-April. Make that weekend a freebie, except for targets, and ammunition. That would at least give people a chance to try the place out."

As they walked outside, Matt met them on the Gator, "You want to ride out and see what we did for the thousand-yard target? I wanted to show you something out that way, anyway."

The old man shrugged. "Sure, why not." Jesse headed back into the building as the old man climbed into the Gator, "I can't believe how nice that turned out. And I can't help but wonder how much Toad spent on all that equipment."

Matt chuckled. "I think he got it for damn near nothing, just for hauling it off. The daughter just wanted it gone, saying it was nasty and a fire hazard. Toad offered her a decent price, but she said just give her scrap value, and get it out within a week. He paid the movers more to get it over here than he paid for it."

"Damn! Even with the moving costs, sounds like a helluva deal." As they trundled up to the berm, the old man saw a steel plate propped up on the ground, and an oddly shaped box sticking up behind it, with what looked suspiciously like a housing for a camera on top. "Video camera?"

"Yep, battery powered, wireless camera. Got an antenna mounted on top of the firing point cover, with power, the control head, and a hangar for a little TV over the firing points, so the spotter can see the hits."

"And hope like hell nobody shoots the camera, right?"

Matt laughed, "That's why the AR five hundred steel plate is propped up in front of it!" Driving around the back of the berm, he said, "And I had them go ahead and dig out that seep that was back here, since we needed some extra dirt for the berms," pointing to a couple of acre depression, with about three feet of water in it. "I'm surprised nobody ever did anything with that."

The old man replied, "It was always on the 'to do list', but since we didn't use this for pasture I just never got around to it."

***

A grand opening banner hung from the front of the building, and about thirty cars and trucks were in the parking lot as the old man walked down to the range. It was still fifteen minutes before they were supposed to open and he chuckled to himself as Yogi bounded along chasing whatever he was chasing through the grass. *Enjoy the turnout, it won't last. Still not sure this is a good idea, but it's their money. Maybe I can get Toad to work on some of the stuff in the safe, though. Gotta ask him what he charges.*

As he walked into the shop, a harried Jesse came over, blowing hair out of her face. "Good, you're here! Aaron brought the MRAD down, so you can fire the first shot to officially open the range!"

"What? Hell, we've been shooting…"

Jesse held her hand up. "That was private and testing. Please Papa? A lot of folks want to see you shoot!"

"Oh good, nothing like a little pressure in the morning, and me with a couple of cups of coffee in me. Shouldn't it really be Matt and Aaron? After all, this is their idea!"

Jesse grabbed him by the arm, pulling him toward the back room. "Papa, we've all agreed you should be the one to officially fire the first shot."

"You going to spot for me?"

Jesse smiled. "Of course. Just like old times."

"Let's go do this, then. Where's the rifle?" Jesse pointed to the gun case sitting on the ammo pallet, and the old man popped it open, picked up the MRAD and verified it was safe, then looked around. Jesse handed him three rounds, which the old man slipped into his shirt pocket.

Aaron had already taken a shooting mat out to the firing point, and the old man headed out the front door, rifle in a hunter's carry. That got people's attention, and a couple of dozen folks followed as he and Jesse walked down to the thousand-yard firing point. The old man pointed to the box of foam ear plugs. "If you don't already have noise protection, you might want to grab a set of foamies and put them in. Since I got roped into this, might as well make it a little more interesting than just watching an old fart shoot."

Propping the rifle up on the shooting bench, he continued, "This is a Barrett MRAD, chambered in three thirty-eight Lapua." Taking one of the rounds from his pocket he said, "I'm shooting a two hundred fifty grain bullet, at a little over twenty-eight hundred feet per second. Which is about three times the speed of sound. That's the big *crack* sound you'll hear. Now at six dollars a pop, these aren't cheap." Pulling out his spare 1911 magazine, he popped a round free. "Now, this is a forty-five, it's old, fat, and slow. This is two hundred grains of hollow point, but it is actually subsonic, only going about eighty-fifty, nine hundred feet per second. Of course, it has a lot less powder." He handed them to one of the people standing there. "Pass them around."

A few low whistles were heard, and he chuckled. Holding up a little Kestrel meter, he flipped the shield on the anemometer, and it started whirring. "This is a pocket weather station. At a thousand yards, the more information you have, the better your chances of making an accurate shot." Glancing down he smiled. "And it looks like I get lucky, the wind is directly behind us, which is *not* normal around here. And the humidity is twenty percent, it's sixty-four degrees, and we're right at three thousand feet above sea level. That tells me I'm gonna be looking at somewhere around twenty-five MOA up to hit the target."

He picked up the MRAD and tweaked the scope to the thousand-yard setting, then backed it off one click. "So I'm actually going to be aiming almost twenty-one *feet* above the target."

A round of oh's and ah's, and a few laughs were heard, as he pointed up to the TV screen above the firing point. "That is the target, from about ten feet. It's that little white dot you can just barely see way out there. It duplicates a normal sized male torso and head." Jesse handed the two rounds back to him, and he finished up, "And now, I'll actually attempt to hit that target. Please make sure you have your ear protection in, 'cause it's about to get loud. Please stay behind me, and Matt, if you will, would you act as the range officer?"

Matt stepped up. "More than happy to!"

The old man put the rifle down on the mat, got down behind it and wiggled into position, opening the bolt and waiting.

Matt looked down range, then left and right, saying, "Range is now hot. Ready on the right, ready on the left, ready on the firing line. You may fire at will."

The old man slipped all three rounds into the magazine, inserted it in the rifle, closed the bolt and wiggled down again, as Jesse sat cross legged behind him, looking through the spotting scope. She glanced up at the two flags, one at three hundred yards, another at six hundred yards and went back on the scope.

"Range is clear, winds are steady ten knots at six o'clock. Hold is twenty-five up."

They heard the old man mumbling, and he said, "Target!"

"Send it," Jesse replied.

CRACK! The recoil pushed the old man back, and he rode it as they heard a distant *ting* from the target, and a black splash appeared dead center on the target in the TV screen.

The old man worked the bolt as Jesse said, "Hold is good, dead center."

"Target."

"Send it." CRACK!

The old man rode the recoil, running the bolt and coming back on target as another *ting* was heard and another black splash overlapping the first one appeared.

"Target."

"Send it." CRACK!

One more *ting* rang out, was heard, and a third black splash appeared in the center of what would have been the head of the target. The old man safed the MRAD, and got up slowly, as the folks applauded and some of them shook their heads in amazement. The old man smiled. "I guess we're officially open, right?"

Matt smiled. "Yep, we are officially open. And folks, before you think this is easy, those three shots are based on probably sixty years of experience at shooting, and thousands of rounds down range. Not trying to deter anybody from trying a thousand yards, but come talk to us before you do, so we can see if your rifle is even capable of it!"

A little boy piped up, "Can I look?"

The old man laughed, "You want to look through the scope?"

The little boy nodded solemnly, and he put the rifle up on the shooting bench, removed the bolt, and used a sandbag to get the scope on the target, wiggling it until the rifle was firmly seated. "Okay, come here." The little boy came forward timidly, and the old man asked, "What's your name?"

"Enrico."

"Hop up here, Enrico." After the boy climbed up on the bench, the old man said, "Now put your head down behind the scope, no a little further back. Can you see through it?"

"Yes!" Enrico said happily, "It looks big through this…"

"Anybody else want to look?"

All the kids came forward, one at a time, and Enrico's dad asked, "How much does something like that cost?"

The old man scratched his head. "Well, all up… er, everything here, the MRAD, the Leupold sniper scope, the Kestrel, and the spotting scope is about ten thousand dollars, retail."

Enrico's dad whistled. "Wow. That's…"

The old man grinned crookedly. "A lot of money. This is actually a police rifle, the sheriff bought it for the office and I'm the custodian, for now."

Enrico tugged at the old man's arm. "Have you ever shot anything with it?"

"I shot a car a couple of years ago that we needed to stop. I hit the engine and it quit on the interstate."

"Cool!" Enrico said. "What else…"

Enrico's dad pulled him away. "Come on, let's go shoot our twenty-twos. That's what you wanted to come and do, right?"

"Yes, daddy."

***

Everybody sat around the kitchen table, the old man and Matt drinking coffee, everyone else with tea, and the remains of a pecan pie on the counter. Jesse groaned, as she rubbed her calves, "Oh my aching feet. I didn't expect that many people to show up, much less to keep coming!"

Aaron laughed ruefully, as he popped his leg loose and rolled the sock off his stump. "Your feet, my stump. We need a couple more RSOs. I don't think I sat down for over fifteen minutes the whole day!" Glancing at Felicia, he said, "That was a damn good idea to get Lucy to babysit, and Khalil worked out well helping out with the targets and running ammo out of the back. Did we remember to pay them?"

Matt nodded. "Yep, cash on the barrel head. I gave them ten bucks an hour, and as far as I'm concerned that was money well spent!"

Jesse asked, "Did you pay that out of the register?"

"Nah, I took it out of my pocket."

Jesse grumped, "Stop doing that. That is a business expense. I'll take the money out of petty cash, and give it to you tomorrow. Maybe we can hire Khalil when he comes back for the summer, and we're probably going to have to hire help, especially on the weekends, if today is any example."

The old man chimed in, "I wouldn't be counting your chickens just yet. You've got one day, and a free day at that, as an exemplar. Wait three months and see what happens. I'll help RSO on the weekends for a while."

Jesse smiled. "Thank you, Papa."

Felicia sighed, "I can help out too, but I'm not that good behind the counter. I don't know enough…"

Matt and Aaron talked over one another. "We'll teach. You'll be fine. It's just a matter of…"

Felicia waved her hands in surrender. "I *will* learn, but you have to remember, I didn't grow up with guns, nor do I have the experience you," waving her hand at everyone else, "have. Kids, I'm good with. Translating, I'm good with. Paperwork, I can do. But telling which gun is which? Not right now."

Matt leaned over and hugged her. "Good with kids works for me." He kissed her on the temple. "Speaking of which, we've got two we probably need to carry to bed."

Felicia groaned, "Yes, I guess so." She got up and picked up the cups and glasses, as Matt headed for the living room. Jesse got up and helped pick up the plates and opened the dishwasher, loading the dishes as Felicia rinsed them.

Matt came back in the kitchen grinning. "Y'all have to come see this."

Aaron got up, hopping after Jesse as the old man steadied him. They stood quietly in the doorway, looking at the sprawl of kids and dogs intertwined on the floor, and Jesse said softly, "Oh damn, that… That would be one hell of a picture, but I know it would wake the kids up."

Felicia and Matt gathered up Esme and Matt, Junior, extracting Esme from under Boo Boo's paw. Jesse picked up Kaya and took her to bed, as Aaron hopped after her, leaving the old man standing in the door, looking down at Jace asleep leaning against Yogi, who was also sound asleep. A tear rolled unbidden down his face, and he quickly swiped it away, as Jesse came back. "See you in the morning."

Jesse pecked him on the cheek. "Night, Papa."

Clay Retires

The old man grumbled, as he and Jesse got in the car, "Why the hell do I have to get in uniform? I could have worn a coat and tie!"

Patiently, Jesse explained again, "Papa, the sheriff wanted you to be the sheriff's office representative at Clay's retirement. That means a uniform." Jesse picked at hers. "I'm even wearing mine."

"I haven't worn an actual uniform in… Shit, I don't remember… Since the last time Jose got elected. And that was for the swearing in."

"At least yours still fits. I swear these pants shrunk."

The old man laughed. "I'd say it's more like you're spreading out."

Jesse took a playful swipe at him, as he turned onto Hwy 18, and stepped on the gas. "Gonna be about three hours. If you want to take a nap, go ahead."

"Thank you. I could use it. Kaya still doesn't sleep through the night."

The old man turned onto I-10 and headed west. Glancing over, he realized Jesse was already asleep. As he squirmed around, trying to get comfortable, his thoughts went back to the first time he'd met Clay. *Thirty, no thirty-one years ago. Why is it I can remember that, but I can't remember what I did yesterday… Clay had just come on the Rangers, and Amy and I were on our way back from El Paso. Don't remember what I had to do at Ft. Bliss, but she'd rode along, wanting to do some shopping.*

We'd stopped back in Alpine, cause she wanted to go by the general store, and we ran up on a robbery in progress. She'd gotten clear, and I tackled that sumbitch. Turned out he was slick as a greased pig, and I finally got him on his belly, but I didn't have any cuffs with me, and I couldn't let go of anything to get my backup .38 out of my back pocket. I was kinda holding on, waiting for somebody to get there, when I saw a pair of highly polished black Justins stop about a foot away, and heard Clay ask if I needed a hand. Clay swears I said shoot the sumbitch or give me a pair of cuffs, but I do remember seeing a S&W 19-3 come down into view, as it poked the Mex in the cheek, and Clay saying something very quietly to the effect of either get shot or give up in Spanish, as he cocked the pistol and put his finger on the trigger. I remember he said I might want to turn my head, that way I wouldn't get splattered with brains.

The perp went absolutely limp at that point, and Clay handed me a pair of cuffs, that I quickly used before the Mex, Sanchez? Yeah, Hector Sanchez went rodeo again. Once I got up, Clay straightened up and asked me who I was. I handed him my creds, and we chatted as we waited for Brewster County to show up...

The old man chuckled at the memory, and others that seemed to fast forward as he drove quickly toward El Paso. Bored, he started humming a tune, one of Amy's favorites from the 1970's. Apparently, he was humming louder than he thought, as he woke up Jesse, who asked, "Papa, what's that tune?"

Self-conscious, the old man stopped. "That was one of your grandma's favorites, by a singer named Jim Croce, it was called 'Time in a Bottle'."

"I don't remember ever hearing you sing, or play music, now that I think about it. Why, Papa?"

"After Amy passed, I kinda lost interest. And when you were old enough to start listening to music, my hearing was bad enough that I just hear it as white noise. If I actually turned it up loud enough for me to hear, I'd blow the speakers," he said with a laugh.

Jesse looked over at him. "I didn't realize it was that much of a problem."

He shrugged. "Too many gun battles, too much shooting with no ear protection. I've turned into a pretty good lip reader over the years."

"Do you even have hearing aids?"

"Somewhere in a drawer in the bedroom. Don't use them, they're a pain in the ass, and fall out all the time."

Jesse yawned and stretched, looking at her watch, she asked, "Where are we?"

"Almost to Sierra Blanca."

"Damn, Papa, how fast are you running?"

"You were asleep, and I was bored. The sun is shining, and it's a beautiful day for a drive. I've slowed down now."

Jesse sighed, "One of these days, you're going to get a ticket."

The old man laughed, "Wouldn't be the first one. Nor probably the last one. And I pay them too!"

Jesse nodded back off, until the old man pulled into the Ranger station in El Paso, and parked. She woke up, quickly fixed her hair, and reached over, putting a hand on his arm, "Thank you for driving. You wouldn't believe how much better I feel with that little bit of uninterrupted sleep."

He smiled. "Okay, you're bright and chipper, so you get to be the public face of the office. Let's go see Clay retire. Remind me to tell Ronni about the fandango on the second, cause I know Clay won't remember anything, especially today."

Jesse laughed as they got out of the car, and walked toward the building. The old man whistled as he scanned the parking lot. "I wonder who's working the highways and byways of west Texas today? Looks like damn near every department and office is represented!"

"I'm pretty sure whoever is on the various departments' shit lists are pulling doubles today, Papa."

As they walked in, they saw a small sign, directing them to the main conference room, and once they got there, they found a standing room only crowd. Jesse disappeared into the crowd, looking for Ronni, as the old man circulated toward Major Wilson, Clay, and Levi, who were standing near the podium.

He finally got to them, and said, "Major, I'm sure you're gonna be glad to get rid of this slacker and get a real Ranger, aren't you?"

He shook the major's hand, along with Clay and Levi's as the Major replied, "Well, Levi does move along quite well, and being a former Marine, in addition to a Harrier pilot, I'm less worried about him doing anything crazy with the chopper."

Levi shrugged, and Clay laughed. "Levi, don't tell the major about our training flights…"

The major rolled his eyes and asked, "Anybody else come from Pecos?"

"Nah, just me and Jesse. Jose couldn't make it, there was some political crap going on with commissioner's court today, and he was going to cover that, so I got tagged."

Clay said, "Smart move on Jose's part. I remember some stories about you and commissioner's court."

The old man assumed an injured expression. "There was nothing ever proven…"

Ronni and Jesse walked up, and the old man hugged Ronni, saying softly, "Proud of you for sticking with Clay all these years."

Ronni kissed him on the cheek and whispered, "Thank you for pulling his ass out of the fire a few times too."

Major Wilson looked at the clock on the back wall. "Hate to break up this mutual admiration society, but we need to get this show on the road." Raising his voice, he said, "Let's get started folks, take seats please."

Jesse found a seat on the aisle, but the old man ended up on the back wall, standing next to Levi, as the ceremony got underway. As they were doing the presentations, and awards, he leaned over to Levi. "You know you got some pretty big shoes to fill, don't you?"

Levi nodded, "Yeah, especially since I've worked with Clay since I've been on DPS. Frankly, I'm a little worried about measuring up."

"Don't be. Remember, you aren't Clay, he was old school, like I am. You're the new breed, so to speak, and y'all have a different way of doing things than we do. Feel free to lean on Clay, though. He's got a lot of contacts, and I know he'll share them."

"Oh, he already has. Both the good ones, and the bad ones. And I've got a slight advantage, in that I've been patrolling down here since I got out of the Corps."

The old man nodded. "That's what I mean. How do you like having a chopper?"

Levi grinned. "It's gonna make my life a lot easier. Especially down on the border. I didn't know Clay learned to fly as an Army Warrant, but he's been a great instructor, and that's just flat a fun little bird to fly!"

The old man grunted, "Huh, didn't know that. Come to think of it, I never asked. Interesting that he's never said anything."

Levi smiled. "He's got a trick or three up his sleeve, even now. I wouldn't have known had I not asked about the old cap with the Warrant Officer emblem stuck down between the seats. He seemed kinda embarrassed that I knew what it meant."

The major got back up after Clay gave a short speech, in which he thanked Ronni for staying with him, and saying he was honored to have worked with all the fine law enforcement personnel in west Texas. The major pulled out a presentation case from under the lectern. "Clay, one last thing, and then we'll close this out. Now we all know you are a revolver man, and you hated going to, as you called them, the plastic fantastics, so we found this beat up, scratched up old Smith nineteen-three to send out the door with you."

Clay gingerly opened the box, and an inadvertent, "Oh damn!" slipped out.

The major, smiling broadly, continued, "Yep, found this guy, David Wade Harris, up at Granbury to do some scratching on it. And those grips are fake ivory, since we all know it's illegal to possess or trade ivory these days, but we hope you like it."

Reaching under the lectern again, he pulled out another box, saying, "And here's a BBQ rig to go with that scratched up old gun. It's all black, and comes from Kenny Rowe over in Arkansas. Now you can give that pretty little snubbie you call a BBQ gun back to Ronni."

Laughter and applause broke out as Clay stood, stunned looking at the pistol. He finally stepped back to the lectern, saying in a choked voice, "Thank you. Thank you, Major, and everyone who contributed to this… Amazing piece of work. Thank you." He turned, walked over to Ronni and sat slowly, forgetting the leather sitting on the lectern.

The major handed the leather to Ronni, and said, "Okay, cake and ice cream for anybody interested. Maybe we can even get Clay to give up the pistol long enough to let folks look at it." That prompted a round of laughter, and general movement toward the side of the conference room, as people queued up for the refreshments.

Jesse had made it to the front of the line, and hugged Clay and Ronni, then slipped over to grab a slice of cake and a cup of coffee. She then walked back to where the old man, Levi, and Brian Cameron, the special ranger, were standing. "Where you do want to sit?"

"Where ever you find a place. We'll be along shortly. Did they do good on the pistol?"

"Just wait until you see it, Papa! Clay is over the moon."

They finally got to the front of the line, and as he shook hands with Clay, said, "So you like that beat up old pistol?"

Clay laughed. "Of course I do, John! I've lusted over yours for years, but I never wanted to spend that much money."

Brian picked it up, looked at it, then looked more closely. "Isn't your brand the Lazy B?"

Clay nodded. "It is, why?"

Brian pointed to the left side of the barrel. "He put your brand on here, see? Right there."

"Damned if he didn't." Turning to the old man he asked, "John, did you have anything to do with that?"

"Who, me? Would I do something like that?"

Ronni interrupted, "Of course you would John. And thank you for doing it. Now, go get your dessert and coffee, I want to get off my feet."

"Yes, ma'am. I be going." The old man got a small piece of cake and a cup of coffee, and joined Jesse at the corner of a table. "Brian pointed out the brand. I was hoping he wouldn't find it till later."

Jesse shrugged. "Well, he would have found out sooner or later, at least this way, we aren't getting a three AM phone call!"

Bucky wandered over, a cup of coffee in hand. "When are you going out John?"

"End of September. I'm too old for this shit, and all these young punks coming up," he cut a sideways glance at Levi, "don't understand how us old farts operate."

Levi laughed, "Yeah, right. I heard enough of that crap in the Corps. The *old* Corps was better, we did it better back in the *old days*, yada, yada. I know you guys get things done, and don't necessarily worry about the paperwork till later. Sadly, now days, the paperwork *is* the driver, and actually getting things done… Well, let's just say it's the *other* number one priority. By the way, that's some *good* fake ivory."

That generated a round of laughs, and Bucky nodded. "I know nothing, saw nothing, heard nothing. But you're right, it's the same with CBP and DEA these days. Cross the I's and dot the T's and then *maybe* you get permission to do your job."

Jesse laughed, "Um, Bucky, if you're crossing the I's and dotting the T's, that might be part of your problem."

Bucky threw up his hands. "Oh hell, you knew what I meant! I'm ready to go too. It's long past being fun anymore."

"You got your thirty in, right? Over thirty?"

"Yeah, hell, I've actually got forty in, with my military service. I think it's time for me to start seriously looking at trotting my happy ass out the door."

The old man looked up curiously. "What would you do Bucky? I've never heard you mention any hobbies, and you're still renting that apartment in Laredo."

Bucky smiled. "Well, I've got a place up in Wyoming, it's forty acres, with a trout stream. That's what I really want to do, trout fish. I bought the place twenty years ago, and I've got relatives up there that take care of it, and rent it out to trout fishermen on occasion."

Jesse asked, "Fish? Really? I didn't think you even liked fish. I seem to remember we never served fish if Papa said you were coming to dinner."

Bucky shrugged. "Like to catch them, don't like catfish. I grew up in the northeast, and they don't eat catfish. And most places that *claim* they are serving trout, aren't. So I just don't eat fish unless I catch it. But let me tell you how good a fresh caught trout, cooked over an open fire, in the morning…"

Levi interrupted, "We get the idea. And I gotta agree." Getting up, he asked, "You ever fish the White Mountain's area?" They walked off, talking fishing, as the old man finished his cake and coffee.

Jesse said, "I reminded Ronni about the fandango, and she's going to make sure Eddie and Iris come. I haven't seen their little boy in a while, and I'm sure Jace wouldn't mind a playmate for a few hours."

"It's on y'all to keep track of the kids. I've already done that," the old man said with a smile.

Jesse stuck her tongue out at him, and she heard a voice asking, "Is this old man being mean to you again?"

She looked up in embarrassment to see Major Wilson, a smile on his face. "Uh, not any more than usual. We're going to do a fandango on the second of July, since the fourth falls on a weekday, if you and your wife can make it. Michelle said she might, depending on the work schedule."

"We'll have to see. As you know, things are picking up, and we're busier than hell right now. And, of course, Austin is on a rampage about overtime."

The old man shook his head. "What a surprise. Do they not get that criminals don't punch a time clock, or only do shit between eight and five?"

The major snorted. "I've got to remember that one. John, I'm worried about the border, especially down in the Big Bend area. We simply don't have enough officers down there, even with the DPS and Game Wardens doing rotating duty down there."

"That bad?"

"Last week, they found ten dead over at the old Warren place. The well was dry, and apparently they drank out of a polluted stock tank. It was… Messy."

The old man winced. "And let me guess, they'd been dead a while?"

"Yeah, Brewster County deputy saw buzzards."

The old man glanced at his watch. "Hate to do this, but we need to head back. Actually, I'm surprised I haven't gotten any calls yet, today."

"Understood. I heard about your retiring in September, I will be there."

"Thanks, 'preciate that. Let's go make our manners, Jesse; then we'll hit the road."

After a round of goodbyes, and three different conversations in the parking lot, they finally got back on I-10 and headed for Fort Stockton.

Three hours and four phone calls later, the old man pulled into the ranch. "We're here. Wakey, wakey."

Jesse mumbled, and sat up. "Was I imagining things, or were you actually on the phone?"

"I was on the phone. It's like people lose their minds if I'm not there. Three, count 'em, three of the phone calls were on paperwork drills! Gah!"

Jesse stretched. "Well, we're home. Turn the damn phone off!"

The old man opened the car door, only to have Yogi jump in his lap. "Soon, trust me, soon. Down dog! Dammit, this uniform was clean!"

Insults and Injury

Aaron reached down and bumped the seat forward, trying yet again to get comfortable. Grumbling to himself, he looked at the clock on the dashboard as he sat on the side of I-10. *Two more hours. Why is it second shift seems to drag on-and-on? First isn't bad, it's all daylight, lots of people moving around, things to do. Third is okay, other than Friday, Saturday nights, usually that's the fight scene, plus the drunks, and…*

A Mustang blew by Aaron at well over the speed limit, barely missing the Tahoe which was well off on the shoulder, as it swerved back onto the Interstate. Aaron pulled out quickly, jumping hard on the Tahoe's accelerator, but it still took him over a mile to catch up to the speeding Mustang. Now, it was more or less staying in its lane, but pacing it, he got an 89mph average speed. Lighting it up, he said, "Lights, gray Mustang, twenty-fifteen? Texas Tag, Initiating stop," for his body cam and mic. Picking up the radio mic, he said, "Dispatch, two-fourteen, stopping twenty-fifteen gray Mustang, mile two-oh-eight."

The Mustang slammed on the brakes and swerved violently toward the shoulder, as Aaron dropped the mic, cussed, and frantically steered to avoid crashing into the back of the car. He managed to miss it, but was now ahead of the Mustang. He glanced in his rearview mirror, saw that it was, in fact, stopping on the shoulder, and turned down into the median. Running back west for a hundred yards, he flipped back around, crossed to the shoulder and stopped behind the Mustang, climbed out of the Tahoe, and walked up to the driver's side window, his Maglite on his shoulder, and his hand on his pistol.

Shining his light into the window, he saw a twenty-something brunette staring owl eyed at him. He said, "License and proof of financial responsibility, please."

She fumbled for her purse, spilling the contents in her lap, and finally gave him her driver's license. He glanced at it. "Um, the insurance papers, Ms. Diaz."

She turned to him. "Whuzzat?" He almost took a step back from the strong odor of alcohol.

He confirmed the car was not running, and said, "Ma'am, please step out of the car."

She smiled sloppily. "M'kay." He stepped back, and she managed to get the door open, finally got the seat belt off, and struggled upright. "Now, wha… What occifer?"

"Please step to the back of the vehicle, please. I would like you to perform a field sobriety test for me."

She leaned heavily on the side of the car as she stumbled to the back, then leaned against the trunk, asking, "You want me?"

Patiently, he said, "I want you to perform a nystagmus test. Have you been drinking tonight?"

She giggled, "Oh, yes! We were having a divorce party! Whazza nys… N… wha'ever you said?"

Aaron shook his head. "Ma'am, I am arresting you for driving while intoxicated, please turn around and place your…"

She kicked out hard at him, hitting his leg and screaming, "Don' you toush…" as she tried to rake his face with her fingernails.

Aaron managed to catch her arm and use the leverage to turn her, then planted her face down on the trunk, as he grabbed his cuffs. Getting the cuffs on one arm, he had to wrestle with her for a minute or so to get the other arm, as she sobbed and flailed at him. "You sonnabish… I did'n do nuffin'. Lemme go you mothfu… Ow!"

He finally got the second arm and cuffed her wrists, then started to lead her around to the side of the Tahoe. She took one step, screamed and collapsed in pain. "What's the matter with you now," he asked.

"M'foot… It *hurts*, youuu broke my foot! You bassard!" she screamed. Shining his light down at her foot, he could see blood and two toes obviously not pointing in the right direction on her bare foot. Looking around, he didn't see her little slip on shoe.

Picking her up, he carried her to the back door of the Tahoe, sat her in the seat and said, "Stay there." Closing the door, he walked back to the Mustang. Getting on the radio, he said, "Dispatch, need an ambulance and a tow truck, mile two-oh-eight. One female in custody, DWI, injured foot, apparent broken toes. Will need a blood test at the hospital."

Dispatch came back, "Copy two-oh-four. Um, ambulance?" Rummaging through the Mustang, he found the insurance paperwork, noting that it was registered to her, and found one empty bottle of Mezcal in the floorboard, and one half-full one in the passenger's seat.

He keyed the mic. "Dispatch, two-oh-four. Yes, ambulance. I carried her to the vehicle and she obviously has two broken toes, at least. She is unable to walk."

Dispatch said laconically, "Two-oh-four, roger, enroute. McMillian towing is up."

Twenty minutes later, McMillian's driver had the Mustang on the roll-back, and Aaron said, "Impound yard. Here are the keys, lock it up if you would." The driver nodded and quickly pulled off, leaving Aaron sitting for a minute in relative peace and quiet. With a sigh, he dropped Ms. Diaz's purse in the seat of the Tahoe and walked forward to the ambulance. Leaning in the back door, he asked the medic, "Y'all ready?"

The medic fastened the last restraining strap across the alternately screaming and crying woman and nodded. "Yeah, the sooner we get her out of here the better. Hopefully, *before* she pukes. I've already talked to ER, they are waiting with the resident to do the x-ray and splint the foot, so you can take her to jail."

"Thanks! Let's roll. I'll follow you."

Aaron jumped in the Tahoe and keyed the mic. "Dispatch, two-oh-four, enroute hospital, following ambulance. As soon as Ms. Diaz is treated, I'll be bringing her to receiving."

"Two-oh-four, ten-four."

Aaron chuckled. *That'll teach her to kick an officer. Damn glad the body camera was on for this one!* That brought back an even older memory, from the physical training when going through the academy in Houston. *That prick Hudson, he was going to use me as the demonstration dummy, and take me out as a lesson to the rest of the class. I guess he forgot which leg was the prosthetic, or thought I'd try to protect it.*

He laughed aloud, remembering what had happened next. *Hudson had called me out front, then told the class about unprovoked attacks, trying to distract me with his hand waving shit… When he tried the leg sweep, I just planted on the pros, and when he failed to sweep me, got pissed and tried a takedown. Problem was, I was a step ahead of him, and locked his ass down, forcing him to tap out, before I dislocated his shoulder. The cherry on top was, he broke his foot when he tried to sweep me, and he ended up on disability for the rest of our training.*

Pulling into the emergency room parking, he followed the medic through the door, stopped at the nurse's station. Angelina smiled up at him. "How goes it, Aaron?"

"I'll let you know. Did you call Jesse?"

Angelina chuckled. "Yes, I did, and we'll get together tomorrow. The party is going to be fun! So, what have you got?"

Aaron shrugged. "Apparent DWI, she got frisky, kicked me in the leg, and broke at least two toes. Need a blood draw, but she's argumentative, fighting, the usual bullshit."

"Who?"

"Diaz, Dorita, one each. Twenty seven. Something about a divorce party."

"*Mierda*, that must mean Estrella is going through with it."

Aaron cocked his head, "Huh?"

Angelina waved it off. "Never mind, just some issues I'll have to deal with, later. Lemme get you taken care of. I'm assuming you want the foot splinted, blood drawn and then you're taking her to receiving?"

"That's the plan."

"Okay, sit. She's in exam one, right there. I'll be back"

Fifteen minutes later, Angelina pushed a now crying Ms. Diaz out of exam one in a wheelchair. "Where's your car?"

Aaron replied, "I'll bring it up to the door. Give me a couple."

"Okay, I'll get Will to cover security for her until you pull up."

Aaron nodded and went out the door, got the Tahoe and brought it back to the ER door. He hopped out, came around and opened the back door, then helped a sobbing Ms. Diaz in, without a word. Slamming the door, he smiled at Angelina. "Thanks! Now comes the fun part. No crutches?"

Angelina laughed, "In her condition? Not unless you want her to face plant every ten feet. I know you have chairs over there. Use one!"

"Yes, ma'am."

Aaron drove quickly over to the sheriff's office, pulled in the sallyport, got out, and went looking for the wheelchair they had in there. Finding it, he came back out, helped a still sobbing Diaz into the chair, and wheeled her back into receiving. The clang of the jail door reminded him once again he was glad he didn't work the jail. Those clanging doors would drive him nuts!

Forty minutes later, he'd finished the paperwork, turned Ms. Diaz over to Corporal Spicer's gentle ministrations, and the female drunk tank. Looking at his watch, he only had fifteen minutes left of shift, and smiled as he headed back out the door. He drove over to the gas pump, filled the Tahoe up, and did a quick vacuum job on it. Parking it nose out, he grabbed his bag and headed into the office. Another thirty minutes, a quick turnover with Ortiz, and he was out the door and headed for the house.

Dammit, I forgot to ask Danny how his cousin is doing. His thoughts drifted back to the academy again, and the physical training. After the incident with Hudson, Aaron had been made an assistant instructor for combatives, even though he was a student. Another student in his class had been Danny's little cousin, Carmen. *Five foot nothing, maybe a hundred pounds, soaking wet, good Catholic girl. And one of those classic Spanish beauties, what the hell was she doing in the academy? She wasn't afraid of anything, but her normal response was to take a shot at any male's balls as soon as she could.* Aaron smiled, remembering some of the sparring training, and the extra hours he'd worked with her. He'd found out she grew up the youngest of five, with four older brothers, hence the ball strikes. A couple of months of teaching her how to use her speed and quickness, and she'd turned into a holy terror in the combatives, even taking him down twice. *And I wasn't pulling my punches…*

***

He pulled into the yard, eased the door closed and walked quietly up the steps, but as soon as he stepped on the porch, he heard the woofing from the other side of the door. Shaking his head, he quickly opened the door, let Yogi and Boo Boo out, then sat on the top step while they ran around for a few minutes.

"Come on dogs. Time for bed," Aaron called. Yogi and Boo Boo came around the corner of the house and ran up the steps, tongues lolling as they sat, waiting for him to open the door. "Quietly, you two," he said as he opened the door, letting them in, and following them, locked the door behind him.

He was surprised to see the old man sitting in the office as he walked down the hall. "John? What's up?"

The old man grumbled, "Taxes. Gahdamn quarterly tax payments. I told Jesse I'd get this caught up, and I've been putting it off. She got the kids down a couple of hours ago, and went to bed then. The store is keeping her busy, and more tired than she admits. How was your shift?"

Aaron shrugged. "Well, I had to take one to the hospital after I arrested her, she broke her foot on my prosthetic."

The old man swung his chair around. "What?"

Aaron explained, and the old man shook his head, laughing, "Hoo boy. That's not one I think I've ever heard before. Did you document it?"

"Yep, and it's on both bodycam and car video."

"Okay, do me a use of force/incident report tomorrow, so I can get documentation in the file before we get sued."

"Use of force? Why? I didn't use any force!"

"I know that, you know that, but you took an injured arrestee to the hospital with an injury acquired in the process of a stop. We'll have to document that for TCJS. While it isn't *technically* a use of force, that's the first document that comes to mind. Make sure you note that there is video, and give me the time, so I can annotate that on the videos."

Aaron grumbled, "I'll do that, guess I better come in early, right?"

"Nope, just come in for your regular shift, and do it before you go on patrol. I'll let the sheriff know in the morning, in case we get any calls from her lawyer."

Aaron threw up his hands. "I can't win, can I?" He turned and banged his head on the door frame. "I'm going to bed. I give up."

The old man laughed. "Welcome to twenty-first century policing. Document, document, and document. Catching criminals and random miscreants is now second place to making sure the forms are filled out, the I's dotted, and T's crossed."

Aaron smiled ruefully. "And to think, I thought the Corps was bad. Little did I know. Good night."

"Night," the old man said, as he turned back to the computer, grumbling to himself.

Aaron slipped into the bedroom as quietly as he could. Stripping off his gunbelt, and uniform, he sat down in the chair, peeled his prosthetic off, and hopped over to his side of the bed. Trying to ease into bed, he sighed as he laid his head on the pillow. Jesse asked muzzily, "How'd it go?"

"One arrest for DWI, and she kicked me and broke a couple of toes."

"Wha? Who?"

"Some girl named Diaz. Dor…"

Jesse sat up, "Dorita?"

"Yeah. Some divorce party, or so she claimed. You know her?"

"She was a year behind me in school. I guess Estrella is going through with it."

"Huh?"

"Dolores Ruiz. She was a classmate of Manuela's, and married a guy from Van Horn. Lots of domestic issues, or so I've heard. They separated earlier this year. Guess Dolores had finally had enough. I think she was staying with her sister down in Alpine."

"Dunno. Anyway, she's in jail for now."

"M'kay." Rolling over, Jesse gave him a hug and a quick kiss. "Glad you're home safe."

"Love you, me too."

Jesse snuggled against Aaron, and was asleep almost immediately, leaving Aaron staring at the ceiling, and wondering how Jesse had known all the details of what was going on. He gave a mental shrug. *The wives network in the Corps was bad enough, I can't imagine how bad it is when you've grown up with the girls. Hell, I don't even want to know, especially what they say about us.*

Jesse rolled over with a huff, and Aaron spooned with her, lightly kissing her hair, as he thought. *I still can't believe how lucky I am. And how tough Jesse is. She never gave up on me, she's been my rock through everything these last five years. I don't deserve her.* A tear ran down his cheek as he dropped off to sleep.

July 4th

Since the Fourth fell on Tuesday, they decided to have a fandango on July second, inviting the neighbors and friends to come in for it. The old man had called the Ramos brothers to do the briskets, ribs and trimmings from the longhorn he'd shot in March, plus enough extra for a hundred people. They'd decided to add pulled pork, and sausages, in addition to some chicken for those *few* that didn't eat red meat. Matt and Aaron took over setting up the working parties with Ernesto, Ricky, and a crew of local boys doing the grunt work necessary to set up for the hundred or more people that were expected.

Trey and Beverly had come in last night from Dallas, along with Toad and Cindy from Alpine. The girls had declared a girls' day out, and taken off for Marathon and points south, leaving the kids and dogs with the guys. Matt, after a losing battle with trying to feed and change Matt Junior had given up and called Lucy, who jumped at the chance to earn double money that Matt had promised, and she showed up a half hour later. Aaron sweetened the pot, asking if she'd watch Jace and Kaya too, promising to pay extra. Lucy smiled, nodded and marched the kids off to play in front of the house, much to the relief of Matt and Aaron. Toad just laughed, and the old man smiled at their antics, since he knew how much Lucy normally made, figuring she'd get almost as much for a few hours today as she normally got for two or three days of babysitting.

***

The next day, the women had gone shopping for the necessities they wanted for the party, and the men pitched in to get the yard set up, with Trey and Toad taking over the tractor and trailer, hauling tables, chairs, poles and lighting from the barn. The old man was amazed at how strong Trey was. Toad was driving the tractor like he'd been born to it, and Trey was picking up the round tables out of the trailer and setting them on the ground, where it took two of the boys to roll them into position. Once the tables had all been pulled out of the barn, they started moving the chairs, first loading them in a human chain in the barn, then reversing the order when they got back in the yard. Matt and Aaron were spraying the tables and chairs off, then wiping them down as they got set up.

He'd had a pang of memory, thinking back eight years to Francisco driving the tractor and trailer, tables and chairs were brought out of storage, washed down and set up between the old house and new house. And the way Juanita had run the household and food, as only she could.

The old man sat on the back the back steps, enjoying the shade, thankful that it wasn't over a hundred. Actually, he was even happier that it was a cool spell and only in the mid-90s with low humidity. A few puffy clouds floated over head as he sat watching Felicia arrange things, and wondered how she knew exactly where everything went. She finally walked over, "*Señor* John, we are going to need beer and ice. Who normally gets that?"

The old man chuckled, "You mean you don't know? I'm amazed at how well you've done with setting everything else up!"

Felicia smiled shyly. "I just use the book Juanita left."

"The book?"

Felicia replied, "I'll be right back." She went to the foreman's house she and Matt shared and came back moments later with a three ring binder, handing it to the old man. "Juanita, she wrote many things down. So did Francisco, and Felix has added to it."

The old man opened it with a tremble in his hands, and teared up when he saw Juanita's familiar handwriting. He flipped a few pages, seeing how she'd de facto managed the ranch, with notes and drawings of where everything went for the fandangos, notes on cooking and particular foods visitors liked. Reminders about pasture rotations in Francisco's sprawling hand, and later Felix's notes on calves and now Matt and Felicia's notes on the ranch. He cleared his throat. "I didn't know this existed. I just assumed Francisco and Juanita kept a lot of stuff in their heads…"

Felicia took the binder back. "Sorry, I thought you knew…"

The old man shook his head. "No, I never went in the house after she died. Francisco took care of all of her stuff, and after he died, Felix took care of everything. I always respected their privacy, just like I do y'alls."

Felicia cocked her head. "So that's why you've never been in the house in three years?"

The old man nodded. "Exactly. It's none of my business what you do in your house."

Felecia rolled her eyes. "*Señor* John, you *own* the house! How could you not check on it?"

Matt interrupted, "We're going after beer and ice, do we need anything else?"

The old man used the distraction to make an escape into the house, heading for the office and a little peace and quiet.

Felicia and Jesse supervised Ricky and his friends as they strung lights, plugged them in, and replaced the bulbs that had blown out. The old man sweetened the pot by giving the boys money to buy fireworks, promising them they could set them off in the south forty, on the rifle range, after dark. He'd also called the volunteer fire department and asked them to bring a truck out, just in case. Of course, they got free food too, and that was enticement enough.

Matt and Aaron were standing in front of the pasture gate, debating what to do with it, when Trey suggested just taking it off the hinges, and moving it. While they were arguing about it, Trey looked at it, saw that the pins pointed up and just picked it up and set it to the side of the cattle guard.

About three, the ladies started arriving, and numerous comments in Spanish and English flew around the kitchen and the yard as the ladies bustled around, setting the tables, prepping the serving and cooking areas, and bossing the men around. Trey found the old man, Toad, and Aaron hiding on the front porch, and sat on the steps, looking frazzled. "What's the matter Trey?" Aaron asked.

"Those women don't have *any* filters! I mean, damn, I'm a nurse, but…"

The old man laughed. "A bit graphic are they?"

Trey shuddered. "Yes, and damn specific too! I mean…"

"They are country women Trey. Matt and Aaron got that a few years ago. There isn't anything they won't discuss in public, because they grew up, by and large, on ranches. They've seen things and done things most city folk can't even imagine."

Matt came through the front door, beers in hand. "Sounds like you need one Trey!" That prompted a laugh from everyone and Trey did drain about half the beer in one swig, as Billy pulled in and parked the airport loaner in front of the house.

He laughed when he got out of the car, casually dressed, and reached up, smoothing his pony tail. "Hiding out, I see."

The old man replied, "Dammit, Billy, you should have called. One of us could have come got you. What did you do with the pilots?"

"I sent them home. I figure it's going to be a long enough night that I'm going to be sleeping on the couch somewhere."

"Nah, we'll find you a bed… Somewhere…" The old man said with a grin.

Forty-five minutes later, the men were still hiding on the front porch, when Jesse brought a bucket of Shiner Bock for them. "Y'all need to get cleaned up, no more beers until later, just in case anybody gets stupid."

Jesse went back in the house, and the old man proposed a toast. "Once more into the breach dear friends, and absent comrades!" They all touched bottles and sipped appreciatively.

Shortly thereafter, cars started arriving, and Ricky and Ernesto managed the parking as Jesse and Aaron played hosts. Beverly and Cindy corralled the kids, while the old man kept Yogi and Boo Boo occupied chasing tennis balls in the side yard. The women were ferrying food from the kitchen and Ricky and Ernesto brought the coolers from the barn with the drinks, setting them at the end of the serving line. Finally, the old man, Aaron, and Jesse walked to the front of the tables. "Well, I think about everybody that's coming is here, so let's have a quick prayer and get to eating. Padre, if you would?"

Everyone bowed their heads, and the padre said a short prayer in English and Spanish, thanking God for his guidance and asking his blessing. The line moved quickly as the Ramos brothers filled plates with the barbecue of folks' choice, and they moved to the next table with all the trimmings. Matt, Felicia, Aaron, Jesse, and the old man hung back and waited for the line to go down, sipping iced tea and keeping the kids occupied by feeding them their dinners. Jesse and Felicia had decided their regular dinner would be better, and if they wanted to try the BBQ, it would be little bits, rather than stuffing themselves.

The line finally got short enough for them to go up, as Trey, Beverly, Toad, and Cindy came back to the big table, with Cindy and Beverly taking over the kids for the moment. "Y'all go get your food. We'll keep the kids occupied for a few minutes."

The old man smiled as Jesus Ramos said, "*Señor*, there is plenty of food, we can keep feeding for another round at least."

"I'd expect nothing less. Y'all done good, Jesus. Thanks again for coming out and putting the barbecue on for us! We need …"

Jesus nodded. "We've already prepped twenty-seven plates and set them aside, we did thirteen beef, thirteen of pork, and one veggie for the strange lady dispatcher, so that should make 'em happy. We've already fed the VFD too."

Jesse added, "We'll load the extras on later, and the sheriff says he'll drop them by the office, so we don't have to worry about it."

The old man loaded up on the brisket and pulled pork, then barbecue beans, and potato salad. With a full plate, he looked longingly at the fresh-cut French fries, salad, tortillas, rice, fresh jalapenos, pickles, onions and bread, *Well there are always seconds*. Jesse laughed as Aaron held up the line, while he tried to decide which sides to get, saying, "You can come back you know, it's not like there isn't going to be anything left."

The old man, Billy, Clay and Ronni, Eddie and Iris, and the sheriff and his wife, all headed for the table that had been left for them. It was funny to watch them, with the exception of Billy and the padre, jockey to sit where they could see the doors and the drive into the yard.

Billy leaned over to Clay and Ronni. "Sorry I missed your retirement, I was stuck in court in California, and couldn't get away."

Clay laughed, "I don't remember much about it, but I do appreciate the thought. Was the trip successful?"

Billy nodded. "Oh yeah. Very successful. The state decided to settle the case the day before we were supposed to go to court, and it took a couple of days to get all the details ironed out, but it's all good."

Jesse looked around, thinking, *Everybody is looking at the table with Papa and the others, and wondering what they are talking about. I think this is the first time they've gotten a table… Well, a table by themselves. Eddie and Iris are the youngest ones there, and they're both in their forties. Papa and Uncle Billy are in their seventies, Clay and Ronnie are… Sixties? And Jose is almost sixty. Everybody has grey or white hair, except Iris, and even her red hair is getting some grey in it. What are we going to do when they're gone?* Jesse shook her head, and looked at Aaron, then Jace and Kaya. *We're it. Whether Aaron realizes it or not, we're going to have to step up. God knows, I don't want that to be anytime soon!* Jace tugged at her arm. "BBQ?"

Jesse finished cutting his brisket into bite sized pieces, then smiled ruefully. "Here ya go. Use your fork."

Felicia cocked her head as she watched Jesse, and Jesse quickly shook her head. Felicia glanced over at the table with the old man and the others, then smiled sadly, as she fed their kids.

Beverly leaned over, wrinkling her nose. "What *is* that smell?"

Jesse looked at the kids, then sniffed, and started chuckling, "That's the smell of money."

"What?"

As everybody else started sniffing, Jesse finally said, "That's crude oil you're smelling. Actually, probably some of the gas that's bleeding off."

Trey rumbled, "Yeah, *that* is a smell I could get used to!"

Once the music started, Jesse perked up, and actually got Aaron on the dance floor a couple of times, but he absolutely refused to try the Two-Step. "I love you Jesse, but I'm not about to try that. I'm not sure how well I can maneuver the prosthetic in those convoluted steps, and I sure as hell don't want to step on somebody, or fall down."

Jesse shook her head, laughed and said, "Okay, but I'm going to dance!" She actually dragged Uncle Billy out for one round of Two-Step, and he begged off, feigning being exhausted, much to Jesse's dismay.

At one point, the old man got a few of the ranchers off to the side, along with Aaron, Matt, and Eddie. The old man opened the conversation with, "The reason I wanted to talk to y'all is none of us is getting any younger. I don't know about anybody else, but it looks to me like we're all having trouble finding hands, and of the ones we find, most of them are older."

Pete Halvorson, the next ranch up the road said, "Yep, and some of them are just waiting for an oilfield job to open up, and they're going to jump to that. Then when the patch falls flat, they come crawling back, wanting their jobs back. And don't get me started on horses. If it wasn't for Eddie, I'd be down to two, maybe three swaybacked nags, not a damn one worth their weight in hay as cow ponies. There isn't a single good horse wrangler in the area, not to mention we're down to one farrier left in the area!"

Bob Nichols, from the Bar N said, "What? When did that happen?"

Eddie said, "Mr. Wright told me last month he was done. He got kicked by a horse down at Marathon six months or so ago, and it messed up his hip. His wife is gone, and he said he's moving to San Antone' with his oldest daughter. He's apparently already sold his place, 'cause I saw some different cars there last week, when I was delivering a colt down to Sanderson."

Don Yarborough, from the Diamond Y, added, "Yeah, and it's getting on to calving season. I've been trying to catch up with Tom, but he's ignoring me tonight. I think he's afraid I want him to come back to work."

The old man winced, "If you're that desperate… Damn… I don't have a good answer. Maybe some of those kids from Sul Ross? Maybe get them up here to work on the weekend?"

Don nodded, "Hadn't thought of that. I keep forgetting they've got that range management program down there. I may just do that."

On that note, the group broke up, and everyone started to head for their trucks, picking up their wives on the way.

After they finished, everyone started packing up and picking up, as Jesse and Aaron bid everyone a good evening and thanked them for coming. The ladies quickly and efficiently finished the twenty-seven plates for the sheriff to take back to the station, and everything else went into the fridges or freezers based on Felicia's direction. By midnight, everything was pretty much done, with the exception of the tables, and the old man gave Jesus Ramos a check for his help and profuse thanks for doing the cooking.

Jesse collapsed in bed, and Aaron rolled over. "Tired?"

"Yes. Mentally more than physically, but at least the kids are out like a light. I never realized how much work actually went into one of these, and how many people were coming to me wanting to know what to do. If it weren't for Felicia, I don't know what we'd have done."

Aaron folded her in his arms. "You done good!" He kissed her softly, as she snuggled into his chest.

In the kitchen, the old man and Billy sat over cups of coffee, and Billy said, "John, we're not getting any younger. I know you're going to retire this year, and I'm seriously considering it. I'm not having fun anymore, and the idiot judges we got, thanks to the last administration, don't seem to actually want to enforce the laws, much less send anybody that isn't white to prison, or set judgements against them."

The old man rolled his shoulders. "I hear you. I just don't know what I'm going to do…"

"Well, the kids' gun store seems to be going pretty well."

"It's making a little money, and Jesse's already hired Khail, and put him to work. I'm wondering if…

Maybe it's time to let the cows go. It's not like I make much off of them."

Billy shook his head. "No, you want to keep them to get the ranch deductions."

The old man finished his cup, and stood. "Maybe. 'Fore long, I don't think I'll have to worry about it."

Billy looked up sharply. "What? Is there something you're not telling me?"

"Nah, just feeling old and grumpy tonight." He picked up Billy's cup and washed it. "See you in the morning."

As the old man walked down the hall, he heard Aaron comforting Jesse. Apparently she'd had another nightmare, and he wondered if it had been brought on by the fireworks. *It took me ten years to stop diving for the ground anytime I heard fireworks. I hope Jesse can remember the good, and bury those nightmares. Or at least have them less frequently, not that they'll ever go away.* Shaking his head sadly, he slipped into his bedroom and shut the door softly.

Grinding Through

Jesse huffed, blew a stray strand of hair away from her face, and picked up the next batch of papers El Paso PD had forwarded from Deen's apartment. *Bank statement, bank statement, water bill, electric, internet... Oh, wait. Phone bill.* She deposited the bank statements and other bills in one of the piles on the conference table, picked up her coffee cup and headed back to the kitchen. Taking the last cup, she grumbled, "He who takes the last cup, makes the new pot. *Why*, do I always seem to get the last cup?" Digging around in the cabinet, she found a can of Folgers and filters, setting them on the counter, she dumped the old grounds in the trash, put the new filter full of coffee in the brewer, and hit the brew button.

She checked her watch, groaned, and steeled herself to go back to the paperwork battle. When she walked back into the conference room, Matt was sitting on the other side of the table, smiling. "What are you so happy about?" she grumbled.

"Broke the code on the phone. It was Deen's TPO employee number. I've got at least forty incoming and, so far, twenty outgoing calls, and a few SMS messages, but all those look work related."

"I'm glad *somebody* is getting something done. Came up cold on the banking info. His checks are direct deposit by TPO, and all of the deposits are from

TPO. They match his payroll records, and his withdrawals are all at a branch that was a block from his apartment. I called the branch and they knew him. Seems like his big withdrawals were always just before he went back in the field. Other than that, he used his debit card at the grocery, the cleaners, and that's about it."

Matt nodded. "Ties in with what Owens told us."

"Did the Rangers get anything off his home computer?"

"Nope, he apparently seldom used it. Most of the emails were from the company, a couple from an old military buddy, and two from that cousin we identified, Harber? No, Haber. She was bugging him to come see her, which she'd already told us when we did the phone interview, remember? No real media presence, one dormant Facebook account, one old Yahoo email, and one work email was it."

"Oh, right. She was his emergency contact at TPO. Gah, now I know why I never did a murder investigation. This is a PITA! This is what, the fourth shift that we've worked on this background stuff?" Sliding the report across the table, she said, "Here's the autopsy. Death by gunshot. One hollow-point forty-five round, Speer Gold Dot. Fired at less than a foot, upward angle, approximately thirty degrees. Powder residue on his shirt, along with stippling from the unburned powder. Round clipped the aorta, causing Mr. Deen to bleed out in less than a minute. Possible defensive wound, powder residue on the left palm, but not definitive."

Matt replied somberly, "It's not fun, but it's necessary. At least we're getting help from the Rangers and El Paso PD, otherwise we'd be driving all over hell and gone. And don't forget, we've got to be back down at TPO thirty-seven this afternoon. Owens is going to meet us there with one of Deen's friends."

Jesse sighed, "One of his few friends. That must have been one lonely man. Parents dead, no brothers or sisters, the one cousin that seems to be his only family point of contact. Ex-wife hasn't seen him or talked to him in over ten years, no kids. He really didn't have anybody, other than Owens, that he appears to have ever talked to."

"Apparently, quite a few oil field folks are loners, guess this is one more proof of that. What did you find on the bank stuff?"

Jesse handed her notes across. "So far, one checking account, eighteen thousand in it. One savings account, one hundred thirty thousand in that one. TPO HR, grudgingly mind you, did admit he was in the four-oh-one K, with slightly over four hundred thousand in it."

"Huh, not a big spender in the last fifteen years, then. Apparently, at one time, he was a boozer and a fighter. He had an arrest record going back to the mid-eighties for fighting and two arrests for drunk and disorderly. Owens confirmed those, and I think Owens was probably with him, or at least I got a sense of that. The stopping point for both of those appears to have been his divorce, nothing after that."

Jesse cocked her head. "Get anything off his personal cell?"

Matt grimaced, "Nope. Calls to and from Owens. One call a month ago to his cousin. A string of texts, but they were all work related. One text from his cousin, something about a family reunion, never even answered it. Only four numbers in his contact list. Owens, his cousin, TPO Operations, and his bank. That was it." Waving a sheet of notes, he said, "El Paso PD came up dry, too. Neighbors knew him to wave and say hi, but that was it. Bar around the corner recognized him, but said he only drank cokes and watched college football. Pretty much a dry hole there too."

"Wow, so he *really* was a loner." Jesse glanced at the clock on the wall. "Well, better pack this up, we need to head out to the patch." She started putting the spread-out paperwork back into file folders, as Matt put his sheets back in the evidence bags with the respective phones.

***

They pulled into TPO 37's rig a little after lunch, with Matt backing the Tahoe in next to Owens' truck. Owens leaned against the front fender, somberly watching them, as they got out. "Afternoon, Deputies."

Jesse took the lead. "Good afternoon, Mr. Owens. Thank you for…"

Owens interrupted, "It's Jim. And I was wondering… Well, have you found anything?"

Matt shook his head, as he watched a middle aged Hispanic walking toward them. "Nothing that is moving us forward, sir. I still need the unlock code for the Iridium though."

Owens smacked his head. "Ah crap. I thought I gave that to you, It's the numerics for TPO Ops." Pulling his phone out, he read off, "Eight, seven, six, six, seven, seven. TPO Ops."

Matt nodded. "Thanks."

Owens turned to the Hispanic. "Jesus, the deputies would like to talk to you about Rick."

By unspoken agreement, Matt stuck out his hand. "Thank you for coming out to talk to us. I'm Deputy Carter, this is Deputy Miller. And you are?"

Shaking Matt's hand, he answered, "Jesus Garcia. I worked with Rick and the rest of the boys for the last six years."

"The rest of the boys?"

Jesus answered, "*Sí*." Waving at the other men moving around on the rig, he continued, "We all work together. Same, same people, six year now."

Matt whistled. "Damn, isn't that kind of unusual?"

Jesus grimaced, "We… We are all, how you say, recovering."

"Recovering?"

"Mostly booze. Jason, drugs. Danny, booze and drugs. We keep each other sober. Nobody else wants to work with us. Fine by us. Is quiet, and we get job done."

"How long did you know Mr. Deen?"

Jesus thought for a moment. "Probably fifteen year. I fight him once on a rig. He beat some sense into me."

"What about the others?"

"Probably close to ten year. Jim, he put us together six year ago. Call us his go-to crew. We get hard jobs, don't screw up."

Matt questioned him for another fifteen minutes, then asked, "Did you know or work with anybody that rode a motorcycle, anybody that got fired lately, that might have blamed Deen?"

Jesus shook his head. "No. We don't know who get fired. We work together. Not pay attention to other crews."

***

Two hours later, they were both sweating but had completed the interviews with all of the crew on the rig. Jesse turned to Matt. "Now what?"

Matt shrugged. "Good question. Nobody knows anybody that rides a motorcycle, and this crew obviously got along. Doesn't seem like anybody had problems with Deen, in or out of the company. Let's go back and I'll pull the data from the Iridium, and we'll go see John."

"Sounds good to me, I need some A/C about now. You know, we probably should have used their office to do the interviews, right?"

Matt shook his head. "Nope. No telling who would have listened, or even tried to record it. This way, we had them out in the open and they didn't get a chance to compare answers. Let's go find Mr. Owens and get out of here."

They trudged slowly over to the rig office, and found Owens on the phone, obviously not happy. "I don't care what you have to do, I need two more guys for forty-four, and I need them by tomorrow! If you can't get 'em, I'll pull these guys off thirty-seven and send them up there." They heard a mumbled response and Owens started to slam the phone down, but stopped and put it very gently back in the cradle. "What can I help y'all with now?"

Jesse replied, "Nothing, sir. Just wanted to let you know we are done. Still wondering if anybody rides a motorcycle that might have interacted with Mr. Deen."

Owens threw up his hands. "Beats the hell outta me. Only thing I can do is ask Ops if anybody that works on the yard rides one. That would be the only other place he might have known somebody that rode one."

"We'd appreciate that, sir. Sorry we took up so much of your time."

Owens waved them off. "Not your fault, you're doing the best you can, it's just that I'm short people, and HR is screwing around with the hiring. I need people now, not in two weeks!"

Matt said, "Good luck with that, we'll go through the Iridium phone, and I should be able to release that back to you next week."

As they started for the door, Owens asked softly, "Anything on the equipment or the truck?"

Matt and Jesse glanced at each other, and Matt replied, "Nothing that we are aware of. It's like everything disappeared into thin air."

Owens huffed, "Probably went across the border then. Well, that's why the company has insurance, I guess."

***

A half hour later, cups of coffee in hand, they were camped in the old man's office, waiting for him to get out of a meeting with the sheriff. Yogi was sitting with his head on Jesse's leg, as she petted him distractedly, while she and Matt played Twenty Questions over what they had and hadn't found. Matt finished his notes on the Iridium, shook his head and disgustedly shoved it back in the evidence envelope, "Nothing. All work numbers, both incoming and outgoing, except a nine one dial at nineteen thirty on the… Shit! We've got a time for the murder, if I'm right. I wonder if he was trying to dial nine-one-one?"

Jesse sat forward. "How does that factor in with what Doc estimated was the time of death?" Jesse opened her notes, searched for a minute and said excitedly, "That's in the window!"

The old man came in, asking, "What's in the window?"

Matt and Jesse both tried to answer, and Matt finally said, "Found a nine one dial at nineteen thirty on the Iridium that fits with the date of the murder and might give us the time of the attack, if I'm right. I think he might have been trying to dial nine-one-one."

The old man sat slowly in his chair. "What makes you think that? And where would a nine-one-one call go from an Iridium?"

Matt replied, "In the US, it would actually connect to nine-one-one. I know that for a fact."

The old man cocked his head. "How?"

"I've used one before for an emergency evac during an exercise."

"Okay, what else do you have?"

Jesse started the review of the paper and bank records, Matt did the phones and what had come in from El Paso PD, and they laid out the timeline they had come up with, based on the phone data, interviews, and personal connections from all the data.

The old man didn't say much, wrote a couple of notes and grunted a couple of times, but let them get all the way to the end.

"So, we have a spent Speer Gold Dot shell case, no prints on same, which means the perp didn't take the time to pick it up, or didn't bother looking. That might correlate with the nineteen thirty attempt at nine-one-one, it was, no never mind. Sun would have still been pretty high, so that doesn't work. Interviews with the crew didn't turn up any problems, nor did the El Paso PD canvass. In other words, what you're saying is we have an unknown perp, maybe riding a Harley, or some type of road bike, who may or may not have ridden through an open gate, and murdered one Rick Deen."

Jesse slumped. "That's pretty much what we came up with Papa. And he's a... was a loner."

The old man reached for the phone, set it in the middle of the desk, hit speaker and dialed Clay's cell. Three rings later, they heard a tinny, "John?"

"Clay, this is John, with Jesse and Matt. Want to chat about the Deen investigation?"

"Standby. They heard a click and a pop, then an even tinnier reply, "Okay, I've got Levi on here with us. You want to start?"

Matt and Jesse ran through their respective findings yet again, with Clay and Levi asking the occasional question. After they finished, Clay added, "Had CBP pull the tapes for the southbound lanes, three trucks matched your stolen truck, two with US plates that went down and back, and one with a Mexican border zone plate. It got flagged for no windshield sticker, but the driver claimed he'd taken it to the dealer for a new windshield and transmission work, so they let him go. That might have been your truck. Or it might have been stripped and parted out. Either way, it's disappeared. Same, same on the computers. Nothing's shown up in any pawn shops. Considering those are oil field computers, our IT guys in the JOIC[2], say they may have been sold to somebody looking to see if they can get any industrial data on TPO's operations or procedures."

The old man said, "So dead ends?"

"Pretty much. And the Fibbies came back with the same thing you did on the motorcycle tread. Generic Avon Cobra tire, which fits most of the touring bikes. The oil patch was Mobil One, twenty W fifty. Again, generic to most touring bikes.

Jesse said, "We did ask about other people that might have ridden a motorcycle and work at TPO."

Levi replied, "Good thinking. I'm pretty sure Deen did spend time at Ops. We'll send you what we have, and we'd appreciate your forwarding what you've documented, too."

Matt and Jesse chorused, "We'll do that."

"Okay, talk to y'all later. John, give me a call tonight."

---

[2] Joint Operations Intelligence Center

"Will do." The old man punched off the speaker. "This one isn't going well." Holding up his hands he said, "Not your fault. Just too many missing pieces. Y'all go write up what you've got and we'll keep pluggin' on it, for what that's worth." Matt and Jesse gathered up their papers, silently left the office, and started looking for open computers they could use to finish their documentation.

Fun and Games

Aaron made one more check of the paperwork, then hit speaker and redial on the phone again. After three rings, it was actually answered. "DFW airport police, Sergeant Smith."

Aaron crossed his fingers. "Sarge, Aaron Miller, Pecos County Sheriff's Office. I'm coming up to DFW tomorrow with a marked unit, flying to New York for a prisoner pickup. I was wondering if there was someplace I could park it for about forty-eight hours, and logically expect it to be in one piece when I get back."

He heard a sigh on the other end of the phone. "What time will you get here?"

"Um, gotta be at the gate by eleven hundred, so probably zero nine-thirty. That should give me a chance to clear through TSA and all that stuff."

"You got all your paperwork in hand?"

Aaron chuckled. "Actually reviewing that checklist right now. I can be there earlier if necessary."

"Nah, get here by nine-thirty, you'll be good. We can run you over, and expedite you thorough TSA and Security. Gimme your badge number."

"Two-eight-three."

"Last four?"

"One, six, three, three,"

"Okay, got 'em. I'll put you in the system for verification now, so that should be done by tomorrow morning."

"Thanks, Sarge! See you tomorrow."

"*De nada.* We got to take care of our own."

Aaron put all the paperwork back in the envelope, got up, and walked slowly from patrol down to the jail captain's office. Knocking on the door, he asked, "Got a minute, Captain?"

Captain Harmon replied, "Sure, come on in Aaron. Sorry to stick you with the PT trip, but I'm out of transport folks, and you're basically the one available male officer."

Aaron shrugged. "Never done one, at least in the civilian world, so it's going to be new experience."

Harmon laughed, "That's one way to look at it. Got your county card? Paperwork? Vehicle? Transport leg braces and transport belt?"

"Yes, sir. All of the above. The transport stuff is in its own bag. Just wondering if you had any last words of advice."

Harmon leaned back in his chair. "Well, I wouldn't wear a uniform. Just wear what you do when you testify in court."

Aaron cocked his head. "No uniform?"

"Nope. You're doing a prisoner transport. If you're in uniform, regardless of where you are, people are gonna see cop and expect you to handle *their* little issues. If you're in jeans, boots, decent shirt with a jacket over your gun and badge, you're just another Texas mope schlepping through the airport. Same thing coming home."

"Okay."

"Last thing is, you're gonna have to deal with the airport and airline weenies. Try to get boarded first. They'll probably put you…"

"In the last row of the airplane. Put the prisoner in the outboard seat. Take him to the bathroom before we board, 'cause we ain't moving again till we land. Try to be the last people off."

Harmon laughed, "Yep, you've done this before in the Corps, right?"

Aaron smiled. "Only a couple of times. But we were in uniform, with a nightstick, and permission to use them as appropriate."

Harmon sighed, "Not any more. But do what you have to, to keep Chavez quiet. Last time we had him, he was a mouthy little bastard."

***

Jesse walked out to the Tahoe with Aaron. "Drive safe. And at least let me know you got there, okay?"

Aaron hugged her. "I will. Sorry to get you up…"

Jesse put her fingers over his mouth. "Kaya got me up, and I know you need your coffee."

"Thanks. I should be back tomorrow night, hopefully by ten. I'll call you before I leave DFW."

Aaron kissed her and got in the Tahoe, waving as he left the yard. Six hours later, he pulled into the DFW police parking lot, hopped out and groaned as he stretched. An officer came out the side door, "Miller?"

"Yep."

"Stick your unit up against the fence over there," he said as he pointed to an empty slot. "Keep your keys. Grab your bags, and I'll run you over to your airline."

"Thanks." Aaron quickly pulled the Tahoe into the indicated spot, grabbed his coat out of the back seat, slipped it on, and pulled his bag and the transport bag out. Locking the Tahoe, he dropped the keys into the side pocket of his bag, making sure, once again, the transportation paperwork was there.

A cruiser pulled up beside him and the window slid down. "Throw your stuff in the back. What airline?"

Aaron did so, then climbed in the front, sticking out his hand. "American. Thanks again Sarge."

"Willie Smith," the sergeant said, shaking his hand. "We try to make it as easy as we can on folks coming through here. Your calling ahead of time was definitely appreciated. You know what gate?"

Aaron pulled the tickets out of his jacket. "Uh, B forty-three."

"JFK?"

"Yeah, flight two-thirty-two."

Sergeant Smith picked up the mic. "Dispatch, car nine, can you give American Ops a call and confirm the gate for flight two-thirty-two, DFW to JFK, please?"

"Standby, nine."

Smith pulled out of the parking area and started weaving through the back roads that lace DFW, totally confusing Aaron in the process. Dispatch finally came back, confirming gate B-43, and moments later, the sergeant pulled to the curb in front of the terminal. Aaron started to thank the sergeant, but he interrupted,

"I'll walk you in. Makes it a lot easier on everybody. 'Sides, ain't nobody going to screw with my car," he finished with a laugh.

Smith walked Aaron through the TSA checkpoint, down to the American lounge, and spoke to the young lady behind the desk. Walking back over to Aaron, he said, "You're good until the flight gets here. Lizzie will take care of you."

"Thanks, but I gotta ask?"

He chuckled, "She's my daughter-in-law. Her hubby, my son, is with Fort Worth PD. Just don't get shitfaced. I know about how you military guys drink on airplanes…"

Aaron rolled his eyes, "Yeah that would work well. Thanks again!" Sergeant Smith left, and Aaron walked over, "Thank you Lizzie. I appreciate it."

She smiled up at him, "Least we can do. Coffee and munchies are free. I'll let you know if anything changes with your flight."

***

Aaron had just settled into his seat, after putting his hat in the overhead, and was texting Jesse, when he heard, "Well, shit. They let *anybody* on these damn airplanes these days."

He looked up to see Clay Boone's smiling face staring down at him. "Where the hell did you come from, Clay?"

Clay slipped into the seat behind him. "El Paso. Goin' up to NYC to work with their Organized Crime folks. They got one of the big *Sinaloa* boys, Vasquez, and I've had a coupla go 'rounds with him before. Chief up there wants me to come play good cop, bad cop with him. We've got a list of warrants on that boy that would choke a mule. What about you?"

Aaron laughed, "I'm the spare body. Going up to pick up one Raoul Chavez, he's wanted for robbery and murder in that shooting down in Old Town last year."

"The precinct meeting you?"

"Supposedly. If not, I've got an address and a credit card."

Clay laughed. "Where are you staying?"

Aaron shrugged. "Don't know yet. I was going to wait till I got up there and get something close to the precinct if that's possible. Plus, I'm a little paranoid about making reservations ahead of time, especially that anybody like bad guys can search, and find my ass."

Clay replied, "Well, worse comes to worst, I think I've got a double room. I'm at the Holiday Inn, on the Lower East Side. Chief Burris said it's close to One Police Plaza, which is where I'll be working out of."

"Okay, I have no idea where that is, in relation to… Uh… The hundred fifteenth precinct. That's where they're holding Chavez."

"We'll figure it out when we get there," Clay said.

Two and a half hours later, they deplaned at JFK, and Aaron and Clay looked around as they cleared the gate. They didn't see any officers that looked like they were waiting, so they headed for baggage claim. Clay peeled off to hit the men's room, as Aaron looked for the correct baggage claim. Aaron finally found it, and stood where he could see the door and the bathroom, to wave Clay over. He started to reach into his pocket for the phone number when he heard a voice behind him say, "You reach for anything, I'm gonna bust a cap in yo' ass. Turn around slow."

Aaron turned and was confronted with two officers, he promptly dubbed Mutt and Jeff, due to their size difference. Predictably, the little one had his hand on his duty weapon, as the bigger one started moving to get behind Aaron. "Hey, I'm a police officer. I've got my creds in my hip pocket."

"Sure, sure. And I'm da Archbishop of New Yawk. Youse God damn hicks think those little carry badges work up here, but they ain't shit boy. Dammit, Tommy, get behind him and take that piece away from him, I ain't gonna wait all day."

Aaron heard Clay's voice from behind him. "If I were you, sonny, I wouldn't do that. You're liable to get hurt."

The one he'd dubbed Jeff sidestepped enough to see Clay, saying, "Move along old man, ain't none of yo' business. This is police business."

Clay smiled. "Oh, that's where you're wrong." Clay hooked his thumbs on his lapels of his jacket, and opened it slowly, "I'm Texas Ranger Clay Boone, and the officer you're trying to jack up is Deputy Sheriff Aaron Miller, Pecos County, Texas. Now, I would suggest that your boy Tommy here step back around where he's next to you and I can see both of your shining faces. *MOVE!*"

Tommy involuntarily jumped, then stepped carefully back around in front of Aaron as Jeff fumed, half pulling his pistol. "How the fuck do I know who you are, old man?"

"I'll happily show you my creds, along with Aaron's, as soon as you reholster that pistol and calm down."

Behind Aaron, another voice with a strong New York accent, said angrily, "What the fuck is going on here? Clay?"

Clay answered, "Michael! Nice of you to show up, two of your *finest* and I use the term loosely, were going to take Deputy Sheriff Miller's weapon, or I should say, *try* to take it."

The voice continued, "Oh, for fuck's sake. Where are you two nitwits assigned? And Deputy Miller, you can relax."

Aaron half turned, noting that the area had cleared out and thought, *What the fuck gave me away? Or did my jacket come open and somebody see and report it? Shit... This is not the way I wanted to start my day in New York City...*

Jeff replied, "We're out of da' One Fifteenth, Chief. We wuz supposed to meet some Texas cop."

The man mountain, identified as Michael by Clay and who was sharply dressed in a three-piece suit, asked, "Named?"

Jeff scrabbled in his pocket. "Uh, Miller, Chief."

Sarcastically, the large man said, "Like maybe Deputy Sheriff Aaron Miller?"

"Yes, Chief."

"Youse guys get the fuck outta here. *I* will bring Deputy Miller and Ranger Boone by. And tell the Inspector that I expect her to be there when I get there, *Capish*?

A thoroughly dispirited Jeff replied dully, "Yes, Chief." He and Mutt, who had never said a word, left the baggage claim, with Jeff berating Mutt, waving his arms, and looking back over his shoulder.

Aaron and Clay grabbed their bags, followed Chief Burris out to his car. Thirty minutes later, after being regaled by the chief about his and Clay's history, which apparently went back almost twenty years, they pulled up in front of the one hundred fifteenth precinct headquarters. They walked in, Chief Burris in the lead, and he pointed Aaron to the desk sergeant. "Check in with him, while I have a few words with Inspector Avado."

Aaron walked over to the desk sergeant. "Uh, I'm Pecos County Deputy Sheriff Aaron Miller." Handing the sergeant the transfer paperwork, he continued, "I'm here to pick up Raoul Chavez; we have an arrest warrant for him for murder in Texas."

The desk sergeant reached over. "Sergeant Luciano, pleased to meet 'cha. Lemme see what you got." Flipping through the paperwork, he turned around and yelled, "Hey, Lou! Got the man for Chavez." Turning back to Aaron he asked, "When you want him?"

Aaron said, "How about tomorrow morning? I can be here at nine. I have an eleven thirty flight. Is that enough time?"

An older, balding, rail thin lieutenant came wandering over. "Al Martinez. Glad you're taking that piece of shit off our hands. He's been in Ad Seg for a month, 'cause of his mouth. He's lucky he's still alive.

Nine is fine. We'll have him packaged and ready to go. You bring irons with you?"

"Irons?"

"Restraints?"

Aaron ducked his head. "Um, yeah, got leg and waist restraints, and extra cuffs."

Martinez said, "Good, always did like dealing with folks that come prepared. Ah, sorry about the reception you got at JFK. Those two aren't our best and brightest, but they were the closest car."

Aaron shrugged. "I think it's being handled…"

Martinez grimaced. "Oh yeah. Those two will never get out of patrol, ever, as long as Chief Burris is in the department."

Chief Burris came out, followed by Clay. "You ready Deputy? Martinez, you got a handle on it?"

Martinez replied, "Got it, Chief. We won't fuck it up."

Aaron stuck out his hand. "Thanks, LT. I'll be back at nine in the morning."

Martinez shook it, asking, "You want us to send a car?"

Chief Burris interjected, "I'll handle the deputy's transport."

"Yes, Chief."

Burris headed for the door, Clay and Aaron trailing. Once they were back in the car, the chief turned and asked, "Where are you staying, Deputy?"

Clay said, "He's bunking with me. I've got a double room at the Holiday Inn."

"You want to come up to the house for dinner with Clay?"

Aaron replied, "Thanks, but no, sir. I want a good night's sleep, so I can be alert all the way back."

"Okay, we'll drop you at the hotel."

***

Aaron popped awake at six a.m., he'd never even heard Clay come in last night, or if he did, he didn't remember it. He got up quietly, took a quick piss and jumped in the shower. After he finished, he fumbled through his luggage, found his clothes and retrcated to the bathroom. After getting dressed, he came out and heard Clay mumble, "What damn time is it?"

"Six-thirty, Clay."

"Oh, shit. I've got the hangover from hell. I'm too old for this shit…"

Aaron stifled a laugh. "I'm going down to grab some breakfast. Should I drag my bags now?"

Clay groaned, "I'll get up. Michael told me a car would be here at seven thirty. Better take your bag."

Aaron said, "Lights coming on." He flipped the lights, quickly packed his bag, checked the bag with the restraints, confirmed everything was still there, and headed out the door as Clay staggered slowly, hair awry, toward the bathroom.

Clay made it down to the lobby a couple of minutes before the staff car showed up, Chief Burris at the wheel. He looked the worse for wear too, and smiled ruefully. "Morning, Deputy. You were smart. Us old farts got stupid last night. We'll go to my office, and I'll get one of my people to run you up to One Fifteen, okay?"

***

Twenty minutes with Lieutenant Martinez, and Chavez was all his. Martinez had told him they'd made sure Chavez didn't get much sleep, and they'd rolled him out at 0400 to shower, shave, and eat. Once Chavez had been put in the restraints, he taken two steps and locked up his leg restraints. He would have face-planted had Aaron not had been holding the waist strap. Aaron reached down and released the pins, saying, "Chavez, don't try extending your legs, next time, I'll let you fall."

Chavez mumbled something under his breath, but walked carefully down to the car. Aaron slid him into the back seat, buckling him in. Then he got in the front seat, and turned so that he could watch his prisoner. At JFK, Sergeant Leland walked them through security and left with a jaunty wave. "Good luck, boyo! Don't envy you this day."

***

Three hours in the last row of the airplane, thankfully with Chavez sleeping most of it, then having to take Chavez to the bathroom at DFW. Adding in waiting for and juggling the bags had left Aaron's nerves on edge. *At least Chavez slept through most of the flight, thank you NYPD! This shit wasn't this hard in the Corps. Now if I can get a ride...*

Aaron saw an officer at the baggage claim as he retrieved his gear, and walked over. "Excuse me, I'm..."

The officer said, "Deputy Miller, right? Sergeant Smith told me to keep an eye out for you. Got a car outside, if you've got everything."

Aaron said, "Yep, would you mind walking Chavez, or taking the roller bag? I could do both, but I'd rather have a hand free if I need it."

The officer laughed. "I'll take the bag. Come on."

They went out and loaded a groggy Chavez into the car and the officer drove them back to the airport police building. Pulling up behind Aaron's Tahoe, he guarded Chavez while Aaron loaded his bags in the back.

Six hours and one pit stop later, Aaron pulled into the sallyport. He almost fell out of the Tahoe, stiff as a board, and buzzed the entry door, "Miller, with one. Chavez. Can somebody give me a hand?"

He heard the clank of the door unlocking, and Smith and Grande, two of the jailers came out, Grande rubbing his hands together. "My, my. Raoul Chavez, welcome back, *mi amigo*!"

Aaron followed with the paperwork, turning it over to Officer Smith, who said, "You look like shit, Miller. Go home. We got this turd."

"Thanks, it *has* been a long day." Aaron barely remembered the drive home. *I'm getting too old for this. What the hell is happening to me?* He remembered kissing Jesse, but that was it. He was face down and asleep in minutes.

Laredo

The old man groaned, rolled over, and sat up in bed, momentarily wondering where he was. Then he remembered he was in a hotel in Laredo. *Gah, what time is… gotta teach today.* He fumbled for the light switch on the lamp by the bed, finally found it, and flipped it on. His watch said 6 a.m. as he grumbled to himself. He got up and started the little four cup coffee pot. Doing his business while the coffee brewed, he stretched to get the kinks out.

The coffee pot burped, farted steam, and finally gurgled to a halt as the old man laid out his fresh clothes. He poured a cup of coffee and the first sip reminded him, yet again, how bad hotel coffee really was, *Dammit, this tastes like drippings from… Sawdust…* Thirty minutes later, he was dressed in his familiar gray Dickies. Flipping his gun belt around his hips, he made sure the magazine was firmly seated in the 1911, press checked it to ensure there was a round in the chamber, pushed the safety back on, and re-holstered it. Throwing the dirty clothes and his Dopp kit in his bag, he slung it over his shoulder, scanned the room one more time, put on his hat, and left.

***

Bucky polished off the last of his Huevos Rancheros as the old man sipped coffee at Danny's.

"So, John, when are you officially pulling the plug?" Bucky asked.

The old man shrugged. "I'm looking at the end of the fiscal year, so end of September. It's not like it makes a whole lot of difference."

Bucky cocked his head. "Why not? You've got to start collecting your retirement, so what date gives you an extra year?"

The old man chuckled. "Bucky, I'm already collecting Social Security, and my county pay has been a dollar a year since day one."

Bucky's mouth fell open. "A… A dollar? What the hell? What did you get when you were with us?"

"Dollar a year." The old man shrugged. "I've got money coming in from the ranch. Never needed much else. The Social Security basically buys dog food for Yogi and Boo Boo."

Bucky sat back in amazement. "John, you are one crazy bastard! I cannot believe…"

The old man interrupted him. "Don't say anything about it, okay? I'm planning on going out like I came in: quietly."

"Am I at least going to get an invite?"

"Sure. You, Clay, probably Billy, and that's about it." Glancing at his watch, he continued, "Bout time for us to go. Since you're the money man, you get breakfast, and I'll get the tip."

Bucky rolled his eyes. "Okay, smartass."

***

The old man ran through the camera sets on a break to make sure he knew where all the controls were, checked the lesson plan to make sure there weren't any major changes, and slipped out of the room as the students started filtering back in. Officer Michelle Spears gave him a quick hug as she walked by. "Great to see you, Captain. You'll be up in about thirty minutes. I'll give the lead in and background, then introduce you, if that's okay."

"Sounds good. I'll be back in a half hour."

The old man started down the hall when he heard one of the students ask, jokingly, "Who's that old dinosaur? Some local yokel on a tour that got lost?"

He started to turn back when he heard Spears ask, "You aren't really that stupid, are you?"

"What?" the student asked.

"One, this is a secure area. Two, that dinosaur, as you called him, is one of the legends down here on the border. He's been doing this for over thirty years, and he was seconded to DEA when it was the wild-west below the border."

The student snickered. "Sure…"

Spears snapped, "Hey, asshole, I wouldn't be here if it wasn't for him. He shot two cartel guys off my back, from a helicopter down on the border. I've seen his graveyards. He's also written papers on how to investigate smuggling, taught at Quantico, and taken smugglers and druggies down world-wide. Where are your graveyards?"

The old man smiled and kept walking as Spears continued to dress down the student and his buddies.

A half hour later, he slipped in the back of the classroom, nodded to Spears, and leaned against the wall as she wrapped up her lecture on cues to smugglers. She finally said, "And now, I'd like to introduce Captain John Cronin, from the Pecos County Sheriff's Office. He's going to go over visual cues, methodologies, and tippers and tricks the smugglers use. Captain?"

The old man walked to the front of the class. "Morning, all." He got a few mumbled replies as he stepped to the podium and cued up the cameras. "This brief is limited distribution, confidential, and close hold due to the specific technologies we're going to be covering."

Bringing up the camera feeds, he walked through each location, whether they were hidden or not, and their contribution to the overall security scheme at the border. "Now, these four, in the upper left, are in plain sight. They are obvious to anyone that looks up. Each one covers a head on shot of a lane. Notice how the officers move to make sure they aren't obscuring any details as the vehicles roll into the lanes."

Pointing to the second row of cameras, he continued the lecture. "These aren't nearly as visible, and these are all pan, tilt, zoom, which allows the operators to focus in on specific details of vehicles. The third row is concealed in the lanes themselves, allowing a look at the underbody of the vehicles. These are some of the most productive ones."

One of the students raised his hand. "Why is that?"

The old man replied, "After a while, an operator can pick out odd details, especially modifications or additions, or even trap doors built into the bottoms of larger trucks. Sometimes, they can even pick up modifications to car bodies, or people strapped to the undercarriage."

There was a snicker from the back of the room, and the old man held up a finger. "Lemme show you." Quickly selecting the camera for lane four, he hooked recorded data, and the previous month. Running to the right date and time, he started the clip and leaned on the podium as the replay started.

As a truck pulled into the lane, the class saw two groups of four people, one ahead of the rear axle and one behind the rear axle, literally tied into netting that held them up against the frame of the truck.

A chorus of, "Holy shit! You got to be kidding me," and other exclamations erupted as they watched feet, a K-9, and then officers crowd under the truck.

"That was forty grand worth of smuggling by the coyotes, right there. Five grand apiece is what those people paid to be smuggled across. They were supposed to be picked up by another truck that afternoon, and delivered to Dallas."

Cueing up another date and time, he said, "This one is a bit different: here, you can see the trap door." Switching to another set of cameras, he pulled up the same date and time, and started the playback. "Here's the rest of that story. Note the load. It's floor to ceiling, and over half the trailer deep." Running the playback fast forward, he finally slowed it down, "Here's the actual smuggling space. Eight feet by ten feet, and they had twenty-one men, women, and children stuffed in there. No airflow, except the two little vents on the front of the trailer, no water, no sanitary…"

After a few more videos, he looked at the clock on the back wall. "Looks like it's time for a break. We'll take ten and go into the rest of the lecture after that.

One of the students came up to the old man and asked diffidently, "Captain, I understand you were a Green Beret back in the day?"

The old man chuckled. "Long, long ago, and far, far away, but yes."

"I'm Matt Hambright, I was in the Tenth before I got out," he said, proffering a 10th Special Forces challenge coin.

The old man smiled, reached under his shirt, pulled out the elephant hide pouch and slipped out the silver 5th Special Forces coin he'd carried for over 50 years. "This is mine."

Hambright's eyes widened, "Damn, is it really pure silver? We heard stories…"

"Yep, and the general actually did give them to us in person. Did you deploy downrange?"

Handing the coin back, Hambright replied, "Five times. Three Iraq, two Afghanistan."

The old man winced. "That wasn't a lot of fun. We only did Nam. I spent most of my time up on the trail with the 'Yards."

"Just out of curiosity, did you guys really have your choice of weapons? We heard stories at the museum at Fort Bragg."

The old man laughed. "Oh yeah. I was weapons and communications. We trained on anything and everything. I carried an AK most of the time."

"An AK?"

"Readily available ammo, not distinctive in a firefight, and good in the jungle. Considering that we got resupply maybe every couple of weeks, I never even took the AR in the field. Did you ever know a Colonel Wojokowicz?"

"You mean General Wojo? Yes, sir. He's over the Warfare Center at Bragg." Curiously, Hambright asked, "Where do you know him from?"

The old man looked around. "Oh, when he was the Defense Attaché in Thailand. Looks like we need to start." Sticking out his hand, he continued, "DOL, Hambright. All right, folks, if you'll take your seats, we'll get back to it."

Hambright sensed there was more to that story, but said, "DOL, Captain," and returned to his seat.

The old man punched up the first picture. "Okay, for this part of the lecture, we're going to look at various methods the cartels and other smugglers use to move drugs."

***

An hour and a half later, the old man was half hoarse, but had answered most of the classes' questions. "Sorry we ran a little long. I hope this has helped you a bit, and just remember, when in doubt, flag a supervisor. And remember, your hunches are usually based on *something* whether you consciously know it or not." Looking at Spears, who was standing in the back of the class, he suggested, "Fifteen?"

Spears nodded. "Make it a twenty-minute break. We're actually a little ahead of the overall schedule."

The classroom cleared out as Spears walked to the front of the classroom. "I hear you're retiring, Captain."

"Yep, end of September. I should have already been gone. I hear you made thirteen."

It was Spears' turn to laugh. "By the skin of my teeth. If it hadn't been for my military time, I'd probably be an eleven forever. But Bucky has me running some local surveillance ops and we've been pretty successful, so that helped. Especially since that was a thirteen/fourteen team lead position."

"Hispanic or…"

"Primarily looking for Taliban, ISIS, and Abu Sayaf. I've been working with EPIC on the *Sinaloa* routes, and we bumped some of the stuff we found to the Coasties. They got almost a hundred Chinese in one sweep, based on an Intel hit where the cartel guy was discussing moving Taliban bodies by ship from Acapulco, at sea rendezvous, then into Long Beach as ship's crew on a Libyan flagged cargo ship. Didn't know there were already Chinese being smuggled on it."

The old man laughed. "One never knows what you're gonna find. Was there also heroin found?"

Spears cocked her head. "Uh, I think so…"

"That's something worth remembering. None of the cartels do just *one* thing. It's always multiples: they figure the odds are better that one entity will slip through, especially if there is a decoy ahead of them. Remember how many decoys you've seen here?"

"Huh, a few. I hadn't thought of it that way, but it makes sense."

"Now I'm betting the Coasties are checking arrival times for Long Beach, and I'm betting there was a ship scheduled in just ahead of that one. It needs to be checked too, and probably has smuggled contraband on it. Not much, but just enough to warrant a full search. I'd also bet it was planted or on loaded at the last port."

"I need to get smarter on that. What would you recommend I do, sir?"

"Get Bucky to send you TAD to LA. DEA has a pretty robust presence out there, and you could pick their brains and get in on some good busts while you're at it. They work the border, too, and are tied in with the Coasties and Navy LEO Dets."

Spears shrugged. "Oh well, why not."

The old man glanced at her. "Problems?"

She blushed. "Well, I finally met a nice guy…"

"And if you TAD, it'll kill the relationship?"

"I don't know, it's just that… Well, he's really nice. I met him at the range."

"So he's a shooter? Who with?"

Spears laughed. "Actually, he's an accountant. But he shoots three gun."

"An *accountant*?"

"Apparently, he and his brother inherited the family ranch, but it's only big enough for one person. He and his brother flipped a coin, and he lost. So he went to school and became an accountant, while his brother went to school for ranch management. They seem to get along fairly well, and I've met his brother and his brother's wife." She pulled out her phone, flipped through her photos, selected one, and turned the phone around.

The old man looked at the picture. "Damn, he looks like a Tactical door kicker! I wouldn't have bet on him being an accountant if you hadn't told me!" *Sounds like this one might be serious. If she's meeting family… But I don't know what this younger generation is doing. I remember what Aaron did to track Jesse down, so maybe, just maybe she's going to be lucky with this one.* "If I were you, I'd just lay it out for him. I'm betting he would understand, and if he's serious, he'd be supportive."

"Maybe, maybe I'll try that and see before I go to Bucky."

The old man glanced at his watch. "Well, if we're done, I need to hit the road. It's six hours back to the house, and I told the sheriff I'd be in to work tomorrow."

Spears gave him a quick hug. "Travel safe, Captain. Will you come back for the fall class? I think it will be in early September."

"We'll see. God willing and the Creeks don't rise."

The old man grabbed his hat, waved, and headed out the door. He swung by Bucky's office, but he wasn't there. Pulling out his wheel book, he ripped a page out of the back, wrote a quick note to Bucky, and dropped it in his chair. He left the parking lot, got on I-35 North and settled in for the drive back to Fort Stockton.

Letting his thoughts wander, he reflected on the years and people he'd encountered working with the DEA, FBI, and various LEOs around the world. He almost missed the Highway 83 exit, shook his head, and thought, *Stop it with the wool gathering. You need to pay attention to your driving before you end up in the middle of nowhere, wondering how you got there.*

Marine Corps Ball

Aaron looked in the mirror at the FBO and chuckled as he tied his tie. Matt asked curiously, "What's so funny?" Matt was running his finger around the inside of his collar, trying to loosen it a hair so he could still breathe, and was looking at his reflection.

Aaron replied, "Remember every boot Marine's wish?"

"Which one? There are a lot of them, if I remember right."

"To marry a nympho that owned a bar."

Matt stopped and looked at him. "What brought that on?"

Aaron shrugged. "Dunno. Maybe it's getting back into this monkey suit for the first time in three years. Or it could be that we're going to the Marine Ball after having flown from Fort Stockton on a Lear jet, owned by one of the top lawyers in Texas, if not the US, and I'm married to a beautiful woman who's borne two children and owns a ranch with oil wells."

Matt smiled. "Yeah, we both came out pretty well, didn't we?"

"And we're going to the Ball in a limo, get to see Toad, and Colonel, dammit, General Moore. We get to show off Jesse and Felicia, and who knows who else is liable to show up?"

The old man stuck his head in the rest room door. "Limo is here, if you two are through pimping. The girls are already loaded up."

With one more quick uniform check, both of them threw their jeans, other clothes, and boots in their bags, following the old man out to the parking lot. The trunk of the limo was open and they dropped their bags in it, then closed the hatch. Billy and the old man were already seated in the limo, as Aaron and Matt climbed in carefully, trying not to brush either Jesse's or Felicia's dresses or mess up their uniforms. "Remember doing this in the bathroom at the club?" Aaron asked.

Matt laughed, "Just like the inspections. Driving to the inspection with a uniform hanging on hangars, getting dressed in the parking lot and never sitting until the inspection was complete."

Billy snickered. "Figures, damn Jarheads can't figure out how to actually keep a uniform clean long enough to make it through inspection."

The old man laughed at that. "Billy, I don't think we stood more than maybe five or six inspections our entire time in the service. I can only remember *one* that I stood, other than basic, that was actually Class A's."

The limo driver pulled smoothly away from the curb, depositing them twenty minutes later at the Marine Corps Reserve Center on Pollard Street. After everyone unassed from the limo, Billy leaned in and said something to the driver, who nodded and pulled away from the curb. "He'll be back at eleven to pick us up. That should be about right, time wise."

Jesse fussed with Billy's bow tie. "Uncle Billy, how come you *still* don't know how to tie a bow tie?"

"Oh, I can tie one, I just don't like to. 'Sides, this is about y'all, not us two old Army farts. Although I will be interested to see Toad actually in a uniform."

The six of them walked up the drive, then into the main bay, where the Ball was being held. A quartet of Marine musicians played softly in one corner, and they spied a bar set up in the opposite corner of the bay, where Billy and the old man headed. Aaron and Matt stood looking around, until Matt finally spotted Toad, talking to two Marines near the head table. "I've got eyes on." Leading the way, Matt snuck up behind Toad, quietly slipping an arm around his neck and pulling back slowly.

Toad faked a dramatic death, as Aaron realized the two men he'd been talking to were General Moore and now-Lieutenant Colonel Ragsdale. Cindy came back carrying two glasses of what Aaron figured was Coke, and Jesse immediately hugged her.

Aaron's thoughts were confused. *Damn, the Col… General looks like he's aged ten years, but Rags, he doesn't look a day older. Hard to believe…* "General, Colonel, may I present my wife, Jesse?"

General Moore took in both Aaron and Matt with a glance, shook Jesse's hand, and said, "It's a pleasure to see you again Mrs. Miller."

Jesse smiled. "It's good to see you sir, and congratulations on the promotion. Colonel Ragsdale, how is Melissa doing?"

Colonel Ragsdale smiled. "She's well, Jesse. Still teaching school and loving it. She would have loved to be here, but couldn't take the time off. We're back at Pendleton now, and the General was good enough to invite me to join him on the airplane coming down here."

Matt made his manners with both the general and the colonel and started to drag Toad off, when Billy and the old man joined them. Aaron smiled at the general's reaction to Billy Moore and his pigtail, saying, "General, Colonel, this is Mr. Billy Moore. He's a lawyer out of Houston and this is John Cronin, my father-in-law."

They all shook hands, with Billy quipping, "Must say General, you Marines clean up pretty good. Us old Army farts can't hold a candle to you, and frankly, don't want to."

General Moore grinned and asked, "Where are you originally from? And you were actually in the Army? I thought that had height minimums."

"North Texas, just outside Amarillo. Yep, did my two years and ran away from it as fast as I could."

Jesse interrupted, "Uncle Billy! Stop that! General, Uncle Billy was a Green Beret, and so was Papa."

The general smiled. "I've read your resume. Can we chat for a minute?"

Aaron and Jesse took that as an indication they were dismissed, and went looking for Toad and Cindy. They'd already found a table, and tilted chairs up for eight, ensuring they would all be sitting together later. Toad slapped Aaron on the back, hugged Jesse and continued, "So, when I heard through the grapevine that General Moore was coming, I thought what the hell, why not get everybody together? It's not like you guys have been doing anything Corps related in the last three years, and maybe you actually missed it. The invite to Mr. Moore was a spur of the moment thing. Cindy and I figured he might appreciate it, too, considering what he's done for folks."

Matt said, "It's kinda nice to do this once in a while, and Felicia had only seen the one Ball at Pendleton, so it worked out. What have they got you doing? And how long have you had the stripe?"

Toad smiled. "Technically, we're a reserve Arty Battalion out of fourth; in reality, we're doing Intel support down here, and I'm the unit armorer and Intel number two. We've got the equivalent of a Scout/Sniper platoon that drills out of here, so I get to stay busy."

Cindy smiled at him. "And I'm working sixty-hour weeks with the DA, so between us, we're lucky if we get one day a week off. Toad's drill isn't really that much of an imposition, considering that it's only one weekend a month."

The music changed, and people started taking seats, as Billy and the old man came through the crowd to their table. The color guard presented the colors, the POW/MIA tribute was read and Marine Corps Order 47 from Commandant Lejeune in 1921 was read. The salads were already on the table and everyone dug in as the caterer started delivering the main meals. Aaron asked Billy, "Interesting conversation with the general?"

Billy smiled enigmatically. "When a general officer wants to talk to me, it's *always* interesting. He's really unhappy with the way you were treated."

A caterer placed the chicken plate down, and Billy started in on that, leaving Matt and Aaron in the dark as to what had really been said.

Once the main meal had been served, the cake was rolled out, and the General was introduced as the guest speaker. However, his first words snapped everyone to attention, "Ladies, gentlemen, honored guests, Marines, before I give my little speech, I need to right a long simmering wrong. Gunnery Sergeant Aaron Miller, front and center."

Wonderingly Aaron got up and marched to the lectern, stopping three feet short, saluting and saying, "Gunnery Sergeant Miller, reporting as ordered, sir."

The general picked up a medal case off the lectern, turned and said, "Adjutant, the citation if you will."

Major Smith, the adjutant, cleared his throat and started reading the citation. "The President of the United States takes pleasure in presenting a third award of the Silver Star to Aaron M. Miller, Gunnery Sergeant, United States Marine Corps for services as set forth in the following." Taking a breath, he continued, "For extraordinary heroism while serving as Alpha Team Leader, Marine Special Operations Battalion, First Marine Division, First Marine Expeditionary Force in support of Operation Enduring Freedom on twelve June twenty-eleven. Gunnery Sergeant Miller's team was part of a joint Afghan/US patrol that was ambushed, near FOB Apache in an Afghan village compound."

Aaron flashed back to the fight, thinking, *It was a village, maybe unnamed, but it was a damn village.* He felt the sweat start as the battle unrolled in his mind.

Just as I was about to cross that second alley, ten or twelve Taliban fighters spilled out of it directly in front of me. He had to struggle to stay at attention, and keep his hands from automatically moving as they would have on the M-4.

The adjutant continued, "Gunnery Sergeant Miller effectively deployed his team under fire to break the ambush. He encountered twelve enemy combatants in an alley. Enduring intense enemy fire and without regard for his own personal safety, Gunnery Sergeant Miller succeeded in dispatching all twelve combatants while taking a major wound to his lower leg."

He started firing into them. It was up close and personal at less than fifteen feet, and he'd gotten on the trigger just a tick quicker. He'd seen their expressions as they died, and almost missed the RPG. He'd shifted to the RPG shooter and put three rounds into his chest as he felt impacts on his vest. The RPG shooter started to fall, but he'd triggered the RPG and it headed toward the ground. He'd felt impacts on his left arm and left leg and started falling. Figuring he'd been shot in the leg or hit by the exploding RPG, he'd done a tucked roll, landed on his belly, and continued to fire into the massed Taliban.

"Though seriously wounded, and under continuous fire in the open alley, he maintained control and directed the assault to where the ambush originated, causing the ambush to be broken."

He'd rolled over and propped himself up against the wall of a compound, remembering the smell of fresh blood that almost overpowered the smell of gunpowder and voided bowels. He'd been amazed he could still hear, too. Doc was trying to work on him, but he'd stopped them, "Fight's still on. Doc and one stay here. Johnson, you're in charge. Get McKenzie up there where he can see and call in the A-10. Mac, get up as high as you can, get a view and if they can do it, have the A-10 hit whatever GRG they can. The rest of you, stay low and hit your targets in the face. Maximum firepower, blow them out of the ambush if you can. Mac, use the gun on the MRAP to keep their heads down until you're ready." The last thing he remembered was the A-10 and smelling jet fuel.

The adjutant concluded, "By his outstanding display of decisive leadership, unlimited courage in the face of heavy enemy fire, and utmost devotion to duty, Gunnery Sergeant Miller reflected great credit upon himself and upheld the highest traditions of the Marine Corps and the United States Naval Service."

General Moore pinned another Silver Star on his chest, whispering, "You okay? Were you back there?"

Aaron nodded. "Yes, sir. But I'm okay now."

"Okay, now we pose for pictures. Smile, if you can."

The general mimed pinning the medal on again, they shook hands again, and finally the general said, "Dismissed. But don't leave before I talk to you."

"Yes, sir." Aaron marched slowly back to his seat, and sat carefully as Jesse reached over and grabbed his hand, tears in her eyes.

"I'm sorry, Aaron."

"What? Why are you sorry?"

"For what you had to experience."

He squeezed her hand in return.

The general opened a notebook on the lectern, cleared his throat, took out a piece of paper and stared at it for a second. "I have a prepared speech here, but I just decided I'm not going to give it." Closing the notebook, he continued, "I'm going to violate a confidence here, and I have my reasons. One of the things we are taught as Marines, is that we take care of our own. Part of that is why we celebrate the cake cutting the way we do, and it is actually part of the Marine Drill Manual."

Waving the piece of paper, the general continued, "Gunnery Sergeant Miller was one of my Marines, in First SOB, when the action occurred that he got his third Silver Star for. The paperwork was submitted within two weeks for an award," he said, waving the paper again, "and it went up the chain. What is worse, is that it went *out* of the chain. For those who don't know it, there is a joint awards board in the Puzzle Palace that issues awards for all services. Under this last administration, it came down to spreadsheets and nose counting on awards and levels. The Marines were called on the carpet, since *we* were accused of giving out too many high awards for valor, compared to the other services. You might remember, Marines were involved in the heaviest fighting, Fallujah, Helmand, the northern FOBs, the whole nine yards."

Waving the piece of paper again, he continued, "*This* award went up as an award for the Medal, or at the least a Navy Cross. It was approved out of HQMC as a Navy Cross, but when it went to the joint board, they, in their infinite wisdom, said the spread sheets based on rank and award prohibited, yes, *prohibited* the Marines from awarding the Navy Cross to Gunnery Sergeant Miller, because we'd already had too many. They downgraded it to a Silver Star. When we tried to fight it, we were told to play nice. I did. Which was wrong of me. I should have stood up for Gunny. But what makes it worse, is that this award was *never* actually issued to Gunny. By the time they were through playing games, he was on his terminal leave, so it just got slipped into his personnel jacket, no harm, no foul."

Dropping the paper on the lectern, he gripped the edges. "I didn't find out until four months ago this had happened, and that was only because of the gunny network inside the Corps. I determined then to do what little I could to right that wrong, and this presentation tonight is part of that. The other thing is, I will give Gunny Miller the original award recommendation. He can frame it with the award, throw it away, or burn it. That is up to him."

Continuing, he said, "The real takeaway for each of you sitting here tonight is remember: we are Marines. We take care of our own, and we do the right thing to stand by our fellow Marines. Master Sergeant Matt Carter, retired; Gunnery Sergeant Moretti, you fulfilled that obligation tonight, and the Marine Corps thanks you. Adjutant, the cake cutting if you will."

The adjutant stepped to his microphone. "Ladies and gentlemen, the Marine Corp's birthday cake-cutting ceremony is important to all Marines, as it is an annual renewal of each Marine's commitment to the Corps . . . and the Corps' commitment to our nation's quest for peace and freedom worldwide. The birthday cake is traditionally cut with the Mameluke sword, as a reminder that we are a band of warriors, committed to carrying the sword, so that our nation may live in peace. The Mameluke sword gets its name from the cross hilt and ivory grip design, similar to swords used for centuries by Ottoman warriors. The Marine Corps tradition of carrying this sword dates from Lieutenant Presley O'Bannon's assault of Derna, Tripoli, in 1805, where he is said to have won the sword of the governor of the city."

An old Gunner and very young Private stepped to the cake, and made a slice with the Mameluke sword, as the adjutant continued, "As is our custom, the first piece of cake will be presented to our guest of honor, General Moore."

Major Bellieu, the commanding officer, presented the first piece to General Moore, who sat it on the lectern. The major cut a second piece and handed it to the old Marine Gunner, as the adjutant said, "By tradition, the second piece of cake is presented to the oldest Marine present. Ladies and Gentlemen the oldest Marine present is Gunner Hobson, who was born in Duluth, Minnesota in July nineteen sixty-five. He will present the piece of cake to Private Yvonne Lopez, who was born in El Paso, Texas November first, nineteen ninety-nine. This symbolizes the passing of experience and knowledge from the old to the young. It also emphasizes the need to take care of our young before we take care of ourselves."

Once the three pieces had been dealt with, everyone else lined up and got their slice of cake, beverage of choice, and the DJ started tuning up in the corner.

Conversations

Billy leaned across the table. "Congrats Aaron, but don't feel bad, you're not the first one to get screwed on a medal, nor will you be the last."

Aaron shrugged. "I don't really care." Flipping the medal, he continued, "This and two bucks will get me a cup of coffee, maybe…"

That prompted a round of laughter, as a Marine Sergeant and his wife walked up to the table. Toad stood up. "Heath! Glad you made it, man." Waving his arm at the table, he said, "Folks, Heath and Amanda Boyd. Heath is one of our resident cyber folks."

Billy, always the wiseass, said, "Nope, can't be. He actually has a tan. Real cyber geeks never see the sun!"

Heath laughed. "Well, when I do drill, I damn sure don't see the sun, they keep my ass *deep* in the systems. I just hope they don't lock me in Sunday night when they leave."

Matt smiled. "So, what do you do in real life?"

Heath replied, "I run the family farm, and Amanda runs our water company."

"Your *water* company?"

Amanda smiled. "We have an aquifer spring on the property and years ago the family would sell water from it to travelers. It's called Dorado Spring Water.

We're not big, and don't want to be, but it's a nice little bit of income."

Aaron cocked his head. "Straight reserves?"

Heath nodded. "Joined in twenty-ten. Did boot and cyber training, then here as a drilling reservist."

Doing the math, Aaron said, "So you're not young and stupid, like we were…"

Amanda laughed. "Not young, for sure. Stupid is debatable…"

Aaron winced, "I didn't mean it that…"

"Well, there might have been a discussion or two at night about the advisability of his joining up, but I do support what he's doing, even if he did leave me in the lurch for a year," Amanda replied, hugging Heath.

Jesse smiled. "Yep, the stupid runs strong in them, doesn't it?"

Cindy snickered, "Among other things!"

Matt glanced at Felicia, who just smiled at him. He shook his head. "Uh, can we start over? Hi, I'm Matt." Matt got up and stuck out his hand, and Heath shook it as Aaron and the others also got up. They shook hands all around, and Heath said, "Folks like you *are* the reason I joined at my so called, advanced, age. I didn't want to sit on the sidelines and not do my part."

Matt chuckled. "Well, be glad you're here and not there. Being downrange sucks rocks. Always has, always will."

Amanda caught Jesse's look and gave her a pained smile in return. Jesse made a motion and said, "Potty break." All of the women got up and left the guys sitting at the table, staring at each other.

Aaron said, "I'll never understand that. Why do they *all* have to go together?"

The old man laughed. "It's because they want to talk without us overhearing them. Haven't you ever noticed how Jesse and Felicia will either stop talking or change the subject when one of us walks in the room where they are?"

Matt nodded. "Yeah, I've caught them doing that. Felicia just says 'girl talk' and gives me The Look."

Billy chuckled. "At least you're getting it in English. Try Vietnamese, or some dialect they seem to know that isn't in the books. Especially when they find out you can speak the language. I swear, my wife didn't speak to me for probably a month after I asked her about something I overheard her and her mother talking about!"

Heath chimed in, "Imagine an office full of women, which is what I have to deal with at the water company. It's estrogen central in there: not safe for man nor beast."

***

Jesse turned to Amanda as they got in the rest room. "Worried about him having to deploy?"

Amanda nodded. "Scared to death. I don't want to lose him. How… How did y'all handle it?"

Cindy and Felicia both started to speak, then stopped. Cindy finally said, "I'm in the same boat you are. Toad and I got married after he got off active duty. I'm just hoping and praying he doesn't have to go again. He's been four or five times, I think."

Felicia said, "I married Matt while he was still active, but he was at Pendleton, so I haven't had to deal with it. He retired rather than put his troops in what he called an unwinnable position."

They all turned at looked at Jesse, who thought for a second, and finally said, "He… Well, I didn't like him deploying, but that's what he got paid to do. I knew the guys on his team, and they all wanted to come back as much as he did. Aaron, well, all of them, Matt, Toad, and the others I met, they aren't *nice* people when they put on the uniform. Their job is to break things and kill people, before the enemy does that to them. That's why they train like they do. Aaron didn't want to get out, but he realized he was actually holding his folks back and putting them in harm's way with the prosthetic. So, he took the medical retirement, and here we are. I just did what I could to keep busy and kept in touch through the Wives Club. It's amazing how much information gets circulated through those channels. *Most* of it is true, and correct. But sometimes BS slips in. I was lucky I had two senior Marine's wives I could lean on too."

She shrugged, continuing, "Things are winding down now, so that's limiting the deployments for the active folks, and I think Toad said they're pretty much on a two-week-a-year active duty for their training schedule for the next couple of years."

Amanda, brushed her hair, and nodded. "That's what Heath was told, and I didn't know about the Wives Clubs. Thanks for sharing that."

Felicia cautioned, "Be careful, though, there can be both good ones and bad ones, according to Matt."

Cindy took a card out of her clutch, and said. "Here's my card, if you've got questions, give me a call."

Amanda took it gratefully, "I will."

Cindy checked her lipstick, smiling. "If you get down here, give me a call, I can probably break away and have lunch."

"Okay."

***

The women came back to the table, to find Heath, Toad, Matt, and Aaron moving glasses, salt and pepper shakers, and the ketchup bottle around, deep in conversation, as Aaron described what happened to him in the unnamed village in Afghanistan. Jesse shook her head. "Boys and their toys…"

Amanda and Cindy laughed, but it was tentative laughter, while Felicia just rolled her eyes. "They never stop. It's like they have to have a way to visualize what they are talking about."

Jesse looked around, but didn't see the old man or Uncle Billy, and she glanced at her watch, wondering if they'd left. She shook her head. *No, it's not time. They're off somewhere quiet. I remember now, neither one of them likes a lot of people around, unless they know everybody personally. But I don't see anybody here being a threat… But Papa has never really talked about what he's been through, at least not in detail. I wonder if grandma went through this with Papa, did he ever talk to her?*

She finally saw them, off in a corner, their backs against the wall, talking to the general and the colonel, and relaxing. She wouldn't have been so happy, if she'd known Billy was giving the general an ear full.

The general wasn't chewing nails, but he was getting closer, as Billy explained the rest of the story, as he called it on Aaron's hearing. The general finally exploded, "How the fuck…?"

Billy continued, "General, that is what happens when the bean counters and administrivia types get in the middle of the real warfighters. Administrators administrate, they make damn sure all the paperwork is done, I's dotted, T's crossed. They never look beyond that, there are no humans in their equation, merely numbers on a page, or forms to be filed. I blame part of what happened to Aaron on his being shipped to an Army base, not for the quality of care, but for the loss of command continuity. Once the bean counters got into it that made it doubly worse. Their only concern was the cost, what pot of money those funds were going out of, and into. As long as their bottom line matched, they didn't care."

Billy took a sip of his bourbon and branch. "And that bean counter in DC that did the first filing, all he was doing was checks in the box. He probably didn't care or even realize Aaron was drugged to his eyeballs. He got the check in the box and moved on to the next name on his list."

The general replied, "But he's supposed to have been a Marine! He should have…"

The old man interrupted, "General, have you ever been given a job so onerous that all you wanted to do was get it done and go home? Knowing you had to get up the next day, and do it all over again?"

"Yeah, my last job, if I were honest with myself."

Colonel Ragsdale looked at the general in amazement, "Sir?"

The general shrugged, "I'd rather take a beating every day than what I was doing in the Pentagon. Pushing paper for the J3 was just painful. We were supposedly providing guidance for current operations and plans, but every damn thing we did had to be reviewed by the lawyers, and we'd end up having to change it. The whole ROE clusterfuck was because of the lawyers and the collateral damage concerns. That's how we ended up with an ROE that if the enemy dropped their gun, they were no longer a combatant…"

Billy nodded. "Not surprised. Give a lawyer an inch, they'll take a mile deep, mile wide swath and obfuscate to the point that no one but another lawyer can understand it."

The old man added, "That's why Matt Carter retired. He told me he couldn't knowingly lead troops into that environment."

The general nodded. "He wasn't the only one. We lost a lot of senior enlisted, and quite a few mid-grade and senior officers that turned down command slots and retired. That was a pretty dark set of days." Looking at the old man, he asked, "Mr. Cronin, how did y'all handle it in Vietnam?"

"Well, sir, we were pretty much out on the pointy end. We got general orders to do things, but we were small teams. Usually a twelve-man A-team would have an outpost, a couple of hundred indigs for support that we'd train as guerrilla forces. And we'd do what they called hearts and minds support, we did medical care, built schools, and that kind of stuff. Some of us ended up in the jungle, doing surveillance on the trail, and that was usually one, sometimes two Americans, a village of 'Yards or Hmong, that would report convoys and troop movements along the trail, sometimes coordinate strikes, and run ambushes if you had a way to exfil or extract."

The old man pointed to Billy. "He was Intel and crossed as a medic, I was weapons and communications, and our ROE was pretty loose. Get the job done, and do the paperwork later."

Ragsdale said, "If I remember correctly, that generated a lot of medals…"

Billy laughed. "Yeah, get killed, get a medal. Seventeen Medals of Honor, eight hundred or so Silver Stars, and over thirteen thousand Bronze Stars. We lost eight hundred thirty-four Green Berets over the fifteen years we were in Vietnam."

"Out of how many?"

"I don't know that anybody ever counted…"

The general said, "I see you both have the Silver Star rosettes, I'm assuming y'all got them, and probably some others, right?"

The old man just smiled, and the general realized he was looking at a warrior, he couldn't help but wonder how many people these two old men had put in the ground. Shaking his head, he said, "Well, at least with the new administration, we're seeing a significant change back to a more realistic ROE, and the lawyers are gone."

Billy glanced at his watch. "Sorry General, we need to head out before our coach turns into a pumpkin. Thank you for doing right by Aaron. He deserved it."

The four shook hands, and the old man and Billy headed back for their table, as Ragsdale turned to the general. "Damn, I'd have hated to cross either one of them back in the day. I've got a feeling…"

The general nodded. "Yep, stone killers. Both of them. I looked up Moore, he was seconded to what I'd guess was Studies and Observations Group for what looks like a year. I'm betting if you dug on Cronin, you'd find that same gap in his records."

Ragsdale whistled. "SOG? Damn… Yeah, but did you notice how much SA they still have? Their eyes never stopped moving."

Major Smith walked up, interrupting them, and they dropped the subject, but not before the general took one more look at their table.

***

Billy clapped his hands. "Okay, children, it's time."

Jesse managed a credible pout. "Aw, Uncle Billy we were just getting started…"

Matt and Felicia got up, with Felicia shaking her head, "Kids…"

Aaron got up, picking up the folder with his commendation and the award box, as he gulped the last of his coffee. "I need to hit the head: now, or at the airport?"

"Airport," Billy said.

Heath and Amanda, along with Toad and Cindy, made the rounds, with handshakes, hugs, and promises to get together later. Toad said, "Mr. Cronin, I appreciate your coming. And I wanted to thank you for letting Matt and Aaron set up the gun store. I'll be over next weekend, and I'll get those guns finished up."

"Y'all are welcome any time. I didn't get a chance to ask, but I'm hoping you're enjoying teaching."

Toad rolled his eyes. "Oh, there are times… Next time we're up there, I'll tell you some stories."

The old man saw Billy pointing at his wrist, and said, "We're being summoned." Giving Cindy a hug, he said, "Y'all take care. Cindy, you need anything up our way, just give me a call."

She hugged him back. "I will, sir. Thank you."

With Billy in the lead, they trooped out and found the limo, loaded up, and rode quietly back to the airport. Matt smiled. "I'm glad you finally got your recognition."

Aaron lifted the medal case and commendation. "Yeah, that and two bucks will get me a cup of coffee."

"Three dollars in Houston, now," Billy chimed in, provoking laughter.

After a quick pit stop at the FBO, they loaded up and headed back to Fort Stockton. The short forty minute flight was still long enough for everyone but the old man and Billy to go to sleep, and the two of them talked quietly most of the ride back. The pilots greased the landing at Fort Stockton, and Billy laughed as he gently kicked Matt and Aaron's feet. "Y'all are lightweights."

Aaron groaned, "Already?"

"Y'all wake up your wives. I'm not going to be responsible for that!"

Matt chuckled. "Chicken?"

"Smart. I'm not a lawyer for nothing." Getting the women up didn't prove to be an issue, and they got off quickly. As Billy closed the door, the engines spooled up, and the Lear taxied out for the final leg back to Houston.

Twenty minutes later, they pulled into the front yard at the ranch, and were met by Lucy, who opened the front door, letting Yogi and Boo Boo out. The dogs romped happily, and jumped up on the old man and Jesse, as Aaron kept dodging, "No, Boo Boo, no! Not on the uniform!"

Jesse finally said, "Aaron, it's not like you have to wear it again tomorrow, and it's going to the cleaners, she's just glad to see you."

"I… Yeah, you're right. It's just habit." He bent down, and Boo Boo promptly hit him in the chest, knocking him on his butt, as Jesse, Lucy, and the old man laughed.

Later, in bed, Jesse rolled over and hugged Aaron. "Congratulations, I'm proud of you."

She kissed him, and he held her tight. "Thank you, and thanks to you and the kids, I keep the nightmares at bay."

Underfoot

Jesse pushed a stray strand of hair out of her face, then bunched it and put a scrunchy around it. Looking around the display area, she spotted the old farts, as she thought of them, comfortably ensconced around the coffee pot. Walking over, she asked, "Tom, would you mind helping out behind the counter?"

Tom, looked up startled. "Me?"

"Yes Tom, you! You know guns, I've seen you helping people on the sly, thinking we aren't seeing what you're doing. And I'm too damn busy to help everybody. Besides, it's time you earned your coffee."

Ed, Bob, and Joe, the other three old farts laughed, and Ed snickered, "You go Tom. Take one for the team."

Tom got up slowly, rising to his full five foot six inches, minus the badly bowed legs, which really made him about five foot four. Hitching his jeans up, he asked, "What you want me to do Mizz Jesse?"

"Just what you've been doing. Help people. For a broke down old cowboy, and one that claims he hates people, you seem to do a pretty damn good job of guiding people to make good decisions."

Tom shrugged. "Kinda like herding cows, but they talk back. I jus' answer their questions." He stumped over to the end of the counter, followed by Jesse, and asked quietly, "Why me?"

Jesse leaned hipshot on the end of the counter. "Matt's doing ranch stuff, and Khalil is going to be heading back to school in a month. We're busier than I thought we would ever be, and I need to keep the books, do the BATF paperwork, and pay the bills. I can't afford to get distracted in the middle of that. We'll even pay you, how about twenty dollars an hour, plus coffee?"

Tom's eyes got big. "You're going to *pay* me? Just to stand back here and talk to people?"

Jesse shook her head. "Yes, we're going to pay you. Why shouldn't we?"

Tom leaned forward confidentially. "Well, if you're a gonna pay me, you might want to know Ed and Joe are both retired Army DIs, and Bob is a dab hand tinkerer, he fixed my old Colt after it got out of time."

Jesse glanced over at the other three, and mumbled, "Damn… Right under our noses…" That thought was interrupted by the cowbell over the door jangling as a mixed bag of folks came through the door as soon as Khalil unlocked it, some making for the coffee pot, others for the gun counter, and a couple of the young ones, for the play area at the far end of the display area.

Tom said, "I ain't doin' kids. Don't know how. I'll do big people."

Khalil caught Jesse's eye and waggled his fingers, asking which direction she wanted him to go. Jesse pointed to the kids' area, and Khalil started that way with a nod. She hated dumping what she thought of as *kiddie patrol* on him, but he wasn't twenty-one yet, so there were issues with him being behind the counter.

Fernando came through the door in a rush. "Sorry I'm late, had a flat…"

Jesse waved him off. "No problem. Shit happens. I don't know how busy we're going to be, but we may be shorthanded. Especially if a lot of folks want to shoot today. If you need help, grab Ed or Joe to help you out, and let me know how they do, okay?"

Fernando grinned. "I can do that. I'll go get the ranges set up."

***

At noon, Matt brought tamales, rice and beans, along with the usual jug of iced tea, and set them in the conference room, then walked over to the counter, catching Jesse's attention. "Soup's on."

Jesse sighed, "Good. I'm starved, and I haven't slowed down all morning. This has just been nuts!"

"What's up?"

"I don't know for sure. I think it's folks that are buying while the prices are down. I've got ten signed up for a class this weekend, and it's only Tuesday."

"Why's Tom behind the counter?"

"I hired his ass. That old fart knows guns, and turns out he's damn good with people, too!"

"Hired him?"

Jesse bristled. "Well, who showed up to work today? Me, Khalil, and Fernando. You're doing ranch stuff, Felicia is watching the kids, Aaron is sleeping, and there were ten people at the door when we got ready to open. I don't want folks to have to wait, and the old farts *have* been underfoot, damn near since day one, but they have *also* been helping out on the side, anyway. I may hire all of them!"

Matt held up his hands. "Whoa! I'm not…"

Jesse laid a hand on his arm. "Sorry. It's… well, that time of the month, and… Dammit, we need help. Apparently, it's been under our noses the entire time, and we just didn't realize it."

Matt cocked his head, and Jesse continued, "Two retired Army DIs apparently, both of whom are former range officers, and a shade tree mechanic, who've been drinking our coffee since damn near the day we opened.

"Damn… Are you going to put them on the payroll?"

"Of course. Part time, full time, whatever they'll do. I'll take care of the paperwork today. We need to find somebody to replace Khalil, too, he's got to go back to school, and I need to give Felicia some breaks with the kids too. She's been a godsend, but it's not fair to her or you to stick her with four kids every day."

Matt held up his hand, "Jesse, she understands, and the kids are good together. She knows how hard you're working to make this place go, and the ranch itself." Jesse just nodded, and Matt continued, "Let me see if Ernesto has any friends that want to work part time. What are we going to pay them?"

Jesse cocked her head, "Well, we're paying Fernando twenty an hour, and I don't think it would be fair to pay them any less."

Matt winced. "That's a lot, just to work the counter or do range… Never mind. Safety… I wasn't thinking." Glancing at the clock on the wall, he continued, "I gotta go move cows. Tell Fernando we'll be working north of the thousand-yard range this afternoon."

"You want to close it?"

"Yeah, let's do that just to be on the safe side."

"Okay."

***

Aaron came through the door at a little after five to see Tom, Ed, Bob, and Joe sitting at the table, filling out paperwork, with Jesse standing over them. Aaron cocked his head. "Should I ask?"

Jesse grinned. "Meet our newest employees."

"What?"

"I hired all these old reprobates today."

Ed grumbled, "Hey, I resemble that."

Tom laughed, "You *are* that, Ed."

"Ah shaddap, you're not anything to look at yourself, ya old fart."

Aaron interrupted, "Why, may I ask?"

Jesse replied, "Well, it's actually pretty simple. They've been drinking free coffee since damn near day one, and we were shorthanded today. I put Tom behind the counter. Ed and Bob, who, by the way, are both certified NRA instructors and range officers, in addition to being retired Army, worked the ranges with Fernando, and Joe put on five sets of sights and sighted in three rifles for customers. I've already told them we're hiring them as part-time employees, so they can work when they want."

Aaron took one look at Jesse's expression, and said, "Yes, dear."

He was saved as Toad and Cindy came through the front door, surprising everybody. Jesse said, "You're early!"

Cindy laughed, "I took a half-day, and Toad was done at nine this morning. He's been frothing at the mouth to get whatever he was working on finished."

Toad, with an injured expression, interrupted, "I was not frothing, drooling maybe, but not frothing!" He shook hands with Aaron, then slapped him on the back. "How goes it?"

Aaron chuckled. "Same ol', same ol'… Another day in the trenches." Turning to the guys still sitting at the table and watching the byplay, he said, "And these are our new employees. Tom is…"

Tom got up, whipping off his cowboy hat. "Ma'am, Tom Kline. Broke down ol' cowboy. Now, I guess, I'm a gun seller." He shook Toad's hand. "You're Matt and Aaron's buddy, right?"

Toad laughed. "I wonder sometimes." Ed, Bob, and Joe got up and introduced themselves, hands were shaken, and Toad disappeared into the back room, with Joe in trail.

Jesse grabbed Cindy. "Come on, let's go up to the house. You guys finish the paperwork and leave it on the table. I'll get it in the morning. Aaron, would you make sure everything is closed down and lock the door on your way out?" She gave him a peck on the cheek, as she and Cindy went out the door, whispering and laughing.

Aaron rolled his eyes. "Women…" It prompted a laugh from the guys as they went back to filling out the paperwork.

Bob said, "I noticed you didn't say that until they were out of hearing…"

Aaron chuckled, "I *have* learned a few things. And I do appreciate you guys being willing to help out."

A loud 'Gahdammit!' was heard down the hallway, and Aaron shook his head. "This ain't good. It usually takes Toad at least fifteen minutes to get this pissed."

Tom asked, "Why?"

"Toad's an armorer first, and a gun builder second. Something isn't fitting exactly like he wants, and he's getting pissed. Which means he's about to…"

A loud '*clang*' echoed down the hall, and Aaron continued, "Get out the *big* hammer." He started down the hall, with the guys following him into the shop portion of the building. Tom hung back a little, not sure if he wanted to be in the shop with a pissed off Marine, but finally shrugged and straggled in behind the others.

Toad was standing at the workbench, mumbling to himself as he screwed an action into a barrel held in the barrel vise, while Joe, eyes bugging a little bit, stood by, holding a big wrench in his hands. Aaron looked around and asked, "What was that all about?"

Toad glanced up. "Damn McMillan makes their stocks tight," he griped, gesturing at the A5 stock lying on the bench. "I test fitted the action, and couldn't get the sumbitch back out. Had to have Joe give it a whack. Ain't doin' that again until I've got a barrel on it, and can get a *good* grip to pry it out if I need to."

"Remington seven hundred?"

"Yep, long action. Reamed the receiver threads, squared the receiver lugs, squared the receiver face, lapped the bolt lugs, and squared the bolt face. Once I get this barrel on, I'll try that again."

"Schneider?"

With a grunt, Toad put another 1/8th inch turn on the action, then stepped back. "What else? I know his barrels, been using them my entire career. Now comes the fun part."

"Um, I'm gonna send the guys home, no need for them to stand here and listen to you cuss."

***

An hour later, Aaron's phone beeped with a text: YOU COMING TO SUPPER OR NOT? Aaron quickly typed, BE THERE IN 10! Turning to Toad, he said, "We're being summoned. It's chow now or the couch later."

Toad looked critically at the almost completely assembled rifle on the bench. "Oh well, I couldn't sight it in tonight anyway. Guess we might as well go eat."

Aaron shook his head. "Does Cindy let you get away with that at home?"

"Oh, hell no. Most nights, I'm cooking, since she's usually late getting home. I forgot *once*, that was all it took. Found out she doesn't like pizza."

"What? She doesn't like…"

"Apparently never has, and quote, never will, unquote."

Toad flipped off the light, and followed Aaron out as he locked up the shop. Stepping out on the front porch, they saw that it was already twilight, and Aaron said, "At least the business isn't losing money."

Toad looked at him, surprised, "What brought that on?"

"We've been running on a shoestring, basically with no employees other than family, and Khalil and Fernando. I guess Jesse's decided we can't do anymore ourselves, without… I dunno, burnout? I was getting to the point that I was starting to dread having a day off from the office, knowing I'd have to come work down here. I can't remember when we actually took a day, maybe the fourth was the last time."

"Damn, that was four months ago! Y'all haven't taken a day off since then?"

"Well, *technically* Sunday and Monday are days off, but we do church, then come back here and do stocking, cleaning and maintenance, and I'm usually on the schedule one way or the other on Monday. And Jesse usually comes in then to do the books, and take any deliveries, so no…"

As they started up the steps, Aaron continued, "Don't say anything, please." Toad nodded as they walked in the house. "Lemme dump my junk and I'll be right there."

Toad was pounced on by Boo Boo, closely followed by Yogi, then Jace. Toad picked him up and flipped him in the air, prompting childish laughter and, "Again!" Toad continued playing with him as he walked into the kitchen, nodded to the old man and plopped Jace in his high chair.

The old man handed Toad a glass of tea, and smiled. "What are you building now, Toad?"

"Thanks! Putting together an M40A-5 for one of the guys I drill with. He's a scout sniper, but because of the weird rules, he can't check his gun out to practice with, other than on drill weekends. So, he wants something to take to the range on a more regular basis."

"Smart move, but kinda expensive isn't it?"

Toad shrugged. "I'm building it for him at cost, but don't tell Cindy."

A pair of arms came around Toad's chest and Cindy asked, "Don't tell Cindy what? That you're not charging Michael for building his rifle? I knew that." She gave him a hug, then went to help Jesse and Felicia get the food on the plates.

After dinner, the old man took a cup of coffee out to the front porch, enjoying the cool breeze, the starry night, and the momentary peace and quiet as he sat on the steps. Toad came out and asked, "Mind if I join you?"

"Feel free. You ever play with old guns?"

"How old?"

"Late eighteen hundred's. Say eighteen seventy-three and on?"

Toad cocked his head. "What did you have in mind?"

The old man nodded toward the office. "Got a few old ones in the safe that I'd like to get checked out."

He didn't see the grin that crossed Toad's face, but he heard the wistfulness in his voice. "I'd love to, sir. You pick 'em, I'll fix 'em."

Threats

Jesse looked up as the door dinged, and an older man walked curiously into the gun store. He looked around, then walked slowly over to Jesse. "Ma'am," he said softly.

"Can I help you?"

"Maybe. Mrs.?"

"Miller."

He flashed a badge quickly, and said. "I'm Officer Perkins with Midland, we're doing an investigation on a Matthew Carter. Does he work here?"

Jesse's hackles rose, but she decided to play dumb and see what she could find out. She said brightly, "No, sir. He's the ranch manager. He doesn't actually work here. He's kinda my boss."

"Oh really? What kind of boss is he?"

Jesse saw what looked like one of those spy pens in the man's pocket, so she smiled for the camera and said, "Oh, I like him. He's a big teddy bear. He manages the whole big ranch out here, and our store is just a little part of it."

"Well, we've had some reports that, maybe some money is, you know, disappearing. Have you, I mean do you handle receipts and money here?"

"Oh no. I just run the register. Mr. Carter, he's real particular about that. He handles all the money himself. He keeps the books and everything."

"He does everything?"

"Oh yes, sir. I come in, in the mornings, and I have a set amount of cash and that's it. He cleans out the register at night, and does everything himself. He does all the ordering, and, well I do help keep the gun books, like for the ATF, you know?"

The man shrugged. "So, you do receipts of the guns and put them in the book?"

"Oh no. Mr. Carter tells me which ones to put in the book, and which ones not to."

"Is Mr. Carter on the books as the FFL?"

"I don't think so, I think it's actually a corporation. Something like CR Guns LLC. That way his name doesn't show up."

"Interesting." The man took out a small pad and paper, writing something on the pad, then asked, "Now this is kinda personal, but has he ever, you know, come on to you? Or wanted you to, you know, do things with him?"

Jesse pouted. "No, not really, but he is pretty attractive. His wife is a little bit bitchy though."

"I understand he is a part time cop down here?"

"Yes, he does a couple of weekends a month, I think."

All of a sudden, Jesse remembered the conversation a few months ago about Matt and Danny being threatened by somebody up in Midland. "He likes that, but he says he couldn't afford to live on a cop's salary."

The man perked up. "He say why?"

Jesse smiled blandly. "Oh, I think his wife's got expensive tastes. She's Mexican, you know."

"Do you know if she's a legal Mex?"

"I'm not sure. We've only been open a few months, and I don't really know her, but like I said…"

"She's a bitch." Putting the pad back in his pocket, along with the pen, he swept his jacket back far enough for Jesse to get a glimpse of a badge and a holstered Glock. "Now Mrs. Miller, we need you to keep quiet about this, okay?"

Jesse shrugged. "Okay."

"Oh, do you happen to know a Deputy Ortiz, Danny Ortiz?"

Jesse thought to herself, *This asshole is crooked as a dog's hind leg. He's, shit I can't remember that asshole that threatened Matt and Danny, but this guy is working for them.* She wrinkled her nose. "Yeah, I don't like him. He's given me a couple of tickets. Like for nothing. He's one of those that is, what do they call it, *La Raza*? Or something like that."

"*La Raza*? Are you sure?" he asked with excitement creeping into his voice.

Jesse shrugged again. "I think that's what he was saying, he was calling somebody about moving some shit, while he was writing me a ticket."

The door dinged, and Tom came in, prompting the man to say quietly. "Remember, this is in confidence." He turned and walked quickly out of the store.

Jesse dodged around the counter, and grabbed a pair of binoculars off the display. Running to the front window, she got the tag and description of the car, as it pulled out of the parking lot.

Tom asked, "What's going on?"

Jesse held up a finger as she ran back to the counter, grabbing a pen, she quickly wrote the tag number and description before saying, "Some asshole playing games. I think he was a PI. Hang on a minute."

Dialing the phone, she waited impatiently until Felicia answered. "Felicia, what was the name of that asshole from Midland that threatened Matt?" A couple of seconds later, she said, "Yep, that's it, Charles Ryan. Thanks, bye."

Scribbling the name on the pad over the other information, she looked up at a perplexed Tom. "Matt got threatened a couple of months ago, by the father of an idiot he arrested. I think they are actually trying to do something."

Tom bristled. "Anything you want me to do?"

"Not yet, Tom. Not yet."

***

Jesse sat in the office, pulling up the video of the interview, mumbling, "*Fucker, you are about stupid. You didn't check shit before you came in, and didn't even realize you were on camera the whole time.*" She picked the camera from behind the counter, and hit play, leaning back and tapping a pencil against her teeth. "Gotcha you piece of shit!"

Jesse pulled the video off to a separate file, and saved it, then burned it to a CD. She got back on the internet and did a global search for Charles Ryan, then whistled at the number of hits that came up. She realized she didn't know what he looked like, and changed the search to the name and Midland. That narrowed the search and she started going through the hits.

Huh, bought Wildcat Ranch in 2011. Where did he get the... Ah, sold some kind of computer software company up in... Boston? What the hell? Why did he come to Texas?

Tom knocked on the door frame. "Uh, Jesse, need you to do the book on the gun I just sold."

"Okay, be right there. Tom, you know anything about Wildcat Ranch?"

Tom cocked his head. "A little bit, why?"

"Hold that thought." Jesse got up and came out front. "What are we doing?"

"Mizz Yarborough wants that little Glock forty-two."

Jesse walked up to Mrs. Yarborough. "Mrs. Glenna, you sure you want that? I thought you liked your thirty-eight."

Glenna Yarborough smiled. "Jesse, Don told me I could get what I wanted, and I'm seventy. That old thirty-eight is getting too heavy for me, and Tom let me shoot one of these. He also showed me the trick to racking the slide at my advanced age. And it holds two more rounds than my old thirty-eight."

Ten minutes later, she was out the door with her new pistol, two boxes of practice ammo, and one box of self-defense ammo. Jesse turned to Tom. "I didn't think we have a Glock forty-two on the rental counter."

Tom hung his head. "We don't," he patted his back pocket, "I just let her shoot mine."

Jesse put her hands on her hips. "Dammit, Tom. If we don't have something for them to shoot, let me know! You shouldn't have had to use your own gun!"

Tom shrugged. "Well, it sold her."

"Arrghhh! Alright, alright. I'll order one for the rental counter." Jesse started to turn away, then snapped her fingers. "Wildcat Ranch?"

Tom nodded. "Worked there about twenty years ago, for old man Morton. Good man, lousy rancher."

Jesse cocked her head, "Why?"

"He knew oil and the oil bidness, didn't know jack about ranching. He had the wrong cows, on the wrong grass, and didn't have enough windmills and stock tanks. Spent half my time tryin' to get the damn windmills primed. I finally left to go to Bar R, where I at least got to punch cows."

"Thanks. I need to run to town, need anything?"

"No, ma'am. We'll hold the fort down."

Jesse laughed. "I'm sure you will!" She went back to the office, picked up the CD and her notes, and headed out.

***

Jesse knocked on the old man's door. "Papa? Got a minute?"

The old man glanced up at Jesse. "What's up?" Yogi padded over for a petting as Jesse walked to the desk.

She handed the CD to the old man. "Take a look at this video, this guy showed up at the shop this morning, asking questions about Matt." She sat down and ruffled Yogi's fur, prompting him to sit down by her chair, and snuffle his head into her lap.

The old man took the CD, put it in his computer, and watched silently as the video played. "Perkins? He didn't identify himself further than that?"

"Nope. And he flashed that badge case so quick I didn't get a good look at it."

The old man leaned back, thought for a minute, and typed on the computer for a minute, then pulled out his wheel book. Flipping through it, he hit the speaker and dialed, then sat back. A cheerful female answered, "Midland Police Department, may I help you?"

"Captain Cronin, Pecos County. Is Chief Bullock in?"

"Yes, sir. One moment please."

Background music came on for a few seconds, then they heard, "John, what's up?"

"Bull, got a question for you. Does a PI named Perkins ring a bell? I just sent you an email with a video attached."

"Wait one." They heard clicking on the other end, then a chopped of expletive. "What the fuck? Who is the girl in the video?"

"My granddaughter, Jesse, who is sitting across the desk from me. She's a reserve down here, and played dumb to see what she could get."

"Yeah, that's him. Shit."

The old man cocked his head at Jesse, then asked, "Why shit?"

The heard a sigh. "Out of school, Lon Perkins took the medical way out five years ago, before I could fire his ass. He was in a supposed shootout with two Hispanics, and there were questions about a throw down gun. He claimed PTSD, and got a medical retirement before the investigation was completed. He's… Sleazy, at best. Did you check the DPS Private Security website?"

"No, I didn't have a first name, and I wasn't going to search through thirty or so Perkins'."

Jesse leaned over the desk and pointed at Charles Ryan's name. The old man nodded, and asked, "What do you know about Charles Ryan?" Jesse pointed at the Wildcat Ranch name, and he added, "Might own Wildcat Ranch."

The heard more typing, and Bullock came back, "He's a problem child. Three DUIs, but he's got a high-powered lawyer. His son is a piece of work, too. Got him twice for speeding, and once for marijuana. Thinks he's a big player, but most of the old ranchers up here ignore his ass. Wildcat's got some pretty good producers on it, and I think the contract is with Apache. He bought it from old lady Morton after she moved up to Dallas with her daughter. I think there was a big fight over the mineral rights. Why the interest in him?"

"He threatened two of our guys earlier this year. Said he'd get their asses fired and run out of the county."

"That sounds like Ryan. He's a big talker. Problem is, he's got money to back it up."

The old man's phone beeped. "Bull, I'm getting a call. Thanks for the info, and I'll keep you in the loop if this develops into anything."

"Please do, John. Take care."

The old man hit the intercom. "Cronin."

Maggie said, "Captain, Mr. Lowry from Tractor Supply on line three for you."

"Thanks." He glanced up at Jesse, and hit the button for line three. 'Captain Cronin."

"Captain, this is Jerry Lowry from Tractor Supply, I need to let you know about something. I just had an investigator in here that… Well, he alluded to Matt Carter stealing from you, and selling stuff he'd bought on the ranch account. He said he had…"

The old man interrupted, "Jerry, did he identify himself? Was his name by chance Perkins?"

"Uh, matter of fact, it was."

"Jerry, he's full of shit. This is a disinformation campaign against Matt, trying to get him fired. He didn't by chance say where else he was going, did he?"

"Um, not really. But he was asking who else the ranch did business with."

"Okay, thanks for calling me. If anybody asks you, just tell them it's bullshit, Jerry."

"Yes, sir. Thank you, Captain."

The old man was visibly angry at this point, and Jesse slouched in her chair, wondering what he would do next. That was answered when he pulled out his cell phone, and made another call. "John Cronin, I need to speak to Billy." A pause. "As soon as possible. Thank you."

Flipping the phone on his desk, he rolled his shoulders and stood up, then sat back down. Picking up the piece of paper, he asked, "This the car Perkins is driving?"

Jesse replied, "Yes, I got the plate number, too."

The old man picked up the office phone, dialed and waited. "Captain Williams, Captain Cronin. Need a favor. There is a PI in town spreading crap about my ranch and ranch manager, Matt Carter. I've got his car and tag number, want to see if any of your officers might run across him." A pause, and he continued, "No, I'm not gonna shoot him, I just want to *chat* with him. I'm going to put it out over County too." The old man handed the paper back to Jesse, and motioned toward dispatch, as he nodded to whatever was being said on the phone.

Jesse walked over to dispatch, handed the paper to Lisa and said, "Papa wants a BOLO on this car. Driver is a sleazy PI named Perkins. If anybody sees it, he wants to know."

Lisa looked up at Jesse. "Dare I ask?"

"The sumbitch is spreading lies about Matt, and damaging the ranch's reputation in town."

Lisa's eyes got big, and she said, "Oh, *that* is *no bueno*. It will go out right now." She punched up all call, and read out the make, model, and license, and followed up with, "Notify dispatch, only."

All of the units responded, and she gave Jesse a thumbs-up. "You got it, Hon."

"Thanks."

Jesse walked back across the hall, and gave the old man a thumbs-up, since he was on the phone. She sat back down and heard, "Billy, I don't care. Find out everything you can about Ryan, and see if you can dig out anything on Perkins, especially who is paying his bill. Give me a call back when you get it."

He hung up, got up and grabbed his hat. "I'm going to go wander around. Who's manning the store?"

Jesse got up. "Tom. Ed and Fernando are running the ranges today. I guess I better get back."

The old man nodded. "Yep. I'll see you at supper. I'll let you know what happens. Make sure Matt and Felicia are there."

"Yes, sir." Jesse didn't like the look on the old man's face, but she wasn't about to challenge him. *Papa is not a nice man. I have to remember that. And I don't ever want him really mad at me.* She shivered a little bit as she walked out of the office.

***

"Car four, dispatch."

The old man picked up the mic and keyed up. "Car Four, go."

"Vehicle you're interested in is currently at Rosa's Grocery."

"Ten-four. I'll be ten-seven for a bit."

"Dispatch copies."

It took the old man about ten minutes to get to the grocery store, and he saw the car sitting in the parking lot. He pulled in behind it, and turned off the car, sitting there for a minute, trying to calm himself down, before he did something stupid.

He had no sooner gotten out, when Perkins walked out the store, and yelled, "Hey, move your car. You're blocking me in."

The old man rounded on him. "You Lon Perkins?"

Perkins, seeing the badge and gun, seemed to draw in on himself. "Yeah, uh, sorry about yelling at you."

The old man got right up in Perkin's face, forcing him to step back, even though he was bigger. "What the fuck are you doing spreading lies about my ranch and my foreman?"

Perkins backed up another step. "I'm not spreading anything. I'm invest…"

"Bullshit! I know at least two people you've lied to today, and there are probably more that haven't notified me yet. Who are you working for?"

"My clients are confidential. I have good, reliable information that your foreman is crook…"

"You haven't got shit, boy. You get in your fucking car, drive back to Midland and tell Charles Ryan he better pull in his horns. Both of you are in *way* over your heads. You understand me?"

Perkins bowed up. "He'll run your ass out of the county too! Maybe I'll buy your raggedy ass little ranch, just so I can burn it to the ground. You can't touch me, you do, I'll press charges! I know my rights!"

"Sure you do, just like the *rights* those two Hispanics had, right?"

Perkins paled at that, and stomped around the old man's car, opened his car door and got in. The old man looked up to see Deputy Hart sitting in his Tahoe, at the end of the parking lot. Hart smiled and waved, and the old man shook his head, got in the car, and pulled away. Keying up, he said, "Dispatch, Car Four is ten-eight."

"Dispatch copies."

Later that night, at supper, the old man told everyone what else he'd learned, and the other businesses that had either contacted him or been contacted by Perkins, who was not only spreading lies about Matt, but also Danny Ortiz.

Felicia was almost in tears, and finally said, "*Señor* Cronin, what? What can we do? They will ruin us."

The old man said gently, "No, Felicia, nobody is getting ruined. Billy is working on seeing what he can dig up, and I've already talked to most of the folks that Perkins spread lies to. I'm worried about Danny though. I let him and Angelina know, and I talked to Mama Rosa at the grocery store, but I don't know who else he talked to in the Hispanic community.

Felicia's eyes flashed. "I will find out. May I have them call you, *Señor*? Especially if they have questions?"

"Of course."

Shootist

John Cronin grumbled to himself about why he'd let Aaron and Jesse talk him into *dressing up,* as they called it just to shoot in an Old West match, hell at 73 he was an old man. *Well, technically I guess it's this Single Action Shooting Society thingie,* he thought, sighing as he walked past the coffee pot in the kitchen. No coffee 'til I shoot, he'd decided.

He'd sat down two weeks ago, read the rule book, and then started scrounging around in the safe. He'd figured if he was going to do it, he'd do it right. But he admitted to himself he *might* have gone a tad overboard.

Toad and Cindy had come down, and he'd put Toad to work to freshen up a pair of 1892 Colt Frontier Sixes that were in the back of the safe, and the 1873 Winchester and he'd pulled out along with great grandpa's old Sharps Buffalo gun with the Malcolm scope on it.

Toad had even reloaded some of the old brass rounds for it, along with reloading the turn of the century WCC rounds. The old man chuckled as he thought about Toad's idea to use the old ammo and original boxes. Toad had really gotten into it, much to Cindy's chagrin, as he'd spent the entire weekend greasy and smiling, between the barn and the office safe. But at least the girls had taken a trip down to

Gruene Hall, built in 1878, and Texas' oldest continually operating dance hall. They'd spent the day shopping and wandering the area, kid free, as Matt and Aaron tried their best to corral the kids.

Now, he was trying to decide between shotguns. The Colt was nicer, but it wasn't legal, apparently, *even though it was a real stage coach gun,* since the barrels were only fourteen inches. Hell, it was even stamped W.F. & Co. and numbered. It'd come out of El Paso probably around 1890. He finally settled on the Remington side by side 12 gauge with eighteen-inch barrels, figuring nobody could complain about it. Toad had made up some brass rounds for whichever 12 gauge he would use, since they were all Damascus barrels and not safe to shoot with the modern loads.

The next question was holsters. He had found his grandfather's Sunday-go-to-meetin' single loop holsters and belt, but the belt was a bit short. His grandpa had been a big man for the 1890's, but he wasn't a fat man by any means, and the old man was bigger still. Cronin had called up to Kenny Rowe in Hope, Arkansas. Kenny agreed to do his best to make a new belt, and said he'd *try* to antique it to match the holsters. Knowing Kenny's work, the old man had figured a try would be better than most others. When he got the belt back, it was so close to the original it wouldn't be noticeable, unless somebody really looked hard at it.

He chuckled as he rooted through the old trunks, thinking, *not many people have three or four generations of stuff sitting in the attic or the barn, at least not over here, unless it's a ranch house that's been in the family the whole time. Raul said his family were newcomers and had only lived in their house in Seville, Spain for what had he said? Five hundred ten years? God, I wonder what he's got in the attic? Swords? Armor?*

He'd already pulled out the batwing chaps, and a vest, and put Neatsfoot oil on them for the last couple of weeks to get them pliable enough to wear. In a different trunk, he found a pair of patched jeans and a well patched white shirt that was a close enough fit. The jeans were a little tight and a little short, but they would be tucked in the boots, old style. He debated but finally decided what the hell, went out to the barn, and pulled his Kelly spurs out of the tack room. They had been a gift from his grandpa when he got his own horse and had learned how to care for it. Bouncing them in his hand, he walked across the back yard to the kitchen, whistling softly.

As he walked into the kitchen, he glanced up at the clock and saw that the rifle side matches were going to start in about fifteen minutes. Looking regretfully at the coffee pot again, he carried the spurs in and dropped them on his bed with the rest of what he was now thinking of as the *outfit*. He stopped in the office long enough to swing his gun belt around his hips, pick up the Sharps, and a box of ammo. Putting on his hat, he told Yogi to stay, watch, and he walked out the front door down toward the south pasture with the rifle over his shoulder and a box of rounds in his back pocket. He was surprised to see a large number of cars already in the parking area, he looked up, checking the sky, and smiled. It was what they called a blue bird day, not a cloud in the sky. It was going to be a beautiful day for shooting. And Matt and Aaron had done a helluva job putting together the 'fronts' as they'd called them, on the rifle range. Felix had gotten one of his friends to come out and paint the plywood to make them look like building fronts, and he wondered if it was really all necessary. As he walked down to the pasture, he saw that most of the folks were already in what they called costumes. *Maybe they're right, maybe these folks are that much into this sport, I guess it's a sport… Stop woolgathering and get your act together…*

At the firing line, he slipped the rifle carefully in the rack, joining the people grouped around a short rotund man in a high crowned cowboy hat, with a feather sticking up. He heard him say genially, "Okay folks, Mel Bristow, for my sins as the regional match director, I get to come in early and run the long-range side matches." Pointing to a dour-faced woman standing by his side, he continued, "My wife Edna is the recorder. This is the buffalo gun side match. This match will be offhand." Some of the competitors groaned at this as he continued, "The usual rules, ten shots, two hundred yards, ten minutes, we've got two streamers: one at one hundred yards and one at one seventy-five. Names in the hat, and I'll draw the shooting order. Anybody with a new rifle or that hasn't shot here before?"

The old man raised his hand. "New shooter."

Bristow said, "Okay, I'll get with you in just a couple of minutes." Passing around a pad of sticky notes and a pen, he continued, "Name and rifle, and drop it in the hat, please." Taking off his hat to reveal a mostly bald head, he dropped it on the bench, crown up and walked over to the old man.

Noting the badge, holstered pistol, and lack of costume he stuck out his hand. "Mel Bristow, sir. I take it you're a first-time shooter?"

The old man laughed as he shook hands. "John Cronin. First time at trying this SASS stuff. I've shot a time or two. My granddaughter talked me into this, and I figured why not."

Bristow asked, "Which rifle are you shooting? I need to do a quick safety check."

The old man turned to the rack and pulled out the '74 Sharps, making sure the breech was open as he handed it across. Bristow took it and stepped to the firing table, whistling as he examined the rifle. "This isn't a copy. And I'll be damned if that isn't an original Malcom scope!" Taking a pen light out, he positioned it in the breech and checked the bore. "Wow, this thing's still got good rifling. That's amazing!" Putting the pen light away, he carefully closed the breech, cocked the hammer and gently pulled the trigger as he guarded the hammer. Handing it back to the old man, he said, "That Sharps is in great shape. And the trigger isn't a hair trigger. Seems like a lot of the old ones that were shot a lot tended to wear the sear down to damn near nothing. I take it you're already sighted in?"

The old man took the rifle and set it back in the rack. "Yeah, I put a couple of test rounds through it. This is a family gun that's lived in the safe for a lot of years. My grandfather only did one season shooting buffaloes before he came back to the ranch."

Bristow said, "Well, welcome. Get your name in the hat, and let's get shooting!"

There was a general shuffle as people dropped their names in the hat, and Bristow did the drawing. He scribbled out a list then said, "Okay, here we go: Hartshorne and Jessup, you're up. Eyes and ears. Let's clear the firing line, and get this show on the road. Range is hot."

The old man was up eighth in line, and from what he could observe there were some damn good shots, since with most of the shots, he heard the gongs ringing. The only real delay was when Bristow and the shooters had to go mark the targets and put up new ones for each subsequent relay. It was finally his turn, and he picked up the rifle and walked to the line. Setting the cartridge box on the corner of the bench, he nodded to the lady shooting against him as Bristow said, "Shooters ready?"

The old man replied, "Shooter ready." The lady did the same and Bristow beeped the timer. The old man took a deep breath and methodically loaded the old buffalo gun, settled into his shooting stance, and put the first round down range. Hearing a clang, he smiled and did the same thing nine more times. After the tenth round, he safed the rifle and stepped back from the line, then put the rifle back in the rack.

Bristow said, "That was quick! You got off ten rounds in a hair over five minutes, and all of them were hits. It's going to take Lacy a few more minutes to finish. She usually uses every minute allowed."

The old man shrugged. "No problem. I ain't going anywhere."

After everyone had shot, Bristow compiled the scores, and said, "Well, looks like we've got a shoot off. Mister Cronin and Mister Jessup both went ten for ten in the ten ring. We'll do five shots, five minutes, lather, rinse, and repeat until one of them comes out on top. Cronin and Jessup, back to the line, please."

The old man picked up his rifle and walked back to the line, told Jessup good luck, and settled in. At the beep he loaded and fired, a corner of his mind noting the wind was gusting just a bit. Shots two, three and four went downrange with no problem, but the fifth shot he felt a push from the wind just as he fired. He heard the clang, but knew that one was a flyer. Turning to Bristow he said, "Well, I just lost it. That one's a flyer."

Bristow looked at him sharply. "You're calling a flyer, and saying you lost?"

The old man nodded. "Yep, wind gust: that's probably a nine ring, maybe an eight." The old man racked his rifle and waited as Jessup methodically put the last round down range. As they walked to the target, they chatted about Jessup's costume. The old man found out Jessup had researched it up in Wyoming, and made sure it was period correct, down to the Buckskin coat and even the beading on it. Jessup admitted he was an engineer out at the tire track, and the old man chuckled. "No wonder I lost, I'm up against a damn engineer. Ya can't beat 'em"

Jessup and Bristow both laughed, and Bristow looked at the old man as they reached the target. "You were right. Last round was a nine." Turning to Jessup, he said, "Well, you did it again. Congratulations!" Bristow and the old man shook hands with Jessup, and they walked back to the firing line where Bristow announced the winner for the third time in three meets.

Shouldering the rifle, the old man walked back to the house, put the rifle back in the gun safe, and made a beeline for the kitchen. Getting a cup of coffee, he fed Yogi first. Then he grabbed a couple of biscuits, buttered them, dribbled some molasses on them, and sat down and relaxed.

A harried Aaron came in, grabbed a cup of coffee and plopped down. "Damn, this is worse than cat herding. Buncha damn women don't like the Port-a-Johns, say they can't fit in them, so I opened up the shop so they could use the bathroom in there."

"Took over both of them, didn't they?"

"Yeah, and bitched at how dirty the men's room was. I can't win!"

The old man laughed. "Yep, you can't make 'em happy. So, is this worth it?"

Aaron shrugged. "I think we'll make a little bit. I looked at what the Bar Three charged and we're charging the same amount to camp. We get a couple of dollars of the entry fee, and that's got the rental Port-a-Johns covered. I worked out a deal with Mrs. Redden down at the camp site, she's going to let anybody that needs to pump grey water do it for five bucks instead of the usual fifteen, so I think that will keep them happy. The hotels are happy, got them two room nights of folks, and I know Miguel is happy with the customers that have come in."

"Y'all plan on doing this again?"

Aaron laughed. "Not any time soon!"

Jesse breezed in wearing a faded sun dress, a Cheyenne rig holster belted on, with her great, great grandma's Single Action Army riding in the holster. She was cheerfully twirling a bonnet in her hand. "How'd you do Papa?"

The old man laughed. "Got beat by a young whippersnapper engineer. How much time before the regular shoot starts?"

Jesse looked at the clock and said, "A half hour. Are you still going to try it Papa? Please?"

The old man replied, "I'll do it. I guess I need to change. Can't look too modern, guess I need to look like a real cowboy."

Jesse laughed and pirouetted. "I found one of great grandma's sun dresses that fit. And I think this was her gun belt too!

Looking closer, he said, "Yeah, I think I remember that get up from one of the tintypes. Grandpa always said she was a pistol in more ways than one."

Jesse laughed. "I read her diary." She turned serious for a moment. "I'm glad we're not doing food. That was smart to have the Ramos brothers do the lunch meals both days! I don't care that we're getting nothing from them. Jesus says they're not going to make a lot, but they're covering costs, and getting a little advertising out of it. Apparently, a couple of folks have asked about them catering big parties."

The old man laughed. "If Jesus says they're making a little bit, they're doing well. It's good quality food, people aren't having to leave and come back, and we don't have to clean up."

Aaron ducked his head. "Yeah, we didn't think about trash cans. I'm glad you had those barrels in the lean-to by the barn. That could have gotten messy."

Petty Tyrants

The old man finished his coffee, put the cup in the sink, and walked slowly back to his room. Changing into the shirt and pants, he picked up the chaps, vest, and spurs, and walked back to the office. Laying the vest aside, he strapped the chaps on, then pulled the gun belt from the safe along with the pistols, rifle and shotgun, reminding himself that he needed enough ammo for both he and Jesse to shoot in their respective matches.

He started to slip the vest on, then stopped. Looking at the bookcase, he walked over and picked up his grandfather's Texas Ranger badge and pinned it to the vest. As he did, he could tell it wasn't the first time it had been pinned on there. Slipping on the vest, he settled his hat on his head. Then opening the possibles bag, he loaded it with the ammunition then picked up the rifle, shotgun, and bag. Taking a deep breath, he steeled himself and walked slowly out of the house.

Walking back down to the pasture, he saw that the parking lot was full and there were probably a hundred or more people milling around. He went to the gun rack and secured both the long guns, making sure to mark where he'd placed them, then wandered over where folks seemed to be gathering. He saw Bristow climb on top of a step stool and walked closer.

Bristow welcomed everyone, introduced the range safety officers, and gave an overview of the planned activities. He was about to step down, when the dour woman standing next to him said something, and he said, "Oh yeah, since this is considered a regional meet, there will be people checking costuming today. Edna will be in charge of that. Please remain in your costumes between events. Lunch will be at noon; some good Texas BBQ. I'm already drooling."

That prompted a few raucous comments, which he waved off while Edna glared at the crowd, trying to figure out who had made the comments. John heard a groan from someone behind him, and a sotto voice comment, "Doesn't Bristow realize how much of a PITA his old lady is?" Followed by another sotto voiced comment, "Nah, he's blind to anything she does. Dunno why, because everybody else sure as hell sees it. She's on a power trip." More grumbling ensued, but he wandered over to Bristow and asked, "I'm still a new shooter, do you want to safety check my other guns?"

Bristow replied, "Nah, when you get ready to shoot a stage, let the RSO know. They'll safety check them at that time. I must say you look quite a bit different than you did earlier this morning."

The old man chuckled. "Blame the granddaughter again."

Bristow smiled. "Well, enjoy yourself. We try to make these fun. And after seeing you shoot this morning, I hope you shoot as well the rest of the day."

The old man was seeded to shoot in the third relay, so he had a little time and he spent watching what was happening at each stage. He helped reset targets and had stepped back to the concession area for a cup of coffee when he heard a sniff and a sotto voice comment: "Here's another one that can't make up their mind what costume they want to wear."

He turned to see Bristow's wife standing there, and he said politely, "Excuse me?"

She walked closer, two other women in tow, one with a clipboard. Looking him up and down she said, "What are you supposed to be?"

The old man asked, "What do you mean?"

She sniffed, "You're supposed to be in character for whatever your class is. You look like you just found the cheapest stuff you could and piled it all on." Stepping closer she flicked the badge, "This isn't even the right badge. What is that, some cheap copy? You should have your SASS badge displayed where I can see your number."

Stepping back, she continued, "And those clothes. Try to buy stuff that is at least made here. That cheap Chinese knockoff crap not only looks bad, it won't last through two events. Those holsters don't look safe either. What'd you do? Run over the whole outfit with a truck trying to make all of it look old?" She snorted a horse laugh as the other women dutifully laughed along, then she turned to the one with the clipboard, "Find out who he is and write him up for inappropriate costume."

As she started to turn away she saw Jesse coming, and said, "Oh here's another one. You'd think-"

The old man said quietly, "Who are you, and what makes you think you have *any* say in the way I dress?"

The woman snapped around raised her voice and said, "*I* am Edna Bristow and I am responsible for making sure people are in the correct costume. My husband is the regional match director!" That got people's attention and the crowd in the concession area started paying attention to the confrontation.

The old man took a sip of coffee and asked, "And?"

The woman reached in her bag, pulled out a rule book, and shook it at him, saying, "This is what gives me the authority!"

The old man looked over at Jesse. "Go up to the old house and get the tintype off the fireplace please." Jesse took one look at his face and shot off for the house at a dead run, as the old man continued, "So is this one of those double secret rule books that the average peon is not allowed to see?"

That prompted some laughter and a few titters from the women as Edna turned red. She glared at him and said, "Well, *somebody* has to enforce the rules around here. And since my husband-"

The old man interrupted her. "So, is this an appointed job, or an *assumed* one?" Prompting more laughter.

She sputtered, "What is your SASS number? I am going to get you disqualified!"

The old man saw Jesse coming back and stared silently until she arrived with the tintype. She handed it to him, and he turned it around and stepped into Edna's personal space, causing Edna and the other two women to back up a step. "You want to be precise about my costume do you?" Pushing the photo out, he said, "This is my grandfather. This picture was taken in 1898. Notice the shirt and pants?" He pulled on the shirt sleeve, "These are the same." He pulled on the vest, "Same vest. And this badge you called a fake? It's not. My grandfather was a Texas Ranger between 1895 and 1899. This was his badge."

He handed the tintype back to Jesse and put his hand up as Edna started to interrupt. "I'm not done. Same holsters. Same guns. Same chaps. The only things that aren't *original* 1898 are me, my underwear, boots, and hat! I actually read the rule book. There aren't any *rules* about costumes per se, it's two pages of generic stuff. The rules are more about safety and shooting."

Edna sputtered again, and the old man went on relentlessly, "Now if you want a true critique, let's look at *your* costume. You look like a cross between a Mexican hooker and a storekeeper. That belt is what hookers wore back in those days to keep their money on them. They sewed the silver pesos on the belt, did you know that? I'm betting those aren't real silver Conchos either. The blouse is wrong, too. And that Buscadero rig? It's a border rig from the 1920s, but what you're wearing was actually designed by John Bianchi in the 1940s. And they didn't have wrist watches in the early 1900s."

Edna pursed her lips, glared at him and yelled, "You're disqualified. Get out of here." She turned and scuttled away as the other two women stood open mouthed staring at the old man.

A middle-aged man stepped up beside the old man and said, "Thank you! She's been a PITA ever since her hubby got selected as the regional match director. He's got one helluva blind spot as far as she's concerned, and everybody is afraid to talk to him about her actions."

The old man turned to him. "Ah, I probably should have kept my mouth shut. After all, I'm not a member, and this is my first time to attend one of these, so I don't think she can disqualify me."

The man said, "Oh she'll try, but probably not. Her hubby is going to catch an earful though. That needed to happen. I'm Jake Thorne by the way. Can I see that tintype?"

Jesse handed the tintype to him, as the old man said, "John Cronin. And that picture was taken in front of the house at the top of the hill there." Pointing at Jesse, he said, "Jesse's wearing her great great grandmother's sundress, holster, and gun."

Thorne handed the tintype back. "Yeah, kinda hard to argue with that. Are those the actual guns?"

The old man nodded. "Yep, and the Winchester in the picture is sitting over in the gun rack."

Thorn asked, "You're going to shoot them? They're not just for show?"

The old man laughed. "Oh, hell yes, I'm going to shoot them. They're tools, and tools need to get exercised occasionally. These haven't been." Looking over at the firing line, he said, "And it looks like my relay is up. Excuse me, and nice to meet you." With a wave, the old man trotted over to the firing line.

After the relay brief, he took his place in line, the RSO safety checked his weapons, and he was getting ready to shoot when Edna strode up, telling the RSO, "That man," pointing at the John, "Is disqualified. I've already told him to leave. I'm going to call the police and get him escorted off the property. *Do not* let him shoot."

The RSO looked at him, and said, "What's going on?"

He laughed, "Apparently I questioned her authority, and she didn't like it."

The RSO said, "I need to talk to the match director-"

Cronin interrupted, "Yes, let's. I believe that's a mister Bristow? Please get him over here. I'll wait right here."

Moments later, Mel Bristow came hurrying over, closely followed by Edna. There was a hurried conference off to the side as Jesse came up with the old man's radio, saying, "Papa, it's dispatch. They want to talk to you."

The old man keyed the radio. "Dispatch go for Cronin." As he did so, Bristow, his wife, and the RSO came over.

Dispatch replied, "Captain, we got a call from a female named Bristow that there were some problems with a crazy man out there that needed to be removed from the property. Can you handle it, or do we need to send a unit?"

Edna turned dead white and her husband looked at her in amazement. "You didn't say that did you?" He asked. The RSO took a step back, trying to distance himself as Bristow grabbed his wife by the arm, pulling her off to the side.

The old man keyed the radio, and said, "Ah, Dispatch, situation is under control. Minor misunderstanding. No need to respond a unit." Handing the radio back to Jesse he said to the RSO, "Now I believe I'm up?"

The RSO looked over at the Bristows, gulped, and said, "Shooter ready?"

The old man shot the stage clean but didn't run between the rifle, pistol, and shotgun portions, which caused him to lose time, but he didn't care. It was all about giving the tools a workout and getting a chance to do a fun and challenging shoot. When his time was called, he was four seconds slower than the fastest time he'd heard, so he figured that put him about mid-pack. But the guns functioned flawlessly. Not bad for four guns over a hundred years old, being shot by a man who was almost three quarters of a century old.

The old man eased out of the crush of people and carried the rifle, shotgun, and his possibles bag back toward the house after Jesse had her turn, getting a lot of friendly nods, and thank you's along the way. He couldn't figure out why until later in the afternoon when the plaques were handed out. Mel Bristow was nowhere to be found, and neither was Edna. Apparently, they'd left early, and Hartshorn, a shooter he remembered from the side match this morning was acting as the MC.

The old man was even more surprised to hear his name called, and he walked curiously to the firing line to hear, "Mister John Cronin. The fastest Senior Silver shooter." Hartshorn presented the old man with a small plaque and stopped him as he started to walk off. "Would Mrs. Jesse Miller come up here now?"

Hartshorn clicked the mic off as they waited for Jesse to wind her way through the crowd. He leaned over and said, "Heard about what you did to Edna. Glad you did it. She works as a DMV supervisor over in New Mexico, and has been on a power trip ever since Mel took over as regional match director. He's never believed Edna would do anything wrong, but you kinda brought it to a head today. Mel got his eyes opened in the worst possible way. He told me he's going to resign, and he'll write you a formal apology for what happened today. Maybe it'll teach Edna a lesson--she sure as hell needed one. Nobody wanted to question her authority and risk pissing off Mel, but I think you put paid to that."

Jesse finally made it to the line, and Hartshorn clicked the mic back on, "By popular acclamation, Mister Cronin and Mrs. Miller win for the most authentic costumes. And I think they win for the most authentic weapons, too." Everybody cheered at that, and Hartshorn asked, "Just out of curiosity sir, what's the *newest* thing you shot today?"

The old man looked at Jesse, who just smiled. He took the mic, and said, "Well, I guess it was the ammo. It was made in nineteen oh six." Another round of laughter followed, and he continued, "The newest gun was probably Jesse's: it's a nineteen oh three SAA. The rifle we both shot is a model seventy-three, made in eighteen seventy-six, and the shotgun was an eighteen ninety Remington side by side. My pistols were made in eighteen ninety-two, and are both forty-four forties, like the rifle."

He handed the mic back and he and Jesse moved slowly through the crowd. All in all, it'd been a pretty good day. He thought Grandpa and Grandma Cronin would probably have approved. Now, he was looking forward to a piece of pie and a cup of coffee.

By Any Means

The old man's phone beeped and dragged his concentration away from the report he was in the middle of. Slapping the speaker, he growled, "Cronin."

"Damn, you're in a grumpy mood, aren't you? This is Milty."

The old man smiled. "Sorry Milty, ass deep in a report that doesn't have any good answers. What's up?"

"I hear through the grapevine you're pulling the plug. Is that true?"

"Yep, September thirty."

"You're going to beat me out by three months. I'm going out thirty-one December, myself. Anyhow, you ever have anything to do with Jake Devreau?"

"Devreau? Not that I can think of, isn't he one of your black bag guys? I've heard some rumors…"

"Was. He's a roving inspector out of the Counter Terrorism Branch, but I've also heard him called a lot of things. He's got a rep for getting a lot of convictions, including bad actors in the government."

"What brought this on?"

"Apparently, your name came up in some meeting or discussion. They put out the word for anybody that knew you. Somebody remembered I had worked with you, and you've briefed up here."

"And?"

Milty said, "I don't know. I went in and told him what I knew about what you'd done. He even asked about the Thailand deal, and whether or not you were a shooter."

"Huh."

"Don't know where it's going, if anywhere, but I wanted to give you a heads up."

"Thanks, but I don't know what they'd want with a broke down ol' deputy sheriff. Besides, I've only got a couple of months left."

"Heard that, John. Send me an invite to the retirement, not that there is a high probability I'll make it, but I might try."

The old man chuckled. "Sure. You just want an excuse to get out of town, right? Thanks for the heads up, and let me know if you hear anything else."

"Will do. Talk to you later."

The old man started to respond, and realized he was hearing a dial tone. Shaking his head, he tapped the speaker off and leaned back in the chair. *Wonder what the hell is going on. Never had any interactions with Devreau, at least that I know of. Maybe I pissed off the wrong person, or… Damn, I wonder if they found out about the little Mexico trip? Or Montoya. Shit… I guess I better call him. I'll do that when I get home.*

He turned back to the report on his screen, looked at it for another ten minutes, then sighed in frustration, prompting Yogi to get up and come nuzzle his hand. "Yeah, you want to go out don't ya, boy?"

Yogi whined softly, shoving his nose under the old man's hand, then gumming it lightly. "Okay, okay." He closed the file and shut down the computer, realizing it was 5 o'clock and time to go home anyway. He got up, grabbed his hat off the hat rack and walked over to dispatch, sticking his head in, he said, "Lisa, I've had all the fun I can stand. I'm calling it a day."

Lisa waved, calling back, "Have a good one, Captain. Night, Yogi."

He walked out back, let Yogi water his favorite tree, and got him in the backseat, before climbing in himself. Driving toward I-10, he thought about what he wanted to say to Montoya, when the radio all units alert went off. "All units, shots fired, I-10 east. Mile two-five-one. White late model Ford Transit Van. No tag number. Back window broken out, DPS unit fired on attempting traffic stop. All units, be advised do not attempt to stop. Trail only." The traffic repeated as the old man swung east onto the on ramp for I-10 East.

"Dispatch to all units, pursuit is on Law-one. Two-one-six is in pursuit. DPS is responding from mile two-five-eight westbound."

The old man flipped over to Law-1, catching the last part of a transmission: "Two-five-four, pacing at eight eight mph. Still eastbound."

The old man figured he had three, maybe four minutes to make a decision. Pulling onto I-10, he sat in the right lane, doing about seventy, thinking, *Stop sticks? Not if they're shooting… This car isn't marked. Maybe, I can…* He saw flashing lights in the westbound lane and heard a female voice: "DPS triple one seven, I'm at mile two-five-seven, I see a white van in the inside eastbound lane: is that the suspect?" The old man smiled in relief. Michelle Wilson, now Sergeant Wilson hadn't been the DPS trooper shot at.

"Two-one-six, affirmative. Left hand lane, pacing at nine zero mph."

The old man keyed the mic. "Car four, mile two-five-eight, eastbound right lane. Maybe I can PIT[3] them."

He heard a mic key. "Captain, be careful, they're shooting at cops."

Keying up, he replied, "I'm in my car, no markings," glancing in his rear-view mirror, he saw a white van coming up fast, glancing quickly ahead, he saw another car in the right lane and he quickly pulled out to pass them, "Are they still in the left lane?"

"Ten four. Was that you that just pulled into the left lane?"

"Yep, going to get around this car, got at least a half mile clear in front of me."

He heard Sergeant Wilson key up. "I'm coming up behind two-one-six. Where are you going to PIT them?"

The old man realized the white van was on his ass, and jinked to the right lane. As the van started accelerating around him, he said, "Down, Yogi." He glanced back to see Yogi in the floorboard, accelerated and yanked the wheel left, catching the speeding van just ahead the right rear tire. It started sliding, and he accelerated to push it further left.

---

[3] Pursuit Intervention Technique

The van shot toward the right shoulder, momentarily straightened up, then snapped to the left, and started rolling. He slammed on the brakes as the back doors flew open, and one body was ejected, along with what the old man guessed was a rifle, then some greenish bundles. As the van continued to roll, a second, then a third body were ejected, and a cloud of white smoke flew up. The old man successfully dodged the first body, and skidded sideways to a stop. Quickly checking to ensure that Yogi was okay, he jerked his door open, jumped out and drew his pistol. He was fifty or sixty feet from the van, but wasn't going any closer for now, as he realized there was a white powder everywhere. He heard Hart key up, saying, "Dispatch, two-one-six. Rollover, two-five-eight and a half. Ejections. We're going to need fire and rescue. We've got a white clou… Ah shit. I think we have either meth or cocaine all over the place. Need to block Interstate, both directions, and probably block Imperial Highway at least out to the service roads on both sides of Interstate. Captain is out of his car and okay."

Dispatch replied laconically, "Roger, two-one-six." He heard the dispatch tones for fire and rescue, followed by, "Fire and rescue, respond to I-Ten, mile two-five-eight and a half. Hazmat response required. Be advised, possible drug spill."

Deputy Hart skidded to a stop near the first body. "Dispatch, two-one-six, ten twenty-three." Sergeant Wilson pulled up next to him, swinging to completely block the eastbound lanes, as the old man glanced over his shoulder to see who was coming up. He walked to the front fender, looked at the crumpling and tire going slowly flat, then shook his head. "Dammit. I'm going to need a wrecker."

Wilson trotted over, "You okay, Captain?"

"I'm fine, but it looks like I fucked this one up, Michelle."

"What do you mean?"

Waving his arm, he replied, "Well, looks like I might have killed three, caused a helluva mess, and spread *some kind* of drugs to hell and gone over the Interstate. At least the wind is from the west, otherwise both of us would be in trouble. You got a bio suit in your trunk?" She nodded, and he continued, "You might want to put it on, and make damn sure the mask is tight."

She surveyed the scene, three bodies, green packages, guns and a white powder blowing gently in the wind and said, "Well, I've got to give you credit, Captain, you don't do anything by halves. You need a bio suit? I've got another one in there."

Dropping his pistol to low ready, he said, "Go ahead and dress out, I'll keep watch on these two to make sure they don't do anything stupid, but I really don't want to walk in there unprotected."

Sergeant Wilson trotted back to her car, popped the trunk and returned shortly in what the old man thought of as the moon suit. He noticed she had a couple of pairs of flex cuffs in her gloved hand and said, "Cover me while I cuff them, just in case."

"Will do," he replied, bringing the pistol up to a low ready. She moved in carefully keeping clear of his line of fire, rolled the second body and put the flex cuffs on it. She reached for the neck, and he could see her shake her head. She stood up and gave him a thumbs down, he moved over far enough to be able to cover the third body, then nodded to her, and she approached it, doing the same thing. She stood up again, gave him another thumbs down and cautiously approached the rear of the van, glancing quickly in, she showed him a thumbs up, and walked slowly back. "Those two are gone. I'm going to get my drug kit and see what we've got. The van is full of packages, looks like three different types. I'll be right back."

He heard sirens in the distance, as Deputy Hart walked up. "Damn, Captain, that was impressive! The first guy back there is DRT. Broken neck, and I've secured the AK in my trunk. Only had two rounds left in the mag. You okay?"

"I'm fine and Yogi's fine. Miche… Sergeant Wilson says those two are also DRT. Apparently there were only the three of them in the van. She said it's full of packages too. What DPS officer got shot at?"

"Adam Pierce. He's okay. They got his radiator and windshield, but he was able to lock 'em up, and get out of range."

"Thank God!"

Two ambulances and two fire trucks pulled in behind their cars and a medic came forward, as Wilson trotted by, drug test kit in hand. "What you got, Captain?"

"Three bodies, one over by two-sixteen, and the other two out there in the drugs, or what I *think* are drugs."

"Damn! I don't even know how I'm going to do this one. I guess we need body bags, but how…"

The old man scratched his chin. "Um, maybe put them in the bags, then have fire rinse the outside of the bag off? I don't have a clue either. Better let Doc know, since I know they're going to have to have an autopsy."

The medic chuckled. "Oh he's gonna *love* that."

Sergeant Wilson came back, waving a tube. "Looks like damn near pure cocaine. And from the size of the bag that broke, I'm guessing it's a mule's backpack, so we're somewhere around thirty plus pounds of coke all over the highway."

The old man hung his head, as the fire captain walked up. "Did I hear thirty *pounds* of cocaine?"

Wilson grinned. "That you did, and this is now a full-blown hazmat spill."

"Shit. What am I supposed to do now?"

Deputy Hart replied, "I'd get out the SCBAs and a hand line. You got some washing down to do."

The medic walked over. "Just talked to Doc, can you spray the bodies off before we stuff 'em? Doc says they're already dead, and he knows there is coke everywhere, but I described the mechanisms of injury I could see, and he said wash-down was okay."

The fireman walked off, mumbling, but five minutes later was back with a charged hand line as the medics finished bagging the first body that had been ejected prior to the cocaine blowing up. Looking at the old man and Sergeant Wilson, he asked through the SCBA mask, "Where do you want us to wash this?"

Sergeant Wilson looked around. "Uh, how about downwind, toward the east? Can you wet the whole area down, then kinda sweep it off the road with your water? I've got the pictures I need, and I want out of this damn bio suit!"

The firemen did as directed, rinsing the bodies as they came to them, and ended up washing the now clumping cocaine off both sides of the Interstate. They took turns washing each other down, finally took their SCBA masks off, and wiped their sweating faces. The fire captain came over and said, "Y'all going to put somebody out here to guard this place?"

The old man turned to him. "Why?"

"Cause every doper in a hundred miles is gonna be out here shoveling up the dirt, or getting down on their hands and knees and snorting the dirt. Free cocaine? Shit, I wouldn't be surprised if the word isn't already out!"

***

Three hours later, they'd finally completed the basic investigation, gotten the westbound lanes of I-10 open, and the left shoulder open on the eastbound side, so traffic was finally moving. The old man's car had been towed to the shop, and the Sheriff, Ranger Levi Michaels, and Sergeant Wilson were sipping coffee around the front of Wilson's cruiser, and kibitzing over the amount of drugs that had been removed from the van before it was hauled to impound.

The sheriff had his phone out, crunching numbers on the phone and whistled. "Damn! If I've got this right, we got us about a sixteen million dollar bust right here. Eighty keys of coke, well, seventy-nine keys, eighty keys of meth, and forty keys of high grade heroin. I'm not sure I want to even try to deal with that after the last time." Turning to Levi, he asked, "Need a bust?"

Levi held up his hands. "Not me, I'm just getting up to speed. 'Twas me, I'd give it to DPS. They started this mess."

Wilson smiled. "That would be a helluva start for Trooper Pierce. He's only been on the job about a month. Kinda makes up for getting his car shot up, ya know."

The sheriff shrugged. "Works for me. John is retiring in a few months too, and I don't have a new investigator yet. If it gets the kid off on the right foot, more power to him."

The old man started to chime in when his cell rang. Pulling it out, he answered, listened for a minute, said "Damn!" a couple of times, and hung up. Turning to the group he said, "Glad this one isn't ours, Doc just let me know one of the bodies was a Chinese triad member, if he remembers his tats right."

The old man and Levi looked at each other, then at the others. Levi said, "This takes it to a whole new level. If we've got a Triad guy, this was a major shipment, possibly a new market, or the Chinese trying to muscle in on some of the Afghan heroin that is coming into the east coast."

Wilson said, "Huh. I'll go get Pierce, and I'm gonna direct traffic for a while. Y'all do what you need to, to get him started, please."

Levi chuckled, "Hope he likes overtime, and has a *lot* of patience; he's gonna need it!"

The old man said, "Oh yeah, probably twenty, maybe thirty hours, plus what? A month waiting time for confirmation of the quality of the drugs?"

That prompted a round of chuckles as she stalked off, looking for young Trooper Pierce. The sheriff glanced at Levi. "You need us for anything else? If you don't, I'm gonna give John a ride home, and call it a night."

Trooper Pierce came walking up and said, "Um, you guys wanted to talk to me?"

Levi said, "Y'all get out of here, we'll get this going." He put his arm over the shoulder of Trooper Pierce, and walked him toward the crumpled van. "Come with me, son. We need to have a chat about how you do DPS investigations."

Missed Opportunity

Aaron was bored to tears. The clock on the dash showed 2215, meaning he had another fifteen minutes before he could head back to Fort Stockton, and call it a night. Sector six was fourteen kinds of boring, especially on a weeknight, and even worse since he was sitting north of Imperial, on FM 1053, running radar and looking for anything unusual in vehicles coming across the county line. *Damn druggies, those assholes are why I'm out here. I know the sheriff wants to catch 'em, and it's pretty much a known fact that…*

The radar alert beeped as he saw a set of headlights coming north, it locked at 78mph, and he U-turned across the road as the blur of an oilfield truck went blowing by. He keyed the mic. "Dispatch, two-oh-two, northbound ten fifty-three north of Imperial, white oilfield truck, speeding seventy-eight miles an hour." Flipping on the lights, he said, "Lights, siren" for the body camera to pick up, and wiggled himself more deeply in the seat as he accelerated hard after the truck.

Dispatch came back with a laconic, "Roger, two-oh-two."

A couple of minutes later, he still hadn't gotten the truck to pull over, and he'd crossed into Crane County, keying up again, he said, "Dispatch, two-oh-two, pursuit of white oilfield truck for failure to yield. In Crane County, still on ten fifty-three north, vehicle is not stopping. Standby for Texas plate."

"Roger, two-oh-two. I'll landline Crane dispatch. You want to go up Law One?"

"Ten-four, switching." He reached down and changed the channel, passed the plate number, and heard a Crane County deputy respond.

"Two-oh-two, one-fifty-one. I'm west out of Crane on three twenty-nine. You there yet?"

"Coming up on it, still running about eighty. I've got 'em lit up, but they… Just blew the stop sign at three twenty-nine. Still north on ten fifty-three." Aaron slammed on his brakes, scanned both ways and accelerated through the intersection.

"Roger, see your lights."

Dispatch came up on Law One, "Two-oh-two, plate comes back to twenty-sixteen white Dodge thirty-five hundred. Registered to TPO." Aaron double clicked his mic in response.

Aaron glanced to the right and saw the blue and red lights. "Got you." He glanced back to see the truck slowing and signaling as it pulled off the road. "And they're stopping. Quarter mile north of three twenty-nine on ten fifty-three. I'll be out on the stop."

The Crane deputy pulled in behind Aaron. "One-fifty-one is out on assist for Pecos County."

Aaron got out and waited for the Crane deputy. As he walked up, Aaron stuck out his hand, saying, "Aaron Miller, thanks for the backup. You want driver or passenger's side?"

"Hector Ramos, I'll take passenger. It's your stop."

"Okay, let's do this." They walked up to the truck together, and Aaron reached down pressing his fingers on the taillight, as he glanced over. Ramos was doing the same thing and Aaron chuckled. He shined his light in the flat bed, seeing the normal detritus of oil field equipment, a welder, and five gallon cooler. He unconsciously checked his pistol moved freely in the holster as he got to the driver's door and gently tapped on the window. Turning his light, he saw a bleary eyed, unshaven face staring back at him. "Roll the windows down and turn off the truck please."

The window came down slowly, and the truck was shut off, as a strong odor of alcohol wafted out of the cab. "Sir, I'm Deputy Miller, I stopped you for excessive speed, I clocked you at seventy-eight mph in a fifty-five mph zone. License and proof of financial responsibility, please."

The driver hiccupped, and slurred, "I… Wall… Billfol? Finshul? Whhaazat?" as he fumbled his wallet out of his back pocket, fighting with the seatbelt. He dug through the wallet for a few seconds, spilling items all over the cab, as Ramos looked at the passed out passenger and reached in feeling for a pulse to make sure he was still alive.

He finally handed his license to Aaron, and Aaron said, "Ramos, can you check the glove box for the registration?"

"Will do, this one is alive, but drunk as hell."

Aaron glanced at the license, saw that it was an occupational license, and sighed, *Shit, this is all I need. I'm screwed for getting home anywhere near on time.* "Mr. White, I pulled you over for speeding, but I see you are driving a commercial vehicle on an occupational license, and I need you to step out of the truck, please. I would like to have you do some tests for me."

White looked at him. "Tesh? Wha kinda tesh? We… Joe too ineb… druck to dribe… Gott go work."

"Sir, you need to get out of the truck, please."

White fumbled with the door handle, and finally got the door open, then tried to get out without unfastening the seatbelt. Ramos came around the back of the truck. "Need a hand?"

Aaron grinned ruefully. "Please. I was supposed to be getting off right now."

Ramos grinned, "Sucks to be you. You want me to do the SFST[4]?"

"Am I going to screw you over?"

"Nah, I came on early tonight. If you want to write the speeding, I'll do the SFST, and haul them in. I'm a lot closer than you are."

Aaron smiled. "Thanks, I owe ya one!"

As they were trying to get Mr. White to comply with any of the tests, a black motorcycle whizzed past, turning down the dirt road into the oil patch. Aaron heard the bike slow, then nothing, then start up again. A niggling thought was running around his hind brain, but he couldn't get it to surface, as they finally had to wrestle Mr. White into Ramos' Tahoe, then haul the unconscious drunk over and deposit him in the back with White. After profusely thanking Ramos, Aaron hopped back in his Tahoe and pulled around the now

---

[4] Standard Field Sobriety Test

locked oilfield truck. He turned into the same dirt road he thought the bike had gone down, and saw a reflector hanging from a single bar gate.

He shrugged and backed out, keyed his mic, and said, "Dispatch, Two-oh-two, headed for the barn. Crane has the DWI in custody. ETA is twenty minutes."

"Roger two-oh-one. Status on speeding ticket?"

Aaron shook his head, and keyed the mic. "Roger, wrote it, but he was too drunk to sign it. Also driving commercial vehicle on an occupational license. I'll run that when I get back."

"Ten-four."

***

Sunday morning, everyone gathered around the kitchen table for their weekly breakfast together. As the old man pulled the biscuits out of the oven, and set them on the island, he asked, "Anything more on the Deen killing?"

Matt shook his head. "Nope, nothing but dead ends. But I still wonder about how that motorcycle rider got through that gate. I still think…"

Aaron exploded, "Dammit!"

Everybody stopped and looked at him, including the kids. He looked around ashamedly. "Uh, sorry. I just remembered something from that stop the other night." Turning to the old man, he said, "We stopped a drunk up in Crane, just north of three twenty-nine, and I saw a big bike go by, then turn down the first oilfield road up there. I turned around in that road, and there was a gate, but I didn't check to see if it was locked, or that was where the motorcycle went."

The old man looked up. "Well, shit. It rained last night, so probably no tracks. Do you… That was the one you got an assist on, right?"

"Yes, sir. Deputy Hector Ramos. He was just coming on, and he took the drunks."

"I'll call up there tomorrow, and maybe go pay them a visit. You said it was the first road to the right, north of three twenty-nine, right?"

"Yep."

"Do you remember who the truck was registered to?"

"Trans Pecos."

Matt and Jesse both looked up at that, and Matt asked, "Do you know which part of the patch they were heading for?"

Aaron shook his head. "No, the driver was too drunk to answer anything coherently, and I never got anything from the passenger. But if they were with TPO, I *think* that road I turned down was one of their leases."

Matt glanced at the old man. "Can I go with you, if you go up there?" The old man nodded, and Matt turned to Jesse. "You think Alton would want to work the store tomorrow? And maybe RO if anybody wants to shoot?"

Jesse shrugged. "Probably. If he doesn't, I'm sure one of the others will. I wonder if that supervisor… Jim Owens, yeah, him. I wonder if he's in charge of those leases too?"

Matt answered, "I'll call him tomorrow. If he's not, he probably knows who is."

The old man cautioned, "Let's wait until we talk to Pete, over in Crane and see if he's got anything. Also, I want to make sure we know which lease Aaron saw the bike go down. It might not have been a TPO lease, since Apache is also up in Crane and north to Midland."

Aaron sighed, "Sorry folks. I fu… screwed that one up."

Jace piped up, "Daddy, you screw up?"

Everybody broke out laughing, startling Yogi and Boo Boo, who started barking, setting off another round of laughter.

***

The old man pulled into the sheriff's office, let Yogi visit his tree, grabbed a cup of coffee, and headed to his office. Booting his computer, he searched for a Google map of Crane County. Hitting the speaker, he dialed the phone and waited through three rings, "Crane County Sheriff's Office, Deputy Esposito. May I help you?"

"Pete, John Cronin. How are you doing?"

"JAFM, you know the drill."

The old man laughed, "Heard that. Got a minute?"

"As long as it doesn't involve me working, sure!"

"You got a DWI up there named White? Picked up last Tuesday? It was an assist to one of our deputies, Miller."

He heard typing and a laugh on the other end. "Nope, he bonded out Thursday. That's all you needed, right?"

"Okay, Pete, I get it. You're having a Monday. But I'm trying to work out a murder down here, and it's possible this guy or his buddy have a clue or two. Can I take a ride up there and talk to you?"

Pete came back, "Sure, let us get the usual Monday BS out of the way. Say eleven?"

"Sounds good. I'm bringing one of my reserves that's been chasing this case since he was in on the original response. He's a retired Marine, got his shit together."

"Okay, see y'all then. Lunch is on you."

"Deal."

Lisa stuck her head in the door. "Morning, Captain. It's that time…"

The old man growled, "Gah, one thing I'm *not* going to miss is these damn Monday morning meetings." Getting up, he grabbed his wheel book, went by the break room and got a refill on the coffee. Stumping into the conference room, he took his accustomed seat on the far side of the table, nodding to the jail captain and Attorney Randall.

A half hour into the meeting, it was finally his turn. "Status is basically no change on the Deen murder investigation. One possible lead that I'll be checking out this morning. Did hear back from the Rangers, one Ernesto Rivas is gone. He took a plea bargain for thirty years, and he's rolling on the cartel." A round of hand claps, and a few laughs followed that, and the old man continued, "Anybody interested in my job, come see me. I'm getting short and I need to start a turnover, right sheriff?"

Jose nodded. "Yep. Otherwise I'm gonna appoint somebody." Another round of laughter followed that, and the old man motioned toward the door with his head. The sheriff nodded and he slipped quietly out of the meeting.

Matt was waiting in his office, playing with Yogi and laughing at his antics as he 'fought' with the Kong toy full of treats. "What did you do to him, Matt?"

"Stuffed some peanut butter in there."

"Dammit, he's gonna be going nuts all day with that thing. That means we gotta take him with us." Grabbing his hat, he snatched the toy. "Com'on Yogi, let's go."

Thirty minutes later, the old man turned into the first dirt road north of three twenty-nine. Sure enough, there was a bar across the road, and a reflector. Pulling up to it, he nodded. "TPO fifty-three." Backing up, he headed for Crane as Matt dialed his cell.

The old man could only hear one side of the conversation, but what he was hearing he didn't like. Matt was saying, "No, sir. I understand your firing all of them, but we'd really like…" A pause, then, "Yes, sir. Could we get access, maybe in an hour?" Matt looked over at him, mouthing, "Thirteen hundred," and the old man nodded. "Yes, sir. One o'clock would work. TPO fifty-three. Thank you, sir."

Matt sighed in disgust. "That was Owens, he's the district manager for all these sites. He fired everybody up there when he came in to get the truck and found them, quote, all fucked up, unquote. He said he fired all of them on the spot, and there wasn't a motorcycle there."

The old man shook his head, and murmured, "Another day at the orifice." Minutes later, he pulled into the Crane County Sheriff's Office. They walked through the door, Yogi on his leash, and Chief Deputy Pete Esposito met them at the counter. Shaking hands, the old man said, "Pete, Matt Carter. He's been working the Deen murder for the last month or so."

Esposito shook Matt's hand and said, "That's gotta suck. Whole lot of nothing for evidence, right?"

Both the old man and Matt shook their heads, and the old man said, "Nope. And what we have is so damn generic it fits probably two thirds of the motorcycles, and at least that many people with nineteen-elevens."

Esposito whistled, "Damn, I didn't realize it was *that* bad."

"Even the Rangers are drawing a blank on this one. It's just a one off that nobody… Well, let's just say none of the patterns fit for this one." The old man stood up. "We're going to meet the district manager out at the site, see if maybe there is something out there that might tie in."

Jim Owens was waiting for them at TPO 53, with the gate unlocked. Matt nodded to him as they pulled up, and Owens waved half-heartedly, then walked over to the car, papers in hand, as they got out. "Thanks for meeting us, Mr. Owens, I know you're busy…"

Owens replied, "I… I fired every one of those assholes that was working out here with White. They were all screwed up. Here's the contact information I've got on them, for what it's worth. I can't explain the motorcycle, much less his having access. I'm in the process of changing all the gate codes this week."

Matt took the papers and handed them to the old man. "Mr. Owens, this is Captain Cronin, he's the actual investigator for the county."

"Cronin? Up off eighteen?"

Shaking Owen's hand, the old man replied, "Yep. That's me."

"You were two years ahead of me at school. I remember you now. I thought you'd gone off to the Army and the government."

"I did, for a few years." Glancing at the paperwork, he asked, "How good do you think these addresses are?"

Owens scratched his ear. "Not sure. Phone numbers are probably good. Most of these guys are floaters, don't necessarily even live in Texas. They might be catching on with somebody else, or working off the books."

"Lovely…"

"The one sketchy guy, the one that I'd bet was the biggest druggie, is Jeff Smythe. He's a Brit ex-pat, left the North Sea a couple of years ago, ended up here about a year ago. Knows drilling, but he's… Twitchy… I think he's got a crash pad over in El Paso, and he called yesterday looking for his last check, so that address is probably good."

Matt and the old man looked at each other, and the old man smiled. "Thank you! I know some people that can go lean on him. Is it worth talking to any of the guys here now?"

"Nah, this is one of my old crews. I pulled them back early to man up this rig. They may drink, but that's it."

"Okay, well thanks for the info. I haven't given up on finding the perp on this one."

Owens looked up at the clouds. "I'd appreciate it. Rick was one of the good guys."

They shook hands all around, and Matt and the old man headed back to the car. The old man said, "You drive, I need to make some phone calls."

Surprised, Matt headed for the driver's side, and said, "You know I'm gonna screw up your mirrors and everything else, right?"

"Yeah, fine. I can fix that." Pulling out his cell, he dialed and waited. "Bucky? John. You got anybody you can lay hands on in El Paso?" The old man listened for a minute. "Yeah, I got somebody I need to have questioned in a murder case I've got…"

A Strange Meeting

The old man sat in his office, grumbling over the royalties and trying to figure out what was going on. He finally got on the computer, pulled up the spot market and saw $46.28 a barrel for the day. Digging out his calculator, he punched in the 15% royalty payment due, then searched through the document to find the average production. He finally found it, and punched in 300 barrel a day average, doing the multiplication, he came up with a little over $62,000 a month in royalties. That was within a few dollars of what the quarterly payment total was, and he shoved it back in the drawer, along with the calculator. *May be a good thing they are doing some prospecting and looking at the whole fracking thing down here. Production is less than half of what it was back in the day. At least there is enough money in the bank accounts for Jesse and Aaron to keep the place running through their lifetimes, if it comes to that.*

His thoughts were interrupted by the land line ringing. He glanced at it, saw a 202 area code, then picked it up. "Hello?"

He heard a strange voice on the other end. "Captain Cronin? Jake Devreau here. Do you have a minute?"

The old man looked at the phone, then put it back to his ear. "Uh, sure."

"I'm going to be in Houston a week from Friday, wanted to see if you might be over that way. I'd like to have a private conversation with you."

"I can probably do that. Do you want me to come to your offices in Houston?"

Devreau chuckled. "Oh, hell no, maybe we can meet somewhere for dinner?"

The old man thought for a minute. "Ah, yeah I can probably do that. Let me clear it with the sheriff. I can take a vacation day. I'm assuming this is off the books?"

"Definitely. Here's my cell number, just text me a time and place."

The old man quickly wrote down the number, said, "Got it." And heard dial tone as Devreau had hung up. The old man rocked in the chair for a minute, then spun around, and got up. Walking out on the front porch, he leaned against the post, staring unseeingly at the sunset sky, as Yogi gleefully chased a butterfly in the yard. *What the hell does the FBI want with me? Did they find out about the Mexico deal? Or is this something else entirely? That fuck from CBP trying to get me hung for that shooting Clay and I did, down on the border?*

Yogi's woofing finally broke his concentration, and he looked over to see him jumping in and out, like he was trying to pounce on something. Thinking it might be a snake, he said sharply, 'Yogi, leave it!" Yogi looked up at him, then trotted over a sat on the porch next to the old man, panting happily. Hearing the screen door squeak, and a grunt, he looked around to see Jace halfway out the door, with Boo Boo's nose between him and the door. He laughed and pulled the door open, allowing both of them to come out on the porch. Sweeping Jace up, he asked him sternly, "Where do you think you're going boy?"

Jace squealed as the old man tickled him. "Out, Papa, me go out."

"Isn't it about time for you to go to bed? You've got your pajamas on."

Jace shook his head solemnly. "No, Papa. Not yet."

The old man heard Jesse calling, "Jace? Jace? Where did you get to?"

The old man smiled to himself, before he said, "Out here, with me."

A frustrated Jesse came through the screen door. "Jace Cronin, I told you to go lay down, *not* go running outside to Papa."

With perfect children's logic, Jace said, "But I was going to lay down out here, mama."

Jesse rolled her eyes, took Jace from the old man and marched back toward the bedroom, cussing softly under her breath. The old man pulled out his cell phone, hit the speed dial for Billy Moore, and hit speaker. Finally, after five rings, he heard, "What?"

"Damn Billy, who twisted your tail?"

"Sorry John, long day and half the night working on a case. What's up?"

"You going to be in town a week from Friday?"

"Hang on a sec." He heard rustling of paper. "Ah, yeah. Why?"

"Need to come over and have a chat. Got an interesting phone call tonight. Maybe do Vietnamese for dinner? Table for three?"

Billy didn't say anything for a minute, then he heard a sigh. "Okay. Can do. You going to drive, or do you want me to send the airplane?"

"Would you mind sending the airplane? I'm not relishing a seven hour drive, then trying to pay attention in our meeting. Did you get my email on the royalties?"

"Yep, got the email. I'll have the bird there at two, puts you here by four. You want to come to the office? We can go over the royalty paperwork there. You want to spend the night?"

The old man thought for a second. "Sure, why not. No point in running the pilots ragged on a night flight for no good reason. We may need to have additional conversations."

"Alright, two o'clock Friday next week, I'll tell Mama Trần to get the guest room cleaned up."

The old man pulled out his phone and texted the address of Mama Trần's restaurant in Bellaire to Devreau, then thought, *I wonder if it really is owned by Mama Trần, and just run by… Han? Yeah, Han. I wonder how deep her connections really go? Is this… Stop it John, you're getting paranoid!*

***

Jesse dropped the old man at the airport. "What's going on that you need to fly see Uncle Billy?

"I want to go over the oil lease royalties with him. Production is down, and it'll be easier for him to get answers than if I try to field it."

"Are they shorting us?"

The old man shook his head. "Not that I can tell, but production is half of what it was five years ago. I know wells don't last forever, and they've shut three down, but I want to get a good legal answer as to why. Wells usually last about thirty-five years, but most of these have been in production off and on for almost fifty years. And with them wanting to look at fracking, I just feel like I need better answers than I'm going to get. I'll be back tomorrow. I'll call you before I leave Houston." He gave her a quick hug, and swatted her. "Now git! You've got things to do, and people to see. The bird should be here in fifteen minutes, probably less…" He watched Billy's Lear touch down. "Or right now. I don't need a minder yet."

Jesse laughed, "Yes, Papa, you do." She hugged him. "I'll pick you up tomorrow. Tell Uncle Billy 'hi' for us."

"I will."

Two and a half hours later, the old man and Billy sat at Billy's conference table in his office. The old man sipped his coffee quietly as Billy flipped through the royalty statement, making notes on one of his ever-present yellow legal pads. He finally leaned back, flipped his pony tail off his shoulder and sighed, "Well, from the looks of this, they've cut you back to one well in each section of the lease. What I *think* they are doing is trying to keep the lease active, pending fracking or some other new technology. Otherwise, all of the mineral rights come back to you, and you'd have the option of reselling them to somebody else. Have you thought about doing that?"

The old man shook his head. "Nope. I figure a bird in the hand is worth a whole damn covey in the bush. It's not like I'm really complaining. We're still getting a pretty good return, and there is plenty of money in the bank for the kids."

"Good enough. Lemme make a couple of calls. Go hit the latrine or something."

"Latrine? Damn, Billy, I haven't been in one of those in… Way too many years."

Billy smiled as he picked up the phone. "Yeah, but I got a rise outta you. Now go anywhere else while I do lawyer shit."

The old man laughed, "Okay, okay."

Getting up, he walked slowly out of the office and down to the elevator. It opened as he got there, and he rode down to the lobby, then walked outside. The little coffee shop was still open, and he nipped in, grabbing a cup of coffee just before they closed. He walked across the street to the little park, and sat on one of the benches facing Billy's building. The sun was shining, a few puffy clouds dotted the sky and it was comfortable in the shade. *Where do I go next? What is going to happen tonight? I guess I better tell Billy, and have him come along… Dammit, I'm too old to have this shit happening. I should be sitting at the ranch, enjoying the grandkids. Did you wait too long, old man? Did you push it once too often, and now it's going to come back and bite you? Billy's been looking at me funny since I got here, but he hasn't brought it up once...* His cell phone interrupted his thoughts, and he pulled it out to see a text from Billy, YOU CAN COME BACK NOW. He typed in K, and, dropped the half-drunk cup of coffee in the trash as he got up and headed back into the building.

An hour later, they had sorted out the royalty issues, with Billy recommending he do nothing and let the reduced payments ride. It wasn't like they needed more money. The old man had then poured out his fears, and they'd come up with a plan. Billy would go with him, and stay or go depending on Devreau's attitude.

***

They pulled into the small strip mall that the Pho Viet restaurant was in and parked facing the street. Billy looked over, "Well, I'll be glad when this dinner is over. You've been grouchier than a bear with a damn sore tooth. I really doubt Devreau is going to haul your ass off tonight; there is something else going on. Devreau may be a connected hot shot, but he's been a black bag guy for too many years to just let somebody steer him to a situation. I'm guessing he got hold of something, and won't let it go until he's satisfied."

The old man sighed. "Maybe, but I just don't know Billy. I know they are still pissed, hell, *all* of the TLAs are pissed that I wouldn't reveal my source. He could be coming at me from that angle."

"Nah, if they were going to do that, there'd be a subpoena, or a *request* to come in and chat," Billy glanced at a plain Ford pulling into the lot, "And there he is."

They got out of the car and walked slowly toward the restaurant, as Devreau came from the other direction. They met at the door, and the old man got an impression of caged vitality from Devreau, *This isn't the normal Fibbie. This guy is one of us…* Sticking out his hand, he said, "John Cronin, Mr. Devreau."

Devreau gripped it in a strong handshake. "Jake Devreau." Nodding at Billy, he continued, "And this is the infamous Billy Moore, I take it?"

Billy stuck out his hand. "As if you didn't already know, yes, I'm Billy Moore, and I'm also John's lawyer."

Devreau cocked his head. "Why are you here?"

Billy laughed. "When I know why *you* are here, then I'll know why I'm here."

Devreau and the old man both laughed, and Billy opened the door, ushering them in. They were the only Caucasians in the restaurant, and silence spread like a ripple until Han came out from the back. She hugged Billy, and bowed to the old man and Devreau, welcoming them in Vietnamese.

The old man bowed back, and said, "*Chào buổi tối,* Han."

Han laughed and led them to a quiet table in the back, with empty tables around it. She asked if they would like a beer. They all nodded, and Han brought them bottles of 33 beer. Devreau chuckled, "Haven't seen this in a while." Raising his bottle, he said, "To getting the job done." The old man and Billy's eyes met, and Billy could have sworn he saw the old man physically relax.

They clinked bottles and all three of them drank deeply, as they settled into their chairs. Devreau looked around. "Don't we get menus?'

Billy said, "Not here. This place is owned by my wife's sister. So, we don't get menus, or a bill, nor can we tip the wait staff. This one is on me."

Han began bringing out food starting with *pho,* followed by a number of small plates of Vietnamese delicacies, which kept the conversation to a minimum until the last bits of dessert were eaten. They were all sweating by the time the meal was over, but nobody was complaining. Han brought them cups of coffee to finish the meal, and the old man turned to Devreau. "What did you want with me, Mr. Devreau?"

Devreau looked around. "Is this a safe pla… Never mind… This is probably a lot safer than the office down here." Glancing at Billy, he asked, "How well do you know 'Mama' Trần?"

Billy smiled. "Pretty well, why?"

It was Devreau's turn to smile, "Just curious."

Han came back to the table with more coffee, and Devreau thanked her for the meal. Han smiled and said, "Thank you. Agent Troung, his wife, and daughter also enjoy it. Your agents are always welcome here."

Devreau's smile faltered for a second, then he said, "Thank you, I will let our office know."

Billy laughed. "Caught you out, didn't she."

Devreau smiled ruefully. "Damn Viet Mafia. That old lady…"

"Is my mother-in-law, and my housekeeper. She lives in my garage apartment, so I'd suggest…"

The old man jumped in. "Alright you two. Just fucking stop the dick beating." Turning squarely to Devreau, he asked, "What do you want with me?"

Devreau glanced around. "Might need you for some work. You've got a pretty good rep with a number of folks in some *interesting* places. I'd prefer that we talked privately though."

The old man bristled. "Billy Moore is my lawyer, so anything said becomes lawyer/client. And Billy's been tied into the Intel world for a long time. We were in Nam together…"

"I know. I reached out to a few folks. The two of you have pulled off some shit over the years. I'm not going to ask any questions, because I really don't want to know the answers, okay?"

The old man and Billy both nodded, and Devreau asked Billy, "Do you let Cronin use your airplane?"

"If he needs it, sure."

"How much lead time, and how trustworthy are your pilots?"

"Minimal, and both the pilots and the FA are ex-Navy, so they can, and do, keep their mouths shut."

Turning to the old man, he asked, "How current are you on your long range shooting?"

The old man leaned forward. "What are you calling long range? And what do you mean by current?"

"Let's say, oh, a thousand yards, give or take. When's the last time you shot at that range?"

"Twenty rounds through the thirty ought six last Sunday, and twenty rounds through the MRAD. Both at a thousand. All forty were body hits, why?"

Devreau smiled. "That's impressive. Wind?"

"Yep, there was ten, maybe fifteen knots, quartering…"

"How much lead time do you need to get away from the Sheriff's Office?"

The old man shrugged. "Not much. Jose pretty much lets me do what I need to."

"Okay, you interested in a possible long range shot?"

"Who or what, and where?"

"That will have to wait, but it's bad guys. Are you interested?"

The old man held his palms up. "Interested? Sure, but I need some more info."

Devreau said, "As soon as I get it, I'll let you know." Slipping a phone from his pocket, he slid it across the table. "Check it every third day, seven to eight in the evening, starting tomorrow."

"How long am I going to have to wait?"

It was Devreau's turn to shrug. "I think around thirty days…"

They finished the coffees, and the conversation drifted to the current state of the border, the issues the new administration was working through, and trying to weed out the leakers left over from the previous administration. Billy laughed, "Good luck with that. You'll never get rid of all of them!"

Devreau grimaced. "Yeah, I know. And on that note, I need to call it a night. I have *interviews* with a couple of agents in the morning that aren't going to be fun."

Han bowed them gracefully out of the restaurant, and they watched Devreau drive off. The drive back to the house was quiet, each lost in their own thoughts. Back at the house, Billy flipped the TV on to the news, and poured two shots of Macallan, handing one to the old man as they sat down.

"Well?"

The old man took a sip, and sighed. "I dunno Billy. I'm thinking this is a big hit, and it's going to be off the books."

"Agreed, but where does that leave you, if it turns to shit?"

The old man laughed, "Calling you?"

Billy snorted, "Probably. But you're going to do it, aren't you?"

"Nothing like going out with a bang."

"Oh shaddap, and drink your scotch."

Undercover

Aaron was headed to the patrol unit when Lisa stepped out of dispatch. "Sarge, go see the Captain, he's looking for you."

Aaron nodded. "Now?"

"Yep, something has come up. You can leave your stuff in dispatch, if you want."

"Nah, I'm sure this will be quick, and I'm already late getting on the streets. Thanks, though," he replied with a smile. Lugging his duty bag and shotgun, he turned around and walked quickly back to the captain's office.

Knocking on the closed door, he heard Yogi bark and the old man say, "Come in, come in." Aaron opened the door after juggling the bag and shotgun, and saw a city officer sitting in front of the old man's desk, as Yogi bounded over to him. "Close the door, if you would."

Not sure what was going on, Aaron kicked the door closed as he fended off Yogi. "Down mutt. Not now!" Dropping his duty bag, he carefully propped the shotgun against the corner of the wall and the desk, and sat down, nodding to Sergeant Alvarez from City. "Morning, Sarge. You just coming off shift?"

Alvarez replied, "Yep, two more weeks on nights, then I rotate back to days. I don't think I'll ever get caught up on my sleep."

Aaron and the old man both laughed ruefully at that, and the old man said, "Got an issue we need to handle. Sergeant Alvarez, if you would?"

Alvarez turned to face Aaron, as he picked up the wheel book laying on the desk. "I've already given the Captain a quick brief, but here's what I've got. One of your jailers, the pretty boy, White?"

The old man interjected, "Micah White. He works book in, and is a floater on hold over."

Aaron nodded. "Yeah, the blond kid."

Alvarez continued, "That's him, anyway, one of our units saw him last night, with one of our former customers in the car with him. One Lucinda Ramirez."

"Ramirez, Ramirez, why does that sound familiar?" Aaron leaned back. "Drugs? Meth? But I thought that was Estaban Ramirez, or am I just screwed up?"

The old man said, "He's on a BOLO as a possible meth dealer, he's got a rap sheet that runs about three pages, all drug related. Lucinda was picked up on possession with intent to distribute on some hydroponic marijuana. Did six months, and was released a week ago."

Aaron said, "Okay, I don't remember her, but go ahead."

Alvarez chuckled. "It's a family enterprise. But they're pretty damn sly about it. Anyway, back to last night. Your boy was seen driving Ramirez around, not like a couple, per se, but like he was helping her. I got in on the tail end of it, about two thirty this morning. There was a third person in the car, but he or she never got out. Only Lucinda ever got out, except once at the stop and rob, where both she and White walked into the store together." He popped his neck and sighed, then said, "We had to hang back, since we didn't have any UC cars, but we think she was delivering drugs. Two of the houses where we are pretty sure they stopped are on our watch list. The fact that your boy is involved brings a whole new set of issues, if true."

Aaron looked at the old man. "Why are you bringing me into this?"

"You're going to be the investigating officer. Since we're screening officers to replace me, and your name is in the hat, think of this as your chance in the barrel."

"So if I screw this up, I get to stay on the street?"

The old man and Alvarez both laughed, and Alvarez said, "Apparently, she's either living with him, or at least stayed with him last night. That's not the section of town where we can put a Hispanic officer at all hours in a UC vehicle. You on the other hand…"

Aaron laughed. "So, send the cracker after the cracker, right?"

The old man shook his head. "No, it's appropriate use of officers. And don't say that shit again. In this enlightened day and age, it'll get your ass fired."

Alvarez laughed. "Yeah, us Spics don't like it…"

"Dammit, both of y'all stop it. Alvarez, I need your incident report, and I'm going to put Aaron undercover, starting tonight. Looks like White is working days this week in book in, so we'll see what we come up with."

Alvarez slid a copy of the incident report across the desk. "I came prepared. If you don't have anything else, I hear my bed calling…"

"Nope, and thanks for the catch. Now it's up to us. I'll keep you and CID in the loop."

Alvarez stood up, shook hands and gave Yogi a pat on the head, before quietly exiting the office. Aaron turned to the old man. "What are we going to do?"

"First, you're going to sit down and take notes. Then you're going home and back to bed. You're unofficially on nights for the rest of the week. Officially, you're taking time off for personal issues. And don't discuss this with anyone but me or the sheriff."

"Got it."

"You are on from the time White gets off, until he goes lights out at night. You know how to access the database, right?"

An hour and a half, and seven pages of notes later, Aaron knew more about Micah White than he wanted to, and the same could be said for Lucinda Ramirez. He did have to admit she was a cutie: young, slender, and attractive, except for her criminal record. She'd been in and out of the system for four years, starting at age seventeen, for truancy, and had only gotten worse. Also, she'd apparently been processed in by White, and looking at the video, sadly with no audio, she'd played him from the get go. Other videos showed her flirting with him, when White was working the jail, but nothing that was provable.

Aaron picked up his bag and shotgun and started for the door, but the old man called him back. "Be ready at sixteen hundred, in civvies. Work jeans, dark shirt, and a gimme hat. Go by Henderson's Auto Sales, and pick up the white Ford he'll have waiting." Reaching under his desk, the old man pulled out a bag, "Here are the binoculars, and the camera; it's charged. There are a couple of lenses in the bag, depending on how far away you end up being."

Aaron slung the camera bag, picked up his duty bag and shotgun, and said, "I'll do my best."

***

Aaron didn't get much sleep. He woke up grumpy at three, as Jesse brought him a cup of coffee, saying, "Sorry babe, but you've got to get going. Papa said you're to take the Suburban in and leave it at Henderson's."

Grumbling, Aaron got a quick shower, gulped the coffee, and dressed as directed. He slipped a dark grey t-shirt on, then his pistol belt with the Glock 19 and mag carrier. Over that, he pulled a beat up dark blue wrangler shirt, and found his camo Remington gimme cap. Walking in the kitchen he asked, "Does this look okay?"

Jesse and Felicia turned, and Felicia laughed. "What are you supposed to be?"

Jesse smiled, saying, "He's undercover, at least for tonight."

Felicia replied, "He looks like a down at the heel oilfield guy, or out of work cowboy, except for the haircut."

Aaron rolled his eyes. "So I pass inspection?"

Jesse kissed him. "Yes, dear. Now go forth and do good."

Aaron laughed. "Okay, I'll try." He headed for the door, but stopped and went back into the bedroom, rummaged through one of his bags in the closet, and came up with a small black box. Shoving it in his pocket, he grabbed the radio and shotgun, along with the camera bag, on the way out the door.

Twenty minutes later, he pulled into Henderson's and parked behind the little house that was the office. Ollie Henderson came out as he started around the side of the house. "Captain Cronin called earlier. Here's the keys to the white Ford pickup over there. Didn't clean it up, figuring you'd want to blend in. She's got a full tank of gas, and all I ask is keep track of the mileage. Registration and insurance papers are in the glove box. Just try not to wreck it, if you don't have to."

"Thank you, sir. And no, I don't plan on wrecking it. Trust me!" Henderson flipped him the keys, and Aaron pulled it behind the house, loaded the shotgun and camera bag in the truck, and climbed in. While it wasn't really clean, per se, they'd vacuumed the interior, although the exterior was muddy half way up the doors. Checking one more time to ensure the shotgun wasn't loaded, he slid it behind the seat, facing the passenger's door, and hoped to hell he wouldn't have to get to it quickly. Not sure what to do with the radio, he finally turned it on, slipped it in the center console and slid the speaker/mic down by the seat belt latch. He played with the volume until he could hear it very softly, and pulled out of the driveway.

Driving by Micah White's apartment, he whistled, there wasn't a single place close that actually would allow him to hide effectively. Circling around, he pulled into a hotel parking lot a football field length away, drove all the way to the back, and backed into the last parking spot. Pulling a pair of binoculars out of the camera bag, he braced on the steering wheel, and focused on the apartment. *At least it's upstairs, so he can't go out the back. And from here, I can at least see them, if they're together, go down the stairs.* Glancing at his watch, he figured he had fifteen minutes before shift change, so he pulled up to the front of the hotel and hopped out.

Walking in, he saw an older lady behind the desk, and saw her nametag said Nita, and underneath that, manager. "Ma'am, are you the hotel manager?"

She straightened. "Yes, can I help you?"

Aaron pulled his badge out of his shirt. "I'm Deputy Miller, with Pecos County. I'm going to be doing some surveillance later on some bad people, and I'd like to use the last space in the back of your parking lot to do that." *Damn, John told me not to tell anybody, but I don't want these folks calling the cops on me, and I'm betting they would…*

She smiled. "You're Jesse's husband, aren't you?"

"Yes, ma'am."

"I don't have a problem with that. I'm going off at six, but I'll tell the night manager to ignore you."

Glancing at his watch, he continued. "I need to get going. Thanks again."

"You're welcome."

***

Aaron pulled in behind the tanks north of the sheriff's office and jail, ten minutes before shift change, and dug out the binoculars again. Spotting White's blue Toyota in the parking lot, he leaned back and waited. Fifteen minutes later, he saw White come out, get in the Toyota, and pull out of the parking area. Aaron let another car pull out, then started following the Toyota, thankful he was in a pickup, and could see over the intervening car. White went straight to his apartment, and Aaron saw him go up the stairs as he drove by.

Pulling into the hotel parking lot, he went to the back, backed into what he thought of as *his* parking space, and wiggled into a more comfortable position. An hour later, he was startled to see a man walk through his field of vision, and quickly glanced up. An older man was standing by his window, with a nametag, and a key in his hand. Aaron quickly rolled the window down, "Yes, sir?"

"I'm Albert, the night manager. Nita said you'd be down here, and I was to give you this key. It's for the last room on the bottom floor, in case you need to use the bathroom. She said you probably wouldn't think about that."

Aaron laughed. "Actually, I didn't think about it, until just now. How much is the room? I'll pay for it."

"No charge. Here ya go." Albert handed Aaron the key and headed back to the office.

"Thanks!"

Albert waved and kept walking, and Aaron shook his head in amazement. *Good folks. And of course I now have to piss. Guess I better be quick.* Aaron hopped out, ran in the room, did what he needed to do, and was back in the truck in five minutes.

Another hour went by, and Aaron was rolling his neck, doing isometrics, and trying to ignore the itch in his sock, when he saw White come down the stairs, followed by Lucinda Ramirez. Reaching for the camera, he got a couple of shots of them walking hand in hand to the car, then pulled out and around the block on a parallel street so he could follow them. White headed for the Interstate, but crossed under it and went to the truck stop, pulling into the restaurant parking area. Aaron's stomach rumbled, reminding him he hadn't eaten anything since breakfast, and he cussed himself for not thinking of that earlier, when he had a chance.

Pulling into the gas pumps, he got out, walked into the convenience store side. Picking up some jerky, a bag of chips, and a coke, he quickly paid for them, then headed back to the truck. Moving it out to a parking spot near the exit and settled down to eat what he had. Forty-five minutes later, he watched the Toyota drive by, and followed it back to the apartment complex.

It was getting dark, and after he watched them go back upstairs, took a chance on pulling into the parking lot next to where White's Toyota was backed into a parking space. Aaron jumped out of the truck, GPS tracker in hand, and walked to the back of the Toyota. Getting on his knees, he fumbled around for a few seconds, then got the tracker to stick to one of the bumper brackets. He wiggled it and it stuck, so he got up, groaning, and hobbled back to the truck. Looking around, he pulled out of the parking lot, and drove back to the hotel parking lot.

***

Two hours later, he had to take a leak. Fishing the room key out of his pants, he made use of the room's bathroom and stood behind his truck, doing stretches as he tried to loosen his muscles from sitting for so long. Glancing up, he saw lights go out in the apartment, and he thought, *Maybe they're going to bed early. One can hope…*

Hopping back in the cab, he pulled up the binoculars, focusing on the stairwell. He was thankful the lights in the stairwell were on all the time, so it was easy to spot, *Dammit, now where are they going? Shit, I didn't check whether these lights come on automatically when I start the truck.*

He watched them pull out of the parking lot and turn south toward town, and Aaron quickly started the truck, pulled out of the hotel parking lot, and cut over to get on the same street. He didn't see the Toyota at first, and jumped on the gas, until he realized there were two trucks between him and the Toyota. He saw it turn left at the corner, and sighed with relief. After almost running up on them twice in the next ten minutes, he pulled over and got out the GPS tracker, stuck it on the dash and dropped further back, more worried about being seen than getting photos of their stops. At one quick stop in the Mexican side of town, Lucinda came back to the car with a backpack over her shoulder.

A frustrating hour and a half later, they pulled back into the apartment complex, and he saw White carrying a backpack up to the apartment. He got pictures of it, noting it in his wheel book, and the time.

The lights went on, and Aaron settled back into the seat, trying to get comfortable, then said to hell with it, and got out, walking around the truck, using the room key to go to the bathroom, and finally leaning on the side of the truck, until the lights went out again. Noting the time, he decided they were in for the night, and stopped at the office, dropped the key off, thanked the night manager, and headed back to Henderson's. Retrieving the Suburban, he drove home yawning.
This crap is even less fun than it was in the Corps. And I didn't get shit for evidence, at least to my mind. I need to talk to John and figure out what I'm doing wrong.

Learning Experience

Aaron knocked on the old man's door. "Captain, got a minute?"

"Sure, what's up Aaron?"

"I'm not sure I'm doing this whole surveillance thing right. It's a lot different than what we did in the Corps. I mean, I got through last night, and put them to bed before I came home, but I'm not sure how to really tail somebody with a vehicle, much less a white pickup."

The old man chuckled. "Drag up a chair." Taking a sip of his coffee, he leaned back. "It's all about *normal*, you want to be as normal as possible. The pickup is one of a thousand out there, all white, all dirty, ranch trucks. Did you find the sun shield behind the seat?"

Aaron shook his head, "Uh, no. What good…"

"It's been modified, if you will, so when you put it up in the windshield, from the outside it looks like it's all good. But there is a six-inch spot, about where your field of vision as the driver is, that was scraped down to just the outer layer. You can see through it, not real good, but enough to see major movements. It works if you have to park somewhere during the daytime and just observe. You know about parking on property lines?"

"No, I know to stay as far away as I can, and still see them, but property lines?"

"If you park between two houses, splitting the property line, if people look out the window, or drive by, they're not going to know which house you're parked in front of. If they live there, they are going to assume you're visiting the folks in the other house. Same thing works at night, too. And if you see the perp develop a pattern in their driving, you can parallel, turn early or turn late, and not be behind them all the time. Also, with a truck, you can see over most cars, so this would allow you to stay two, three, maybe even four cars behind whoever you're tracking."

"Oh, so kinda like field trials. Be obvious, but not too obvious."

"Exactly."

"How long do you think we'll run this?"

"Let's go through the end of the week."

A knock on the door frame caused the old man to look up. "Levi, come on in."

Aaron got up to leave, but Ranger Michaels said, "You might as well stay, Aaron. I hear you're going to be taking this job, and you might as well get the good with the bad…"

Aaron replied, "First I heard of it, but if you want me to stick around."

The old man said, "What you got, Levi?"

"Remember that oil field murder you got a few months ago, with the bike?"

"Yeah. Dead end so far, other than Aaron seeing a bike go into one of the TPO sites."

Levi smiled. "Well, we got a description of the biker." Reaching in his pocket he unfolded a piece of paper, reading, "Mid-thirties, early forties, over six feet, thin, long ragged black beard, apparently bald or shaved head, always wears a skull do rag. Also known to carry what appears to be a 1911 on his right hip. Deals primarily Meth, but also has delivered coke and marijuana into the field." Handing the paper to the old man, he continued, "Got this off one of the CIs from Apache, that doesn't want to go back to the pen. This guy works the patch in New Mexico and Texas, and he had a habit that 'Skul' was feeding. New Mexico picked the CI up, and we did a deal to extradite him to Texas."

Aaron suddenly began digging through his wheel book, mumbling to himself, and the old man asked, "What the hell blew your skirt up, Aaron?"

"Shit, I stopped to do a courtesy check on that guy or his twin brother! A couple of months ago, I think. Hang on…" He continued to flip pages, then stopped and smiled, "Got it! Michael Orvis Harris, El Paso. Bike's license is R23973."

The old man quickly ran the plate, and smiled. "Comes back to a house in the 1300 block East San Antonio Avenue, that's down toward the border. Not a real good area."

Levi grinned. "Gimme that again, I'll get somebody from El Paso PD to do a site and surveil on it, until we can get some folks there. You want to do a warrant from here, or want us to do a simple person of interest question and answer?"

The old man rocked back. "I'm not sure... Maybe call in for questioning? This is kinda thin, unless we... We'd need a match on the tire tread, I'd say yeah, call in for questioning, or you folks do an onsite interview and try to get pics of the tread pattern? A sample of the oil would be even better."

Levi rolled his eyes. "Don't want much do ya?"

Aaron and the old man both laughed. "Nothing more than what a good Ranger should be able to accomplish Levi," the old man said with a chuckle.

"Okay, let me go make some calls. Have you told Aaron about the dick pictures yet?" With a wave, Ranger Michaels left the office, a smile on his face, as Aaron turned to the old man with a startled look on his face.

"Wha..."

The old man shrugged. "Well, I was going to break you in slowly on that, but since it's out there, you'll be picking up the ICAC[5] position, in addition to the investigator position. A couple of years ago, I had a case, Manuela Calderone, she was sixteen and committed suicide because of an internet pervert that got her stripping and sending him pictures by threatening her with publishing it on all her friend's accounts. I managed to get to the right folks at the FBI, and they ended up taking him down for child pornography, but we couldn't indict him on manslaughter charges. Anyway, the folks down in Austin sat down with us, and gave us a briefing on the amount of sex crimes in our area, and their need for an

---

[5] Internet Crimes Against Children

officer to be part of their system. I was so pissed, well, let's just say I let my mouth run away, and I ended up volunteering." He reached down and petted Yogi for a minute, as Aaron sat stunned.

"But dick pics?"

"That's part of the job: today, we have teachers having sex with students. We have brothers molesting their sisters, and making them cover it up. We have step-fathers raping and molesting step sons and daughters. We have juvenile rape. We have adult drunken rape of minors. We have buyer's remorse rapes, in which the victim decides later to call the sex rape. We have rape claims when mommy and daddy find out their precious snowflake is having sex, and bully her into claiming it's not consensual."

"Hadn't thought… Well, I guess I didn't think that happened here."

The old man smiled sadly. "More than you know… And these days with cell phones, people are just stupid, and the kids more so. Thirteen, fourteen, sending nude pictures back and forth, and thinking that stuff is gone quickly, that… Snapchat? Yeah, that crap."

Aaron shook his head. "Nope, once it's on the net, it's there forever, depending on who is looking for it. But kids… Damn… I don't think I want to look at those."

"They're all part of the job. *Not* the fun part. It's not catching bad guys, most of the time. It's stupid kids, and stupider parents in a lot of cases. Especially when you point out to them that their child both sent and received that crap."

Aaron got up. "Well, I guess I'll learn. I'm going to grab some lunch and go sleep for a while. I'll pick the truck up at four-thirty and get back on the surveillance."

"Lunch sounds good, let's go to the truck stop. I'm in the mood for a burger. I'll even buy."

***

Five hours later, Aaron rolled over and groaned, prompting Boo Boo to get up and lick him in the face. Pushing her away, he grumbled, "Not on the face, not on the face!" Boo Boo wagged her tail as Aaron sat up, then grabbed his crutches and made his way into the bathroom. After a quick shower and shave, he put his prosthetic on, then finished getting dressed. Opening the bedroom door, he stepped to the side as Boo Boo bolted by, headed for the kitchen and the smell of fresh tamales.

Felicia nodded as he walked into the kitchen. "I'll have a plate ready for you in a minute. Coffee is fresh, and I'll wrap a couple of tamales for you to take with you."

Aaron pulled a coffee cup down, filled it, and replied, "Thanks, you don't have to cook just for…"

Felicia held up a hand. "I'm fixing them anyway, and Jesse said you were on nights, surveillance? I think that's what she said. So, this is your breakfast. Now let Boo Boo out before she chews through the door. Jesse's down at the store, and the kids are napping in the living room, so be quiet."

Aaron let Boo Boo out. "Thank you. I had lunch, but I don't know how long I'm going to be out there tonight. Didn't sleep worth a damn. It always takes me a few days to flip my sleep cycle."

Felicia laughed. "You and Matt both. He's still not waking up when the kids cry. I really think he's deaf! I have to prod him awake, and then he usually brings the baby back to me to do whatever needs doing." She sat a plate in front of him and asked, "You want two or three for later?"

Aaron mumbled around a mouthful of food, "Two please. These are *so* good!"

Felicia smiled as she rolled two more up in aluminum foil and set them by his plate. "I like to cook. It's my contribution to the house." She filled his go cup with coffee, and handed it to him as he got up. "Stay safe, okay?"

Aaron smiled. "Do my best. Tell Jesse I don't know what time I'll be back." With that, he headed for the front door, grabbing a light jacket and fumbling it on to cover his badge and pistol. Thirty minutes later, he was back in the dirty pickup, and heading back toward the sheriff's office, parking in the same place as yesterday, and pulling the sun shade out. He unfolded it and stuck it in the windshield, and found the hole Cronin had told him about. He had to sit up pretty straight to see through it, but it worked, and he was less worried about being spotted. Twenty minutes later, shift change started, and he saw jailers streaming out of the jail. He waited until he saw Micah White pull out, then let three more cars go by as he folded the sunscreen back up, then pulled out in trail. Pulling up the tracker software, he was reassured as the dot moved, and he dropped the phone on the seat next to him.

Three hours later, Aaron was sitting on the street, sun shade in place, and seriously in need of a bathroom, as he contemplated the advisability of large amounts of coffee or any liquid during surveillance. He finally gave up and pulled out, driving down to the convenience store two blocks away, and hurried in to use their bathroom. Coming out, he bought two bottles of water, and headed for the hotel parking lot, figuring it was almost dark and he could set up there again. Glancing at the phone, he was relieved to see the car hadn't moved.

Pulling into the hotel, he saw the lights go off, and grabbed his binoculars to see if anyone would come down the stairs. No one did, and he settled back and ate the last tamale, as he tried to stay awake. Albert, the night manager, came by and Aaron got out of the truck for a few minutes and talked to him, turning down the room key he offered, finally giving up at 0200, figuring Micah and Lucinda were well and truly down for the night.

***

Thursday night, Aaron was back on the surveillance from the hotel parking lot, this time with a room key and plenty of coffee. *God, this is boring... I'm not getting shit done, just sitting here with my thumb up my ass. I wonder if we can do this kind of stuff with video cameras? Maybe set one up here on the motel...* He was jerked out of his muse when he saw White and Ramirez come down the stairs, with Ramirez carrying a backpack. He waited until they were on the move, and the tracking bug showed him which way they were going, before he pulled out of the parking lot. Deciding to do something different, he used the tracking bug and stayed further back, as they drove a random pattern, then finally turned into the not so good section of town. He saw the bug stop, and quickly turned down the street, easing by the car as he observed a man getting in the front seat, another backpack in hand.

He turned into the apartment complex parking lot just down the street and killed his lights, then pulled up the photos he had on the phone. *Crap, I think that was Estaban Ramirez that got in the car. I wonder if he's been under our noses the whole time?* The car started moving again, and as it drove by the apartments, Aaron pulled out and followed them. *Shit, do I call Alvarez or the Captain? If we're in the city, better call Alvarez.* Picking up his phone, he scrolled down and found the sergeant's cell number. He hit it, and speaker, then dropped the cell phone in his lap.

Five rings later, he heard a sleepy, "Alvarez, what you got?"

"Sarge, Miller here, I think I've got Estaban Ramirez and a backpack in the car with White and Lucinda Ramirez."

Aaron heard a grunt, then scrambling noises. "Where are you?"

Looking up, he answered, "Parkview, heading north, back toward town."

"Okay, stay on them, it'll take us twenty minutes to put something together. You want to call SO?"

Aaron thought for a second. "Nah, it'd be better if you do it, then one person is running the whole op, not trying to…"

"Alright, I'm on it. Text me with updates at least every ten minutes, I'll call you back when we're ready. You got a radio with you?"

"Yep, I'm up on dispatch."

"We'll run this on Law One, switch up when you hear the tones go out to county, and start providing updates. By then we should be close, in case they try to rabbit on us."

Two text updates later, Aaron was wondering when they were going to get their act together. White had stopped twice, and Lucinda had gotten out and taken packages up to one apartment and one rundown house, while Aaron duly noted the addresses, as he hung back a half a block. Just as he was getting ready to send another update, his cell rang, and the tones went off, causing him to jump and drop the phone.

He dug it out of the floorboard, answered it, and hit speaker. "Miller."

"Where are you?"

"Westbound on East Fifth, crossing Orient."

Aaron heard him say, "All units, converge on West Fifth and Railroad, we'll do a stop on the tracks." Aaron remembered that he was supposed to switch over to Law One, and changed the channel to hear, "One-oh-three, come down fourth, one-oh-six, you're on sixth. You're the back door. One-oh-eight, meet me at Railroad and Fifth. County units, cover Nelson and Main."

Aaron saw brake lights, and White turn left suddenly. Keying up, he said, "This is Miller, he just turned left, down an alley between Main and Nelson." As he eased by the alley, he said, "White is parked next to another car, facing north in the alley. I think I see two people out of the vehicles."

He heard Alvarez key up. "Go, go, go! Alley between Main and Nelson, cover Fifth and Fourth streets. No sirens, no lights."

Aaron turned left on Nelson, then pulled a quick U-turn and flipped the lights off as he pulled up in front of the cleaners, then eased forward where he could see down the parking lot next to the building. He saw blue and red lights come on, reflecting off the buildings and heard one burp of a siren, then a PA come on, "Turn your cars off. Step out of the cars. You, in the blue Toyota, turn your car off, *now!*

Aaron thought, *Okay White, don't do anything stupid. Just do what they…* Out of the corner of his eyes, he saw somebody come racing around the corner of the next building over, looking like he was humped over, but running full out. Aaron jumped out of the pickup. *Shit… I've been sitting too long, I'm stiffer than a damn board.* Drawing his pistol, he pulled out his tac-light with the off hand, clicking it to the strobe function as he yelled, "Police, stop where you are."

Realizing it was probably Ramirez, he yelled, "Drop the backpack, let me see your hands!" Ramirez looked up and suddenly face planted in the parking lot, twenty feet from Aaron. *Huh, guess there is something to that strobe disorientation stuff…*

Aaron hobbled over to Ramirez, as Alvarez and Deputy Hart came running up, and between the three of them, they got him pig piled, got the backpack off, and got him cuffed. As they stood him up, Alvarez shined his light in Ramirez' face and remarked, "Oh, that's a nasty road rash there, Estaban!" Blood dripped from his obviously busted nose, and he was missing a couple of teeth, in addition to the deep scrapes in his nose and chin, "You have the right to remain silent…"

Ramirez moaned, "I need an ambulance, man. You fucked up my face, I'm gonna sue you, whoever the fuck you are!"

Alvarez grabbed him by the cuffs. "You're going to jail, mi amigo. Aaron, if you want to go, we've got it from here."

Hart picked up the backpack and added, "Nice job! Go get some sleep, Sarge."

Aaron shook his head. "Nah, I want to see what we got. I'll be over there in a minute." He hobbled back to the truck, massaging his leg, took off the light jacket so his badge was visible and got back in. He drove slowly around and pulled into the alley behind the city unit. Getting out, he was gratified to see six people cuffed and on the ground. Walking up, he put his fingers on the left tail light, and reached under the bumper and pulled the GPS tag loose from its location, slipping it in his pocket.

When he got to the front of the Toyota, he saw Hart and Alvarez chuckling over the pile of baggies and a pistol laying on the hood. Alvarez smiled as he turned to him. "Aaron, you just made our night. Meth and coke, couple of kilos of each, which is possession with intent to distribute. That, and ol' Estaban there had him a pistol, which gets him even more charges. He's going away for a *long* time."

Aaron heard Micah White whine, "I was coerced. They made me drive them around, I can tell you…"

Aaron mumbled, "Yeah, coerced by the wrong head."

Hart and Alvarez laughed and nodded.

An Old Gun

It was a slow morning, and Tom and the old farts, as Jesse thought of them, were BS'ing around the coffee pot in the corner. Toad had come in late last night, grumbling that he was getting behind on the orders for custom work, and had dragged Bob back into the 'hole' as the guys called the workroom, needing help with something on a barrel not cooperating with being mated to an action.

The weather had turned chilly, and that had contributed to a lack of early morning shooters, which left Fernando and Ed deciding to clean up the ranges. That reminded Jesse, the brass buyer was due to come by on Monday, so they needed to box up what they'd recovered from the ranges and shoveled into the barrels in the back of the storage area. Seven months had proven that they could stay afloat, as a company, but she was thankful they didn't have to count on the income to live on.

Her accounting background and training caused her to want steady income and outgo month to month, but they weren't seeing it. She was counting noses in the pistol and rifle cases, to see what they might need to order, when a very old, traditionally-dressed Hispanic lady, escorted by what she guessed was a grandson, or maybe great grandson walked slowly to the counter. "*Señora*, how may I help you?" Jesse asked.

A spate of very fast Spanish followed, and the great grandson, said, "My *bisabuela*, she is our *La Matriarca*, and does not speak much English. My name is Manuel, we are *la Sanchez*. We… come from Ozona, to your shop… Store? My English, I am learning."

Jesse replied, "If you will wait, I have someone who can translate quickly. Can you wait ten minutes? Can I offer you a cup of coffee?"

Another fast back and forth, and the old lady and her great grandson went over and sat down by the coffee pot, as Jesse called Felicia on the cell. "Hey, can you come down here for a few minutes? I need you to translate for me." Felicia said she would, since Matt was still in the house, he could watch the kids. Five minutes later, Felicia walked in, and Jesse walked her over to the old lady.

Felicia greeted her with a bow, and they spoke for about a minute, then Felicia turned to Jesse, "She is *La Matriarca* Sanchez, she had her Manuel bring her here, she has heard Mexicans are treated fairly here, and she has an old gun she would like to sell. None of her children, grandchildren, or great grandchildren are interested in it, and she wants to use the money for school clothes for another great grandchild.

Jesse nodded, "Please tell her we will be happy to look at it." Felicia translated, and Manuel went out the door, coming back moments later with a battered leather valise, sitting it carefully in front of his *bisabuela*. *La Matriarca* reached into the valise, and pulled out a huge old pistol, then carefully handed it to Jesse, with another spate of Spanish, and Jesse was pretty sure she caught the words, loaded.

Felicia said, "She says be careful, it's loaded. It's the *pistola* she keeps in her bedroom. She would like to get five hundred dollars for it, if possible. That is what her grandson thinks it might be worth."

Jesse asked, "Can I take it over to the counter?"

Felicia translated, then nodded, and Jesse gingerly carried it over to the counter, placing it on the mat, and making sure it was pointed in a safe direction. Turning on the light over the counter, she was amazed at the condition, and immediately wondered if it was a copy of an 1848 Colt Dragoon. Picking up the magnifying glass, she started looking closer, and almost dropped the glass when she saw the inscription 'B Company No 148'.

Jesse looked up. "Felicia, tell her I must get our gunsmith to look at this, I will be right back." As Felicia was translating that, Jesse made a bee line down the hall to the hole, sticking her head in, she said, "Toad, I need you to come look at a pistol, please."

Toad glanced up. "Can it wait, I'm right in the middle of…"

Jesse glared at him. "No! Now. If this is what I think it is…"

Toad said, "Okay, okay… If it's that important."

She led Toad back to the counter and said, "She told me it's loaded, so be careful."

Toad glanced at it. "Looks like a copy of a Dragoon. Late 1840 design, maybe early 1850. Looks like a pretty good job of aging…"

Jesse handed him the magnifying glass. "Take a closer look." As she stepped back, Felicia watched her, wondering what was going on. Jesse just shook her head, holding up a finger.

Toad was mumbling something, then Jesse heard him say, "Holy shit. This can't… This has gotta be… No fuckin' way."

La Matriarca Sanchez said something to Felicia, who walked over, "She wants to know if there is a problem."

Toad looked up from the pistol. "If this is real, yeah, there is a big problem."

Felicia cocked her head, "Why?"

Toad said quietly, "If this pistol is real, this is a half million dollars sitting here, at the minimum."

Felicia blanched. "What? How?"

Toad said, "Tell her we're looking some things up, and it will be a few more minutes."

"Should I tell her?"

"No, don't say anything about the value. I gotta make some calls." He flipped the pistol over, and said, "Yeah, it's loaded. Don't do anything until I get back."

Toad disappeared back into the hole, and Jesse pulled some pastries out of the fridge, put them on a tray, and took them over to where the old lady and her great grandson were sitting. She offered them, and they both took one, as Felicia explained that it would be a few more minutes. There was another spate of fast Spanish, and Felicia followed Jesse back to the counter, whispering, "She's worried she wants too much."

Jesse just shook her head. "I hate not telling her, but Toad is right. We'll have to wait."

Fifteen minutes later, a shaken Toad came back to the counter, reexamined the pistol and turned to Jesse. "I think… Based on what I could find out, I think this is the real deal. We need to ask her some questions."

Felicia shrugged. "I'll translate, but you'll have to keep it simple. I don't know all the terms and stuff."

The three of them went back to where *La Matriarca* and Manuel were sitting and Toad smiled, looking at her and said, "Ma'am, do you have anything else that goes with this pistol?"

Felicia translated, and the old lady reached into the valise, pulled out a well-used saddle holster, three spare cylinders, an old tally book, and a set of crumbling sheets of paper. Toad looked at them in amazement, then turned to Jesse, mouthing, "It's real!"

La Matriarca pointed to one of the sheets of paper, and one name, P.L. Buquor, as Felicia translated, "She says that is her grandfather. He served under El Captain Hays. She said he served and was called back in 1847 and went back for a year or two."

Picking up the tally book, she started flipping through and looking at Felicia, she again pointed at the crabbed entries, and Felicia translated, "She says this is the book of… What he did, men they tracked and… things they did. And she wants to know what is wrong."

Toad looked at Jesse. "You want to tell her, or should I?"

Jesse motioned Toad to continue, and he turned to the old lady. "We cannot afford to buy your pistol." Felicia translated, and *La Matriarca*'s face fell. Toad rapidly said, "It is worth too much money for us to pay."

When Felicia translated that, *La Matriarca* looked at all three of them, eyes wide, and asked Felicia a question. Felicia said, "She wants to know what you mean. It is only an old *pistola*. What do you mean it is worth too much?"

Manuel nodded. "Why too much, does not make sense."

Toad leaned forward, hands on knees, and said, "Please translate this- Ma'am, that *pistola* as you call it is conservatively worth up to one half million dollars if it can be authenticated. What I see here, it makes me believe this… This pistol is the real deal."

Manuel crossed himself as he heard Toad say it, "*Dios mío, Bisabuela, Dios mío…*"

La Matriarca also crossed herself, and then put her hands over her mouth in wonder. Toad continued, "That is why we cannot buy it. We can help you get it authenticated, and help you with an auction company that can sell it, but you need to decide what you want to do."

Felicia translated that, and listened as the old lady spit rapid fire questions at Felicia, who said, "She wants to know how is this possible? And where should she keep it, she has been keeping the valise under her bed? She said she shoots it once a month, to clean it out, before she reloads it."

Another fast interaction, and Felicia added, "How long would it take to veri… authenticate it?"

Toad replied, "Does she have any other things, papers, anything that might prove… That could… Ah hell, I'm at a loss for words here…"

Felicia smiled, and translated Toad's fumbling question, and the old lady smiled, reached over and patted Toad's hand, speaking directly at him. Felicia translated, "Something like a picture of her grandfather holding it? Would that help?"

Toad nodded. "Of course. But I didn't think they had pictures back in the eighteen-forties."

A quick answer was forthcoming. "A picture, probably from the eighteen-seventies, when he was the justice of the peace. He is leaning on a desk, holding the *pistola* and a rifle." She reached in the valise and pulled out one more piece of folded paper, and an old badge fell out, clanking on the floor.

Jesse picked it up, turned it over, and said, "Oh, damn. How old is this?" She handed it to Toad, who whistled. "Well, that's not… No, I'm not going to say that after seeing this pistol. Ma'am, where did you get this?"

She gently unfolded the creased paper, and Toad and Jesse read the handwriting together-

April 10th, 1875
Burton, Texas

Honored Sir,
I take this opportunity to answer your favor of this instant. While I applaud your willingness to volunteer for this dangerous endeavor, however

we cannot use Texans from this area, due to the possibility of having to take family under fire. However, in honor of your history with the rangers, I would present you, Pasquale Leo Buquor, with this badge, our new symbol. And a symbol of your service to the state of Texas as a member of the original Texas Rangers under Captain John Coffee Hays from March 1840 and April 1847.
Your Obedient Servant,
Signed- Leander H McNelly. Esq.

Toad turned the badge over, looking at it closely. "Eighteen seventy-three. Mexican five peso, silver, five pointed star, plain front, just says Texas Ranger. Damn…"

Toad looked up and said, "We can help you sell the pistol is that if what you want to do. The pieces you have with it, which will help with authentication, is critical to the provenance…"

The old lady interrupted and asked a question, which Felicia translated as, "What is provenance?"

Toad thought for a second, then said, "It's a record of ownership of an antique, like this gun. Your documents and photo can be used to prove the authenticity. Very few of these guns exist, and fewer still with documentation that proves the lineage."

Another quick exchange, and the old lady sat up straighter. Felicia translated, "She is asking if we will help her, and she will send Manuel over with the picture and other pieces. She also asks if we will keep the *pistola* for her, since she is no longer comfortable keeping it under her bed."

Jesse said, "Yes, we will. I will give her a receipt for every item, and I will show her the vault where we will store it."

Felicia translated, "That is acceptable, and she asked how long will it take to sell."

Jesse looked at Toad, who answered, "It may take a couple of months. Once it is appraised, then the lady will have to make a decision who to consign the pistol to, and when the next auction will take place. Stress to her that we can only advise her, we cannot and will not act in her place."

One more back and forth, and Felicia said with a smile, "She agrees, and that is understood. She trusts us to do the right thing."

Toad said, "I will unload the pistol, and clean it before we get it appraised."

With a laugh, the old lady made a gesture and said with a smile, "*Dispara la pistola!*"

Felicia laughed, "She said shoot it."

Toad's eyes lit up, and he smiled from ear to ear. "Really?"

The old lady patted Toad on the arm again, and Felicia translated, "She says that is how she empties it each month to reload it."

Toad rubbed his hands together. "Oh my God. This… Will be unbelievable! I get to shoot… Yes, ma'am. We will only shoot to clear the cylinder."

Jesse photographed each item, noted them in the spreadsheet, and carefully placed each piece back in the valise. Finally, he slipped the pistol into the saddle holster, and closed the valise. She printed off the page as a receipt, signed it, had the old lady fill in her information and countersign it, then led them down to the vault. Placing the valise on a shelf, she turned. "We will call you when we know an appraiser will be here, would you be available to come and meet with him or her, *Señora*?"

The old lady nodded. "*Sin duda allí estaré.*"

Toad looked at Felicia who said, "She said certainly, I will be there."

As they walked back to the front of the store, she said, "*Gracias*, I appreciate your… Assistance. Good bye." They marched out of the store, got in their car and left.

Toad put his hands on the counter and exhaled, as the old farts crowded around, asking, "What the hell was that all about?"

Toad shook his head. "You won't believe it. Lemme make some phone calls and calm down, then I'll tell you, and show you."

There was some grumbling at that, but it was good natured. Toad and Jesse went in the office, and Toad immediately got on the computer, doing search after search, until he narrowed it down, finally saying, "Michael Simens, at Historical Arms is the guy for Colts. I'll call him."

***

Three months later, the old lady, her son, grandson and great grandson sat in the store, in front of the TV, along with the old man, Jesse, Aaron, Matt, and Felicia, while the kids played in the play area, and Yogi and Boo Boo hid under the table. Coffee, cokes, and munchies sat on the table as they watched the internet feed of the auction from Christie's in New York.

The pistol finally came under the gavel, with the auctioneer giving a brief description, "Ladies and Gentlemen, next is lot number two eight five. An authenticated Walker Colt, serial number one four eight, issued to the Texas Ranger P.L. Buquon in 1847. There is provenance associated with this pistol, and it comes unrestored and fireable, as demonstrated by the associated video, also with an original saddle holster, three additional original cylinders, and tools for making bullets."

There was a prolonged murmur of noise, and the auctioneer started his patter at $500,000. It quickly rose to $800,000, stalled for a minute, then finally was gaveled down at $880,000. Jesse broke out a cake that had been made for the occasion, and Matt cracked a bottle of champagne, as *La Sanchez* sat stunned with tears in her eyes.

Turning to Felicia she asked, "How much...?"

The old man answered in Spanish, "*Señora*, it cost you fifty-two thousand eight hundred dollars for Christie's to sell it, which means you made eight hundred twenty-seven thousand, two hundred dollars just now."

The grandson, Pedro, asked, "Why so much? Just to sell one *pistola*?

The old man chuckled. "Actually that's only six percent. Until we got them in a bidding war, they all wanted to charge up to nineteen percent. If we'd had a couple of more people, we might have gotten it sold for no seller's commission. There is also a buyer's premium, which is, I believe, twenty percent for Christie's. So, they made a hundred and seventy-six thousand dollars there, added to your fifty-two thousand eight hundred, commission, they made two-hundred twenty-eight thousand dollars on your pistol."

"Dios Mio! So much for nothing. How much did you charge us?"

Jesse shrugged. "Thirty dollars. That's what we charge for a transfer fee. That, and we got to shoot it."

As they started out the door, *La Matriarca* Sanchez turned and said, "*Que Dios los bendiga y los favorezca y los proteja de todo mal,*" before she stepped out the door.

Toad looked at Felicia, who translated, "She said, may God bless you and favor you and protect you from all Evil."

"Ah, all I understood in that was God. I hope to God she's got good security, considering how much money they have all of a sudden."

The old man replied, "Anybody that screws with her or the family will bring the wrath of the entire community down on them. And they live on a nice little ranch that's been in their family even longer than this one's been in ours. She also has vaqueros that are loyal who *will* shoot first, and ask questions later. They've taken out a few Coyotes down there over the years."

Trouble

The old man sat on the steps, watching the sun rise as Yogi and Boo Boo chased around the front yard, sniffing and investigating clumps of grass. As he sipped his coffee, he reflected on the beauty of the morning, and the peace and quiet. *Used to hate getting up, dad damn near had to beat me to get my lazy ass out of bed. Didn't know what I was missing. A good cup of coffee, a few minutes to enjoy the…*

His thoughts were interrupted by an old Honda Civic pulling tentatively into the driveway, and Yogi and Boo Boo barking as the car pulled to a stop. He could see a female in the car, by herself, so he called the dogs back and put them in the house. When he turned back, he saw an obviously distraught young Hispanic female walking toward the porch, carrying what looked like a CD in her hand.

"*Señor* Cronin? John Cronin?"

"*Sí, cómo te puedo ayudar?*"

She, visibly slumped, then continued in English, "*Señor*, my father said if anything happened to him, I was to bring this to you, and you could help me."

"Your father?"

"*Sí*, Carlos Montoya. He said… I could trust you with my life."

Stunned, he parroted, "Carlos Montoya?"

"*Sí*, he… he was…" She broke into tears. "An accountant, and he…"

"Oh, damn…" the old man said softly. "Please, come in. Would you, um… Coffee? You are Eva, correct?"

"Yes, please, and a bathroom. It was a long drive from Austin. I was scared to stop for anything other than to get a tank of gas."

Commanding the dogs to sit, he opened the door, ushering Eva into the house. He caught a whiff of fear sweat from her, as she handed him the CD. He pointed her to the bathroom, asking, "Do you want anything in your coffee?"

"No, black is fine." She stepped into the bathroom, and the old man slipped back down the hall, setting the CD on his desk, before going back to the kitchen and pulling out a new coffee cup.

A tousled Jesse came walking into the kitchen, scratching her ribs under her bathrobe. "I could have sworn I heard you talking to somebody, Papa."

"You did, her name is Eva Montoya. She believes her father has been killed, and she drove from Austin here for hel…" Eva walked into the kitchen and stopped short. "Eva, this is my granddaughter, Jesse. As I was saying, Eva has come to me for help, and I'm sure can use some female companionship right now. Eva, Jesse is also law enforcement, so you are safe with us. Did you bring any luggage?"

Eva tentatively stuck out her hand. "Jesse? No, *Señor*, I brought nothing but my purse and backpack. I did not even go back to my apartment. When I got the message from *mi papá* I knew I had to leave right then. They will be looking for me."

Jesse handed Eva her cup of coffee, asking, "Would you like a shower and some clean clothes? I think you and Felicia are about the same size."

Eva slumped in a chair. "Yes, if you would be so kind. I can pay…"

The old man said, "They will be looking for you?"

"*Sí, mi papá* knew that regardless of how much he did to shield me, there would be those in the cartel that knew who I was, and more importantly, where I was. That is why… Why we…" She broke down in tears again, and Jesse wrapped her in a hug, but Eva defiantly lifted her head and continued through the tears, "We had a code on the phone. If I ever got it, I was to drop everything and run. Every three months or so, I would get a box of blank CDs in the mail, from Amazon. I was to pull the CD that corresponded to the month from the pack, and set it aside. That CD would be from *mi papá*, and I was to destroy the previous one."

She sipped her coffee, staring off into space, and Jesse finally said, "Let's get you cleaned up. I have a robe you can use, and I will get soap and shampoo. By the time you get out, I will have some clothes for you, if that is okay."

Eva nodded. "Thank you." She got up slowly, and Jesse led her down the hall, with a meaningful glance at the old man.

The old man headed for his office, pulled the current burner phone he used with Montoya out of the desk, and dialed Montoya's number as he booted the computer. After six rings, there wasn't any answer, nor did voicemail kick in like it normally did. Now the old man was truly worried, and waited impatiently as the computer finished booting. Sticking the CD in the reader, he quickly did a security scan on it, and it came up clean. When he went to open the directory, it requested a security code, *Damn… I have no idea… Is this disc even meant for me? What could it possibly be?*

The old man went back to the kitchen for more coffee, and found Jesse and Felicia in the midst of laying out various clothes for the young lady. Jesse turned to him. "Papa, what is going on?"

Distracted, he said, "Let me tell you later. This has some potentially major ramifications, and I may need to act quickly." Jesse started to say something, but the old man's expression caused her to nod, and he got another cup of coffee, then headed back to the office.

After trying various combinations, he sat back, thinking, *What is something that only he and I would know? There has to be… Maybe the meeting?* Typing in the month, day, and year Montoya came to the ranch, he hit enter, and was disappointed to see yet another error. Then he tried spelling out the month, another error. *Dammit… Mexicans do it backward!* He put in the day, then the month, and the year, only to get one more error. Shit. Now what… He cracked his knuckles, and typed in the day, spelled out the month, and put in the year.

He was rewarded with a directory popping open, and he saw a text file labeled Sheriff. He hesitated for a couple of seconds, then clicked to open it. When it did, and he read the first couple of lines, his shoulders slumped.

> *Señor, if you are reading this, I am dead. There has been increasing unrest between the rival cartels, as you know. There has also been an increasing level of challenges from inside this one, with the more militant wanting more control. What you will find on this disk is the total of my knowledge of our group, the financials, where the accounts are located, and a complete list of members, informers, and politicians and military that we control. Also, there is all the information I have from those inside the other cartels, and links, as best I know them. This data may be up to a month old, depending on when you receive it. Do with it as you will. The person that delivers this to you has no idea what is contained on it. Vaya con Dios.*

The old man scrubbed his face, closed that file, and opened one of the spreadsheets at random. Paging through it, he shook his head. *If this is anywhere close to accurate, this is over a half billion dollars… Damn!*

Opening another file, he saw pictures and names, with what was effectively an organization chart, almost twenty pages long. Another file was LFM, another was *Sinaloa*, and they went on and on, listing all the competing cartels in Mexico, and suppliers in Guatemala and Colombia. A mix of Intel and much sketchier organization charts, he was amazed at the amount of data this presented. There were even files on US companies, apparently fronts for the cartels, and they stretched from west to east, and as far north as Chicago.

Jesse came into the office. "I put her to bed in the guest room. Jace and Kaya are at Felicia's house, and Aaron wants to know what's going on."

The old man leaned back. "First thing is to get her car moved. Stick it between the barn and the old house. She's… Well her dad was one of my CIs down in Mexico. Tell Aaron to tell the sheriff I'm working something."

Glancing at the screen, Jesse asked, "Okay, intel?"

"A-1, this is, well, the keys to the kingdom, so to speak. I've got to make some calls. Everybody goes armed."

"Papa?"

The old man sighed. "Her dad was the head of *Los Zetas.*" Pointing at the screen he continued, "Everything is here. All of their organization, their financials, their contacts, *everything*! And a bunch of intel on the other cartels."

Jesse whistled softly. "Damn! What are you going to do?"

"That's what I'm trying to figure out."

Jesse turned, tossing one more statement over her shoulder as she hurried away. "I'll go move the car, and I'll let Felicia and Matt know."

***

Two hours later, Eva knocked on the office door. "*Señor?*"

The old man spun his chair around, "*Si.*"

"I… I need to go to Florida. I need to get away."

"Why Florida, Eva?"

She leaned back and looked down the hall, then said quietly. "I have a place to go. In Florida."

The old man cocked his head, "How do you know it's safe? And how do you plan to get there?"

Eva bit her lip, "I… It's safe. Nobody knows about it."

The old man shook his head, saying gently, "Eva, unless… Unless you have a separate identity, and money, it's impossible to pull something like that off."

"It *is* safe. It's… I have another identity. It's real. And I have money. I can pay."

"I don't want money. But I also don't want you hurt or hunted down. If you need to go to Florida, we can make that happen. I'd like to get some professionals involved, if you really want to disappear. And I'd like to get somebody, a female, here who can help protect you till we can get you to Florida. What do you want to do with the car?"

She shrugged. "I don't care. It's not registered to me, nobody knew about it. If it disappears, nobody will care. It's paid for, and… I don't care. Who would you… use, to help me?"

The old man thought for a second. "I have two trusted, no three trusted friends that will help you without asking details. One of them needs to see this data. Or at least I need to pass it off to him. He would be one of the guards, and one of his people, a female would be another."

Eva yawned. "I'm sorry. I'm so tired. If you trust them, I have no choice but to do the same."

The old man looked up at her. "Eva, will you tell me where in Florida you need to go?"

She chewed her lip again, then said softly, "Miami."

"Thank you. Let me make some calls. If you'd like, feel free to go back to bed."

***

Later, the old man sighed in disgust, closing the news feed he'd opened. He was convinced after seeing the coverage from Cozumel that Montoya was in fact dead. The accidental fire that consumed the entire building had supposedly started on the second floor, and from the remains shown, looked like it had probably centered on Montoya's office. *I wonder if it was a thermite grenade? Those seem to be getting popular with the cartels lately, or was it a Molotov cocktail? Who knows, but I don't see how he could have survived more than a few seconds to a minute in that inferno. I wonder if he knew it was coming and sent that text to Eva just before…*

Reaching for the land line, he dialed Billy's office. After a quick chat with the receptionist, he got Billy on the line. "Billy, I need your airplane if it's available."

"What's going on, John?"

"I need it to pick a couple of folks up in Laredo and come here, then go to a different location."

"When?"

"Today, well, later today. Got some A-1 stuff I need Bucky to look at. And I need to move a package."

The old man heard typing on the other end of the phone, and rustling papers. "Okay, the bird will be there. Should be in Laredo by one. You talk to Bucky yet?"

"He's next."

"Looking at the timing, depending on where you're going, it's going to take a RON for the crew. You got a problem with that?"

"Nope, I'll cover their costs."

"A-1, huh?"

"Keys to the kingdom, A-1." He heard a whistle, then a click on the other end, and a dial tone as Billy hung up. He flipped open his wheel book and found Bucky's office number, and dialed it. Bucky was in a meeting, so he left a message, hoping to get a call back quickly. Since Eva was not around, he pulled two new CDs out and burned copies of what she'd given him, and slipped them in his briefcase. Realizing he still hadn't had breakfast, he shut the computer down and wandered into the kitchen. Feeding the dogs, he took out bacon and eggs and a half dozen left over biscuits and started cooking. Jesse had gone down to open up the store, Aaron was at work, and he wondered, *Is this what retirement is going to be like? Get up, be lazy, have nothing to do?* He laughed to himself. *It's a ranch: there is always something to do.*

Eva came into the kitchen and he gave her a plate of bacon and eggs and a couple of biscuits, which she ate in silence. She finally looked up. "Thank you *Señor*, more than you know."

The old man wondered what must be going through her head. He knew from talking to Montoya that she was probably in her early twenties, and was probably a stunning young lady in better circumstances. Right now, she looked like a haunted waif. "There will be an airplane here this afternoon. We will fly to Miami tonight, as you wanted. Are you sure you don't need any help on that end?"

She shook her head. "No, thank you. I will be fine."

Felicia knocked and came in the back door, kids in tow. "I'm going to put them down for their naps. It's easier here, if you don't mind. Eva, would you like some help with your hair?"

The two of them devolved into a back and forth, in Spanish too fast for the old man to follow, and Eva picked up Kaya, cooing to her as they walked down the hall. The old man shook his head. *Women. Hot and cold, at the flip of a switch.*

***

Bucky leaned back and sipped his coffee. "John, you know this… This is explosive. On both sides of the border. We'll need to bring the FBI in on this."

"I think I know who to call. You want me to make that call now?"

"The sooner the better. It's going to have to be coordinated." Bucky looked around. "Where did Spears go?"

"Jesse took her and Eva down to the shop. I think she's going to give Eva a pistol, she just kinda had that look. Lemme go make a call."

Billy looked up from his computer, smiling. "Yep, this is big. There is stuff in here that ties into a good bit of the BS going on in Houston right now, too."

The old man stretched and walked down to the office, dug through the cards in the drawer, and found

Devreau's card. He picked up the landline, and dialed the cell number listed. Devreau answered grumpily, "Devreau, what you got?"

"This is your Texas guy. I've got a disc you need to get. A-1 and supportable data. Perishable."

"You can't send it?"

"Nope. Can you meet us in Miami later this evening?"

"Us?"

"My lawyer and Bucky and possibly the daughter of the source of this information."

"No problem. You have a place you prefer?"

"Uh, not sure. We're flying in by way of my lawyer's Lear. I'll call you with the tail number. And Devreau?"

"Yeah?"

"They may be hunting for our passenger even as I speak. I have no idea how deep their sources and abilities go but I do know she's scared."

The line was silent for a moment and then Devreau came back on. "Tell your pilot Opa Locka, Signature Aviation. I'm going to arrange to have a discreet transponder squawk issued. That way your flight will not show up or be tracked on Flight Aware. As an added safety margin, I'll also have the Air Force assign you a military training route- you'll have your own private airway from Texas to south Florida. That's about as secure as I can make it for you."

In spite of the seriousness of the conversation, the old man couldn't help but smile to himself. *Jesus, it's good to work with professionals.* "That makes me feel a whole lot better. I'll contact you when we're ready to file a flight plan."

"Works for me," the FBI inspector replied. "I'm clearing my desk for this so if you need anything else. . ."

"I'll call you," the old man assured him.

Florida

The Lear touched down at Opa Locka a few minutes after eight, taxiing through the darkness to the ramp in front of Signature Aviation. They were directed into a parking spot next to an unmarked C-20, and the lineman popped the door open, saying, "Folks are waiting for y'all in the conference room," before he disappeared back into the building.

Spears was the first one out the door, she did an unobtrusive sweep of the area, and waved for Eva to come down. The old man and Bucky followed closely behind her, and they formed a sort of protective guard around her as they headed toward the building. The old man looked back, and finally saw Billy start down the stairs, then jog across the tarmac to catch up to them, "Piss first, then meeting. I'd recommend Spears take Eva wherever she needs to go, and do that immediately. The Fibbies don't need to know who she is."

Spears nodded. "I can do that. Eva, while you're in the bathroom, I'll…"

Billy interrupted, "Car's already arranged. They'll loan you the airport car."

"Okay."

Ten minutes later, Eva hugged the old man, and said, "Thank you for everything, Señor. Don't worry about me, I will be fine. *Muchisimas gracias.*"

The old man hugged her back, "*Vaya con Dios*, little one. Know that your dad did not die in vain."

Eva stepped back, wiping a tear as she nodded and turned to Spears, and they left by the side door. Billy said, "Lotta guts in that one, somehow I do believe she will make it. Let's go see what the Fibbies want to do, shall we?"

The old man nodded and said, sotto voice, "Interesting that nobody came out to meet us, nor are there any employees in here."

Bucky chuckled. "All tradecraft John, you should remember that. If you didn't see anything, or hear anything, you can't be called to account for it."

Billy shrugged and headed for the door marked conference room. "Let's get this over with. I told the pilots to be ready to go at zero five hundred in the morning, and I want to put my tired old ass in bed for at least a few hours." Pushing the door open, he was surprised to only see Devreau sitting at the table. "You it?" Billy asked.

"What, you expected me to bring a crowd for something like this?" Glancing at Bucky as he got up, he said, "You must be Grant, DEA, right?"

Bucky nodded. "That's me. Heard of you, but this is the first time I've seen you." Bucky shook hands with Devreau and sat, taking his laptop out of his backpack.

The old man nodded to Devreau and sat quietly across the table from him. Billy took the head of the table and opened his briefcase, taking out a laptop and two CDs. He slid one across to Devreau, who simply looked at it for a moment before asking, "This it? How many people have seen it, and how many copies are there?"

Billy looked at the old man, who said, "That I'm aware of, three total. Billy has one here, Bucky has one, and now you have one. Nobody has looked at this on any connected system, just stand alone laptops, and my old computer at the house, but I disconnected it from the 'net before I loaded it."

"What makes you think this is anything approaching real?"

"Two things. This is about three, maybe four weeks old, and the man who provided it is dead."

"So?"

"Does the name Carlos Montoya ring a bell?"

Devreau reeled back in his chair, "Holy shit, you're telling me that the fucking head of *Los Zetas* was your CI? *Jesus Christ!*"

The old man got up, reached across the table and grabbed the CD. "I knew this was going to be a waste of time. Let's go Billy."

Bucky held up his hands. "Devreau, check it out. I've looked at the CD, and it's real, as far as I can tell. It matches stuff we had from as deep cover as our CIs could get. We even cross-checked it against old and original information from our NADDIS[6] files going back over two decades. This stuff is five-star."

Devreau shook his head. "Sorry Cronin, I'm not doubting you—I'm just in fucking shock. *Complete* fucking shock. Everybody and their brother's brother has tried to infiltrate the cartels. Now I'm sitting here

---

[6] Narcotics and Dangerous Drugs Information System

in Miami with you and the DEA, listening to you tell me that not only did you have the head *hombre* of Mexico's most notorious cartel in your CI stable, but that you also have the complete goods on their operation here on a CD. " The FBI inspector paused, looked around the room with a momentary thousand-yard stare, then turned his attention back to Cronin. With a slight shrug of his shoulders and complete deference to the old man, Devreau looked at him and asked, "How?"

The old man continued to hold the CD, bouncing it on his palm. "I got his attention. Let's just leave it at that," he replied with a poker face that would've done Amarillo Slim proud.

Devreau relaxed a bit and gave a small crooked smile. "Fair enough, Cronin. And again, wasn't doubting you—well maybe a little, but . . . it's just… Damn…"

The old man handed him the CD, saying, "I'm going to go find a cup of coffee."

Devreau took it and put it in the computer, mumbling, "Montoya? Damn…" He glanced at Billy as the CD booted. "Password?"

Billy chuckled. "Yes, it really was Montoya. And yes, John really did get his attention, twice. The password is, twenty-five April, spelled out, twenty-sixteen."

Devreau typed it in, and opened the first of the files, then scrubbed his face as he looked at it again, then at Bucky. "Financials? All of *Los Zetas'* financials? What else is in here that you can verify?"

Bucky replied, "Open the file named ancillary, that's all the companies they own or control in the US. I can vouch for at least half of those being on watch lists, and a couple under close surveillance."

***

Spears asked, "Are you sure you can get us there?"

Eva replied, "*Sí*, we need one hundred thirty-fifth street to I-95 South, to exit three A. From there it is, how you say, surface streets? Maybe twenty minutes."

"Does somebody know you're coming?"

Eva shook her head. "No, but that's okay. I will be fine…"

Spears glanced over, "Are you sure?"

"*Sí*, I am sure. I am, how you say, good with this identity."

"Nothing that connects the two?"

"No, I will destroy everything that connects. I threw the cell phone out before I left Houston, and I haven't used any of the credit or check cards. I will destroy them and my driver's license tonight. Oh, the car…"

Spears laughed. "We will make the car disappear, you don't have to worry about that."

"Oh, good. And the short hair is a different look for me, all people have ever seen is the long hair. But I will get it styled later, and keep it short."

"Who did your hair?"

"Jesse and… Felicia, they cut it for me, and Felicia gave me clothes that make me look older." They rode in silence for the next fifteen minutes, as Eva fiddled with things in her backpack. Spears glanced down as

Eva laid an ID on the center console, and saw it was a Florida driver's license.

She got most of the name and address before Eva picked it up, and put it in her clutch that she was repacking. Eva looked up and said, "This exit." Another ten minutes of weaving back and forth on surface streets, and Eva had her stop just down the street from a multistory building. Eva reached over and gave Spears a quick hug. "Thank you for everything. *Muchisimas gracias*." She hopped out of the car quickly, and walked toward the entrance of the building, then disappeared inside.

Spears killed the lights and pulled out, driving slowly past the entrance, and saw Eva at the Concierge desk, then being waved toward the elevators. Looking at the façade, Spears saw the name Terrazas Miami. As she turned around and weaved her way back out of the dead end, she repeated to herself, *Rosa Evita Sanchez y Ortega, Terrazas; Rosa Evita Sanchez y Ortega, Terrazas, Rosa Evita Sanchez y Ortega, Terrazas,* until it was committed to memory.

Finally getting back to I-95, she turned back north, and started to call Bucky, but thought better of it. Why let anyone know where they were? They'd pretty much come in covert, if what she'd overheard was correct. No rental car, no tracks, per se. She smiled, and thought, *Girl, I hope you survive. And I truly hope I never see you again. Go with God is right, you're going to need God on your side.*

Spears finally made it back to Opa Locka, and returned the car to the young man at the desk. "Thanks, I appreciate the use of the car, and I probably owe you something for gas. I put it back at the end of the second row in the parking lot."

"Don't worry about it, it's part of the service. And thanks for telling me where it is," he said with a smile.

Hooking her thumb toward the conference room, she asked, "They still in there?"

"Yep, other than bathroom breaks and coffee out of the break room, they've not come out."

Spears nodded. "Well, I guess I better go beard the lions."

The young man laughed as Spears walked over, opened the door, and disappeared inside.

***

The old man glanced up from his coffee as Spears came through the door. "All done?"

Spears nodded and sat down next to the old man, watching Bucky and Devreau going back and forth in low voices over one of the files. They sat quietly, the old man sipping coffee occasionally, as he watched the two go back and forth. Spears was amazed at how quiet he was, sitting at the end of the table, not saying a word. A couple of times, she thought he might be asleep, but he was just watching Bucky and Devreau.

By eleven, they had pretty much divided up the information on the CDs, with each deciding what their respective agencies could use to impact the drug trade and the cartels. Billy had been uncharacteristically quiet, sitting at the table and writing on his ever present yellow pad the whole time.

Spears had gotten up from time to time, wandering around the FBO, and marveling at how the 'other half' lived. *Yep, they truly do live a different life than we do.*

Hell, this furniture is better than anything I've got in my house, and their loaner car is nicer than mine! I wonder… No, don't go there! She was standing in the lobby when the rest of them came out, and watched as Devreau shook hands with everyone.

Billy led the way toward the van as they heard a jet spool up on the ramp. Devreau walked toward it, and climbed aboard without looking back. The driver drove them silently to the hotel, and he and Billy had a short conversation as they unloaded everyone's bag. Billy turned and said, "Okay, van will be back at four in the morning. Be here or you're going to get left."

Billy checked everyone in, handed out keys, and they headed to the elevators *en masse*. Billy and Bucky were on a different floor, and got off first, with Billy being the smartass he always was, leaving a parting shot. "Now y'all stay out of trouble. But if you do get in trouble, don't call me. I need my beauty sleep."

The old man rolled his eyes, and said, "Yeah, right. Beauty sleep," as the doors closed. He asked, "Did you get Eva dropped off okay?"

"Yes, sir. I took her down to some high rise called Terrazas Miami." She stopped for a second, then said, "I saw what I think her other identity is… It's… Rosa Evita Sanchez y Ortega."

The old man cocked his head. "Why tell me?"

Spears shrugged, "Because you really do seem to care about her getting away safely. Don't worry, I'm not telling Bucky or anybody in my chain, 'cause I know they would try to use her, until they got her killed."

"Thank you." The doors opened, and they got off the elevator, walked down the hall and found they were in rooms across from each other. He turned as he said, "Good night, Michelle, and thanks, you're doing the right thing." *Little Havana. That makes sense, and explains what was wrong with her accent, it's Cuban, not Mexican. Interesting…*

She nodded, "Good night, Captain."

***

Inspector Devreau rolled the plastic tube of Tylenol on the airplane desk, back and forth as his mind processed the depth of the information he'd just preliminarily scanned. Having started his career in the Bureau working kidnappings, his success landed him in the counterterrorism division where his legend grew both rapidly and exponentially. Part of his success was his uncanny instincts. But another part of his success was that he played by the book and never broke the very laws he swore to uphold. Bending them, on occasion, was one thing—but breaking them was not an option.

But now. What he had in front of him. Son of a bitch! He whistled softly. This was an opportunity that not just the FBI, but the entire Justice Department had been fantasizing over for years. And here it was… laid out for them on a literal silver platter, in this case, a silver compact disc packed with heretofore never known information on the largest, deadliest, most bloodthirsty drug cartels Mexico had ever produced.

He owed Cronin for passing him the information, but he also sensed that Cronin would like to close this chapter in his life. And Devreau knew exactly how

Cronin would wish to do it. But he, Inspector Jake Devreau, could not be a part of it.

At least not a direct part of it, he smiled as he thumbed a number from memory into his phone. When the voice on the other end answered, he said, "Good evening, Ram."

***

The old man sat quietly in the lobby, a cup of coffee in hand, wondering if he'd done the right thing. *I hope the girl makes it, but I'm not sure giving the CD to both Bucky and Devreau was a good idea. Maybe… Ah screw it, I'm too old to do anything with this stuff, and a month from now I'll be retired and it'll be somebody else's problem.* He glanced at his watch, and wondered where everybody else was, when the elevator dinged, and the pilots came out, "Morning, gents. It looks like y'all at least got a good night's sleep!"

Ted smiled. "For versions of sleep, I did. Of course I had nightmares, since Chuck has the landing in…"

Chuck and the old man laughed, as the elevator dinged again, disgorging Billy, Bucky, and Spears, with a grumpy Billy in the lead. Billy stomped over. "Dammit, I need coffee. Damn machine in the room wouldn't work for shit. Keys?"

Everybody handed over their keys and Billy dropped his bag, then stomped over to the registration desk, where a quiet one-way conversation took place, until the desk clerk disappeared through a door. The old man saw the van pull up and picked up his and Billy's bags and briefcase. "Well, I'm going to go hide in the van…"

A mumble of agreement followed as everyone headed for the door. They had the van loaded and were in with the door closed before Billy finally came out, a Styrofoam cup in hand. Billy was silent for the entire ride to the airport, as the pilots quietly discussed weather, and who was filing what.

Three and a half hours later, they touched down in Laredo and had to wake Bucky up to get off the airplane. He and Spears both mumbled good byes and stumbled down the steps toward the parking lot, as Billy pulled the door closed.

The old man got up and stretched, stuck his head in the cockpit, and asked, "Anybody need coffee?"

Chuck smiled, "Please, sir! Black is fine," handing him a cup as Ted shook his head.

The old man filled his cup out of the thermos, and handed it back into the cockpit, as Billy grabbed the thermos, pouring himself another cup and flopping back in his seat. The old man sat back down and asked, "Well, how do you think we did?"

Billy sipped his coffee, then replied, "I think Mr. Montoya will be well and truly avenged. Well and truly!"

They sat quietly until the Lear got to altitude and Billy pulled out one of his yellow pads, and the old man said, "Spears got a name and part of an address for Eva."

Billy looked at him. "Really? Did she… Who did she tell?"

"Just me. Said she wasn't going to put it in the system, she was afraid they'd get her killed."

"Probably. And?"

The old man thought, *Do I tell him? Why did I even mention it…? Ah hell, somebody besides me needs to know, just in case*, "Rosa Evita Sanchez y Ortega, Terrazas Miami, whatever that is. Maybe a complex? I don't know. I think its Little Havana or close."

Billy scribbled the name and location on a fresh sheet of paper. "I'll see what I can get."

The old man turned. "Billy, I don't want that girl hurt."

Billy held up his hands. "Not going to do that. I have folks that I can check with on the last name. Trust me, I'm not going to get her in trouble."

Good News, Bad News

The old man looked up from the pile of paperwork he and Aaron were shuffling through as Yogi woofed, and saw Ranger Michaels standing in the door, hand up to knock. "Come on in, Levi. What brings you over this way?"

Levi sat down and ruffled Yogi's fur, as he took off his hat. "Well, I've got good news and bad news."

Aaron glanced at the old man and asked, "And this affects us how?"

Michaels grimaced. "That's a good question. Remember Harris, the biker you ID'ed for us?"

"Yeah, why?"

"Well, he committed suicide."

The old man's head snapped up. "What? How in the hell…"

Michaels held up a hand, "Murphy got in the middle of this one, right from the git-go. El Paso ran a few officers by there, but never saw any activity, and we didn't have anybody available to get over there for a couple of days."

"So?"

Michaels hung his head. "A young rook with EPP drove through the neighborhood about twenty-two hundred night before last. And saw the garage door open, and a man working on a bike."

The old man rocked back in his chair. "Oh hell, he didn't?"

Aaron asked, "Didn't what?"

Michaels sighed, "Yeah, he did. He stopped, got out and walked up on the guy. Didn't have his earpiece in, and when the shift sergeant told him to GTFO, Harris heard the radio traffic, jumped up and the rook started to try to stop him, but the bike was in the way. He got to his workbench, picked up a 1911 that was lying under a jacket, and capped himself. Rook said his last words were, "I ain't goin' in a cage.""

"Shit!"

Aaron replied, "I remember him saying that during the assist, I'm guessing pretty bad case of PTSD, probably untreated. He was Army, and I think he'd been in an IED attack…"

Leaning forward, Michaels continued, "So Harris goes down, and the rook starts looking around, not thinking to see if there is anybody else home. Wife comes out with baby, sees hubby dead on the floor of the garage, and she melts down. Rook now has his hands full, and forgets radio procedure, just says shots fired, and nothing else."

The old man shook his head. "So it went rodeo from there?"

Michaels nodded. "Pretty much. But we got a Ranger there within an hour, and there was a kilo of meth, and one of cocaine in the saddlebags. Also did prints on the tire, and got oil samples, and they match the cast and sample taken at the TPO rig. We're still waiting on the forensics from the pistol, but I'm betting it will match, since it was loaded with two hundred grain hollow points, same as what killed Deen."

Aaron asked, "Any follow-up with Trans-Pecos?"

"Yes, and that's where it gets interesting. Turns out he was an employee at their yard in El Paso up until about a year ago, when the patch lost a bunch of workers. He was a welder, and apparently had been a hot shot guy they sent on the road to do welding repairs in the field."

The old man grunted, "So he would have had access to the gate codes. But that still doesn't explain why he shot Deen."

Aaron said, "With PTSD, there is no telling, and now we'll never know. It could have been as simple as a flashback, or…"

Michaels interrupted, "Deen was known to be hard core against booze or drugs, and you said Harris had mentioned a job, I'm wondering if he thought Deen would rat him out to management about drugs or whether the two just didn't get along. We posed that to Owens, the district guy, and he vaguely remembered him, mainly as a good worker in the shop. HR said they laid him off due to lack of work, and his lack of seniority with the company."

"So where does that leave us?"

"Waiting on the bullet match, I guess."

Aaron shook his head, "I wonder why?"

Michaels said, "Well, it appears Harris couldn't get a job, and was using drugs to handle his issues, and it ballooned from there. Wife says she didn't know he was dealing, she thought he was getting hot shot jobs, because he was seldom gone more than a day, and he always took his gear and helmet. Apparently, he was picking up drugs and delivery schedule from somebody somewhere else. She says he didn't have any close friends, other than one guy he served with in Iraq that was apparently in treatment with him at Ft. Bliss."

The old man rolled his shoulders as he got up. "Another one that goes in the maybe file. Those are the ones that are going to haunt me…"

Aaron asked, "Maybe file?"

"Cold cases… Got about twenty of them. Never been able to solve them. They're in the bottom drawer." The old man rubbed his arms as if he was suddenly cold. "I look at them occasionally, still trying to sort 'em out."

Michaels nodded sympathetically. "Clay handed me about fifty, and that was after he'd made copies. I only had, really, two… And both of those got turned over to the Rangers, so I guess I've got two still."

Aaron glanced between the two of them, hesitated and finally asked, "What do you do with them, when you, review them?

The old man walked over to the file cabinet, opened the bottom drawer and pulled out a file. He came back to the desk and dropped it in front of Aaron. "Read through the case notes, trying to find anything I might have missed. Checking old wires against updated UCR[7]s to see if any similar MO pops up. This one," he said, pointing to the file in front of Aaron, "this one has haunted me from day one."

---

[7] Unified Crime Report

Aaron flipped open the file and recoiled from the picture on top. "Damn, what the hell did that?"

Michaels looked over his shoulder and whistled. "Nasty…"

The old man closed his eyes, "'Coyotes and at least one mountain lion, but that was after somebody set her on fire with gasoline. Doc Marshall guessed she'd been dead a week when she was found. To this day, she's never been identified. One little scrap of cloth was found under the body, and he thought she had a white ruffled skirt on. All of her teeth were gone, jaw broken, he thought one arm had been broken, but there wasn't enough to ID her. Spread the word, posters, newspapers, put it on the wire, nothing… We'd gotten a good rain earlier that week, so no vehicle tracks, footprints, fingerprints, just 'yotes and that lion."

Aaron shuddered. "I thought I saw some nasty shit in combat, but damn…"

Michaels nodded. "Gets nasty out here too, especially on the highways. I've got a few nightmares from calls, especially the ones where kids were involved."

The old man picked up the file, dropped it back in the file cabinet and turned. "Okay, enough of this. We'll wait to see what ballistics comes back with, and move on."

"Speaking of moving on, I need to get back on the road. I'm heading up to Austin, another round of training on investigative procedures," Michaels said, as he put his hat back on, and stood.

"Have fun with that. Maybe I oughta send Aaron with you."

Aaron looked at the old man. "Wha… Austin? I thought you wanted me to take that TCOLE class."

"You have to have that one, it just doesn't teach you much. The Rangers teach a much better one, but it's not certified," the old man said with a laugh.

"Now this is starting to sound like the Corps…"

Michaels laughed. "It's all government, which puts the fun in dysfunctional. Always remember that, and you'll get along fine."

"In other words, Semper Gumby, right?"

***

Jesse picked up the coffee pot. "Anybody want more?"

Matt, Aaron, and the old man nodded, but Felicia shook her head. "No *más*. I never drank much coffee, maybe a cup or two in the morning. Living here, I drink way too much!"

Everyone laughed, as Jesse poured coffee, then sat back down. The kids were playing quietly in the living room, as Felicia handed out the pieces of pecan pie. Patting her stomach, she said, "And I eat too much too."

Matt rolled his eyes. "Not going there. Nope."

When everyone had finished their pie, the old man said, "Got a couple of things."

Felicia asked, "Do you want me to stay?"

"Nothing you can't hear. First, Matt and Jesse, Ranger Michaels dropped by today, and we have a possible closure on the Deen case."

Matt leaned forward. "They caught somebody?"

"Not in so many words. The possible suspect Aaron put us on to… Well, El Paso PD screwed it up, and he committed suicide. But everything leans toward him being the perp. Just waiting on the ballistics from the 1911 he carried to sort it out."

Matt sighed. "Dammit. Well, he's getting his justice, just in a different fashion."

The old man nodded. "And he left a wife and a baby."

Jesse said, "Ouch, that's not good. Not at all. How old?"

"Not sure." Glancing at Aaron, he asked, "Do you know?"

Aaron shook his head. "No, and I don't remember Levi mentioning it, either. If I remember right, he was late twenties, early thirties, so the wife is probably similar. But I just don't know."

The old man said, "The other news is good."

Everybody looked at him, and he smiled. "Aaron has been officially approved by the sheriff to be the next investigator for the sheriff's office. It will be officially announced tomorrow."

Jesse jumped up and hugged Aaron. "So proud of you." Kissing him loudly, she rounded on the old man. "So now things are going to be even screwier around here. He's going to be just like you are Papa, working all kinds of hours, isn't he?"

Aaron interjected, "You're proud of me and now you're complaining?"

Matt looked at Felicia. "I think this is our cue to leave. By the way, congrats Aaron."

Matt picked up the dishes and headed for the sink, as Felicia went to pick up Esme and Matt Junior. The old man sat very quietly, realizing his announcement could have come at a better time, and knowing Jesse would get over it. Eventually. He got up, put his dishes in the sink, and decided the better part of valor was to get out of range, so he headed for the porch with his coffee cup.

Ten minutes later, Aaron came out, shaking his head. "I don't get it, she's happy I got a promotion, but she's pissed that I got the investigator job."

The old man chuckled. "It's because she grew up watching me have to go out at all hours, and work a lot of weekends. It was one thing when you were active duty, she could accept that, since everybody else was doing it."

Aaron mumbled something, and the old man continued, "She's worried about you getting enough rest. This job does suck, because you're always on call. It's not like we have a bunch of investigators and take turns. She also wants to have you home, and be able to plan things. I think she's probably more pissed about that, than anything else."

"Lovely, just lovely. Damned if I do, damned if I don't."

The old man whistled for Yogi, and got up slowly. "Yep, welcome to my world."

"How did you handle it with…? Well, with your wife?"

"I gave her a choice: I continued to work, or I quit and would be underfoot every day."

Aaron grinned, "Somehow I don't think I can get away with that, but what did your wife say?"

The old man laughed. "If I remember right, it was something like, don't let the door hit you in the ass when you leave for work in the morning."

Aaron shook his head. "I'd be afraid to give Jesse that option."

"Remember, the sheriff will work with you. He'll give you time off if you give him enough of a heads up. And I'm pretty sure Levi will come in and back you up if needed. It's a team effort, and even though I'm retiring, I'll still be around to answer questions."

"I'll definitely take you up on that. Thank you!"

The old man whistled for Yogi. "Now go face the dragon in her den."

Aaron chuckled. "The couch might be safer!"

***

Aaron got quietly in bed, wondering if it was safe. He heard Jesse huff, and started to say something, when she pounced on him. "Hush. I'm proud of you, and I shouldn't have gone off like that."

Aaron put his arms around her, hugging her tightly. "Thank you. I was worried I was in trouble…"

Jesse replied, "Oh you are," and giggled as she kissed him. Things got interesting from there, and when they finally came up for air, Jesse said, "I love you Aaron Miller. For better or worse, remember?"

Aaron kissed her lightly. "Yes, I do remember that, and I'm going to hold you to that, the next oh three hundred call out I get."

"You bastard…"

Aaron kissed her again, and they made slow love until they were both sated and dropped into a deep sleep.

Jesse woke up when Kaya cried, and looked at Aaron, sprawled on the bed. "Don't you dare do something stupid and get killed. Not here, not now. I couldn't bear that," she said softly as she got up to feed Kaya.

One More Time

The old man was sitting at the desk, paying bills, when the FBI burner phone rang. After the third ring, he hit the speaker button. "Hello?"

"John Cronin?"

"Speaking."

"Jake Devreau, can you get a couple of days off?"

"When?"

"Next couple of days, maybe through Monday."

"Shouldn't be a problem, why?"

"Remember what you passed me?"

"Yes."

"Something that has come out of that."

"Okay, when and where…"

Devreau interrupted, "A white King Air will be at your airport at twenty-hundred tomorrow night. Pack for three days."

"What do I need to bring?"

"Yourself and a bag, everything else will be taken care of."

"Oka…" The old man realized he was talking to a dial-tone. Shaking his head, he hung up, and went back to paying bills. *He's a short bastard, but it's a non-secure line. Makes sense. Do I really want to do this?*

Jesse came in. "Did a phone just ring?"

"Yep, that was the FBI. Something has come up with the data I turned over to them, and they want me to work with them a couple of days."

Jesse cocked her head. "When?"

"They're picking me up tomorrow night."

"What are you going to be doing, Papa?"

The old man shrugged. "Not sure, probably looking at files, or mugshots. Probably trying to ID people from other source data. I should be back Monday."

"Is Uncle Billy involved?"

The old man shook his head. "I don't think so. I think this is LEO only stuff."

Jesse visibly relaxed, "Good!"

Finishing the bills, he leaned back in the chair. *What am I doing? Do I really want to shoot more guys? Did Montoya mean that much…? I guess, in a way, he became a friend. He helped us stop the MANPADS and the terrorist smuggling last year. And he trusted me enough to send his daughter to me, and trusted me with the data on the CD. Fuck it… Why not? I'm an old man, I'm not going to live forever.*

***

The old man knocked on the sheriff's door. "Got a minute, Jose?"

"Sure, what's up?"

"I'm going to be out of pocket this weekend. Should be back Monday, but might need an extra day. FBI stuff."

The sheriff waved a hand. "Take what you need. You've pretty much turned everything over to Aaron, right?"

"Yes, and I've already given him a heads up on this."

"Good enough. Now go away, unless you want to help me with this damn budget request."

The old man held up both hands. "Oh hell no! I thought you were going to bring Jesse in to work on that."

"I did, and she did. But now I'm trying to figure out how to explain this to the county commissioners."

"I thought Jesse explained it to you."

The sheriff hunched his shoulders. "She did, and I wrote notes, but now I can't figure out what the notes mean."

The old man chuckled. "Call her butt back in. Have her put a brief together for you, with notes!"

"John…"

"Going, going." The old man shook his head as he walked back down the hall to his office. "Aaron, I'm going to take Yogi out, be back in a minute."

Aaron looked up from the computer. "Okay. Not like I'm going anywhere. When you get back I've got some questions."

The old man took Yogi to his favorite tree, then let him run for a couple of minutes, before he took him back in. Yogi flopped on his mat, as the old man picked up his coffee cup. "Coffee?"

Aaron nodded. "Please."

Two hours later, Aaron finally leaned back. "Okay, I get the gist of the systems, and I can log in, but how often should I do that?"

The old man rolled his shoulders. "Normally you'll get an alert email, if there is something directly for the office, or a query that goes region or statewide. I always checked a least every couple of days. For El Paso and the other stuff, I checked that at least once a week. Task forces, they normally overload you with emails multiple times a day." The old man stretched. "Let's go get lunch."

Aaron smiled, "Sounds good!"

The old man drove and parked in front of Miguel's. Getting out, he said, "Inside or outside?"

Yogi headed for the outside table they normally sat at, as Aaron laughed, "I guess outside."

Miguel waved through the window, and the old man chuckled. "Well, it's in the mid-seventies, and not too windy, so why not."

Miguel brought chips and salsa, took their orders, and gave Yogi a dish of water, as they continued discussing the various systems and timing Aaron needed to be aware of. Lunch passed quickly, and forty-five minutes later, they were back in the office, and deep in the old man's file system as Aaron took notes on due dates, matching them with the administrivia that came with the reporting requirements to TCJS, the Feds, and other interested parties. Aaron finally said, "How the hell did you keep all that in your head?"

"Years of practice."

"Is any of this stuff written down anywhere?"

The old man laughed. "See those books up on the top shelf?"

Aaron looked up, and said quietly, "Aw, shit. Lemme guess. References, right?"

"Yep, all in there. Pull that inspection manual down, third one on the right."

Aaron reached up and got it, and the old man said, "See the tabs in it? They all relate to things we have to comply with."

Aaron mumbled something the old man didn't hear, as he put the manual back on the shelf.

***

A King Air touched down a little before 8pm, and the old man got out of the truck. "Thanks for the ride Aaron, I'll call you when I get back."

"Okay. You got everything?"

"Yep."

The old man walked slowly out toward the ramp, as one of the ramp rats walked out of the shack, a pair of lighted wands in hand. The ramp rat directed the King Air to a spot in front of the office, and the left engine spooled quickly down. As soon as the prop stopped, the door hinged open, and a large man, backlit by the interior lighting, motioned the old man forward.

He handed his bag up, then climbed in. As the door closed, he heard the left engine start spooling up. He finally got a good look at the man, and saw a large, muscular Hispanic, who stuck out a paw. "Ramon Alvarez, call me Ram."

Taking it, he replied, "John Cronin."

"Come have a seat, we will talk in the air."

As soon as the King Air was airborne, Ram handed a thick manila envelope to the old man. "This is where we are going and who we are to shoot when they arrive."

"What are we supposed to shoot them with?"

Ram shrugged. "I was only told that weapons would be provided. You are the shooter, I am your spotter and protection."

The old man shook his head. "Oh this should be fun. We've never shot with each other. You call mils or MOA?"

"MOA," Ram said with a grin. "I am an old man, I do not do that new stuff."

The old man chuckled. "You're a youngster, compared to me. I do MOA, that's all I've used for fifty years." Nodding to the cockpit, he continued, "They know where we're going?"

"I am not sure, but I think so. They are supposed to deliver us somewhere outside Phoenix, that is all I know."

The old man broke the seal on the manila envelope and slid the contents onto the little fold down table. Two keys slid out, one labeled 'Airstream' and one labeled 'Jeep', "Huh, guess we're in a camper and have a Jeep to drive, for what that's worth. You want to hang on to these?"

"Sure," Ram nodded while sweeping them off the table. He slid them into his shirt pocket, as the old man spread out the documents, a brochure, and pictures.

They looked through the various items, and Ram whistled in surprise as he picked up one of the sheets of paper, "*Madre de Dios*! This appears to be a meeting between all the largest cartels. It looks like they have taken over the entire ranch for the meeting on Sunday. But I wonder if they have moved all the employees somewhere else?"

The old man flipped through the brochure, then pulled one of the photos toward him. "Looks like all private cabins. Maybe one meeting area. Looks like the cabins back up against that ridgeline, and are spaced maybe a hundred feet apart. They've got a pool, too." He flipped the brochure around and pointed to the line of cabins, then the photo. "I don't think this is Google. And I'm not sure what they did with the employees. Maybe just kept the food service ones?"

Ram pulled out the topo map of the area, saying, "That is possible, and also maybe the mail service. These honchos are very particular about their stuff being clean and neat." Taking a closer look at the map, the Mexican remarked, "This is a very rugged area. Right now, it looks like the best place to shoot from is southeast of the ranch, off one of these peaks along this ridge." Pulling a ball point pen out of his shirt pocket, he said, "My guess is that this is maybe a thousand yard shot. And this looks like a six-hundred foot drop over that range." Studying the photo closer, he smiled. "No, I do not think Google gets that kind of expert resolution. But perhaps, *Señor*, we probably should not be asking that question."

The old man nodded. "Probably not." Pointing at the picture, he asked, "Is this a road? It looks like it takes off the main road about a mile or so before the ranch."

Ram looked, then compared it to the topo map. "*Sí,* Phon Sutton Road. It must go to a ranch somewhere down that road." Using his pen, he measured. "We would have to walk in, maybe a mile, maybe two, to get to a shooting position that would be to our advantage."

The old man looked at the photo again. "What about this… Road, or wash to the east of it?"

Ram peered at the photo, comparing it to the topo. "Uh, perhaps a wash. See, here, it feeds into Bulldog Canyon, up to the north."

"We might be able to get a Jeep in there. Concealment, and less of a walk."

Ram shrugged noncommittally, "Maybe. But it would make noise."

"I need to think on this." The old man handed the rest of the package to Ram and leaned back in his seat, steepling his hands under his chin. Ram flipped through the photos of the cartel leaders, flipping them over to read the bios taped to the back, then he too, leaned back in the seat.

An hour later, the copilot came over the PA. "Twenty minutes to landing."

Ram and the old man shuffled all the photos, maps, and assorted items back into the manila envelope, and the old man folded the little table up, then pulled his seatbelt tight. Fifteen minutes later, the airplane touched down with a thump, surprising them, as they saw no runway lights, or any lights, for that matter. The copilot came over the PA again. "Please stay in your seats, we're going to back taxi for a couple of minutes, then we'll let you off."

The old man glanced over to see Ram looking out his window, and the old man did the same, seeing an outline of what might be a runway, as the airplane turned around. Five minutes later, they heard one engine spool down, and the airplane braked to a stop, as the copilot pushed the curtain aside. He pushed a set of NVGs up on his forehead, saying, "We're here. We've stopped adjacent to some buildings and other stuff. This is where you guys get off. We'll be back here twenty hundred local Sunday night. If you're here, you get a ride home. We'll wait fifteen minutes only. Got that?"

Ram and the old man nodded, as the copilot dropped the door. "Careful of your heads. Make sure you've got everything." As soon as they cleared the door, it was retracted, and the airplane started rolling toward the landing end of the runway. The left engine restarted, as Ram and the old man walked carefully toward the buildings they could see in the moonlight. Moments later, with a roar, the King Air rushed by them, then climbed into the night sky.

The old man pulled his penlight out of his pocket and turned it on, lighting the crumbling asphalt path they were walking on, and glinting off an Airstream trailer sitting about thirty feet ahead of them. Almost automatically, they separated, each moving to the side of the path as they approached the trailer. The old man went down the back side, saw a dusty Jeep CJ-7 sitting there, and called, "Clear."

Ram had done the same thing on the other side, and said, "*Sí*, all clear here too." Fishing the Jeep key out of his shirt pocket, he slipped it in the ignition, clicked it to on, and watched the dash lights come on. "It looks like this is our ride." Taking the key out, he pocketed it, and turned toward the trailer. "Now if the trailer key works…"

Once inside, they closed the blinds as soon as they confirmed there was power to the trailer, and the old man took a good look at Ram in the light. "Guess you get the bed, and I'll take the couch. I don't think you'd fit on it!"

Ram bowed. "*Gracias, Señor.*"

The old man just shook his head, plopping the manila envelope on the dinette. As he looked around, he saw a two gun cases, and slid them over to the couch. "What have we here?"

Popping one case open revealed an MRAD in .338, and the other case held a Remington M-24 in .308. Ram glanced at them, and said, "Your choice, *Señor.*"

The old man pointed to the MRAD. "That one. You okay with the M-24?"

Ram smiled. "It is a very good rifle. Better than most I have used." He stepped over to the kitchenette area, and rifled through the cabinets, then turned. "Ah, a GPS. I think we should find out where we are. And it looks like we have our choice of MREs for dinner."

"Where we are would be good."

Ten minutes later, they stood outside the trailer by the Jeep, waiting for the GPS to get a good lock. The old man grumbled, "Damn things take forever."

Ram smiled, as it finally locked, and he flipped screens to get to the map. "We are… Close to highway sixty and highway seventy-nine. It says our altitude is eighteen hundred twenty feet. I wonder if there is a map in the Jeep?"

The old man shook his head, and walked around it, shining his light in various places, he finally opened the glove box, and said laughingly, "Lo and behold!

An actual Arizona map!" Spreading it on the hood, he found Phoenix, and traced highway 60 until it intersected with highway 79, tracing the roads, he found Saguaro Lake and said, "Looks like about an hour by road. Dunno about you, but I'm hungry, and tired."

Ram nodded, "I could eat too."

Thirty minutes later, with the MREs finished, the old man said, "I figure we get up early, find some place to sight in, and go scout the roads."

Ram smiled. "And then, we go kill bad guys, *Señor*!"

Site and Situation

The old man woke up and checked his watch: 0530. With a groan, he sat up, scratched the scar on his chest and got up slowly. He went in the rudimentary bathroom, took care of business and walked back to the kitchenette, running water in the coffee pot and starting it. He heard Ram Alvarez moving around, and said, "Coffee's on."

He got dressed in his usual gray Dickies, and pulled the MRAD out of its case. Quickly disassembling it, he ran a cleaning rag through the barrel, lubed it, and put it back together. Taking the suppressor out of the case, he attached it to the muzzle brake, knowing the rifle would kick more, but it would make the location of the shooter harder to pinpoint.

The coffee pot finished burping and spitting, and he pulled a plastic cup out of the bag on the counter, filling it and going back to the rifle. The sun wasn't up yet, but it was getting lighter outside. He carried the rifle out of the Airstream, setting it on the hood of the Jeep, and pacing off a hundred yards to a tree with a knot that he could see.

Pulling the bolt, he sighted through the barrel until he could see the knot, then raised up and looked through the scope. He smiled as the knot was centered in the cross hairs. Carrying it back into the Airstream, he saw Ram standing at the kitchenette, a cup of coffee in hand. "Looks like this one is pretty well dialed in."

Ram grunted, "We will still need to check zero. We should be able to do that here. I do not believe anyone is working here on the weekend."

The old man nodded. Picking up the Pelican case and opening it, he said, "Looks like M one-eighteen LR for the three-oh-eight, and Black Hills two-fifty grain boat tail for the MRAD."

"How many boxes of each?"

The old man rustled through the case. "Two for each. A Kestrel weather station, and a laser range finder. You bring a pistol?"

Ram opened his shirt. "*Sí*, Forty-four magnum and three reloads."

The old man whistled. "Nice! Model twenty-nine?"

"*Sí, Señor.* Six inch barrel, Hogue grips."

The old man turned. "Nineteen-eleven. Three mags. So we have more rifle ammo than pistol ammo."

Ram said thoughtfully, "And we should not need all that, if we do this correctly."

"Let's hope so. You want an MRE?"

"What are the choices?"

The old man dug through the packs. "Looks like maple sausage or sausage and gravy are the only two breakfast ones."

Ram grimaced. "Sausage and gravy. I know it will not be good, but at least it will be filling." He pulled the M-24 out of its case, attached the suppressor, and headed for the door, "What did you use to bore sight?"

"Across the hood of the Jeep from the passenger's side, there's a tree out there with a forty-five in the trunk and a knot at the forty-five."

"Okay." Ram replied, as he walked out the door.

The old man nodded. "I'll get breakfast started."

Ten minutes later, Ram was back, smiling. "It appears the M-24 is also on."

The old man nodded. "Breakfast is served."

As they sat in the kitchenette, the old man suddenly asked, "Ramon, why should I trust you? You're Hispanic, and we're going after cartel heads."

Ram stopped, his spoon halfway to his mouth, and looked at the old man quizzically. "What do you mean, *Señor*?"

The old man leaned back with a grin, "Well, you and I don't know each other from Adam. You obviously know your way around weapons…"

"Ah, I see, *Señor*, I am known to Jake Devreau. He asked me to help out in this… Evolution."

"You know Devreau?"

"*Sí*, he and my partner in the ranch, up in Cook County, Texas, were in service together. They have stayed in touch, and I have worked with them."

"Your partner?"

"*Sí*, he and Dillon Cole, they were in a special group, Nomads? I think it was."

The old man planted his elbows on the dinette. "Really. That makes things even more interesting. I spent some time with DEA, back in the day."

Ram laughed. "So you and I were on opposite sides, back then."

The old man cocked his head, and Ram continued, "I was once a troubleshooter for Medellin, until I met my wife and came to the right side."

The old man nodded, and dug back into the breakfast. "Good enough."

They cleaned up and got the guns sighted in, with only three rounds each. The old man took six playing cards out of his pocket, careful not to hold them where he would leave any fingerprints. He put one more round through them from a hundred yards, then put them back in his shirt pocket. Repacking the guns in their cases, and throwing a couple of MREs and bottles of water in the Jeep, they then took the spare tire off and propped it against a tree. Ram locked up the trailer, and they set off to scout the roads and see if there was access to the wash at the canyon.

Three hours later, they were back, and making final plans. The old man took out the pictures of the cartel heads, spread them out, and asked, "You know any of these guys?"

Ram shook his head, "No, they are all much too young for me to have known them. Their fathers, maybe."

"You got any problems taking them out?"

"No, *Señor*. Not a bit."

"Okay, I figure another couple of hours, and we'll head back. I like where you found to leave the Jeep, and I figure it'll take us an hour, maybe more to get in position. It's going to be a long night. You okay with that?"

"*Sí, Señor*. It is not raining, and will not be cold. I will be all right. It will not be the first time I have, how you say, *roughed* it?"

The old man smiled. "I'll be grouchy as hell in the morning, but not the first time for me either. Let's grab a couple of hours of sleep then go do this."

***

Four hours later, they started climbing the back side of the cliffs across the Salt River from the ranch. Each carried a pack with a couple of MREs, trash bags, and ammunition, in addition to the range finder, and the Kestrel weather station.

Night was falling as the old man and Ram scrambled up the last pitch to the military crest of the cliff, overlooking the ranch. The old man panted, "Okay, that's enough of that shit. Ain't doing that again."

Ram smiled, white teeth showing in the gloom. "Ah *Señor*, it was only about six hundred feet. And there were good places for hands and feet."

"And you're twenty years younger than I am. Don't want to hear it."

The old man swung the rifle and pack off, then edged up to the top of the crest, with Ram doing the same. "Good sightline. Or at least as good as we're going to get. We'll lase the cabins and the restaurant in the morning, as soon as it's light. Maybe the pool too."

"*Sí, Señor*. How do you want to handle tonight?"

"Well, I don't think anybody is going to come looking for us, and I don't think anybody saw us. Knowing the cartel, they might put security out a hundred yards, in pairs, but that will be about it." The old man glanced over, and it was like seeing the Cheshire cat's grin with Ram's complexion in the dark. "I think we can both sleep, or try to. This is fairly well concealed, and unless somebody walks up on us, they aren't going to see us from any distance. And we'll hear them coming."

Ram nodded. "Especially if they are old men."

The old man chuckled. "Go ahead, rub it in. I just hope the Jeep is still there in the morning."

"It should be. I had never seen the trick of digging the hole for one wheel, to make it look like the tire was flat."

Laughing softly, the old man said, "Learned that one in 'Nam. It still works a treat in most places." Pulling out an MRE from his pack, he settled back to eat dinner, such as it was.

***

The old man groaned softly as he opened his eyes, seeing the faintest hint of light on the horizon to the east. Pulling back his sleeve, he saw that it was 0445, and he mumbled, "Nautical twilight."

Ram replied softly, "Looks like a clear day, *Señor*. A great day to shoot."

"Let's hope so, Ram. I need to piss. I'm going to go down and left. If I'm not back in ten, or you hear a splat, you're on your own." The old man levered himself up slowly, and groaned again as he tried in vain to stretch. Stepping carefully, he slid down to a place he'd picked the night before, and relieved himself as quickly as he could. Climbing back to the crest, he said, "Cheated death again."

Ram snickered at that, and rose effortlessly, saying, "I will return shortly, *Señor*." Ram disappeared silently down the slope, as the old man took out his handkerchief and wiped the MRAD down. Slipping his shooting gloves on, he took a box of ammo out of the backpack, and quickly loaded the magazine.

Ram slipped silently back into place. "You want to lase the targets now?"

Pulling his wheel book out, the old man said, "Sure. Start from the left, call 'em off, then I'll lase, and you can crosscheck." Fifteen minutes later, they had ranges to all the cabins, the restaurant's front door, and the pool area. The old man looked at his notes, mumbling, "Aim low, 'bout thirteen, maybe fifteen degrees down, so take off one MOA, wind is…"

The old man scrabbled through the pack, pulling out the little Kestrel weather station, and turning it on. "Two thousand feet, temp is seventy-seven, humidity thirty-five, wind two six zero at four."

Ram asked, "So about what we saw yesterday, *Señor*?"

"Temp is twenty-five less, and we're two hundred feet higher. I'm dropping two MOA on the BDC, two left for the wind, and aiming at the crotch. I figure that will give me a center of mass hit."

Ram nodded. "What do you want me to do?"

"At this range, I can ride the recoil and get the scope back on target. You can either spot or shoot, up to you." Turning the Kestrel off and putting it away, he reached up and adjusted the BDC to one thousand and backed off two clicks, then put in two clicks of windage. Pulling one of the black trash bags out, he scooped a couple of pounds of sand into it, then eased up to the crest, making sure the scope covers were closed.

Ram asked, "Sandbag?"

"I like shooting off one. Little easier for me to get stable for repeated shots."

Ram quickly did the same, muttering, "This is why I am a *pistolero*! Much less work!"

The old man laughed quietly. "To each his own. I figure we've got an hour or so, but I like to be prepared." He positioned the rifle on the makeshift sandbag, flipped the scope cover open, and refined the position until he had the front door of the middle cabin in his sights. Closing the cover, he squirmed around, moving a couple of rocks, until he had a semi-comfortable place to lay.

Ram copied him, and said, "Wake me up when something happens." With that he pillowed his head on his arms, and went to sleep. The old man shook his head in amazement, knowing he couldn't do that, especially not now.

The old man looked at the sun angle, as the sun came up, measuring where the scope flash would show, and decided it was well away from any place that the security detail below could see it. He was starting to see movement, and cautiously flipped the scope cover up, quickly scoping the ranch. He tapped Ram's boot. "Movement. Security teams are out."

Ram looked at the sun, then quickly scoped the area. "*Sí*, two man teams. Ingram's, probably full auto. Useless. I see a few of the underbosses moving. The bosses are sleeping in, or playing with their women. It is a macho thing."

The old man rolled his eyes. "Seen that before, used it against them before."

Ram rolled over and looked squarely at the old man. "The playing cards. Where did you get them? And what do you plan to do with them?"

The old man *smiled,* and Ram realized he was looking at the face of a stone-cold killer. Deep within his psyche, he was glad they were on the same side. The old man said, "Not sure yet. I've had them a long time."

"So the legend is true?"

"Don't know what the legend is, so I can't say."

Ram snorted, "*Sí, Señor.* But the legend is that *El Lobo Blanco* killed from everywhere, day and night, in all weather, and never missed. One shot, one kill. And always the ace of spades with a hole through it. An ace with a white wolf logo… Like those in your pocket."

Rather than answer, the old man said, "Movement. I've got two, maybe three moving toward the pool. Got a waiter out there, looks like coffee cups." The old man slipped his shooting glasses on, and pushed earplugs into his ears.

Ram rolled quickly back into position, as the old man continued, "Eight hundred yards. Minus two, same wind hold." He reached up and backed off to eight hundred yards on the BDC, then dropped two more clicks.

Ram looked and said, "*Sinaloa* and *Los Zetas* leaders. I see two more, maybe three, heading in that direction." A few seconds later, he said, "LFM and...

Jalisco Nueva Generacion. Can't make out the third one. Interesting, since JNG is an offshoot and now competitor of *Sinaloa*."

"Shoot or no shoot?"

Ram responded immediately. "Shoot. There is no cover. They cannot get away."

"As soon as the other three show up. I'll call it. Let's see how they arrange themselves."

"*Sí, Señor.*"

The old man wriggled into a final shooting position, flipping off the safety and starting to breathe slowly. Ram said softly, "The fifth man is the *Juárez* Cartel's head. That is all the cartels that control the northern border."

"You take the two on the left, I will take the three on the right of the table. Shoot on three. Target. One… Two… Three!" The cracks of the supersonic rounds were louder than the muzzle blast as the both fired together. The old man ran the bolt, taking the second man, and ran the bolt for a third time, seeing one body flopping in the pool, he put a final round in it, watching the blood spread in the water as the body went limp. He quickly scoped and saw both of Ram's targets down, and said, "Let's go." The old man picked up his three spent cases, and noted Ram doing the same.

They eeled back from the crest, and the old man quickly emptied the trash bag of sand over the area where he had been laying. Then got up, shoving the trash bag in the backpack, along with the spent cases. Getting into the pack, he slung the rifle, checked that his pistol was easy to hand, and started down the back side of the cliff, Ram following him closely.

They scrambled down to the point where the cliff leveled out, then went side by side, moving quickly toward the Jeep. The old man working his earplugs out, asked, "How many shots?"

Ram said, "Two. I was a little slower than you on the second shot. I am sorry, I am not a good rifleman."

"No problem. You got yours down, I got mine down. Maybe fifteen seconds, overall. And the echoes should confuse the hell out of them. Now the question is, will they send out search parties, and will the Jeep still be there?"

Ram grinned. "If not, *Señor*, we have a long walk."

The old man grunted and leaned into the backpack, moving as quickly as he could. Forty-five minutes later, they saw the top of the Jeep as they crested the last little rise, and walked quickly down to it. A quick look around, didn't show any problems and they quickly loaded the rifles, putting the backpacks on top of them. Ram started the Jeep, backing it up, and turning, heading down the ATV track in the canyon bottom toward the road.

An hour and a half later, they pulled back into the deserted airstrip, and parked next to the Airstream. Ram unlocked the door, as the old man quickly unloaded the Jeep. The old man finally said, "I need some coffee. You want any?"

Ram nodded as he slipped on a pair of nitrile gloves and started cleaning the M-24. The old man started the coffee pot, then did the same with the

MRAD. Looking across the dinette at Ram, he asked, "You good with what we did this morning?"

"*Sí, Señor*. This needed to be done. We were the instrument to get it done. I will not lose sleep over this, and I will answer for this on Judgement Day, along with my other sins."

"Good enough. I feel the same. We won't speak of this again, nor will I talk about this with anyone else. No one needs to know."

"I agree, *Señor*."

Lost in their own thoughts, they meticulously cleaned and oiled the guns, wiping them down and removing all fingerprints. Ram got up and got a cleaning wipe from the kitchenette, and wiped the cases down as they replaced the rifles. The Kestrel and the rangefinder got the same treatment, and the ammunition boxes were wiped down before they were replaced in the Pelican case. It was also wiped down, then slid back to its original position, next to the gun cases.

The old man poured two cups of coffee, setting one on the kitchenette in front of Ram. "I'll go wipe the Jeep down. Get a shower if you want, and crash for a while. We've got about 10 hours before we are supposed to be picked up." He took his coffee cup, and the wipe, and headed for the Jeep. He heard the water start, then cut off, then start again, as he wiped all the places he figured either of them had touched on the Jeep.

Fifteen minutes later, he'd finished, and took a quick piss before going back into the Airstream. Stripping down, he took fresh underwear and walked softly back to the head, noting Ram was snoring softly on the bed. Getting wet, he quickly washed, then rinsed off. After drying off, he went back to the lounge bed, and was asleep in minutes.

Eight hours later, he woke to the smell of coffee, and some kind of MRE. Ram's Cheshire cat grin caught his eye, as he rolled over and sat up. "Uh, damn. Don't know which hurts more, the back or the legs."

Ram said, "These are definitely not our beds at home, *Señor*. I believe we have an hour and a half before the airplane shows. What do you want to do with the trash? I will wipe the Airstream down, if you take care of that."

"I'll take the trash back to Texas with me. That way, it gets burned, and there isn't anything tying us here, other than DNA. And if it gets to that point, we're screwed anyway."

***

It was eerie, hearing the King Air touching down in the darkness, then seeing the darkened airplane whiz by, as they sat at the midpoint of the runway where they had been dropped off. Two minutes later, it pulled to a stop next to them, the left prop slowly rotating as the door opened and a hand motioned them in. A hand came out, taking their bags, and they climbed quickly onboard, falling into seats as the airplane taxied back to the end of the runway, then turned and rapidly took off into the dark skies.

As the airplane leveled off, a figure stooped next to the old man. "Well, how did it go?"

He looked up in surprise to see Jake Devreau, and said, "Five down. Ram knows who, but I think we took out the heads of all the cartels on the northern border."

"Only five?"

"They were all out by the pool. We took what we had. Bird in hand and all that. I got three, Ram got two."

"I owe you. I know this isn't a lot of payback for what was done to you and yours, but I owe you."

"You owe me?"

"The folks you lost, the attempt on your granddaughter, your stabbing…"

"How did you know about that?"

"It was all on the disk. You done good, Cronin. Thank you."

The old man asked, "What about the stuff we used?"

"It will all be back where it belongs by midnight."

The old man nodded, and Devreau went back to his seat, starting his computer and typing quickly. The old man leaned back and looked up at the overhead. *What the hell just happened? He owes me? What else was on that disk I didn't see…?*

He dozed off until the airplane started descending into Fort Stockton. Coming awake, the old man reached up and realized he had the playing cards in his shirt pocket. Getting up, he went back to where Devreau was sitting. Taking the cards out by the edges, he dropped them on his computer. "If you've got a way to mail these to the five cartels, it might be interesting."

Devreau looked at the cards curiously. "Nice shooting. Why these cards?"

The old man smiled. "Maybe it's time to breathe some new life into an old legend." Turning around, he went back and sat down as the PA came on saying they were landing in ten minutes.

The pulled up in front of the FBO, and the old man climbed down, bag in hand, along with the trash bag. He walked over to the dumpster and threw the trash bag in, then pulled out his cell phone, calling Jesse. When she answered, he said, "I'm back. Can somebody come get me?"

Shootout

Aaron sighed as he turned onto I-10. *Three more days of patrol, three more days of second shift, and then I get a desk. Am I making the right…?*

A black late model Charger blew by him at well over the speed limit, and he grabbed the mic keying up. "Dispatch, two-oh-one, eastbound ten from Hovey Road, pursuit of a late model dark colored Dodge Charger, speeding, no plate yet."

"Roger, two-oh-one."

After a mile or so of slowly closing, he hit the lights and siren, and saw brake lights come on. As he closed quickly on the car, it suddenly braked hard, and pulled off onto the shoulder. "Out with a stop, just east of Mendel Road, plate is Texas, bravo, kilo," Aaron got out of the Tahoe and started walking up, as he continued, "uh, tango, three." He saw movement on the passenger's side of the car and shouted, "Stay in the car, do not…" He unconsciously moved to get out of the light, as flame blossomed three times from the passenger's side door.

He felt an impact low on his left side, and a second in the center of his chest, as he dove for the ground, fighting to get his pistol out. Gravel spurted from the rear of the car as it fishtailed and accelerated off the shoulder, and Aaron managed to get off two shots as the car sped away. "Shots fired shots fired, dispatch. Charger is running east."

Dispatch came back, "Two-oh-one are you injured?"

Panting, Aaron scrambled back into the Tahoe and resumed the pursuit. "Negative, hit me in the vest, I'm okay... I got two rounds off at the car. Guessing more than one occupant. Tinted windows, I was shot at from the passenger's side." Flooring the accelerator, he pounded on the wheel. "Come on you sumbitch, get up to speed." The Tahoe topped out at 130, but he was slowly closing the distance again, and wondering what to do next.

He vaguely heard dispatch go out with an all call on the pursuit, stating the occupants were considered armed and dangerous. Aaron keyed up. "Passing Firestone, still in pursuit," he said, as he closed slowly on the Charger. "Off at Dickinson, still eastbound." In the distance he saw another set of red and blue lights come on, and the Charger dived down a side street. "Now south on… Sycamore." He wrestled the Tahoe around the corner, floored the accelerator again, cussing as the Charger sped away from him.

He saw a stab of brake lights, and a cloud of dust. "Attempted left on fifth, may have dumped it." Jumping on the brakes, he manhandled the Tahoe around the corner, only to see the Charger disappearing in the distance again. "Charger is eastbound on fifth, passing the middle school." He heard other units closing on the area, and said, "Armed and dangerous. Still east on fifth. Late model Charger,

Texas tag bravo, kilo, tango, three, don't have last two numbers."

As more city cars and other deputies got involved, Aaron realized he was leading a parade, so to speak, as first one, then two more cars fell in behind him. "Crossing Railroad, still east on fifth. Car is weaving," he called, as he bounced over the tracks.

Deputy Ortiz called in, "Two-fourteen, I'll deploy stop sticks at fifth and Rooney. In position now."

Aaron also saw two patrol units turn onto fifth heading west, as brake lights came on and tire smoke erupted from the Charger. The driver tried to turn left, but spun and hit the corner of the bank building, as Aaron keyed up, "Ten-fiftied at Fifth and Main, car hit the bank building." As he tried to get the Tahoe stopped, he saw a shadowy figure run toward the back of the building, "Runner headed east on Fifth!" Easing up on the brakes, he rolled through the intersection and half way to Water Street before coming to a stop. He jumped out of the Tahoe, wincing as his feet hit the ground. He grabbed his Streamlight out of the holder, and drew his pistol. A quick scan didn't show a running figure, so he limped slowly toward the drive-up area, scanning back and forth.

A flicker of movement caught his eye, and he turned toward it, extending the light away from his body as he did so. A black male in a dark track suit was visible, partially hidden behind the dumpster at the back of the bank building. "Hands, let me see your hands," Aaron yelled.

The figure crouched, and Aaron sidestepped to get a better view of the man, as he yelled, "Stand up, let me see your hands!" He saw the man come up with his hands, then saw the blossom of gunfire again, and fired two rounds at the man as he felt an impact on his leg and started falling. *Shit, not again! Did I hit the sumbitch?* As he fell on his left side, he lost the Streamlight, and rolled quickly onto his chest. As he brought his pistol up again, he thought, *Damn, why does my chest hurt so bad? Am I having a fucking heart attack, on top of…?*"

He heard somebody key up, "Officer down, shots fired, Pecos County Bank." Aaron kept his gun trained on the dumpster, but no further gunfire came from there, and he rolled over as he heard Sergeant Alvarez yell, "Perp is down. Somebody check on the officer!"

Aaron holstered his pistol and slumped back as Deputy Ortiz ran up. "Aaron? Are you…"

"I got hit in the left leg, Danny," Aaron said, as he groaned and tried to sit up, "and I might have taken one in the vest, too."

Ortiz shined his light down Aaron's leg, and saw blood on the outside of his thigh, "Looks like you were hit in the thigh." Keying his radio, he said, "Dispatch, two-fourteen. Need an ambulance, Fifth and Water, officer needs transport with gunshot wound."

Leland from City was cutting Aaron's pant leg open, and shined his light on the leg, "Looks like a graze, not a through and through." Moving his light up, he said, "I see a hole in your shirt, lower left." He cut the shirt away, and saw the vest had absorbed the round. "One hit lower left abdomen." Moving the light up, he saw that Aaron's body camera was destroyed, and shook his head. "Damn, that was a center punch!" Gently sliding his hand under the vest, he said, "No blood, but back plate deformation."

Aaron moaned, "That fucking *hurt*."

"Sorry man, just trying to see if you're bleeding anywhere else."

Dispatch replied, "Ambulance in route. Land line please."

Ortiz fumbled out his phone as he propped Aaron up, and dialed dispatch. "Lisa, Aaron Miller was shot in the leg, and hit twice in the vest. He's conscious and alert, waiting on an ambulance to transport him." Thirty seconds later, the dying growl of an ambulance could be heard as the other officers gathered round Aaron.

Sergeant Alvarez said, "Good shoot, Aaron, you nailed the perp in the head and throat. He won't be shooting at any of us again, but I'll need to get your weapon for the investigation."

Aaron nodded. "They're taking me to the hospital, I guess. Meet me there?"

"Okay."

Aaron suddenly realized he needed to call Jesse, and pulled his phone out, thankful it hadn't been hit or broken, and he hit Jesse's number. After a couple of rings, he heard her answer and said, "Honey, I got in a shootout tonight. I've been hit in the leg, but I'm okay. They are getting ready to take me to the hospital. Can you meet me there?" He listened for a minute, and said, "No, I'm okay. Really. I think it's just a flesh wound. They're here, and I gotta go. Love you." He slid the phone back in his pocket, and slumped back as the medic and EMT puffed up with the gurney.

***

Jesse knocked on the old man's door, "Papa, Aaron's been shot, and they are taking him to the hospital. He called and said he's not bad. I've got to go!"

The old man grunted, "Get Felicia down here. As soon as she gets here, I'll be there."

Jesse nodded, then realized he couldn't see her. "Okay." Pulling her phone out of her pocket, she dialed Felicia, hitting the speaker button as she grabbed her purse and looked for a jacket. "Felicia, Aaron's been shot and is on the way to the hospital. Can you or Matt come watch the kids until I get back?"

Felicia replied, "Of course, any idea how bad?"

"Aaron called and said he was hit in the leg. That's all I know right now."

"Give me five minutes, and unlock the back door."

"Okay, Papa will be here." With that, Jesse hung up the phone, dropped it in her purse, and checked to make sure she had her credentials and her pistol. Boo Boo whined, sensing something was wrong, and Jesse said, "Quiet girl, don't wake the babies, please."

The old man came out of his room, buttoning his shirt. "Felicia on the way?" Jesse nodded and he continued, "Go, I'll catch up with you there. Drive careful."

Jesse grimaced. "I will, I just hope…"

"Go." Jesse headed for the door, and the old man called the dogs. "Yogi, Boo Boo, come." He walked through the kitchen to the back door, opened it, and let the dogs out. He headed for the office, pulling his gun belt off the rack, and buckling it on. He slipped the radio out of its charger, turned it on, and headed back to the kitchen as he heard the dogs' nails scrabbling on the floor. He met Felicia in the kitchen, and said, "Thank you for helping out."

"*De nada, Señor*. I pray Aaron is okay. Please go and don't worry about the babies."

He nodded and headed for the door. As soon as he got the car started, he keyed the mic. "Dispatch, Car four, enroute hospital."

"Car four, dispatch, copied all. Sheriff has been notified, and is also enroute."

"Rangers been called?"

"Ten-four. ETA is one hour."

***

Ranger Michaels leaned back in the chair, with his note pad in his lap, and reached up, shutting off the recorder sitting on the hospital table. "Thanks Aaron, I appreciate your willingness to give me a statement, especially right now, and without a lawyer present or any pain pills."

Aaron started to shrug his shoulders, but said, "Ow, damn, I hurt. No problem, Levi, I *trust* you. I'd rather get it over with, and hopefully it's all on the dashcam and body camera. You know what's weird? I never heard a single shot he fired, or I fired." Glancing over at his prosthetic lying on the floor, he said, "Not sure what I'm going to do about that. You need it for evidence?"

Michaels looked at it and asked, "Why?"

"Jesse?" Jesse picked up the prosthetic and handed it to Aaron, as the foot dangled loosely. "He shot me in the foot, in addition to the thigh and the vest." Wiggling the foot, he said, "It's not supposed to do that, Levi."

Michaels replied, "Maybe. Can I take it with me? Do you have a spare?"

Aaron nodded. "This is the spare; my good leg is getting maintenance at Fort Sam. But I've got a running leg I can use in the interim."

"Okay, thanks. Um, the not hearing a shot, I think they call that auditory exclusion. You heard it, you just never processed it."

Sheriff Rodriguez said, "You're on admin anyway, until the investigation is completed, so it's not like you're going to be doing any patrolling. Levi, you need anything else from us?"

Michaels said, "Not right now. I've got to go do the scenes. Downtown first, then back out to the original scene. Apparently, Sergeant Alvarez pulled a goodly amount of cocaine out of the car, and they found another gun in the driver's floorboard."

Aaron asked curiously, "Did they get the driver?"

The sheriff and Ranger looked at each other, and the sheriff finally said, "He died at the scene. Apparently you got a round into him, and he broke his neck when they crashed. No seatbelt."

Aaron grimaced. "Damn, I didn't know that."

The sheriff shrugged. "You were a bit occupied at the time. Doc Truesdale says he's going to keep you overnight, just in case. He's a little worried about the chest trauma from the two rounds in the vest, and he's got to stitch up the thigh wound."

Aaron grunted, "Yeah, they do hurt like a bit…"

Jesse said, "You can say bitch. It's not like I haven't heard that before."

Aaron sighed. "I know, but I'm trying to clean up my language, especially around the kids. Speaking of that, who?"

The old man answered, "Felicia is watching them. I'm going to leave Jesse here with you, and I'm going to go examine the scenes with Levi."

Doc Truesdale strolled in. "Are you done with my patient to the point I can hit him with some good drugs and let him get some rest? I swear, I spend more damn time patching up you Cronin's than I do anybody else in town!"

The old man picked his hat up. "He's all yours Doc. I have to go to work, no thanks to Aaron. You and Jesse can fight over him."

Doc rolled his eyes. "Okay John, get the hell out of here so I can get him patched up, and leave him to Jesse's tender ministrations."

***

The old man pulled in behind the Ranger's Tahoe, and climbed slowly out, noting the police tape surrounding the car, stretching down the street to Aaron's Tahoe, and into the drive through behind the bank. He saw that the city had a couple of portable light stands set up. After he signed in, he made his way over to Sergeant Alvarez, who nodded. "Captain."

"How goes it, Luis?"

"Lucky. Aaron was lucky, not once, but twice. And he took the brunt of it, rather than our officers. Hate that he had to put the perps down, but I don't see it as anything but a good shoot."

"Got time to show me the scene?"

"Sure. The Ranger is out back. He's already done the car and driver."

They walked over to the crumpled dark gray Charger, the driver's side door bent around the corner of the bank building. Alvarez bent down and pointed to the back door behind the driver, "Both of Aaron's shots went in there." Walking around the other side of the car, he shined his light and pointed. "See the blood on the wall? Best guess is the driver broke his neck when he hit the wall with his head. When they pulled him out, he had one round in mid-back, probably got the lung. From the skid marks, the car spun trying to make the corner, but it was already weaving the last couple blocks after they crossed Railroad. We'll have to wait for the autopsy, but I'm betting he was bleeding out the whole time."

The old man shined his light in the back, whistling. "Damn, good amount of drugs. Y'all already tested any?"

"We did, came up pure coke. Ranger wanted it left until he can get enough pictures then we'll have to weigh it, test all of it, and put it in evidence."

"Any ID on them?"

"Yeah, two brothers out of Houston. Crips, from the look of them, between the tats and the colors."

"Brothers? As in?"

"Bravo mikes, but actual brothers, too. Twenty-one and twenty-three, both out on parole for drug dealing. From the packaging, looks like they'd made a deal with *Sinaloa* and were doing a pickup and run back home."

"So, felons with guns. What a fucking surprise," the old man said in disgust.

Alvarez shrugged. "Yep. Anyway, perp number two ran around the back of the building." He and the old man walked down the side of the building and stopped at the back corner, looking at a dumpster pulled out at a 45 degree angle. He said, pointing, "Perp two hid there. Aaron's truck is where he stopped and got out, he was moving laterally toward the drive up." Alvarez shined his light in the general direction of the drive-up lanes. "About twenty yards from perp two. He said he caught movement and turned. Perp shot at him, he shot back, and won the battle."

"Any idea where the perp's rounds went?"

"Found a couple of chipped bricks in the front of the library. That's probably where they went. Didn't see any spent bullets, but who knows where they might have ended up."

The flash of a camera momentarily startled the old man, and he looked sharply at the dumpster again, seeing Ranger Michaels standing up, camera in hand. "What are you finding, Levi?"

Michaels looked over. "Did you sign in, Captain?"

"Sure did. Sergeant Alvarez has been giving me the ten-cent tour."

"Okay, come around in front of the dumpster at least ten yards out. I haven't gotten all his tracks marked yet, but I don't think he went that far. Maybe two-three yards."

The old man stepped carefully to where Levi pointed, and saw a body slumped against the wall, a Glock lying on the ground, and a splatter of blood just about where the top of the dumpster would be.

Michaels walked over. "Two rounds: one in the throat, one centered in the forehead. That is some impressive shooting on a two-way range, in the dark. Aaron must not have any nerves, or he's just flat crazy."

The old man shook his head. "No, he's been in combat multiple times. He's a former Marine Sniper, two, no three Silver Stars. His last go-round, he took out a dozen or so Taliban, at bad breath range, in an alley, that was his third. I'd guess a one-on-one was a relief to him, and he was probably pissed they'd already hit him in the vest."

Michaels whistled. "Didn't know his background. I knew he was in the Corps, but he never said anything."

"Just like you don't talk about flying Harriers with folks that haven't been there."

Michaels ducked his head. "Point taken. Still impressive shooting."

"Yep. Aaron practices religiously. As do Jesse and Matt."

"Good to know." Looking over, he said, "Sarge, can you tell the medics to bag this one, I'm done with him, but he needs to go to the hospital for an autopsy."

Alvarez turned and yelled, "Medic up! Bag 'em and tag 'em."

Michaels chuckled. "Gotta love 'em. Now I've got to go find the first scene."

The old man smiled, "O'Brien is sitting on it for you. Just park behind him. You need any help?"

"Nah, I've got it. Just got to finish the documentation, and if I'm lucky, get home before the kids wake up. It's supposed to be my turn to fix breakfast."

"Good luck with that. Thanks for coming as quickly as you did."

"No problem. Tell Aaron I hope he gets better quick."

"Will do, good night, Levi."

The medics came up, rolling the gurney and the Ranger pointed to the body. "All yours. The Doc is waiting on him."

The medic nodded. "Got it. We'll have him there in twenty minutes."

The old man turned to Alvarez. "Well, I'm going to go to the house. Thanks for your support, as always."

"No problem, Captain. It's a team effort. I'll sign you out. Tell Aaron we wish him the best."

"I will. Thanks."

Retired

The old man grumbled as he got in the car with the sheriff. "Dammit, Jose, I need to finish moving the boxes out of my office. My retirement is at three, and that's only two hours from now."

"John, I'm not throwing you out. Aaron can work around a couple of boxes on the floor. Besides, you've been moving stuff out for a week!"

The old man shrugged. "Mostly old wheel books, copies of old files, a few cold case files I copied years ago. I probably should just throw them all out, they don't mean shit to anybody but me."

The sheriff pulled up in front of the church, saying, "Come on, gotta make on quick stop here, then we'll go over to the PD."

The old man continued grumbling as he got out of the car, then stopped and looked at the parking lot suspiciously. "Damn you, Jose, what have you done?"

The sheriff took him by the arm, "Come on, you didn't really think we were going to let you retire and sneak out the door, did you?"

"Hell, I hoped so. I don't want this, it's embarrassing…"

Opening the front door, he escorted the old man in, opened the door to the sanctuary, and the old man stopped dead. It was half full, with a plethora of uniforms, civilian clothes, locals and a couple of people up front that looked familiar. He saw Jesse,

Aaron, Matt, Felicia, Clay and many others as the sheriff led him down the aisle, and he said, "I'm gonna get you for this, you sumbitch."

The four standing at the front of the sanctuary resolved themselves into Bucky, Milty, Tony, and a small Asian man in an expensive suit. Tony, rumpled as always, yelled out, "*Ciao*! Cowboy, *come stai*?" Pulling him into a hug, Tony air kissed him on both cheeks and the old man growled, "Dammit Tony, no kissing, you know that!" as the sanctuary erupted in laughter.

Bucky and Milty shook hands with him, and Tony said, "I was at Quantico, and found out they were coming today on an airplane, so I hitched a ride. Andrea sends her love."

The old man turned to the middle aged Asian man, who set his briefcase down, bowed and said, "*Sawasdee krup*, Captain Cronin. I am Tanongsak Suanatat, I am the first secretary for political and security cooperation at the Thai embassy in Washington. Please call me Tan. Joe said to tell you hello, and no you cannot retire."

The old man laughed. "Did he also ask you to hit me up for some Blantons?"

Tan smiled. "There was a mention of you owing a bottle."

The padre and Major Wilson, Company E Texas Rangers, came out from the back of the sanctuary, and Wilson said, "Bout damn time you got here."

The sheriff said, "Okay, let's get this show on the road. John, come on up to the pulpit with me."

Reluctantly, the old man followed him, as the sheriff tapped on the mic. "Test, test... This thing working?"

Sergeant Alvarez from the PD, standing near the back, gave him a thumbs up.

There was a general shuffle, as folks took their seats, and the sheriff said, "Well, this is probably the safest church in Texas right now." Laughter and chuckles resounded around the room, and the old man noticed the padre come up and sit on the other side of the pulpit. The sheriff went on, "We're here today to retire Captain John Cronin after forty-four years of service to Pecos County, and a few other organizations and places. First I'd like the padre to say a prayer."

He stepped back, and Padre Augustin stepped forward. "I'm not sure a prayer will do much good, but I do ask you to leave my church standing, I've heard about law enforcement parties..." Laughter erupted again, and the padre gave a short prayer, then rather than sitting down, said, "I have probably known John Cronin longer than any of you. He saved my life, and gave me a new direction. I had not seen John in over thirty years before I came here, but we served together in the drug wars in South America. John is one *mucho hombre*, and I am proud to call him my friend." He stepped away from the mic, as the sheriff looked over at John curiously.

The sheriff stepped back to the mic. "Well, I'm Sheriff Jose Rodriguez, and I thought I'd known him a long time, but I guess not. But I do have a story... You see, when I started with Pecos County nigh on to twenty-five years ago, I had a training officer that was this meaner than a snake, white guy, with a crewcut, that I was scared to death of. He never yelled at me, never cussed me, and taught me a lot of sh… stuff that wasn't in the books. Now he's retiring, I'm the sheriff, and I'm still scared to death of him." More laughter, and the sheriff made a quieting motion, "John, I don't know that we've ever done this, but we are retiring your badge number, forty-three. I think that's pretty appropriate, since this is your forty-fourth year here, and frankly, I don't see us being able to actually replace you. So, you can keep your badge."

A round of hoots and applause sounded at that, and Bucky walked to the pulpit with a wave. "Well, I can claim I've known John for forty-two years. I'm Bucky Grant, the Laredo station chief for DEA. We go back to the bad old days, when John was seconded to DEA, and spent some time in South America and other places. It's not often that one can talk about how many pounds or kilos of drugs an officer has been responsible for, but in John's case, the number is a little higher. Roughly, twenty-two tons, yes tons, of illegal drugs John Cronin has been responsible for taking off the streets over his career, world-wide. And he's done it in as diverse a set of locations as Colombia, Mexico, Italy, and Thailand. At least those are the ones I know about…"

Reaching under the pulpit, Bucky pulled out a plaque, and said, "Come on up, John. It's not much, but it's in appreciation for all your contributions to the DEA and safety of the United States."

Another round of applause greeted that, as the old man stepped up to the pulpit. Bucky read, "From the

Department of Homeland Security and the Drug Enforcement Agency to John Cronin, for exemplary service to the United States in various capacities from 1975 to 2017. Here ya go, John." He handed him the plaque and the old man sat back down, laying the plaque on the floor.

Tan got up next, bringing a medium sized box with him. Opening the box, he rustled through it and pulled out a plaque as he said, "I am Tanongsak Suanatat. I am the first secretary for political and security cooperation at the Thai embassy in Washington. Thanks to Mr. Milton, I was able to get a ride here today. I am representing Colonel Cho Wattanapanit, director of the Central Investigation Bureau of Thailand. Colonel Cho was very specific that I read the plaque, then present to Captain Cronin the package in the box, so I will now do so."

The old man got back up and stepped to Tan's side, as Tan looked at the plaque and then at the old man in horror. Putting his hand over the mic, he whispered, "Sir, this… I cannot read this out loud. It is embarrassing."

The old man laughed, "Let me guess, it starts something like here is another useless plaque to hang on the 'I love me' wall?"

Tan chuckled nervously, "Yes."

"Then read it. That's an old joke between Joe and me, going back to the National Academy."

Tan shook his head in amazement, "As you wish, sir." Taking his hand away from the mic, he continued, "This is from the Central Investigation Bureau of Thailand, presented to Captain John Cronin, Pecos

County Sheriff's Office. It says… It says, 'Here is another useless plaque to hang on your 'I love me' wall. In appreciation for your support and involvement in the rescue of twenty-one young Thai women and the capture of smugglers and a large amount of pure uncut heroin during a joint operation with between the CIB, US Marine Corps, and Thai Navy."

Laughter followed that, and Tan lifted a smaller box out of the package, and presented it to the old man. "I was instructed to have you open this. I have no knowledge of what it is."

The old man hefted it, and a small smile crept across his face. Pulling out his pocketknife, he carefully slit the tape over the seams, noting the diplomatic stamps as he did so. Popping the box open, he moved the oiled paper, and his grin spread across his face, as he pulled a 1911 out of the box.

Tan blanched. "Oh my, I didn't know… I…"

The old man laughed as he racked the slide and ensured the pistol was empty. "I wondered what ever happened to this thing. At least Joe had it cleaned." Holding it up, he said, "This was the pistol I used to get my ass out of trouble over in Thailand." Turning to SAC Milton, he continued, "Do I need to declare this as a gift?"

Milty looked puzzled. "Why? I don't see anything." That brought the house down with laughter, and Tan shrugged helplessly as he walked back to his seat.

The old man said, "I'll get something for you to send back to Joe. Please pass on my thanks to him, and to the government of Thailand for the plaque."

Tan nodded in thanks as Milty walked up to the pulpit next, and opened his briefcase. Pulling out some papers, and another plaque, he said, "Well, I guess I'm the new kid here. I've only known John for twenty-seven years, going back to his National Academy class, that I had the *pleasure* of being the proctor for. Between John, Tony, Joe, and that damn sheriff's deputy from over in Louisiana."

The old man chimed in, "Justin Boudreau."

Milty continued, "Yeah, Boudreau. I had my damn hands full. There was enough sh… Stuff going on that it's a wonder I didn't get fired, and they all didn't get thrown out. But one story I do have to tell. There was a class of baby FBI agents in the dorm, on the top floor."

The old man put his head in his hands, then rubbed his face, as Milty smiled at him. "They had just come back from Hogan's Alley, and were down in the lounge, along with this crew of miscreants. Well, there was a card game going on, and the baby agents were getting a little loud."

Tony started laughing, and Milty said, "Tony, you were eyeing that cute little female agent."

Tony shrugged. "I'm Italian, what do you expect?"

The crowd started laughing again, and Milty had to wait for that to die down. "Anyway, Boudreau made a comment about shooting, and one of the agents took it personal. Said he was going to report these guys for gambling, since it was illegal and specifically prohibited on the campus."

The old man said, "Wasn't gambling, we were taking your money, that ain't gambling…"

More laughter erupted, and Milty blushed. "Whatever. Anyway, a challenge got issued, and it was decided that there would be a *competition* between the agents and these four."

Milty shook his head. "So, bright and early the next morning, everybody trooped over to Hogan's Alley, and these four were still hung over. There was a coin flip, and the agents got to go first. They all ran the course clean, and came out bragging, and of course the ante got upped. It became a dinner at the Old Ebbitt Grill in downtown DC, which was pretty pricey back in the day."

The old man shook his head again, and smiled, as Milty continued, "So these four hung over ass... *Individuals*, who, by the way, had never shot Hogan's Alley, cleaned it, and in a faster time that the agents had."

The crowd roared at that, and Milty raised his hands. "And they didn't cheat, either! Of course, every one of them had already been in actual shootouts, and John and Justin were both combat veterans, so they had a leg up on these kids. Anyway, I've got this plaque, John, come on up here."

The old man stood and walked slowly over, as Milty read, "From the Federal Bureau of Investigation to John Cronin, for exemplary service to the United States, in support of FBI initiatives in drug enforcement, human trafficking, and interagency cooperation from 1991 to 2017. Here ya go John."

Jesse snapped another picture with her cell phone, as the old man stepped up to the pulpit. "The real story is we ran the alley two at a time. The Fibbies didn't allow more than one agent in at a time, to keep them from shooting each other. Since we were lowly cops, they didn't care if we shot each other or not." More laughter bubbled up, and he said, "And had it not been for Milty, we probably would have been thrown out. But he was a pretty good den mother, and kept us, if not on the straight and narrow, at least contained. Thank you!"

The sheriff got back up. "Anybody else?" Looking around he saw Major Wilson get up. "Ah yes, the Rangers. Can't forget them."

Major Wilson came up, planted both hands on the pulpit, and said, "I'm Hack Wilson. I'm the commander of Company E, Texas Rangers. I've known John over twenty years, and I will tell you I have not worked with a better or more knowledgeable officer in my entire career. His breadth of local knowledge, along with his experience in the smuggling game, and his ability to see trends and loci of criminal activity have made my job considerably easier. I'm just sad we were never able to get you to come over to the Rangers, John. I think you'd have been a helluva good one."

He stepped toward John, then back to the pulpit. "I don't have a plaque or any of that frou-frou stuff. We can't afford it."

The old man got up and laughed as he shook hands with the major. "Thanks, Major. I never wanted the Rangers because I knew I wouldn't get to stay here, and Amy didn't want to leave."

"I know. But you would have been a hell of an asset to us."

The sheriff got back up, looked around again, and said, "Okay, I think that's it. Time to get back to work, and John's got boxes to clean out of the office, before we kick him out at four."

Chuckles were heard, as he continued, "There's punch, not spiked I hope, in the recreation room, along with a cake. Padre, if you would?"

The padre got up and gave a short homily, and a prayer for everyone's safety.

Two hours of handshakes, multiple conversations, and more pictures with people than he would have believed. Good-byes to Milty, Tony, and Tan, and folks from the surrounding agencies, left him sitting in a daze, a cup of coffee in his hand.

Billy brought a piece of cake and a cup of coffee, and sat across from him. "Does it seem real, yet?"

The old man shook his head. "Nah, it doesn't. I can't believe all the folks that showed up."

Billy smiled. "Yeah, we were worried you'd trip to it and just disappear."

"Where have you been?"

"Working the crowd. Handing out cards. I'm a lawyer, remember?"

The old man chuckled. "Billy, I really doubt there was anybody here today that didn't already know who you are."

Billy shrugged. "One never knows. One never knows. So, what's next?"

The old man looked at Billy. "I honestly don't know. It's going to feel strange to not have to get up and go to work Monday."

Billy smiled. "Well, you've got all weekend to figure it out. Aaron said to tell you he's got your boxes in his truck, and he'll bring them home after work."

"Crap! I don't have a ride! I rode over here with the sheriff. Dammit!"

Jesse walked through the door. "You about ready to go, Papa? The sheriff had to get back and handle something."

Billy laughed, and the old man slugged the rest of his coffee. "Might as well." Getting up, he walked over to the kitchen area, stuck his head in the door, and saw Maria. "Maria, please tell the padre thank you, and I'll see him next week to pay the bill."

Maria smiled. "Captain, you no worry about it, it is taken care of. We will miss you."

The old man's eyes got misty, and he bowed his head. "Thank you, Maria."

Trading Longhorns

The old man cradled the phone and leaned back with a smile, tapping his pencil on the desk. "Hector, it'll take me a couple of days to round up four young cows that will be a good set of trades. I'd like to leave two with you for your bull to get on, and two out of my bloodstock as trades for your bloodstock."

He listened for a minute, then said, "Nope, these are Yates bloodline, not WR, but they are damn close. Same part of the country, back around 1915. I'd like to have that Phillips bloodline bull cover them." Nodding he continued, "Yep, Ol' Red is still servicing cows. I'll put him on the ones you send up. Whichever two catch, we can trade back in the spring."

Chuckling, he finally said, "Okay, Hector, I'll plan on seeing you late Saturday." Going to the safe, he flipped through the pedigrees for the longhorns, finally picking four two-year old cows, and setting them to the side. Grabbing his hat, he wandered out into the back yard, Yogi in tow, and finally found Matt in the barn, literally ass deep in the oat bin. "What'cha got Matt?"

A disembodied voice floated out of the bin. "Found the gahdamn rat hole. Little sumbitches ate through the back corner."

The old man winced. "That's going to be a pain in the ass to fix."

Matt straightened up with a groan, holding a piece of folded cardboard in his hand. "No," he said judiciously, "I think I can put sealer in the hole, then put a tin patch on the inside of the bin, and we don't have to tear it out."

"That would be nice. Can you finish that today?"

Matt glanced up. "Uh, sure. Why?"

The old man grinned. "We're gonna be moving some cows."

Matt cocked his head. "Moving cows? We just moved them back to the north forty."

"We're moving four two-year olds to *Mehico*."

"Mexico?"

"Yep, worked a deal with Hector Velazquez down at *Boquillas Del Carmen*, we're going to swap some cows, partly in trade, and partly to get covered."

Matt fiddled with the piece of cardboard. "Okay, do you know which ones?"

"Yeah, I've got them picked out. I'll take Ernesto and some temp fencing up to the loading gate at the north forty, he and I can get that set, while you fool with the bin. Tomorrow morning, we'll move the cows in, then we need to drag the trailer out and check it."

"The big trailer?"

"Uh huh."

"How old *is* that trailer, John?"

The old man laughed. "Oh, at least forty years. Rebuilt it twice. The last time was the metal floor with the rubber padding. It's all steel."

Matt rubbed his back ruefully. "Oh yeah, I remember trying to pick up the tongue to move it. *Once!*"

"Didn't make that mistake again, did ya?"

"Oh, hell no!"

Ernesto came in the barn, and the old man turned. "Ernesto, can you please go get the Gator and the small flat trailer? We need to move some temporary corral fencing."

"Sí, Señor. From the back side of the barn?"

"Sí,"

Matt said, "I'll finish this up, and come help."

The old man nodded. "Works." He walked out of the barn, grabbing a set of work gloves, and headed around the corner.

***

Three hours later, they had an open-ended pen set up, just waiting for the cows to close them in the pen. Loading the tools in the back of the Gator, the old man said, "Good enough. I'm going to ride up to the cemetery. I'll be back in time for supper."

Matt and Ernesto nodded, and headed back to the ranch house, leaving the old man in peace. He rode Diablo slowly up to the gate, opened it, and rode through. Getting down, he closed the gate and dropped Diablo's reins, then walked over to the little fence surrounding the cemetery, leaning on it as he looked out over the land in the late afternoon light. Finally, he took off his hat. "Amy, I think you'd be proud of me. I finally retired. Now I don't know what to do with myself. I kinda feel like I'm being a pest, sticking my nose in Matt's business, or Jesse's, but I swore I'd stay out of the department. I just didn't realize how hard it would be."

Sliding his hands around the brim, he looked over at Francisco and Juanita's graves. "Matt and Felicia are doing good, but I miss y'all. God knows I miss y'all. Jack and Pat, I know you're watching over Jesse, and now Jace and Kaya. Y'all done good. She's turned into a great mother."

A soft wind caressed his face, almost like a ghostly hand. "Mom, Dad, I'm doing my best to leave things in good shape for the next generation. Dad, you'll be happy to know we're still dealing with the Velazquez family down below the border, and they still have the longhorns."

Slapping his hat on his thigh, he said, "Well, that's about all I got, for now. I just need for y'all to keep guiding me. And help me stay on the straight and narrow."

Another gust of wind passed through the graveyard, and the old man put his hat back on, picked up Diablo's reins, opened the gate and walked him back through it. Closing the gate, he mounted slowly, riding slowly back to the ranch house in the dying light.

He finished grooming Diablo, and put him back in the stall, as he heard Jesse call, "Papa?"

"Coming!" Glancing at his watch, he realized it was almost seven. Sighing, he hit the boot brush at the back door and hurried in. "Sorry. Didn't keep track of the time."

Jesse and Felicia both looked at him, and he saw Aaron smiling behind Jesse. He shook his head. "Hey, I'm retired. I don't even have to wear a watch anymore, if I don't want to."

Matt coughed to cover a laugh, as Jesse said, "Papa, don't start. Just don't. What's the deal you've got cooked up?"

"After dinner. I don't want to be accused of any more delays," he said with a smile.

The old man sipped his coffee, idly playing with his fork on the remnants of the pie crust on his plate. "So we're agreed? Matt, Felicia, and I will load up early Saturday morning, cross at Del Rio, and back up to Hector's place at *Boquillas Del Carmen.* We'll spend the night there, then come back Sunday?"

He looked around the table, and Matt nodded, then Felicia. Aaron glanced at Jesse, then he nodded. Jesse shrugged. "Sure, why not. I can wrangle kids for a couple of days, I just won't do much at the shop."

"Okay. I don't expect any problems, but we'll carry on our creds just in case. I'll call Bucky tomorrow and give him a heads up."

***

Saturday dawned bright and chilly, as Matt backed the C3500 and trailer up to the loading gate at the north forty. The old man and Ernesto started the first cow toward the loading gate as Matt and Aaron stood by the back of the trailer. Aaron leaned over. "I don't know that I'd want to be in a pen with a bunch of Longhorns on foot."

Matt shook his head. "Me neither, but it doesn't seem to faze John. That little popper is all he has, and Ernesto doesn't even have that."

"True, but Ernesto can move pretty damn quick, John, not so much."

Matt laughed as the first cow trotted up the chute, twisting her head sideways to not hook the ramp, and moved into the trailer with almost no hesitation. Matt and Aaron prodded her forward, into the front of the trailer, and a minute later, the second cow was up there, too. Aaron unlatched the interior gate and shoved it across, allowing Matt to catch it, and fasten it closed on his side. Twenty minutes later, all four cows were loaded, the trailer buttoned up, and Aaron and Ernesto were tearing down the temporary corral, as Matt and the old man pulled into the ranch yard.

Felicia kissed the kids, put her bag in the back seat along with Matt's and the old man's, and handed the old man a thermos of coffee. "I'm ready."

Matt, sensing now was not a good time for a smart remark, simply nodded, as the old man told Jesse, "Ernesto and Aaron are tearing down. They should be back shortly. We'll have our phones on to the border, then be on the sat phone if you need us. That'll probably be around noon."

Jesse nodded. "Drive careful."

Matt pulled out carefully, remembering the old man's caution about giving the cows a chance to get their feet under them and adjust to the movement of the truck. A little over two hours later, they stopped in Comstock for a potty break, and the old man checked on the cows, who seemed calm and fairly content. Just short of Del Rio, he directed Matt to pull over. "I'll drive the rest of the way. Everybody got their passports handy? And creds?"

Matt nodded. "Got mine."

Felicia said groggily, "Passport and my ID, just in case." Holding up the old man's battered briefcase, she continued, "And the cows' paperwork."

After a quick pit stop, they drove up to the border crossing, showed their passports and creds, and were allowed to cross into Mexico. Heading south on Hwy 29, the old man grumbled, "Now the suckage starts. It's not more than fifty miles direct to *Boquillas Del Carmen*, but it's gonna take five hours to get there."

Felicia pulled out the map. "There isn't really a direct route is there?"

The old man shook his head. "Nope. Last time we did this, we just trailered the cows down to Lajitas, drove them across the river, picked the new ones up, brought them back across, loaded up and were back home by three."

Felicia asked curiously. "When was that *Señor*?"

The old man thought for a second. "Um, nineteen sixty-four."

Matt snorted a laugh, as Felicia said, "But, *Señor*, that was fifty-four years ago."

Matt watched the scenery, constantly checking the right side of the road, until they were out in the countryside, then started to relax, until he heard the old man's soft, "Now what?" He looked and saw what looked like a roadblock ahead, and glanced over at the old man, who shrugged. "Get ready, just in case." Matt nodded, popping the thumb break on his 1911 loose and easing it in the holster.

The old man slowed, prompting Felicia to start and ask, "What's this?"

"Roadblock. Looks official. Let's hope so." As he slowed to a stop, he was relieved to see that the markings on the two Hummers were Mexican Marines, not *Federales*.

A young looking Marine officer stepped to the open window, "*Capitan* Cronin?"

"*Si.*"

"I am *Capitan* Ortgea, *Mayor* Huerta sends his regrets he cannot meet you, but asked that we escort you to the *rancho* of Señor Velazquez, and suggested your timing could be better."

The old man laughed. "*Mayor* Huerta is too kind, and probably really said something about stupid old men, right?"

The captain held up his hands, smiling. "That I do not know, *Señor*. Shall we go? We will lead and one Hummer will follow, if that is acceptable."

The old man bowed his head. "Completely, *Capitan*, please lead on."

***

Four and a half hours later, the little convoy rumbled over the cattle guard onto the Velazquez spread, and the old man rolled his shoulders, sighing, "We're here. At least, we will be in another mile or so."

Matt nodded. "Quiet trip."

Felicia replied, "And not too soon. I need the bathroom."

The men laughed, and Felicia batted Matt in the back of the head. "Not funny. The world may be your urinal, but *we* are a tad more picky."

"Yes, dear."

The first Hummer pulled into the yard, and the old man saw Hector gesturing toward a loading chute a hundred yards or so to the left. He pulled over there, smoothly backed the truck and trailer into position, and shut it down, as Hector walked over, accompanied by a younger Hispanic woman.

They piled out of the truck, with the old man grabbing his back and doing his best to stretch, as Hector walked up. "Hector, *mi amigo*!"

Hector, spare and wiry, with a full head of gray hair, grabbed the old man in a bear hug. "*El Lobo Blanco* returns to the scene of his crimes!"

Matt and Felicia looked on in bemusement, as the two pounded on each other, and Felicia whispered, "I think they have known each other for a long time." Matt could only nod, as he checked out the surroundings, noting the layout of the ranch buildings, and the not too obvious fortifications.

The Hispanic woman hung back a few steps, but with a smile on her face, until Hector said, "John, I don't think you ever saw Isabella after she was born, did you?"

The old man cocked his head. "No, Sofía was still pregnant the last time I saw her. My pleasure, Isabella." He touched his hat, and continued, "Let me introduce my ranch manager Matt Carter and his wife Felicia."

A round of how do's, handshakes, and Felicia whispering something to Isabella ended with the women heading for the house, as the old man said, "We got an escort that I wasn't expecting. Is there any place to put them up?" he asked, pointing to the Mexican Marines.

Hector smiled. "*Capitan* Ortega is my wife's brother's youngest. He called ahead. And he brought food for his troops. We will be fine. Sofía is busy driving the kitchen help crazy, preparing dinner. May I suggest we unload the cows, and let Mateo, my foreman, and Luis get them in a big enough pen to let them stretch out?"

After a great dinner, they sat around the outdoor fire pit, cigars and brandy in the men's hands, and the women enjoying glasses of Port.

Hector, a few sheets to the wind, said, "So, *El Lobo Blanco*, we are together once again. Hopefully we are older and wiser than the last time we were together."

The old man tipped his glass. "Hopefully, and I don't go by that anymore. Haven't for over thirty years, Hector."

Hector giggled. "But still the bogeyman to the cartels, or so I hear. Ah, the things we did…

Captain Ortega cocked his head. "*El Lobo Blanco*? I thought that was a legend. I did not know you served, *Tío* Hector."

Hector smiled. "Not many do. But enough about us old men." Turning to Matt, he asked, "I understand you were an American Marine?"

Matt nodded self-consciously. "I was, sir. For twenty years. Retired as a master sergeant."

Felicia smiled and followed-up with a spate of rapid fire Spanish, that prompted Captain Ortega's eyes to get big, and for him to sit forward. After a little back and forth with Felicia, he asked, "Master Sergeant, would you be willing to talk to my troops? For a few minutes only?"

Matt cocked his head at Felicia, who just smiled, and said, "Sure. Not sure what I can do to help. Want to do that now?"

"If we might?"

Matt and the captain disappeared, and the old man shook his head. "That wasn't nice Felicia."

Hector, Sofía, Isabella, and her husband Manuel all laughed, as Felicia replied, "He deserves the recognition. I am proud of him and what he did. And he's not old!"

The old man asked, "Any problems with the Coyotes or cartels, Hector?'

Hector flip flopped his hand. "Not really, not anymore. We ride armed, and they are careful not to cut any fences. They have learned the hard way."

"The hard way?"

Manuel laughed. "One set decided to cut a fence and take a short cut. *El Matador* took offense. They did not survive."

"*El Matador*?"

"The prize bull. He stomped and gored them to death. Now they stay in the lanes, quietly."

The old man grinned. "Ah, now I understand."

***

A bedraggled Matt came into the kitchen, and the old man said. "Coffee, right here," as he shoved a cup at him.

Matt groaned as he took the first sip. "Oh man, I needed that."

The old man chuckled. "What time did y'all finally quit?"

"Dunno, maybe oh two hundred. We ready to go?"

"Yep, just got to load the cows. We did all the paperwork last night while you were playing Marine."

Matt hung his head. "Sorry."

"Don't worry about it. Maybe you helped them a little bit."

The women came into the kitchen closely followed by Hector, and a quick breakfast of *Huevos Rancheros* was served.

Mateo knocked on the kitchen door, and Hector answered, followed by a quick back and forth in Spanish. Hector turned, "Your cows are loaded. I'm sure you want to check the trailer, and I will go make sure Alejandro has his men ready to go."

The old man nodded. "Let me grab my bag. Matt, Felicia, you ready?"

Sofía, Isabella, and Felicia had a quick conversation, too fast for the old man to follow, and Felicia said, "Momentarily, by the time you get the truck checked, I will be ready."

The old man and Matt checked the trailer, ensured the interior gate was closed and locked, and checked all the tire pressures, as the Marines loaded up their Hummers. Captain Ortega came over. "Thank you for the training, the troops really enjoyed it." Turning to the old man, he continued, "*Capitan* Cronin, it has been an honor. We will escort you back to *Ciudad Acuña*."

The old man nodded. "Please convey my thanks to *Mayor* Huerta. I wish you and your troops the best."

Felicia and the women hugged, and Felicia climbed in the back seat, as the old man and Hector shook hands, then clasped each other. "Stay safe, my friend."

"We will, Hector. See you in about six months."

"*Vaya con Dios.*"

As the old man got in the truck, his nose was assailed by the odors of fresh Mexican food. "Oh we're going to eat good going home!"

Eight hours later, they pulled back into the home ranch, with Matt and the old man still laughing about the young Customs and Border Protection Officer that wanted to get in the trailer and check the inside of it for drugs. Matt glanced back to see if Felicia was asleep and asked, "So, what is that whole *El Lobo Blanco* thing?"

The old man shook his head. "Something long dead. Maybe someday."

Matt shrugged. "Ortega seemed to think you were something special. He kept asking questions about you, and what you'd done."

"Stuff gets blown way out of proportion, you know that as well as I do."

Felicia sat up. "Are we there yet?"

They both answered, "Yes, we're here."

"Good. I have a Christmas tree to put up."

Epilogue

The old man stepped out on the front porch and leaned against the post, slowly sipping his coffee in the morning chill, looking up at the plethora of stars visible in the dimness of the morning. *Another year, another Christmas. Nobody is going to be up for a while, maybe I'll go up to the cemetery. Guess it'll just be us this morning, with Matt and Felicia going to her family's Christmas morning stuff. Kinda quiet, which will be nice.*

He drank the last of the coffee, whistled softly for Yogi, and held the door open for him, then followed Yogi down the hall. Stopping in the office, he pulled his gun belt down, flipped it around his waist, and checked to see that the 1911 was free in the holster. Grabbing his hat, he picked up the coffee cup and continued on to the kitchen. Taking down a battered tin mug, he filled it with coffee, grabbed a couple of carrots, and headed out the back door.

Setting the coffee cup on top of the corral gate, he went in the barn and led Diablo out, feeding him a carrot, then saddling him up. He stuck the other carrot in his coat pocket, with just the end sticking out, playing a little game with Diablo. Diablo whuffed, nudged the old man's arm aside, and gently pulled the carrot out of the pocket, whinnying softly, as if laughing at him. The old man rubbed his nose, then slipped the bridle in his mouth, and led him to the corral gate. Diablo craned down and sniffed Yogi, as the dog bounded around in front of him.

Mounting up, the old man reached over and picked up his coffee cup. "Gently now, Diablo. I don't want you to spill my coffee." Diablo bobbed his head up and down, almost as if he was agreeing, and walked softly out of the yard. The old man noted there weren't any lights on in Matt and Felicia's house, and smiled.

Fifteen minutes and one gate later, the old man reined up at the cemetery. He sat for a couple of minutes sipping the coffee, as the sun started peeking over the horizon, painting it in lighter blue and rose colors. Tying the coffee cup to the saddle horn, he got down and ground reined Diablo, then walked slowly up to the gravestones.

It was still too dark to actually make out the names, but he knew them and their locations by heart. Taking off his hat, he stood in front of Amy's stone, and said, "Well, another year, hon. Jesse and the kids are doing well, healthy and happy. Can't ask for more than that. The only other thing would be for you, Jack, and Pat to be here with us, but I know that can't happen. I only hope you're looking down and liking what you're seeing. I still miss you, Amy. Always have, always will."

He walked a couple of steps and stopped between Francisco and Juanita's stones, with Rex's little stone off to the side. "Forgot to tell you, I took a little revenge for y'all. Maybe I'll be going to the hot place for what I did, but I got some back for y'all. And Hector asked about you. He said say a prayer for you, so I will. Something from Psalms ninety-one seems appropriate, especially today."

He bowed his head. "*Thou shalt not be afraid for the terror by night; nor for the arrow that flieth by day; nor for the pestilence that walketh in darkness; nor for the destruction that wasteth at noonday. A thousand shall fall at thy side, and ten thousand at thy right hand; but it shall not come nigh thee. Only with thine eyes shalt thou behold and see the reward of the wicked. Because thou hast made the Lord, which is my refuge, even the most High, thy habitation; there shall no evil befall thee, neither shall any plague come nigh thy dwelling. For he shall give his angels charge over thee, to keep thee in all thy ways. They shall bear thee up in their hands, lest thou dash thy foot against a stone. Thou shalt tread upon the lion and adder: the young lion and the dragon shalt thou trample under feet. Because he hath set his love upon me, therefore will I deliver him: I will set him on high, because he hath known my name. He shall call upon me, and I will answer him: I will be with him in trouble; I will deliver him, and honor him. With long life will I satisfy him, and show him my salvation*. Amen."

***

Jesse yawned as she walked in the kitchen, seeing the empty coffee cup in the sink, she looked around for the old man or Yogi, but didn't see either of them. She poured herself a cup, and headed for the front door, Boo Boo in trail. Opening the front door, she was surprised to see the porch empty, as

Boo Boo scooted out to do her business. Jesse shook her head. *Maybe Papa went back to bed, but that's not like him. And I didn't hear Yogi scratch at the door, either.* Boo Boo came back up on the porch, tail wagging, and she let her back in the house.

Jesse walked to the back door, opened it and looked out, but didn't see him or Yogi, but a light was on in Matt and Felecia's, so she picked up the phone and called over there. Felicia answered, and she asked, "Is Papa over there?" Felicia said no, and Jesse wondered where he was. She'd seen the truck out front, she hit the speaker as Jace came toddling in. "Okay, thanks. When are y'all going over to Angie's?"

Felicia laughed. "Whenever the babies wake up, all three of them."

Jesse snorted. "Matt complaining about the riding again?"

"Oh God, yes. Even Ernesto was laughing at him, saying he rode like a sack of potatoes. But they got the entire north forty checked, along with the south pasture over the last two days."

Jesse heard a baby cry in the background, and said, "Sounds like at least one of the babies is awake!"

Felicia laughed again. "Matt Junior, as usual. Let me go take care of him. We'll be back around two, probably."

"Okay, we'll do y'all's presents then. Merry Christmas!"

"*Feliz Navidad*, bye."

Jesse hung up, then picked Jace up. "Come on little man, we need to go check something." Walking out the back door, she went to the barn, and saw the empty stall. *Huh, Papa must have gone up to the cemetery. He's been doing that a lot lately. Well, I guess we'll wait until he gets back to do Christmas.*

Jace whined, "Cold, mommy."

Jesse turned and headed for the house. "I know little man, sorry, but mommy needed to check something. Let's go get you warm, and your sister up. You know what day it is?"

"Uh-uh."

"It's Christmas! We get to open presents this morning."

"We do that now, mommy?" Jace asked.

"No, we have to wait for Kaya, and daddy, and Papa. Then we open presents."

"Okay, mommy." They stepped back in the house and Jesse put Jace down. He asked, "I feed dogs now?"

Jesse smiled. "Yes, you can feed the dogs now."

"But Yogi is not here."

"He will be back. You can feed Boo Boo now."

"Okay." Jace went over to the dog food bin, carefully scooped out a scoop of dog food, and put it in Boo Boo's bowl, saying, "Eat, Boo Boo." Boo Boo dug in with relish, as Jace put the scoop back in the bin and carefully closed the lid.

Just as Jesse heard Kaya cry, she saw movement outside the back door, and realized it was the old man, riding back into the yard. *Yep, he went up to the cemetery. At least he's back, and not everybody is up yet. Maybe I can get Kaya up before Aaron wakes up.* "Jace you want to go help Papa?"

"Uh huh."

She quickly put his jacket on him, took him to the back door, and yelled, "Merry Christmas, Papa. I'm sending Jace to you." She picked up a carrot and gave it to Jace. "Go see Papa."

The old man smiled. "Merry Christmas, come here Jace. You want to help me unsaddle Diablo?"

Jace charged down the steps. "Me help, Papa, me help!"

***

Thirty minutes later, the old man led Jace back into the house, and found Aaron sitting at the kitchen table, bouncing Kaya on his knee as Jesse made breakfast. "Morning sleepy head, Merry Christmas!"

Aaron smiled. "Merry Christmas, John. Jace you ready to open presents?"

Jesse interrupted, "Not until after breakfast."

The old man chuckled, as he poured another cup of coffee, setting the old tin cup in the sink. "I can wait."

Jace fed Yogi, then climbed up in Aaron's lap as Kaya toddled around the kitchen, chasing the dogs, while Jesse finished breakfast. The old man pulled out silverware and plates, saying, "I guess Matt and Felicia, and the kids are gone to Angie's. I didn't see the truck."

Jesse nodded. "They will be back around two-ish. We're going to do dinner at five."

Aaron laughed. "I hope there is going to be lunch in there somewhere!"

Jesse turned, spatula in hand. "I'm going to 'lunch' you! Damn men…"

The old man, Aaron, and Jace laughed, as Kaya tugged on Jesse's pants. "Up?"

Breakfast went quickly, and Jace said, "Presents now?" prompting more laughter.

Aaron picked him up. "Okay, presents now!" Jace took off for the living room, followed by everyone else, and the dogs. The old man sat in the rocking chair, watching the kids tear into the presents, wrapping paper going everywhere, dogs barking, and Aaron and Jesse laughing as they handed the kids more presents.

The old man finally asked, "How late were y'all up last night putting stuff together?"

Aaron grinned ruefully. "I think Matt and I got the bicycle finished about two this morning. Esme's damn Easy Bake Oven was a PITA, but we finally got it to work. But that bike…"

The old man got up and walked into the office, then came back with two wrapped presents, "Here, these are for y'all."

Jesse grinned and pulled two presents out from the back of the tree. "Two for you, Papa," turning back, she pulled one more out, handing it to Aaron. "And one for you."

While the kids played in one of the boxes, strewing the packing peanuts everywhere, Aaron opened his presents. First was the present from the old man, and Aaron whistled. "That is a helluva duty belt, John!"

"Yep, Kenny Rowe made it. It's not quite a BBQ rig, but it's pretty damn nice. But you can't get fat," he said with a smile.

Jesse opened hers and gasped. "Papa, where?" holding up a big five stone turquoise bracelet, "This is beautiful!"

"It's from the nineteen-fifties, Yazzie family. I called a buddy and he found it for me."

"It's *heavy!*"

Aaron opened his other present. "Damn, what is…?"

Jesse laughed. "It's a Bolo, dummy. And there should be something else in there."

"Oh." Digging further in the wrapping paper, he came up with a set of turquoise cuff links that matched the Bolo. "Oh, nice!" Leaning over he kissed Jesse. "Thank you."

"Papa, open yours!"

The old man grinned, picking them up and shaking them, then opening the lighter one, taking out a new Silver Belly, and trying it on. "It fits. I guess my other one is getting a bit ratty." He opened the heavier present, and took out a new pair of black Lucchese boots. Rubbing his hand over it, he asked, "Ostrich?"

"It better be," Jesse said. "And I kept the invoice in case they don't fit, but they are the same size as your others. And before you say anything, yes, you needed a new pair of boots, too."

The old man laughed. "Yes, dear granddaughter."

Aaron pulled a small box out of his pocket. "It's not much, but…"

Jesse opened the box and started crying. "Aaron, you didn't have to."

"I know I didn't have to, but I always felt bad that I couldn't get you a decent engagement ring. It's late, but I figured better late than never."

Jesse threw her arms around him, and they kissed as the old man got up and headed for the front porch, mumbling, "Kids…"

***

Jesse looked around, and didn't see the old man, but his coffee cup was missing, and she headed for the front door. She found him sitting in the rocking chair, watching Yogi and Boo Boo cavorting as he talked to Billy on his cell, "I can set something up. Maybe in a couple of weeks. I'll let you know. You want to be there?"

She heard Billy's scratchy response through the speaker on the cell, "Oh hell yes. I want to lay eyes on him. If I get the chance, I'll even provoke him."

"Good enough. Well, tell Mama Trần Merry Christmas, and I wish all of y'all a Happy New Year."

"Same to you John, and tell the kids the same."

"Will do." The old man looked up as Jesse sat down in the other rocker. "Kids down?"

Jesse sighed, "Yes, they are played out, which means they'll be up half the night now. What are you and Uncle Billy plotting?"

The old man looked over with a feral grin, "Billy and I plotting, God forbid."

"Papa! Really?"

"Billy's found some stuff on Charles Ryan, the guy that wants to get Matt and Danny fired. There's some questionable dealings, especially his buying Wildcat Ranch. He's also found out he likes to have lunch three or four days a week at the Petroleum Club in Midland. So he wants me to set up a lunch with some old friends up there, and get him a look at this turd."

Jesse smiled, "We haven't been up there in a long time. I remember when you used to take me up there and call it our date for the month."

The old man took a sip of coffee. "Yes, daddy was proud of that deal. He was one of the founding board members. I still remember that big old house the club used to be in, it was a sad day when they razed that old place. Granted the new club is doing better, but that was a piece of history."

Jesse nodded, "I remember seeing pictures of that old red brick house and the beautiful interior. It's sad that it couldn't be saved."

The old man shrugged. "Time marches on. And so does the oil bidness."

Curious, Jesse asked, "Who are you going to invite?"

"Probably Charlie Waters, Cliff Erwin, and Johnny Chapel. They're all old farts like me, and are on the board. Plus they are both ranchers and oilmen."

Jesse sighed, "I almost wish I could go along."

The old man snapped his fingers. "Oh that… Would be perfect. Could you and Felicia put the grands in daycare for the day? Then we could all go!"

"What about the store?"

"Leave Tom and Fernando in charge. Hell yes, that'll work great for what Billy is planning." The old man got up slowly, "I need more coffee, and something to eat." Whistling for the dogs, he turned toward the door, as Jesse got up and joined him.

ABOUT THE AUTHOR

JL Curtis was born in Louisiana in 1951 and was raised in the Ark-La-Tex area. He began his education with guns at age eight with a SAA and a Grandfather that had carried one for 'work'. He began competitive shooting in the 1970s, an interest he still pursues, time permitting. He is a retired Naval Flight Officer, having spent 22 years serving his country, an NRA instructor, and a retired engineer who escaped the defense industry. He lives in North Texas and is now writing full time. This is his fifth novel in The Grey Man series.

Other authors you make like are on the facing pages…
I highly recommend all of them!

You can either use the Amazon link or search for them on Amazon.com under books or Kindle.

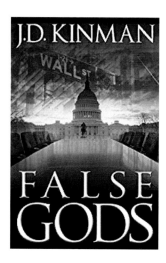

http://amzn.to/2Cx2eOs

http://amzn.to/2CvPIis

http://amzn.to/2CwX9Wy

http://amzn.to/2BFWmpt

Made in United States
North Haven, CT
11 May 2024